DR ZINETTI'S SNOWKISSED BRIDE

BY
SARAH MORGAN

THE CHRISTMAS BABY BUMP

BY
LYNNE MARSHALL

CHRISTMAS WITH A HOT DOC

Snow, seduction—and miracles made at Christmas!

As the snow starts to flutter,
and the fairy lights begin to twinkle, there are
two delicious doctors on the lookout for the perfect
someone to share a festive kiss under the mistletoe!

DR ZINETTI'S SNOWKISSED BRIDE
by Sarah Morgan
Can Medic Meg tame the roguish Dr Dino Zinetti
before the clock strikes Christmas?

THE CHRISTMAS BABY BUMP
by Lynne Marshall
Discover how a Christmas bundle of joy is just the cure
for steamy doctor Phil and obstetrician Stephanie!

*This Christmas they'll all unwrap a gorgeous present
they never expected to receive!*

First published in Great Britain 2010
Harlequin Mills & Boon Limited,
Eton House, 18-24 Paradise Road, Richmond, Surrey TW9 1SR

© Sarah Morgan 2010

ISBN: 978 0 263 87926 1

Harlequin Mills & Boon policy is to use papers that are natural, renewable and recyclable products and made from wood grown in sustainable forests. The logging and manufacturing process conform to the legal environmental regulations of the country of origin.

Printed and bound in Spain
by Litografia Rosés, S.A., Barcelona

'You did well, Meg. You probably saved that boy's life.'

'Well, I don't paint my nails or bake cookies, but I have some skills.' But maybe her skills weren't enough in this case. Suddenly she wanted to lean against that broad chest and just sob. She didn't care that she'd been resisting his advances for months. She just wanted to feel those strong arms close around her. 'Dino—'

'It's a good job I am here, no? A weak, feeble girl like you is going to need a big strong guy like me to help you out of this mess.'

Her traitorous desire to lean on him vanished instantly. 'I don't need any help from you.'

'*Sì*, of course you need my help.' His mouth curved into a slow, sexy smile. 'It's just you, me, and this little private room. This isn't quite how I pictured our first night together, but I can be flexible. Do you have any mistletoe?'

'If I had any mistletoe all I'd do with it is force-feed you the berries—'

Without warning he leaned towards her, and for one breathless, heart-stopping moment she thought he was going to kiss her. His eyes glittered dark with sexual promise and Meg felt something she'd never let herself feel. Then she came to her senses and gave him a hard shove.

'You said you weren't in the mood,' he purred. 'I was going to put you in the mood.'

Sarah Morgan is a British writer who regularly tops the bestseller lists with her lively stories for both Mills & Boon® Medical™ Romance and Modern™ Romance.

As a child Sarah dreamed of being a writer, and although she took a few interesting detours on the way she is now living that dream. With her writing career she has successfully combined business with pleasure, and she firmly believes that reading romance is one of the most satisfying and fat-free escapist pleasures available. Her stories are unashamedly optimistic, and she is always pleased when she receives letters from readers saying that her books have helped them through hard times.

RT Book Reviews has described her writing as 'action-packed and sexy', and she has been nominated twice for a Reviewer's Choice Award and shortlisted twice for the Romance Prize by the Romantic Novelists' Association.

Sarah lives near London with her husband and two children, who innocently provide an endless supply of authentic dialogue. When she isn't writing or nagging about homework Sarah enjoys music, movies, and any activity that takes her outdoors.

**Sarah Morgan also writes for Modern™ Romance.
Her sexy heroes and feisty heroines
aren't to be missed!**

CHAPTER ONE

'I CAN'T believe you f-found me. I'm *s-so* cold, Meg. Are we going to d-die?'

The boy's words were barely audible above the angry shriek of the wind and although she'd been standing still for less than two minutes, Meg could feel the icy fingers of cold reaching inside the padded layers of her high-performance jacket.

Normally she would have relished the opportunity to pit her wits against the vicious weather, but she hadn't planned on doing it with a badly injured teenager.

'We're not going to die, Harry. I can't possibly die yet because I haven't done any of my Christmas shopping…' She raised her voice so that he could hear her, knowing he needed reassurance almost as much as he needed emergency medical care. 'And there's a lump of mouldy cheese in my fridge I keep meaning to throw away. If my mum finds that, she'll kill me, so we need to get back home as soon as we can.' Ignoring the voice in her head reminding her that the wind chill decreased the temperature to minus fifteen and that the teenager had nasty injuries, Meg tore open the top of her backpack and dragged out the equipment she needed. 'I've called the rest of the mountain rescue team. They're on their way. In the meantime, I'm going to get you out of this wind and keep you warm.' As if challenging that promise, the wind gave a furious howl and buffeted her body. She reached out and steadied herself with her gloved hand, putting her body between the wind and the boy.

Behind them were snow-covered layers of jagged rock and beneath them the side of the mountain fell away into a deep ravine where icy water formed a death trap, waiting to finish off what the rocks and the wind had started.

Meg pulled the collar of her jacket over her mouth and tried to catch her breath, ignoring the nagging worry that it was going to be impossible to evacuate him from this treacherous site with the wind so high.

Her priority had to be shelter. The rest could wait. If she didn't get him out of this biting wind in the next few minutes, there wouldn't be anyone alive to rescue.

She gave a whistle and Rambo, her German shepherd search-and-rescue dog, nosed his way over to the boy and sat in front of him, offering still more protection from the wind while Meg found what she needed.

'Right, Harry, prepare for luxury.' She shouted to make herself heard. 'What we need now is a nice, warm living room with a roaring log fire and a pretty Christmas tree, but this is the best I can do at short notice.' She flipped the portable tent she'd removed from her backpack and for a terrifying moment the wind caught it and almost pulled her off her feet. 'Oh, for... I need to eat more chocolate. I'm not heavy enough.' As she felt her feet lift off the snow, Meg yanked the fabric hard and managed to anchor it. Within seconds she and the injured boy were inside. 'Unfortunately no log fire and no Christmas tree,' she panted, brushing the snow away from her face, 'but this is better than nothing. All right, now I can look at you. What have you been doing to yourself, Harry? You look like an extra from a cheap horror movie.'

It was worse than she'd thought. In the fading light she could see the wicked gash on his head and the purple bruising spreading across his skin.

Harry lifted his bloodied hand to his head. 'Is it bad?'

'I've seen worse.'

'But you work in the emergency department, so that's not much comfort. You see people with half their bodies missing.'

'You're going to be fine, Harry.' Meg pulled off her glove and undid the straps of her backpack. 'You're going to have a bit of a headache tomorrow, but it's nothing that a few days in bed won't solve.' She kept her voice matter-of-fact, but she was listening to his responses, watching for any signs of confusion or disorientation as a result of the head injury. 'Were you knocked out?'

'I—I think so.'

'Do you know what day of the week it is?'

'Yes, it's Sunday,' he mumbled, 'and I'm going to be in a shit load of trouble for going out into the mountains.'

'Harry Baxter, you are not supposed to swear in public.'

He closed his eyes and leaned back against her backpack. 'Aren't you going to yell at me and ask me what I thought I was doing, coming up here on my own?'

Aware that hypothermia could kill him long before the head injury, Meg was busy covering him with extra layers. Another scarf. A coat. 'That's your mum's line, sweetheart. Rambo and I just do the rescuing. We leave the lecturing to others.'

At the mention of his mother, Harry's face went from white to grey. 'She's going to be worried sick. I told her I was only going out for an hour.'

'Yeah, well, that's part of being a mum. Goes with the territory.' Meg examined the wound on his head, took a photograph with her phone and then covered the injury with a sterile pad held in place with a bandage.

'Why are you taking photographs of me?'

'Because it will save the trauma team having to remove the dressing to see the wound. Just a precaution.' In case he needed to be taken straight to Theatre.

The tent flapped against her and Meg pushed back against the fabric, relieved they had at least some protection from the raging blizzard. They weren't exactly cosy, but at least they were out of the deadly wind. 'When you're a mum, you sign up for worry on a long-term basis. Someone on the MRT will have called her and told her we've found you. There's not much else I can do for your head, so I'm going to take a look at this arm of yours now. Tell me what happened when you fell. Can you remember?'

'I slipped on a patch of ice and fell over the edge of the gully. I remember falling and falling and then I smacked my head against a rock.' The boy opened his eyes and looked at her dizzily. 'When I woke up I had blood on my face and my wrist was a really funny shape. I could see the bone.'

Meg kept her expression neutral. 'Right. Well, that's something we're going to need to fix. You can't go around with a wrist that looks like that—you'll gross everyone out.'

His face was a strange shade, now somewhere

between white and grey. He clutched her arm with his good hand. 'I thought I was going to die on my own here. I couldn't believe it when I heard Rambo barking. You're so cool, Meg. Dog-girl.'

Meg moved aside the extra layers and gently pulled up the sleeve of his jacket so that she could take a better look at his injuries. 'Harry, when you're a bit older you'll realise that calling a woman "dog-girl" isn't going to win you hearts.' There was an obvious fracture of the bone, his wrist shaped like a dinner fork. 'I don't mind "wolf-girl" but I draw the line at "dog-girl", if it's all the same to you.'

'That's what I meant. I know that's what the mountain rescue team call you because you and Rambo are such a good team. And you're so fit—not fit as in fit…' He coloured, backtracking wildly as he realised how his words could be construed. 'I mean fit in the sense that you run up the mountains without even getting out of breath, and…I…' His voice tailed off and his eyes drifted shut.

'Talk to me, Harry!' Meg felt a stab of alarm as she looked at the bruising on the side of his face. 'Tell me what you want for Christmas.' *Had he lost consciousness? Had he—?*

'At the moment?' He kept his eyes closed, as if it were too much effort to open them. 'Just to be lying in my bedroom. I have a funny feeling I'm never going to see it again.'

'You're going to see it.' Meg dug her hand into her backpack and pulled out the first-aid kit she always carried with her. 'Although if your room is anything like my Jamie's, I bet you can't see the floor anyway. What is it about boys and untidy rooms?'

'I can find everything in the mess. I like mess.' His voice was faint. 'Meg?'

'Right here, honey.'

'We're not going to make it, are we? No one is going to be able to get us down from here. Tell me honestly—I really want the truth. I'm thirteen now, not a kid.'

Still a kid, Meg thought, a lump in her throat. 'We're going to make it, Harry. I promise you that.' But it wasn't going to be easy. Looking at his badly injured wrist and the swelling on the side of his face, she felt her heart lurch. There was no way she was going to be able to walk him off this mountain. And he was right about the bone. It was sticking out. She took another photograph for the trauma team, quickly emailed it to her colleagues in the emergency department and then covered the wound with a sterile dressing and bandaged it in place. Outside the tent the wind howled and suddenly she felt horribly alone. What had started out as a relaxed training walk for her and Rambo had turned into a deadly storm and a seriously injured casualty at risk of hypothermia.

If she hadn't decided to walk today...

Pushing aside that thought, she pulled out a thermometer and checked his temperature. It was dropping and she'd used every layer she had. She was just wondering whether she could risk giving him her jacket when she heard Rambo bark.

Meg felt a rush of relief. 'He's telling me that reinforcements have arrived. That must be the mountain rescue team. You just hang in there for a few more minutes, Harry. We're going to get you something for the pain and then get you out of this ravine.'

Tucking the coat around him, she went on her hands and knees and poked her head out of her tent. Through the swirling snow she saw powerful male legs, and then a man squatted down to her level and she found herself staring into glittering dark eyes that made her heart flip.

'Well,' he drawled, 'if it isn't wolf-girl.'

Meg was so relieved to see him that for once she didn't react. 'Dino, thank God you're here! Where are the rest of the team?'

'Just me so far.' His voice calm, he swung his backpack off his back. 'But quality is always better than quantity. Except in my case, you get both.' He gave her a sexy wink. 'Relax. What you need is a big, strong man and here I am so your worries are over, *amore*. I will handle everything now.'

Meg gave him a withering look. 'I'm not, and never will be, your *amore*. And I don't need you to handle anything. I can handle it myself. I've been handling it while you've no doubt been out to a fancy restaurant for Sunday lunch with some skinny blonde.'

With a maddening smile, he pushed past her into the tiny tent. 'She was brunette.'

'This tent isn't big enough for you and me,' Meg gritted, but he ignored her, his leg brushing against hers as he settled himself next to the injured boy. His wide shoulders pressed against the flimsy tent and there was barely room left to breathe, but that didn't seem to bother him. And, for once, it didn't bother her either. Not that she would ever have admitted it, but she was really relieved it was him.

Dino Zinetti might be too good looking for his own good, he might drive her crazy and make her feel horribly uncomfortable, but he was also a skilled doctor and an experienced mountaineer.

'You chose lovely weather for your trip, Harry.' He

sat next to the injured boy, the same eyes that had been seducing her moments earlier now sharp and focused, the sexy smile replaced with a reassuring one. 'You seem to have got yourself in a spot of bother. You're lucky wolf-girl happened to be out today on one of her lone walks.'

Harry's lips were turning blue. 'I made a mistake. I called her dog-girl.'

'Ah...' Dino's eyes crinkled at the corners. 'In a couple more years I'll give you some tips on the right and wrong things to say to women.' His tone was relaxed and easy, in direct contrast to his fingers, which were working swiftly, checking pulse, pupils and other signs. 'Do you know if you knocked yourself out?' He questioned the boy, interspersing reassurance with questions designed to aid his clinical judgement.

'He might have done. GCS of fifteen when I got here but that's a nasty gash on his head. I think he needs a CT scan. Do you reckon the helicopter might still make it, or is the weather too bad?' Cramped in the confines of the tiny tent, Meg found it unsettling to be pressed so close to him. 'Are we going to have to wait it out for a few hours?'

'You want to leave this place?' Smiling, Dino checked Harry's pupils, asked him another couple of questions and then turned his attention to the broken wrist. 'Are you telling me this isn't the most romantic place you've ever spent a night? A beautiful woman, alone with two strong men?'

'One strong man. I don't think I count.' Harry gave a weak smile. 'You're pretty smooth, Dr Zinetti. When I'm older, I want to be like you.'

'Trust me, you don't.' Meg squashed herself against the tent to make as much space as possible. 'Not unless you want to walk around with a permanent black eye courtesy of all the women who have punched you. Dr Zinetti is Italian so that's how he gets away with being so politically incorrect. You don't have that excuse. And you do count, Harry.'

'I don't think so. I don't feel too good…' Harry's eyes drifted closed and this time didn't open again.

Meg felt her heart do an emergency stop. Instead of focusing on not allowing any of her body parts to touch Dino, she concentrated on Harry. 'He—'

'Take a breath, wolf-girl,' Dino said calmly. 'There's a spare jacket in my backpack and a space blanket. Get them both on him because his temperature is dropping and I don't want to add hypothermia to his list of problems. Time to call in the cavalry.' He reached into his pocket and pulled out a satellite phone while Meg tucked the extra insulation around the injured boy.

As Dino talked to the search-and-rescue team, giving GPS co-ordinates, she was thinking about how worried Harry's mother would be.

'They're going to scramble a helicopter.' Dino rocked back on his heels, frowning as the tent flapped against his back. 'I think he needs a faster trip to hospital than we can give him on a stretcher.'

'The wind is too high for the helicopter.'

'It's dropped slightly. They're going to give it a try, although of course it won't be easy given that we're in a gully.' He gave a humourless smile. 'Let's hope the winchman likes a challenge. Is Rambo all right with noisy helicopters?'

'Of course. He's flown in them more times than you.' Meg was looking at Harry, worried about his pallor. 'Dino—'

'I know. I see. I agree with you that we need to

get him to hospital and do a CT scan. I've rung the department.'

'Who is on duty this evening?'

'Sean Nicholson. And the helicopter crew picked up Daniel Buchannan when they received our call.'

In the confines of the tent, their faces were close. She could see the thickness of his eyelashes and the beginnings of stubble on his jaw. It was a face so handsome that no woman passed him without taking a long, covetous look. Except her. Resolutely, she looked the other way. The day she started noticing that he was handsome was the day she was in trouble. So he had sexy eyes. *So what?* 'So you're not going in the helicopter?'

'No. I'm staying with you, wolf-girl.' Suddenly those sexy eyes were deadly serious. 'What were you doing up here, Meg? Hardly the weather for an evening stroll. Blizzard, drifting snow, wind chill…'

'Perfect evening for a walk.' Meg didn't bother telling him that was how she liked the weather. Wild and crazy. She'd given up explaining herself to people years before. 'Anyway, you should be thanking me. If I hadn't decided to walk, I wouldn't have found Harry. I didn't plan to come up this far but Rambo picked up the scent.'

'You should be at home, baking cookies or painting your nails.'

Even though she knew he was intentionally trying to wind her up she was still shocked by the emotion that rushed through her body. Why did comments like that still bother her so much? Reminding herself that it had been nothing more than a flippant remark on his part, Meg pulled a face. 'I'd rather be blown off a ridge in a force-nine gale than paint my nails. *Not* that I expect you to understand that. The women you date can't walk and blink at the same time. The one today—could she talk and eat her lunch?'

'Jealous, *amore*?'

'No. I'd rather poke myself in the eye with a fork than have a romantic lunch with you.'

'Is that so? You have strange aspirations, Meg Miller.' Humour in his eyes, Dino watched her for a moment and then turned back to Harry, checking his temperature and other vital signs again. 'His GCS is dropping.'

'Perhaps we should—' Meg broke off as Dino put a hand on her arm.

'Listen. No wind. Must be the eye of the storm.'

All she could hear was the throb of blood in her ears. She told herself it had absolutely nothing to do with the touch of his hand on her arm and the fact that they couldn't move without brushing past each other. Forcing herself to focus, she realised that the tent was no longer flapping so violently. 'I can hear the helicopter.' She stuck her head out of the opening and saw lights approaching high above them. 'They'll have to hover above the gully.'

'I'll make sure everything is strapped down.' Dino crawled out of the tent to help the helicopter crew and Meg's gaze lingered on his shoulders. She was an athlete, she told herself. It was natural that she'd admire honed muscle and a powerful physique.

He stood on the narrow, snow-covered path, ready to assist the winchman. As the helicopter hovered above the narrow gully, the downdraft caused the sides of the tent to flap and whip up the new snow. Given the potential hazards, there was no wasted time. The winchman was lowered out of the helicopter and together the three of them strapped Harry securely to the stretcher, protecting his back and his neck. As he was winched back up into the helicopter, Dino held the guide rope to help prevent the potentially lethal swing of the winch rope into the sides of the gully. Once Harry was safely inside the helicopter, the crew released the guide rope and disappeared into the darkness.

Meg felt the adrenaline drain away and relief take its place. It was almost weakness, this response after the event, and she slid back inside the tent and sat for a moment, breathing slowly, trying not to think of all the alternative scenarios that tried to destabilise her sense of calm.

What if she hadn't found him?

What if Dino hadn't come?

She covered her face with her hands, dimly aware that Dino had gathered up the guide rope and was now back in the tent with her. 'I've known Harry since he was born. My mum knows his mum. I used to go round and help bath him when I was a kid.'

'Lucky Harry.' Dino stowed the guide rope in his backpack and then gently removed her hands from her face. 'You did well, wolf-girl. You probably saved his life.'

'Well, I don't paint my nails or bake cookies, but I have some skills.' But maybe her skills weren't enough in this case. What if he had a depressed skull fracture? What if they didn't get him to hospital fast enough? Now that the immediate crisis was over, the fear that had been pressing against her threatened to overwhelm her. Suddenly she wanted to lean against that broad chest and just sob. She didn't care that he was a notorious heart-breaker and that she'd been resisting his advances for months. She just wanted to feel those strong arms close around her. 'Dino—'

'It's a good job I am here, no? A weak, feeble girl

like you is going to need a big strong guy like me to help you out of this mess.'

Her traitorous desire to lean on him vanished instantly. 'Do you honestly think I need your help?' Anger stoked the fire inside her that had burned down to no more than a few glowing embers. 'I don't need any help from you.'

'*Sì*, of course you need my help.' He started piling the equipment back inside his bag. 'You are too small and delicate to walk down this mountain without assistance. The wind has dropped, but not for long. You wouldn't be fit enough to walk as fast as you'd need to. We will stay the night here, and I will protect you.' His mouth curved into a slow, sexy smile. 'It's just you, me and this little private room. This isn't quite how I pictured our first night together, but I can be flexible. Do you have any mistletoe?'

Anger flushed away the worry about Harry. 'If I had any mistletoe all I'd do with it is force-feed you the berries. I'm not in the mood, Dino—'

Without warning, he leaned towards her and for one breathless, heart-stopping moment she thought he was going to kiss her. His eyes glittered dark with sexual promise and Meg felt something she never let herself feel. She felt strangely disconnected, as if she were being controlled by some invisible force outside herself. Then she came to her senses and gave him a hard shove.

'What the hell do you think you're doing?'

'You said you weren't in the mood,' he purred. 'I was going to put you in the mood.'

'I meant that I wasn't in the mood for your flirting,' she croaked, 'not—anything else.' It was disconcerting to realise that her hands were shaking. She knew that if she'd been standing up, her knees would have been shaking, too.

'That's what you meant?' Those sexy eyes teased her. 'Then you need to be more specific when you communicate.'

Her lips were tingling and the blood was rushing around her body. 'Don't *ever* do that again, Zinetti!'

'Do what?' Dino smiled and trailed a finger over her cheek. 'I haven't done anything yet. Maybe this is a good moment to teach you all the practical applications of the use of body warmth in the prevention of hypothermia.'

Meg skidded to the furthest point of the tent, too aggravated by her own response to notice his brief, satisfied smile. 'I wouldn't spend a night cosied up with you if we were the only two people left on the planet. I'd rather *die* of hypothermia.'

'Beautiful Megan.' His voice was soft. 'A woman like you should have a man in her life, but you do everything alone.'

'That's the way I like it.'

'Because you are afraid?'

It was like dropping a lighted match into a haystack. 'Dino.' Meg hauled the anger back inside herself. 'You're the one who should be afraid. Get out of my tent. I want to go down, now. I can't stand another five minutes stuck on this rock face with a smooth-talking Italian. You're more lethal than the weather.'

To her surprise he didn't argue with her. Instead, he helped her pack up the equipment with his usual ruthless efficiency and then switched on the headlamp on his helmet.

Meg was so furious, so tumbled up inside that she barely noticed the steep descent. Dino stayed a metre in front of her all the way down, which gave her plenty of time to glare at his shoulders and plan various methods of revenge. Maybe she'd do something really embarrassing when he was surrounded by a bunch of nurse groupies. Maybe she'd even give him that kiss he'd been teasing her with. She could fry his brain and teach him a lesson. Just because she didn't paint her nails, it didn't mean she didn't know how to kiss, did it?

They trudged and stumbled through the deep snow and the inky darkness until they reached low ground and all the time Rambo panted alongside her, his shape a reassuring presence in the vicious weather.

It was only as they were striding across the safety of the valley floor that the adrenaline ceased to pump round her body and her brain started to work properly. And then she realised what Dino had done.

She stopped for a moment, cursing herself for being dense and slow.

Dino turned with a frown. 'Not a good place to stop, wolf-girl. Something wrong?'

'You did that on purpose, didn't you?' The wind gusted, almost blowing her over. 'You made me angry, you—'

With a maddening smile, Dino shrugged and carried on walking.

Meg glared after him, feeling like a fool. He hadn't wanted to kiss her. It had just been a ploy to stop her worrying about Harry. She strode after him and caught up with him at the car. 'There are times when you really drive me mad, Dr Zinetti.'

'I rely on it. Need any help with that backpack?' He slid his own off his back and threw it into the boot.

'I can handle my own backpack.' She spat the words. 'And I can handle myself up a mountain. I don't need you—' She almost said 'messing with my head' but just in time she decided that she didn't want him to know that the thought of kissing him filled her with anything other than feelings of boredom.

'You were going to cry, wolf-girl, and I didn't want a hysterical woman on the mountain with me. I'd rather deal with ten fractured skulls than one hysterical woman.'

'I was *not* hysterical and I was *not* going to cry.'

'You were getting really wobbly and there's no way I could have got you down this mountain in that feeble state.'

'*Feeble!*' Meg took a breath as the extent of his manipulation sank in. 'You never intended us to spend the night on the mountain—'

'I enjoy extreme mountain survival as much as the next macho guy…' he closed the boot '…but I was worried about you. You don't exactly carry much body fat. Keeping warm would have been a challenge. Talking of which, we need to get out of this wind.'

He'd goaded her and then he'd almost—and she'd almost—'I hate you.'

'No you don't.' He placed an arm on either side of her so that her back was pressed against the car, with no opportunity to escape. 'You're afraid of what you feel for me, *amore*, and that's understandable because it's very powerful.' He dragged his gloved hand over her cheek, a thoughtful look on his face. 'Interesting, isn't it? Wolf-girl, who never lets a man near her, suddenly feeling the chemistry.'

For a moment, Meg was transfixed by those night-black eyes. 'No, it isn't interesting. The last thing I need in my life is a Mediterranean macho man. You're not my type and I'm certainly not yours.'

'You don't know me well enough to make that judgement.'

'Maybe I don't want to know you.' She shoved at his chest but he didn't budge. 'Dino...'

Rambo growled low in his throat and Dino smiled and released her.

'I have more sense than to come between wolf-girl and her wolf.' He spoke quietly to Rambo in Italian and Meg felt her stomach flip because, although she wouldn't have admitted it in a million years, the words sounded so lyrical and sexy.

'He's protecting me.'

'I know. He's an excellent dog. But you don't need to be protected from me. I'm not the enemy.' Not remotely afraid of the dog, Dino stroked Rambo's head gently. 'He's never growled at me before.'

'You've never pinned me to the car before.' She tried not to show how flustered she felt. It was as if his powerful body had imprinted against hers. Even though he'd moved she could still feel it, hard and heavy. 'He growled at you because I pushed you and you didn't move. He was giving you a warning. Which makes two of us.'

'Will he let you give me a lift? I left my Lamborghini outside your cottage.'

'You drove the Lamborghini in this weather?' Meg glanced at the ice and snow covering the road and then back at him in disbelief. There was a devilish gleam in his eyes and his face was breathtakingly handsome in the moonlight. 'The roads are lethal.'

'Like you, I love a challenge.'

And that was why he was dangerous. Like her, he loved the adrenaline rush. 'I'm tempted to let you walk from here to the brunette who is probably waiting for you at home. The cold air will do you good.'

'No one is waiting for me at home, Meg. And I'm going to the hospital. They're overstretched and I want to check on Harry.'

Feeling really stupid, Meg let out an exasperated breath. 'You see? It's things like that I find really infuriating! Just when I'm ready to dismiss you as shallow you do something really—really...' She floundered and then shrugged. 'Decent. Go on. Get in before I change my mind. Rambo, don't eat him. He's going to help Harry. That's the only reason we're letting him live.'

Trying not to think about the moment when he'd almost kissed her, she drove her four-wheel drive down the narrow roads that led towards her cottage. 'I can't believe you drove the Lamborghini.'

'I was at lunch, remember? With a woman.'

'So the Lamborghini is an essential part of the Zinetti seduction technique?' For some reason it irritated her and she changed gears viciously. 'Do some women really fall for that?'

'All of them. Could you slow down before you kill us both?'

'I've driven these roads since I was a teenager. You must mix with some shallow women.'

'I do my best. You drive too fast, Meg.'

'Coming from someone who owns a Lamborghini *and* a Ferrari, that's a bit rich. Don't tell me—you're such a chauvinist you hate being driven by a woman.'

Dino's fingers were gripping the seat. 'I hate being driven by anyone.'

'That's because you're a control freak.'

'*Sì*, I admit that. I like being the one in charge.' He

glanced towards her, laughter in his eyes. 'I like to be the one on top, so to speak.'

'Well, that confirms I'm not your type, because I like to be the one on top, too.' Meg increased her speed, taking pleasure from his sudden indrawn breath. 'Two control freaks together is a recipe for disaster.'

'Or a recipe for explosive passion. Shall we find out which it is?'

Just for a moment her concentration lapsed and she felt the wheels of her four-by-four lose traction as she hit ice. She resisted the impulse to hit the brakes and steered into the skid, regaining control of the car within seconds. 'That was fun.' Her heart was pounding and her mouth was dry. 'At least it shut you up. Are you all right?'

'You mean apart from my heart attack?' His sardonic drawl made her smile and she slowed her speed.

'Why did you leave your car outside my house?'

'When Harry's mother realised he was missing, she called the team. Then she called your mother because she remembered that the gully is a favourite walk of yours and Harry often watches you and Rambo training up there. She hoped you might already be out, which you were. I dropped by to get your route from your mother.'

Meg tightened her grip on the wheel. 'So this is all my fault because he followed me?'

'No. It's Harry's fault. He went for a walk in the winter without the right equipment.'

'He was unlucky.'

'No, he was lucky.' Dino pulled off a glove and flexed his fingers. 'You found him. Could have been worse.'

She was concentrating on the road but she could feel

him looking at her. 'It was Rambo who picked up the scent. I didn't even know he was missing.'

'We were about to call you when you called us.'

'So how come you got to us so quickly and the others didn't?'

'I was about to head into the mountains myself. I guess we spend our free time the same way.'

'So your date didn't end the way you wanted it to.'

He smiled. 'It ended exactly the way I wanted it to.'

Which meant what, exactly? He'd already said the brunette wasn't waiting for him at home. Trying not to think about it, Meg pulled up outside her cottage. 'Home, sweet home. And you're still in one piece.'

'Miracles do happen. Thanks for the lift. Are you working tomorrow?'

'Yes. Look, Dino…' She hesitated, torn between getting away from him as fast as possible and doing the right thing for Harry. 'Don't take the Lamborghini. We've had so much snow in the past few hours and your car isn't good in bad weather. I'll drive you to the hospital. If they're as busy as you say, they could probably use my help as well as yours. Just give me time to explain to Mum and see Jamie.'

Meg slid out of the car and crunched her way through layers of snow to the front door of her cottage. She stood for a moment, looking at the lights burning in the windows and the rose bush groaning under the weight of snow by the front door. In a few more months it would be frothy with white blooms, turning her home into something from a picture postcard. The summer tourists who overran the Lake District like a million invading ants had been known to stop and take photographs of her house because it was so quintessentially English. To her it was home and she loved it. Now, with Christmas only two weeks away, there was a wreath on the door and scarlet berries on the holly bush. And mistletoe.

Meg frowned.

Who had added the mistletoe?

The door opened before she even started to delve for her key and her mother stood there, an apron tied round her slim waist, a mug in her hand. 'I've made you hot soup, Dr Zinetti. You need something to warm you before you go back to the hospital.'

'*Molto grazie*. You are truly a life saver, Mrs Miller.' Dino emerged from behind her and took the mug in his gloved hand, the steam from the soup forming clouds in the freezing air. 'I'm grateful.'

'I'm the one who is grateful. You brought my girl safely home.'

'I brought myself home, Mum. Do I get soup, too?' Irritated, Meg dragged the hat off her head and immediately saw Dino's expression change as he followed the crazy tumble of her hair with narrowed eyes.

She tensed, thinking that he was probably comparing her messy, tangled hair to the smooth, blow-dried version he'd stared at across the lunch table a few hours earlier. For a moment she wished she'd left her hat on and that thought annoyed her because she'd long ago come to terms with who she was. When other girls in her school had been learning about lipstick and moisturiser, she'd been learning to map read and use a compass. While they'd spent their weekends shopping for clothes, she'd been up on the mountains. Her only interest in clothes was whether they were wind resistant and weatherproof. She knew about wicking layers and the importance of not wearing cotton. She didn't know whether grey was the new black or whether jeans should be straight cut or boot cut. And, more to the point, she didn't care.

Meg turned away, irritated with him for looking and even more irritated with herself for caring that he'd looked.

What could have been a decidedly awkward moment was broken by her mother's disapproving tone.

'Megan, I found mouldy cheese in your fridge.'

Meg gritted her teeth and vowed never to let her mother babysit again. 'Is Jamie still awake?'

'Mummy?' Right on cue a small figure dressed in a Batman costume barrelled into her, crushing her round the waist. 'We decorated the house. We've put mistletoe everywhere.'

'I'd noticed.' Why was everyone suddenly so obsessed with mistletoe?

'Grandma says the berries are magic. If you stand under them, exciting things can happen.'

'Is that right?' Meg dropped to her knees and hugged her son. Immediately she felt her mood soften and the tension in her limbs evaporate. He smelled of shampoo and bedtime and his smile was the best thing she'd seen all day.

As long as she had him, everything was all right with her world.

'Hey there, Batman.' Dino was smiling. 'Have you saved Gotham City lately?'

'Loads of times.' Jamie wrapped his arms round Meg's neck, shivering in the thin costume he insisted on wearing to bed but grinning up at Dino anyway. For some reason that Meg didn't even want to think about, in the months that she'd been working alongside Dino, her son had developed a serious case of hero-worship for him. 'Why? Do you need any help?'

'When I do, you'll be the first person I ask. I need to get back to the hospital.' Dino retrieved his car keys from his pocket.

'Did you drive the Lamborghini? Wow, that's so cool. It looks like the Batmobile. Can I sit in it?'

Meg tensed. 'No, Jamie, you—'

'Just for a minute—pleeease?'

Anticipating Dino's inevitable rejection and Jamie's subsequent disappointment, Meg shook her head. 'Dino has to go, Jamie. He's a very important doctor and he's needed at the hospital. And, anyway, I know you love cars but the temperature is minus five and you're in your Batman costume. You need to get back inside.'

'Batman doesn't feel the cold.'

'You heard Dr Zinetti, he has to get back to the hospital now. Another time, perhaps.' Having made his excuses for him, she expected Dino to leave, but instead he handed his empty mug back to her mother.

'Does Batman have a cloak or some sort of coat? Anything you could wear over your outfit?'

Jamie frowned. 'I'm not cold. Batman is tough and strong.'

'I know,' Dino didn't miss a beat. 'But the neighbours might be watching and you don't want them to know who you really are. A superhero likes to keep his identity a secret.'

Jamie turned his head and looked at the neighbouring cottages. 'You think they might be watching?'

'I think you can't be too careful when you're saving the world.' Dino's expression was serious. 'If you have something warm that will cover up who you are, we could sit in the Batmobile for a few minutes and discuss tactics.'

'Really?' Jamie's face lit up like the lights on a

Christmas tree. 'Wait there.' He sped into the house and returned moments later in his warm ski jacket, trainers on his bare feet. In his hand was a plastic Batman figure. Seeing the excitement in his face, Meg frowned.

'Jamie, you can't—'

Ignoring her, he hurled himself at Dino, who caught him with a laugh, swung him round and then lifted him onto his shoulders and carried him to the car.

Gripped by a fear that she couldn't control, Meg watched as cracks appeared in her tightly controlled life. Jamie's delighted giggles cut through the night air and she plunged her hands into the pockets of her coat, resisting the temptation to snatch him back. *Keep him from harm.*

'Dino is good with him.' Her mother handed her a mug of soup. 'I can't believe he's actually managed to get Jamie to wear a coat. It's more than I've been able to do all day. This is worse than the Tarzan phase when he ran around in nothing but his underpants for two whole months.'

Meg found it difficult to move her lips. As much as it pained her to admit it, she agreed—Dino was brilliant with Jamie, and that was a whole big problem in itself. 'Yes.'

'It's a pleasant change for Jamie to have a man about the place. They look good together, don't they? Doesn't it warm your heart to see it?'

'No, actually.' Meg had never felt colder in her life. 'It just reminds me how little Jamie knows about the real world.' How easy it was to be hurt. *The more you gave, the more you could lose.*

'Chill, Megan.'

Meg turned her head to look at her mother. 'Since when did you start speaking like a teenager?'

'Since I started working at the youth group,' her mother said cheerfully. 'I love it. They're so vibrant and full of hope. Gives me something to do when I'm not helping you with Jamie. Oh, look at Jamie jumping in the seat! He's enjoying himself, Meg. He likes Dino. And Dino likes him.'

'Yes, because it suits him right now. And will until the next female distraction walks across his path and he has someone better to play with than my son. What then?' Meg's tone was savage. Her worries suddenly overflowed, like a river bursting its banks. 'Presumably I'm the one who is going to have to explain to Jamie why Dino doesn't have time for him any more. I'm going to have to break it to him that men often have a short attention span.' She shivered as Dino fired up the engine, indulging her son's passion for supercars. The Lamborghini gave a deep, throaty growl and Jamie bounced around in the passenger seat in paroxysms of delight.

Aware that her mother was staring at her in astonishment, Meg licked her lips. 'Sorry,' she croaked, 'I'm tired. Maybe that was a bit of an overreaction.'

'Just a bit? Megan, you're a basket case when it comes to men.'

'I know.'

'Just because Hayden couldn't keep his trousers zipped, it doesn't mean all men are the same. You need to move on, Megan.'

'I've moved on. I'm living a good life with my child.' Huddling down inside her coat, Meg watched as Dino switched off the engine and let Jamie play with the wheel for a few minutes, pretending to be a racing driver. 'Why does Jamie have to be interested in cars? It's the one thing I know absolutely nothing about.'

'He's a little boy.' Her mother's face softened. 'A gorgeous, fantastic boy and you have to help him grow into a gorgeous, fantastic man. That's your job. Part of that is letting him mix with men.'

'He does mix with men.'

'I'm not talking about the mountain rescue team. They treat you as one of the lads. I'm talking about man-woman stuff. He needs to see men as part of your life. When did you last go on a date?'

'You know I don't go on dates.' She blew on her hands to warm them. 'And there's no way I'm introducing a string of men to Jamie. What happens when they dump me? Jamie gets hurt. No way.'

'Maybe they wouldn't dump you. Have you thought about that?'

Meg stared straight ahead, her breath forming clouds in the freezing air. Her brain fielded the memories that came rushing forward to swamp her. 'My job is to protect my child. That's what mothers are supposed to do.'

'Are you protecting him? Or are you protecting yourself?' Her mother's voice was casual. 'Talking about protecting yourself, it's lucky Dino was able to find you and help you out on the mountain today.'

'I didn't need his help. I could have managed on my own.'

'Megan, when are you going to realise that you don't win awards in this life for managing on your own?' Her mother looked tired suddenly. 'You're a fantastic mum, but Jamie needs a man in his life and, frankly, so do you. It's time you stopped shutting everyone out. If you can't bring yourself to trust another man quite yet, at least make a New Year's resolution to have sex.'

'Sex?' Scandalised, Meg shrieked the word just as Dino scooped Jamie out of the car.

It echoed through the silence, the sound somehow magnified by the cold emptiness of the night.

Across the snow Dino's eyes met hers.

And she knew she was in trouble.

CHAPTER TWO

'MUMMY, what's sex?'

Oh, brilliant. Cursing her mother for landing her in such deep water, Meg tucked the duvet around Jamie. 'Well, sex can mean different things.' This was one conversation she did *not* want to have right now—not while memories of Dino's irresistible dark eyes were still fixed in her brain. 'It can mean the same thing as gender—whether someone is male or female.'

'So Rambo is male sex.'

'That's right.'

'And you're female sex.'

'Right again.'

Jamie reached for his drink of water. 'So what else does it mean?'

Meg wondered whether to simply change the subject and then decided that wouldn't be right. This was part of being a single parent, wasn't it? You dealt with these things on your own. 'When a male and a female come together to make a baby, that's called sex, too.' She decided that was enough detail for a seven-year-old, at least for the time being.

'Grandma thinks you should make a baby.'

Meg gulped. 'No, Jamie, that's not what Grandma thinks.'

'Yes, she does. She's told me loads of times she thinks you should get married and have more babies. She's always talking about it.'

Meg contemplated calling her mother upstairs to sort out the mess she'd created. 'Jamie, I'm not getting married.' She took the cup from him and tucked the duvet around him. 'Honestly, if I ever decide to get married, you'll be the first to know.'

'The man you're marrying would be the first to know. I'd be second.'

'Sometimes, my little superhero, you're too clever for your own good.' Meg kissed him on the cheek and then reached across and snapped the light on by his bed. 'Which story do you want?'

'Batman. So if you're not getting married, why did you yell the word "sex"? And why was Dino laughing so hard?' Jamie snuggled under the duvet, his hair still rumpled from play-fighting with the Italian doctor. His Batman toy was still in his hand. 'I don't get what's funny.'

'Nothing's funny. I was talking to Grandma. She was being…well, she was being Grandma.'

'She also told me it isn't normal or natural for a young woman of your age to be on her own,' Jamie parroted. 'I pointed out I live here too, but apparently I don't count.'

'You count, Jamie.' Meg picked up the book they'd been reading the night before. 'Believe me, you count.'

'I wouldn't mind if you got married. Especially if you married Dino. That would be super-cool.'

Meg thought about the heat they'd generated in the small tent on the mountainside. 'Cool' wasn't the word she would have chosen. 'Jamie, I'm not marrying Dino. We're not even…well…'

'You're not dating?'

'What do you know about dating?'

'It's when a boy and a girl hold hands. Sometimes they kiss and stuff. I know you don't do it.'

'Right. Well, that's because I haven't met anyone I want to…' she cleared her throat '…hold hands with.'

'Maybe you will now we've hung all the mistletoe everywhere. Grandma says you just won't let a man close enough to hold your hand.'

'Grandma talks too much.'

'But it could happen?'

Not in a million years. 'Maybe—of course, you never know what will happen in this world.'

'Could it happen by Thursday?'

'Thursday?' Meg blinked. 'Why Thursday?'

'Thursday is Dad's Day at school.' He sounded gloomy. 'You're supposed to bring in your dad or some other important man in your life and they're all meant to talk about their jobs for five minutes.'

Meg felt as though ice water had been poured down her back. 'There are lots of kids in your school whose parents have split up.'

'Not in my class. Only Kevin and he still sees his dad every weekend. I'm the only one whose dad doesn't actually visit. Freddie King says I must be a total loser if even my own dad doesn't want to be with me.' Jamie sat up and scrubbed his hand over his face. 'I know you told me to be ass-ass—'

'Assertive.'

'That's what I meant—assertive, but it's hard to be assertive when he's telling the truth.' His little mouth wobbled.

'It isn't the truth, Jamie.' Meg felt boiling-hot anger replace the freezing cold. 'Dad didn't leave because of you,' she muttered thickly, pulling him into her arms and hugging him tightly. The plastic Batman dug into her back. 'He left because of me. I've told you that a thousand times. He left before you were even born, so how could it have been about you? Technically, you weren't even here.'

'The thought of me was enough to scare him away.'

'It wasn't you who scared him away, it was me. I wasn't who he wanted me to be.' Meg eased him away from her. 'Your dad wanted a really girly girl, and I'm, well, I'm not like that. I've never been that great with hair and dresses and make-up and all that stuff.'

But other women were.

Do you really need to ask why I had an affair with Georgina? Because she's glamorous, Meg, that's why.

Meg sat still, shocked by how much it could still hurt, even after more than seven years.

Jamie snuggled under the covers, clearly reassured by her words. 'But you can do all the important things. You're like Mrs Incredible. I mean, not with the stretchy arms, but you can climb, and slide down ropes and stuff. That's cool.'

Mrs Incredible. Meg swallowed down the lump in her throat. 'Well, *you* think it's cool, but some people think it's more important to know about the right shade of nail varnish than be able to rescue someone off a mountain in a blizzard.' She stroked his head quickly and then stood up, too agitated to sit still a moment longer. She prowled around the tiny bedroom, picking up socks and more Batman toys, trying not to remember how hard she'd found it to fit in at school. She didn't want her child to go through the same thing. She didn't want him to feel that same sense of isolation. 'It's going to be OK, Jamie. Tomorrow I'm going to talk to your teacher and ask her what on earth she was thinking, having Dad's Day at school. It just makes kids a target for bullying. We'll sort it out, I promise. We'll come up with a plan.'

Jamie was silent for a moment. 'I sort of had a plan. I thought of something.'

'Good. That's what I like. A plan. It's great that you sort things out by yourself. Tell me.'

'I want to invite Dino.'

Meg froze. 'To Dad's Day?'

'Why not? He lets me ride in his car, he's always nice to me when we have to go the mountain rescue centre and that time at the hospital he let me wait in his office and got me a whole bunch of toys to play with. And he knows about cars and stuff. I like him. He's nice.'

Nice? Meg thought about Dino Zinetti. Hair as dark as night, a mouth that was masculine and sexy and eyes that knew just how to look at a woman.

'Nice isn't the word I'd use.'

Jamie looked shocked. 'You don't think Dino is nice?'

'I'm not saying he isn't nice, honey.' 'Nice' seemed like such an inappropriate word to describe a man as hotly sexual as Dino, but somehow Meg managed to get her tongue round it. 'He is—er—nice, but, well... he's just not the right person to take to Dad's Day.'

'It doesn't have to be your dad. Just a man who is important in your life.'

And she didn't let Jamie have a man who was important in his life, did she? This was all her fault. Torn apart by guilt, Meg stood still. 'Jamie, listen, I—'

'You work with him every day. Will you ask him, Mum? He just has to come for an hour and chat about what he does.'

Ask Dino to come to the school? Meg felt the Batman toy bite into her palm as she squeezed it tight. 'He wouldn't do that.'

'He might. You didn't think he'd let me sit in his car, and he did. You don't know if you don't ask.'

'I can't ask, Jamie.'

Jamie's face fell. 'OK. I'll just go on my own. It'll be fine.'

Meg felt like the worst mother in the world. 'All right, I'll ask him.' The words were torn from her, dragged from inside her by the raw power of maternal guilt. 'But he might be busy.'

'I know. He's a consultant in Emergency Medicine and he's a member of the mountain rescue team *and* he won a gold medal in the men's downhill at the winter Olympics when he was nineteen.'

'I beg your pardon?'

'He won a gold medal. Didn't you know?'

'No,' Meg said faintly. 'I didn't. We don't talk about personal stuff that much.'

'You should. He's really cool, Mum. Did you know that when he was my age he could eat six doughnuts in under a minute?'

Meg thought of Dino's athletic physique, a result of his active, outdoor lifestyle. 'No, I didn't know that either. Presumably he gave that habit up before he won the men's downhill. Go to sleep now.' Why on earth had she allowed herself to say she would speak to Dino? She'd rather dig a hole and bury herself in it. 'Jamie, listen to me—'

'I'm so glad you're going to ask him, Mum.' Jamie pulled the duvet up to his neck, a blissful smile on his face. 'I was dreading school this week, but now I'm really looking forward to it. Dino's the best. If he comes and talks to my class, Freddie will never tease me again. Do you know it's only fifteen more sleeps until Christmas? Isn't that great? I've written my letter to Santa. I did it with Grandma. We put it in the fireplace. Do you think he'll take it tonight?'

Meg opened her mouth to tell him that there was no way she could ask Dino to Dad's Day. 'I'm sure Santa will take it. Is it really only fifteen more sleeps?' Her voice was croaky and somehow she just couldn't form the right words. 'That is great. I guess I'd better start doing some Christmas shopping.'

Hi, Dino, what are you doing on Thursday?

Hi, Dino, don't take this the wrong way, but would you consider...?

Meg rehearsed various ways of asking him as she walked through the main entrance of the hospital the following morning. As if she didn't have enough pressure from her mother, now she had it from her son, too.

Why did she have to find a man? It was just nonsense. Jamie's life was full of men. Just not one special man. And that was a good thing. Relying on one man could leave you flat on your face, as she'd discovered to her cost.

Jamie had already had one man walk out of his short life. She wasn't going to allow it to happen a second time by encouraging him to spend time with a man as notorious for his unwillingness to commit to relationships as Dino.

They were doing fine, the two of them. They were a great team. She was the one in control of their future.

But she couldn't shift the heavy weight of guilt and she'd hovered for an extra five minutes at the school gates, fighting the temptation to seek out Freddie and tell him to stop torturing her child. She'd stood and watched Jamie, a tiny figure, swamped by his warm jacket. *The only boy in his class who wasn't bringing a Dad to Dad's Day.*

She'd wanted to go into the school and yell at them for being insensitive, but Jamie had begged her not to. Now she was wishing she'd overruled him.

Should she have rung the school? Freddie's mother? She worried about it all the way to work and was still worrying when she visited Harry in the observation ward. He was in a corner bed on his own. 'Hey, lay-about. I thought I'd say hi before I start work.'

His face brightened when he saw her. 'Wolf-girl!'

'Better not call me that. They're funny about animals in hospital—they might throw me out. Here...' Meg handed him a book she'd bought from the hospital shop, 'I've no idea if you've read it, but I thought it had an interesting cover. Monsters ripping people apart. Perfect teenage reading.'

'Thanks. Cool.' Harry put it on his lap and reached for some chocolate from his locker. 'Want some?'

'At nine in the morning? No, thanks. I don't mind being wolf-girl, but I draw the line at elephant-girl, and if I start eating chocolate for breakfast that's what I'll be. How's your head?'

'Hurts.' Harry chewed. 'But they did that scan thing and said my brain is all right.'

'I know. No skull fracture. I rang last night to check

up on you.' She looked at his bedside table. 'Who bought you the torch and the whistle? Your mum?'

'Are you kidding? Mum's never going to let me out of her sight again.' He looked gloomy. 'No, the torch and whistle were from Dr Zinetti. He dropped them off before he went off duty last night. Or it might have been this morning—it was definitely after midnight.'

He'd been at the hospital that late? Meg's tummy gave a little lurch. 'I suppose your mum was upset.'

'She freaked out. I'm grounded. No more walks on my own. Dad went totally mental.' He looked so forlorn that Meg took pity on him.

'When you've healed, you can walk with Rambo and me.'

'And me.' The deep, male voice came from right behind her and Meg felt her heart bump against her chest. Was it the Italian accent? Or the fact that last night he'd got too close for comfort? Or was it just her mother's fault for mentioning sex?

She closed her eyes briefly, feeling sick at the thought of telling him Jamie's request. Imagining how he would interpret such an invitation, Meg slid lower in her chair. Could anything be more embarrassing?

'Hi, Dr Zinetti,' Harry grinned. 'Thanks again for the torch and the whistle.'

'Basic walking equipment.' Dino sat down on the chair on the opposite side of Harry's bed and helped himself to chocolate. 'I'm going to run a survival course in the New Year. I've booked you on it, no charge.'

Harry sank back against the pillows. 'No way will Mum let me go to that.'

'Meg will speak to her.' Dino winked at her. 'Put in a good word. She's going to be taking a session on training a search dog.'

Meg recoiled. 'No, I'm not. No way am I standing up in front of a bunch of strangers and—'

'You're an important part of the MRT. We want you there.' Railroading over her objections, he ate another piece of chocolate. 'And you're an expert at what you do.'

'Yes, well, just because you're good at something it doesn't mean you can talk about it. I'm useless at speaking in public.' She hated being looked at. Hated being the focus of attention. 'My tongue ties itself in a knot.'

'Does it, now?' his gaze slid to her mouth and lingered. 'I'm a doctor. I could look into that for you if you like.'

Was he flirting with her?

Meg felt her cheeks turn a fiery red. No, he wasn't. Men didn't flirt with her. They slapped her on the shoulders and offered to buy her a drink. She was one of the lads. Hating herself for feeling flustered, she scowled. 'I can't speak to large groups.'

'That's fine, because I'm thinking a maximum of ten. And then we're going to do some practical sessions outside. How to survive a night in the mountains, that sort of thing. We need you and Rambo for that. The work of the search-and-rescue dog is important.'

Meg wanted to tell him that anything other than one on one was a large group in her book, but she didn't want to look like a wimp. Although with strangers she definitely *was* a wimp. 'I'd be rubbish. I wouldn't have a clue what to say.'

'We'll work it out together.' Something in his frank, appraising gaze made it hard to breathe and Meg forgot about Harry, who was happily munching his way through a chocolate bar in the bed right next to them. She forgot that she'd been awake all night worrying about Jamie and Dad's Day. Because of the way Dino was looking at her, she forgot everything.

A warmth spread through her limbs and Meg was aware of every beat of her heart. And then he smiled.

At her.

Her insides melted.

The corners of her mouth flickered and she was about to smile back at him when a soft, feminine voice came from behind her.

'Dr Zinetti. It's so good to see you again—is there anything I can do for you?'

Meg turned to find the ward sister smiling at Dino. She knew her vaguely. Melissa someone or other. Always giggling with the crowd of girls from Radiography.

Staring at the woman's freshly glossed mouth and smooth hair, the feeling of excitement left her. A cold feeling spread through her body. Turning away quickly, Meg dipped her head, feeling really awkward and furious with herself for being so stupid.

Dino hadn't been smiling at her.

He'd been smiling at Melissa, standing behind her. And it didn't take a genius to see why.

Melissa was the sort of woman who men found interesting. She was someone who took the trouble to straighten her hair before an early shift and apply lip gloss whenever a good-looking doctor walked onto the ward. Her uniform was slightly shorter than regulation, but not quite short enough to draw comment.

She was exactly like gorgeous Georgina.

Feeling the past rushing forwards to mock her, Meg

suddenly wanted nothing more than to escape. The world was full of women like Melissa, she knew that all too well, just as she knew that the world was full of men who salivated over smooth hair, perfect nails and glossy lips.

Suddenly she felt grubby and unkempt. She was wearing the scrub suit she always wore for work in the emergency department—no doubt Dino was making several unflattering comparisons.

Her palms damp and her heart thudding, she shot to her feet and gave Harry a quick smile. 'I'm off. Be good.' She didn't look at Dino. He was probably occupied ogling Melissa's glossy mouth and, for some reason she didn't want to examine too closely, she didn't want to witness that.

'I heard about your heroic rescue, Dino,' Melissa was saying, and Meg quickened her pace as she walked towards the door. Within minutes they'd blatantly be arranging where and when to meet. Then Melissa would be giggling with her colleagues, planning what to wear.

Feeling as though she belonged to a different species, Meg hurried along the corridor towards the emergency department.

What had possessed her to promise Jamie she'd invite Dino to Dad's Day?

It was a totally ridiculous idea. And it wasn't going to happen.

No way. There were a million easier ways to make a complete fool of yourself.

She was going to have to find a different solution to Jamie's problem.

* * *

'Meg, wait—' Wondering what had caused her to run this time, Dino strode after her as she sped towards the door. He caught up with her easily and grabbed her arm. 'Wait! I want to talk to you.'

'I have to get to work.' Without looking at him, she shrugged him off and carried on walking. Her mouth was tight and she looked as if she was going into battle.

With a soft curse he caught up with her again and this time spun her round to face him, his hands hard on her shoulders.

Forced to stop, she made an impatient sound in her throat. 'What?' Her eyes were darkened by anger. It was like looking at the sea before a storm and Dino racked his brains to think what he could have done to whip up such a response from her. He'd always unsettled her, of course. He knew that, and he'd been biding his time. *Treading carefully.* Letting her get used to being around him.

For a moment he was tempted to tell her in blunt phrases exactly what it was he wanted from her, but his experience with women had taught him when to speak and when to go slow. With Meg Miller he was moving so slowly he was virtually standing still. *One step forwards, two steps back.* 'Why did you run off?'

'I didn't "run" anywhere. I have to get to work, so I left.'

In the middle of a conversation. In the middle of the first intimate exchange they'd ever shared. She'd been about to smile at him. For the first time since he'd met her eight months earlier, she'd almost acknowledged the connection between them. And then it had snapped. She'd snapped it.

It was like trying to tame a wild animal, he thought. You just had to be patient and let them come to you.

Shame that he wasn't that patient.

'Your Jamie is a great boy.' He stuck to a safe subject. 'He loves cars so much. I was the same at his age.' He'd expected her to relax, but instead the mention of her son seemed to increase her tension.

'Thanks for indulging his interest and letting him sit in your Lamborghini.' She was stiff and polite. 'That was kind of you when you must have had a million better things to do with your time.'

What was it about him that scared her? 'I wasn't being kind. I like his company. He's a great kid. You're a great mum. He's lucky.'

She stared at him for a moment and suddenly, out of nowhere, a sheen of tears veiled her eyes. Without saying anything, she jerked her shoulder away from his grasp and started walking again.

Cursing in Italian, Dino followed her. '*Accidenti,* will you stand still for one moment? *Mi dispiace,* if I upset you, I'm sorry, but I don't understand how. Jamie *is* a great kid and you *are* a great mum.' He blocked her path and she wrapped her arms around herself and stared past him, not meeting his eyes.

'Thanks.' She was all rigid formality. 'Is that what you wanted to say? Because I have to—'

'No.' He ignored the fact that they were standing in a busy corridor with half the hospital staff hurrying past. 'Why do you always run from me, Meg? I know you're not a coward. You were out there last night in howling winds, staring down at a vertiginous drop and you didn't even quiver.' He was still stunned by how well she'd handled the conditions on the mountain the previous night. But now there was no sign of the guts and bravery she'd shown in a blizzard. She looked jumpy and distracted, as if she had a thousand problems on her mind and no idea how to handle any of them. 'If we're talking about work or mountains, you have plenty to say, but when I change it to something more social, you clam up. Why?'

'Sorry. I'll try to be more sociable.' Her smile was false. 'It looks like we might have more snow. I do hope that won't make your drive to work difficult, Dr Zinetti.'

Curbing his exasperation, Dino stared down at her, studying the smooth skin of her cheek and the way her lips curved. 'I don't want to talk about the weather.'

'Sorry. We'll talk about something else. How did you like my mother's soup?'

'The soup was delicious. She obviously knows what hungry climbers need when they come home.'

She relaxed slightly. 'She ought to. Both my dad and my grandfather were in the mountain rescue team.'

He already knew that from the other guys, but he didn't say so. Instead he felt a buzz of triumph that reserved, buttoned-up Meg Miller had finally revealed something personal about herself. 'So it's in the family.' Dino moved to one side as the chief pharmacist hurried past. 'Same with me. My dad used to be a mountain guide. He took people up the Matterhorn.' *Give something back. Conversation. To and fro. Try and get her to relax.*

Her brow furrowed. 'The Matterhorn is in Switzerland.'

'Part of it is in Switzerland. The best part is in Italy. You're lucky you have your mum to help you. Jamie's lucky to have such close family.' He hesitated, wondering how far he dared push it. 'Does he ever see his father? Are you still in touch?'

He watched, cursing himself as her expression changed and her body tensed.

'No. All he has is me. So he's not that lucky, is he? And I really don't understand why everyone is taking this sudden interest in my love life.' Her voice rose and he saw the sudden flare of anguish in her eyes, which was rapidly replaced by horror that she'd revealed so much. Within seconds it was masked and she was businesslike. 'I really have to go.' Dodging him, she hurried along the corridor towards the emergency department, leaving Dino standing in silence, regretting bringing up the subject of Jamie's father.

He'd touched a nerve.

And he still hadn't asked her what he wanted to ask her. He'd had the tickets in his office for six months and he'd known instantly who he wanted to take. And he'd been waiting for the right moment to invite her.

A wry smile touched his mouth and the smile was at his own expense because this was the first time in his life he'd ever had to ask a woman a question and not been sure of the answer.

Determined to catch up with her and finish the conversation, he strode into the department and was immediately met by Ellie, one of the sisters in charge of the emergency unit.

'Oh, thank goodness!' She grabbed his arm and pushed a set of notes into his hand. 'Three-month-old baby with severe breathing difficulties—I've taken her into Paediatric Resus. Mum's demented with worry. Meg's already there because you know how good she is with babies and worried mothers.'

So there would be no chance to finish their

conversation for the next hour or so, Dino thought grimly as he strode towards Resus. But later...

He pushed open the door and immediately picked up the tension in the atmosphere. Meg had already attached the baby to a cardiac monitor and a pulse oximeter and was giving oxygen. Despite the obvious crisis, her voice was gentle and soothing as she talked to the mother, explaining what she was doing. For a fraction of a second Dino watched her, transfixed by the change in her. There was no sign of the prickly, defensive exterior she showed to the world. With the baby and the mother, she was gentle and warm. Infinitely reassuring. If he'd been brought in to the department injured, he would have wanted Meg by his side. Once again he remembered how good she'd been with Harry. It was as if she lowered her guard around people who were vulnerable while the rest of the time she hid behind layers of thick armour plating.

'It happened to me,' she was saying. 'My Jamie was exactly three months old, just like Abby here. The oxygen levels in Abby's blood aren't quite as high as we'd like and she's really having problems with her breathing, poor thing, that's why I'm giving her some oxygen right now.'

'Did your son recover?' The mother's voice wavered and Meg reached across and gave her shoulder a squeeze.

'Celebrated his seventh birthday last week. Cheeky as ever. Addicted to superheroes. Batman, Superman, Spiderman—you name it. He saves the world at least a hundred times a day. Ah—here's Dr Zinetti right now.'

Dino strode into the room, noticing that Meg's anxiety and stiffness appeared to have vanished. She even looked pleased to see him.

Whatever else she might think of him, at work they were a good team.

'Dino, she's had a cold and runny nose for twenty-four hours and it's been getting steadily worse. She hasn't fed at all today, she has nasal discharge and a wheezy cough. Sats are ninety-four per cent so I've started her on oxygen because I can see she's struggling.'

'I can't believe how quickly she's got worse.' Abby's mother looked terrified, her face almost grey from lack of sleep and worry. 'Is she going to be all right?'

'I'm going to take a look at her right now.' Dino gently lifted the baby's vest so that he could look at her chest. He watched for a moment, noticed that the chest was visibly hyperinflated and that there were signs of intercostal recession. 'Was she born at full term?' He asked the mother a number of questions and then listened to the baby's chest.

'Is she bad?' The mother was hovering, stressed out of her mind. 'I'm worrying that I should have brought her in sooner but I thought it was a cold.'

'You've done the right thing. Because she is little and she has tiny airways, she is struggling at the moment.' Dino folded the stethoscope. 'I can hear crackles in her lungs, which suggests that this could be bronchiolitis. It's a respiratory infection caused by a virus. It's quite common at this time of year. There's nothing you could have done to prevent it.'

She looked at him, desperate for reassurance. 'You're sure?'

'Positive. But in Abby's case it is quite severe so I'm going to run some tests and keep her on oxygen for now.

I'm also going to contact the paediatric team because she's going to need to be admitted for a short time.'

'She needs to stay in hospital? It's nearly Christmas.'

'Hopefully it will only be for a few days.' Meg's voice was gentle. 'She's having to work quite hard to breathe, and if she isn't feeding then we need to keep her here and give her some help. Honestly, it's the best place for her to be. Whatever treatment she needs, we can give it right here. You know you wouldn't be able to relax if she was ill like this at home. You'd be hanging over her cot, listening to her every breath and just worrying.'

'Oh, yes, that's exactly what I've been doing.' The baby's mother looked dazed. 'I need to phone my husband—he's gone into work. He didn't realise she was this bad—neither of us did.'

'Why don't you do that right now? We're going to take some blood samples,' Dino took the tray that Meg had already prepared. 'That will help us work out exactly what's wrong with her and how we're going to treat her.'

'You're going to stick needles in her?' The mother looked appalled, her eyes full of tears. 'I should be there for her, hold her...'

Dino took one look at her ashen face and knew that if she stayed, she'd probably pass out. He was about to say something when Meg spoke.

'I think the most important thing right now is to call your husband. That's a bigger priority. You need the support. The weather isn't great out there so it might take him a while to get here. I'll hold Abby while Dr Zinetti takes the bloods.'

In one sentence she'd given the mother permission to leave and not to feel guilty. Admiring her skill, Dino waited while Abby's mother left the room. 'You're so good with worried mothers.'

'There's nothing worse than watching someone stick needles into your child. Can I ask why you're taking bloods? I got the tray ready just in case, but we don't usually do that for bronchiolitis. I thought it was a clinical diagnosis.'

'I want to check her blood gases. She has marked chest wall retraction, nasal flaring, expiratory grunting and her sats are dropping, despite the oxygen.'

'She's certainly a poorly girl.' Meg slid her hand over the baby's downy head. 'All right, sweetie, we're going to do this together and Uncle Dino is going to get that nasty needle in first time and not miss.'

'No pressure, then.' Dino ran his finger over the baby's tiny wrist and arm. 'If I manage it first time, I get to choose the time and the place.'

'For what?' She handed him a tourniquet.

'For our first date.'

Her cheeks flushed, Meg squeezed the baby's arm gently. 'I don't go on dates.'

Neither did he. Usually. He wondered what she'd say if she knew he was every bit as wary as she was. For the past two years he'd kept his relationships superficial. It was a measure of how much he liked Meg Miller that he was willing to risk the next step. 'Perhaps it's time you did.' Dino stroked his finger over the baby's skin, found what he wanted. Smoothly and confidently he slid the tiny needle into the vein. 'There. First time. I win the challenge.' He murmured softly to the baby in Italian and glanced up to find her watching him.

'I'm glad.' Her cheeks were flushed. 'I would have hated you to have missed, but I don't want you to take that the wrong way.' Meg turned her head to check the baby's pulse and blood pressure on the monitor. 'She really is very sick. I've rung PICU and warned them that they'll need to isolate her.'

Dino took the samples he needed and dropped them onto the tray, his eyes on the baby. 'I'm still not happy with her breathing. She may have to be ventilated.'

'Paediatric team on the way, including the anaesthetist.'

'The problem with working with you,' Dino drawled, 'is that you're so efficient there is no opportunity for me to impress you.'

'You got the needle in first time—that impressed me. And anyway…' she pulled a sticker from a sheet in the notes and stuck it onto the form for the blood test, '…you don't need praise from me. You already have quite a fan club going, Dr Hot. I gather fourteen nurses have asked you to the Christmas ball so far. Is that all the bloods?'

This would have been the perfect moment to ask what he wanted to ask, but the situation was too tense to contemplate having a personal discussion. Later, he promised himself. Later, when they weren't working, he was going to remind her that she owed him a date. And no doubt she would fight him all the way.

In the eight months he'd worked at the hospital he'd noticed that Meg didn't really socialise. She worked and then she went home to her son. On the few occasions she joined the rest of the mountain rescue team for a drink, it was either early, in which case she took Jamie with her, or it was late and she popped in quickly while her mother was babysitting. At first he'd wondered if her attitude was driven by financial concerns, but as he'd got to know her better he'd realised that there was a great deal more to Meg's hermit-like existence than an urge for thrift.

Someone had hurt her. Presumably Jamie's father. *Relationships,* he thought. *Complex and difficult.*

He watched as she moved around the room, calm, quiet and efficient. When it came to work, she never failed to impress him. What surprised him was the difference between her confidence levels in a work or rescue situation and her confidence levels in a social situation.

Abby's mother arrived back in the room at the same time as the paediatric team and Dino pushed aside thoughts of Meg, briefing his colleagues as they transferred the sick baby to PICU. He was walking back to Resus when Meg grabbed him and dragged him into an empty cubicle.

'About this date,' she whispered fiercely, her gaze flickering to the door to check no one was passing, 'there is somewhere I really want to go and I'd really like you to take me.'

Astonished that it had proved that easy, Dino smiled. *'Molto bene,'* he purred. 'Of course. Anything. Romantic dinner? Or something less public perhaps. I could cook for you. My place.'

Instead of reacting the way he expected, she chewed her lower lip nervously for a few seconds. 'I want you to come to my house at eight-thirty on Thursday morning.'

Dino watched her carefully. He could see the pulse beating in her throat. *Feel her nerves.* 'I'm all for injecting variety into the dating scene, *belissima,* but isn't eight-thirty in the morning a slightly unusual time to eat dinner? Unless you're suggesting breakfast?'

'Don't get any ideas. We won't be eating anything.'

She pushed her hair out of her eyes and he noticed that her hand was shaking. 'Look, I know you won't want to do this, but—' She sucked in a deep breath, like someone summoning up courage to do something they found terrifying. '—Thursday is Dad's Day at school and Jamie doesn't have anyone to take. I know you're not his dad but that doesn't matter because it just has to be an important man in his life, and I know you're not exactly important, but—'

Dino covered her lips with his fingers. 'Meg, take a breath.'

'Sorry. Look, I'm sorry I asked—just forget it.'

'I'm glad you asked. And the answer is yes. Of course I'll go to Dad's Day with Jamie. I'd be honoured.'

'You would?' She stared up at him, her breathing rapid against his fingers. 'You'll go? Seriously?'

'Yes. Of course. I think he's a great kid.' It took a huge effort of will to remove his fingers from her soft lips. An even bigger effort not to replace them with his mouth. 'Just tell me what's expected of me.'

'I have absolutely no idea. All I know is that you have to be incredibly impressive,' she blurted out, 'so that Freddie stops telling him he's a loser because his dad doesn't want to see him.'

Dino felt anger flash. 'Some kid is calling him a loser?' *Was that the reason for the tears he'd seen in her eyes earlier?* 'Someone is bullying Jamie?'

'I don't think so. Not really. Hard to tell. The line between bullying and boy behaviour can be blurred.' She rubbed her fingers with her forehead, her eyes tired. 'I'm trying to stay calm and rational about it. But I've discovered that rational thinking goes out of the window when it's your child. Kids are really mean. And I know I have to get my head round it and in the end Jamie has to find his own way of dealing with it, but…' Her voice was thickened as she struggled not to break down. 'He's so little, and when it's your child it feels *horrible,* you have no idea. I just want to go and find Freddie and yell at him, but I can't do that.'

'Describe him to me,' Dino said coldly. 'I'll do it for you.'

'No.' With a tiny smile, she shook her head. 'What I want you to do is make Freddie and his dad look as small and insignificant as possible, while making yourself look like a cross between Mr Incredible and Batman.'

He raised an eyebrow. 'Does that mean I have to wear a tight red Lycra suit and a black cloak?'

She gave a choked laugh. 'You'd be arrested. I don't know what's the matter with me. I don't really want to make Freddie and his dad look small, and I *hate* myself for having to ask you to go so that Jamie can be like the other kids. I've always taught him that he doesn't have to be like everyone else—that people are allowed to be individuals—and here I am playing some silly game of impressing people.'

'Well, that's a great theory,' Dino drawled, 'but I guess sometimes it's just nice not to have to fight the world on everything.' And that was what she did. He was sure of it. She was standing between the world and her child. 'I'll do it, Meg. No problem. I can't promise red Lycra, but I do promise to help Jamie. Will you be there?'

'No. Mums aren't allowed. I'll be outside, biting my nails.'

He took her hand in his and lifted it—and had a brief glimpse of bitten nails before she snatched her hand away, her cheeks pink.

'I thought you could pick him up from home…' She thrust her hands behind her back. '…in your Batmobile. That should attract some serious attention at the school gates.'

'Particularly if it carries on snowing. The Lamborghini is a nightmare in the snow. I'm likely to crash right through the school gates if the conditions don't improve and that isn't exactly superhero behaviour, but I'll see what I can do. You really do want to give them the full treatment, don't you? In return,' Dino drawled, 'you'll do something for me.'

The relief in her eyes was replaced by caution. 'What?'

'This isn't our date. Next time it's my choice. We go where I decide, when I decide. And it won't be at eight-thirty in the morning, Meg, so you'll need to book a babysitter.'

He'd been patient long enough.

CHAPTER THREE

'MUM, he was *awesome*. When he stripped off his jacket he was wearing this tight suit *just* like Mr Incredible, and he was all muscle, and Freddie's mouth was like this…' Jamie dropped his jaw to show her. 'And he had a proper six-pack and everything and then he was telling us about the suit and he said that you need to wear that for speed so that you go as fast as possible when you're skiing. He wore it in the Olympics! You should have seen Freddie's face when Dino got out his gold medal. He opened and closed his mouth like a fish and his dad sort of spluttered a bit and went very red in the face and quiet.' Jamie chatted non-stop while he sprinkled glitter onto the Christmas card he was making. 'And then he talked about when he worked as a mountain guide in Italy, where he comes from, and there was this avalanche…'

Listening to Jamie talk, Meg felt a rush of gratitude towards Dino. Whatever he'd said and done at Dad's Day, it had obviously been the right thing.

'Don't use too much glue or the card will be sticky.'

He stared at the card dubiously. 'Do you think Grandma is going to like this? We could have bought one.'

'Home-made is better. She's going to love it. So what else happened?'

'All the kids thought his Lamborghini looked *exactly* like the Batmobile.' Jamie added stars to the card. 'And he let me wear his Olympic medal.'

He'd let him wear his Olympic medal? *Wasn't that going a bit over the top?*

'So, anyway, I invited him over for pizza night, Mum.'

'Who?'

'Dino, of course.'

'You invited him for pizza night?'

'Yes. Pizza is Italian, isn't it? He told me he likes pizza.'

Trying to reconcile the smooth, sophisticated Dino she knew with a version that ate pizza, especially *her* pizza, Meg closed her eyes.

Feeling as though she was being sucked into quicksand, she picked up the tube of glitter. 'He wouldn't want to come over, sweetheart. He was probably just being polite.'

Jamie's smile faded. 'You mean he doesn't really like us?'

'No, he likes us,' Meg said quickly, 'of course he likes us. Especially you. I *know* he likes you a lot. I'm just saying that a man like Dino is busy, and he's probably got better things to do than eat pizza with us.'

'So why did he say he's really looking forward to it? And it isn't just me he likes—he likes you a lot too, Mum. He kept asking stuff about you all the time while we were in the car. Do you think he wants to marry you and have sex? Is it because Grandma and I hung extra mistletoe from the door?'

The glitter slipped through her fingers. 'No—no, I

don't think that's what he's thinking and I don't think the mistletoe makes any difference. What do you mean, he was asking stuff about me? What kind of stuff?'

'Mostly questions about what you do when you're not working. I told him I'm a lot of work, so when you're not working or out on a rescue, you're usually looking after me. Mum, there's glitter all over the floor.'

Meg started to clean it up. 'Well, it's certainly true that I'm usually looking after you. Apart from the fact you eat enough for eight boys, you create masses of laundry. I couldn't believe the state of your rugby kit this week.' She kept talking so that she didn't over-analyse the fact that Dino had been asking about her. 'Did you leave any mud on the field?'

'Freddie tackled me. He pushed me right into the mud.'

Freddie again. 'Well, maybe Freddie won't be so quick to jump on you now he knows your best friend is a superhero.' She emptied glitter into the bin. 'So what night did you invite Dino? Just so that I make sure there is some pizza for him to eat.'

'Tomorrow, because it's a Friday and pizza night is always Friday. And he's expecting your extra-gooey chocolate cake. I told him it's the only other thing you can cook.'

'Right.' This was a man who dined out in the finest restaurants. His favourite food was probably lobster. And she was giving him pizza and chocolate cake. In a house festooned with mistletoe.

'Thanks so much for what you did yesterday.' In the middle of the constant bustle of the emergency department, Meg handed Dino a set of notes to sign. 'You made Jamie's week. Actually, you probably made his year. The whole class is talking about your car and your Mr Incredible suit. I must admit I find it surprising you can still fit in a suit you wore when you were nineteen.'

'It was a tight fit.' Dino scrawled his signature on the page. 'I've filled out since then.'

She looked at his shoulders and then looked away again quickly. 'I can imagine.'

'Send this guy to fracture clinic. Did that man in cubicle 4 get transferred?'

'They found him a bed on the medical ward.' She wasn't going to think about his shoulders. 'Dino, it was really sweet of you to tell Jamie that you love pizza, but you really don't have to torture yourself like that. I'm honestly not expecting you to come. I'll make some excuse—tell him you had some emergency or something.'

'No, you won't.' Frowning, Dino rose to his feet and slid his pen into his pocket. 'I love pizza. I'm looking forward to it. And I think Jamie is great. He has a good sense of humour and he's very observant about people. And I'm looking forward to your food.'

'All right, that is *seriously* bad news.' Meg gulped. 'I ought to warn you that I am not that great a cook. Pizza is about the limit of my repertoire, and I only manage that because Jamie's pretty good with toppings. He gives me a list and I buy them and then he just throws them on. He even tells me when it's cooked. If he left it to me, the whole thing would be burned.'

'Are you trying to put me off?'

'I'm just warning you that this isn't going to be a gourmet evening. I'm sure you're wishing you'd never said yes.' Of course that was what he was wishing. He must be desperate to back out. Why would a good-looking, single guy want to waste a precious evening off eating home-made pizza with a seven-year-old boy and his mother? 'I know how persuasive Jamie can be and it was kind of you not to hurt his feelings but, seriously, it's OK. I'll handle it with him.'

'What time does pizza night start?'

Meg stared at him. 'Y-you're coming? Seriously?'

'I wouldn't miss it. What time?'

'Oh—er—indecently early. Six o'clock. Jamie goes to bed around eight so we have to eat around then. That's way too early for you, I'm sure, so maybe we should just—'

'Six it is.'

She looked at him helplessly. What was this all about? Why did he want to eat pizza at her house? *Why had he helped her child?* 'Dino—'

'Would you mind talking to the relatives of the child who fell off his bike? They're worried about their son being discharged home. They need a head injury information sheet and some of your special brand of "I'm-a-mother-too" reassurance.'

'Right. I'll do that.' He was behaving as if there was nothing strange about the fact that he was coming round for dinner. As if it were something they did all the time. She had no idea what was going through his mind. Unless it was the fact that her mother had yelled the word 'sex' across the whole valley and he thought he may as well make the most of what was on offer. Perhaps he'd decided that the mistletoe was some sort of hint. On the other hand, a man like Dino wasn't exactly going to find himself short of offers or opportunity. Mistletoe or no mistletoe, he didn't need to settle for a girl who didn't paint her nails.

One thing she knew for sure—once he'd tasted her food, he wouldn't be coming back for more.

Dino pulled up outside the cottage and tried to remember when he'd last eaten a meal at six o'clock in the evening. Locking the car, he smiled. *Probably the same time he'd last eaten pizza.*

Another fresh fall of snow had dusted the path and he saw a small pair of blue Wellington boots covered in pictures of Spiderman abandoned on the step.

As he waited for Meg to answer the door, he studied the wreath. It was a festive twist of ivy, pine cones and fat, crimson holly berries. Looking closer, he saw that it was just a bit haphazard, and suddenly had a vision of Meg and Jamie making it together, laughing at the kitchen table. A family preparing for Christmas.

He was eying the mistletoe thoughtfully when the door was dragged open and he was hit by light and warmth.

Jamie stood there, a grin on his face, Rambo wagging his tail by his side. 'You made it. Come in.' Unselfconscious, he grabbed Dino's hand and pulled him inside. 'You have to choose your topping. Pepperoni, olive, ham or mushroom. Usually I'm only allowed to pick three but Mum might let you have more as you're the guest.'

Dino followed him into the kitchen and found Meg, red in the face, making pizzas on a scrubbed wooden table.

'Hi—you made it. That's great.' She looked flustered. White patches of flour dusted the front of her apron and the arms of her jumper. Her hair was clipped to the top of her head and tumbled around her face in a riot of haphazard curls.

Her eyes changed colour, he noticed, according to her mood. Tonight they were a deep, sparkling blue like one of the lakes on a summer's day. 'I bought you something to drink.' He held out the bottle and she looked at it and gave a hesitant laugh.

'Champagne? I don't know what you're expecting, Dino, but what we have here is a basic pizza with a few toppings. Nothing fancy.'

'Champagne goes with everything.' He looked around him. Her kitchen was warm and homely, delightfully haphazard, like everything else in her life. At one end of the table there was a stack of papers and unopened post, which she'd obviously cleared to one side in order to make the pizza. Brightly coloured alphabet magnets decorated the door of the fridge and the walls were adorned with Jamie's paintings and photographs.

Intrigued, Dino strolled across the room to take a closer look. There were photographs of Meg and Jamie wrestling in the snow. One of Jamie in his school uniform, looking proud. Jamie and Rambo. Meg and Rambo. A family.

Something pulled inside him and suddenly he felt cold, despite the warmth thumping from the green range cooker that was the heart of the kitchen. This was what a childhood was supposed to be like. A million small experiences, explored together and retained for ever in the memory. A foundation for life. In comparison to the rich tapestry of family life spread around the kitchen, his own experience seemed barren and empty. His mother had paid expensive photographers to record various carefully selected moments and the subsequent pictures had been neatly catalogued and stored. Whatever artwork he'd brought home from school had been swiftly disposed of because his mother had hated clutter of any sort. The walls of his home had also been adorned with priceless paintings that no one could touch. His mother would no more have displayed one of his childish drawings than she would be seen without her make-up.

Pushing aside that bitter thought, Dino opened a glass-fronted cupboard and helped himself to two tall stemmed glasses.

As he popped the cork on the champagne, he realised that Meg was watching him as she shaped dough into rounds.

'Sorry, we're in a bit of a mess.'

'I like it.' He poured champagne into the glasses. 'This is a lovely cottage. How long have you lived here?'

'The house belonged to my grandfather. When he died my dad fixed it up and then they rented it to tourists for a while. Then I had Jamie and needed somewhere to live, so they stopped renting it out and it became mine. I love it here. The views are incredible, the walking is fantastic and in the summer we sail on the lake, don't we, Jamie?'

'Grandma bought me my own boat. It's a single-hander.' Jamie climbed onto a stool. 'Do you like boats, Dino?'

'I've never had much to do with boats.' He put a glass of champagne down next to her hand. 'But I know I'd love sailing.'

'Sometimes I capsize. That's the best part.'

Meg finished the last pizza base and gave a sigh of relief, as if preparing the food had been a test she'd faced and passed. 'OK, guys, over to you.' She pushed two of the bases across the table towards them and picked up her glass. 'Cheers. What do you say in Italy?'

'*Salute!*'

Her glass made a gentle ringing sound as she tapped it against his. '*Salute*. To superheroes and pizza night.' She sipped the champagne. 'Oh, that's so good. I've never tasted anything like it. Where did you get it from? Is it expensive?'

'I picked it up last time I was home,' Dino avoided the question, putting the open bottle in the fridge. He looked at his pizza base. 'I'm going to need some help here, Jamie. Do you have any advice for me?'

Jamie was holding a bowl of tomato sauce. 'I can do yours for you if you like.'

'That would be great, thanks. You obviously have more experience than me.' Dino sat down on a chair, watching Meg. Her face was pink from shaping dough and a few more wisps of blonde hair had escaped from the clip on her head. He'd seen her handle the most complex medical situations without working up a sweat, but here in the kitchen, she was definitely sweating.

'OK, Jamie, I'm ready for tomato.' She pushed her pizza base towards her son. 'You know what to do. Not too much or you'll make it soggy.'

Dino leaned across and helped himself to an olive. 'So how was school today, Jamie? Any trouble from Freddie?'

'Nope. Not today.' Jamie carefully spread tomato sauce on the three pizzas. 'He wants to be my friend now.'

'That's good.'

'Not really. It's only because he wants a ride in your car.' Jamie picked up a bowl of grated cheese and Dino looked at Meg. She was staring at her son and there was so much love in her eyes that he felt something squeeze his insides.

'You're pretty wise about people for someone who

is only seven years old. I wish I'd known that much at your age.'

Jamie pulled a face. 'Yesterday he didn't want to be my friend, and today he does. I haven't changed. The only thing that's changed is that he knows you're my friend.'

'That doesn't matter, Jamie.' Meg's voice was husky. 'As long as he isn't being nasty, that's the important thing.'

'I think the reason he picks on me is so that he doesn't get picked on himself.'

Startled by that insight, Dino put down his glass. 'What makes you say that?'

'The way people behave...' Jamie sprinkled cheese over the pizza bases. 'There's usually a reason. My mum taught me that. People are complicated. What you see on the outside isn't what's on the inside.'

'Right.' Dino looked at Meg but she was busy chopping mushrooms.

'You can't always believe what people say,' Jamie said stoutly, plopping olives and pepperoni onto one of the pizzas. 'Sometimes people say things they don't mean. And sometimes they don't say things they do mean. Do you want pepperoni and olives?'

'Sì, grazie,' Dino said absently, his mind on the conversation. *Sometimes people say things they don't mean.* Was that what had happened with Jamie's father? 'So who is your best friend at school?'

'Luke Nicholson.'

'Sean and Ally's youngest son.' Meg took another sip of her champagne. 'Luke is a really nice boy. Sean's been taking the two of them climbing. Jamie, that's enough for one pizza. Do one of the others now.'

Jamie loaded the other pizza bases with toppings. 'If

we lived in Italy, could we eat this all the time? I bet you made loads of pizzas with your parents when you were little, Dino.'

Dino thought about the atmosphere of his parents' home. On the rare occasions he'd been allowed to join his parents for dinner, it had been an excruciatingly formal occasion with no concession to the presence of children. His sister and he had endured countless long, boring evenings when he would rather have been playing or asleep.

'I didn't make pizza, but I always wanted to.' At the time he hadn't imagined that kids did that sort of thing with their parents, but clearly he was wrong.

Jamie pushed a base across to him. 'Go on, then. The cheese and tomato is the hard part and I've done that for you. You just have to choose what else you want.'

Smiling, Dino sprinkled olives, pepperoni and mushrooms and Meg slid the pizzas into the oven.

Jamie jumped down from his stool. 'I'm going to watch TV until it's ready. Don't let them burn, Mum.' He vanished from the room and Meg gave Dino an apologetic glance.

'Sorry.' She started clearing the various bowls from the table. 'Not what you're used to, I'm sure.'

'No. It's better.'

'Don't patronise us, Dino.'

'Is that what you think I'm doing?'

'You just admitted you didn't eat pizza when you were a child.'

'Not because I didn't want to. Usually my sister and I ate alone in the kitchen with one of the nannies while my parents entertained in the dining room.' He looked around her kitchen. 'And the kitchen was nothing like this one.'

'You mean messy.'

'I mean homely.' He picked up one of Jamie's paintings that had been tidied to one side of the table. 'He's such an important part of your life. The evidence is everywhere.'

'That's because I don't spend enough time cleaning the place.' She blew the strands of hair away from her eyes. 'I'm not a natural housekeeper.'

'You're proud of him. It shows. And the place looks fine to me. No kid wants to live in a mausoleum.'

Startled by the sudden abruptness in Dino's voice, Meg risked asking a personal question. 'Is that how your house felt when you were growing up?'

Dino pushed his chair away from the table and stretched out his legs. 'We had paintings wired to alarm systems that connected straight through to the police station. Once I brought half the Rome police force round to the house by kicking a football indoors.'

'Ah.'

'My parents' child-care strategy was that children shouldn't be seen or heard. Which meant that basically we lived separate lives.'

A tiny frown creased her brow. 'I admit that doesn't sound great.'

'It wasn't.' Dino spoke quietly, not wanting to disturb too many of the memories. 'So perhaps now you'll believe me when I say I'm enjoying pizza night.'

'Oh, well—good.'

'You do this every Friday?'

'Yes. Unless I'm working.' She washed her hands and removed her apron. 'I wanted to thank you again for what you did yesterday. It's made all the difference to Jamie. And to me. It was such a relief to see him bouncing out of school today instead of slinking along.

I can always tell what sort of day he's had by the way he walks out of the building.'

'It was tough not intervening. I wanted to pick Freddie up by the collar and give him a talking to.'

'I think you found a more effective way of silencing him. Hopefully it will all calm down now.' Reaching up, she closed the blind in the kitchen. 'It's snowing again. Did you hear that they've issued an avalanche warning? Can you believe that in the Lake District?'

'We have had half a metre of snow in some places. Add to that a high wind and you end up with drifts that are only loosely attached to the mountainside. The snow pack needs time to consolidate.'

'I suppose you're used to it, having been brought up in the Alps. Apparently it's lethal underfoot. Some of the edges are literally breaking away and if you're standing underneath at the time, you're in trouble. They're warning people not to venture out. But people will, of course. There's always someone who thinks they're cleverer than the weather.' The conversation was light, skating over the surface of the personal, but he felt the undercurrent of tension and he knew she felt it, too.

Since that moment in the tent on the mountain, everything had changed.

Every interaction they shared had another level—something deeper.

Sensing that this wasn't the moment to explore that further, Dino looked at the dog stretched out in front of the range cooker, enjoying the warmth. 'Is Rambo trained to search in snow?'

'Yes. Whenever we have snow we do extra training because obviously there aren't that many opportunities around here. But it's a different skill. A search dog is trained to find the person, bark, and then return to the handler. They carry on doing that until they've drawn the handler to the body.' She bent down and stroked Rambo's head, making a fuss of him. 'When they're working in snow they have to stay with the scent and dig. He's good at it.'

'How long have you had him?' Dino crouched down to stroke the dog too and Meg immediately pulled her hand away.

'He was my eighteenth birthday present from my parents. I was already involved with the mountain rescue team. I used to help out manning the base and I worked as a volunteer body. That means losing yourself on a mountain so that the dogs can practise finding you. Then, when I had Rambo, I trained him. It took longer than usual because halfway through I discovered I was pregnant and that—well, let's just say that complicated things.'

He wanted to ask her how, but he was afraid of triggering the same response he'd seen a few days earlier when he'd asked if Jamie's father was still on the scene. 'So you moved into this cottage?'

'My dad died the same year I had Jamie.' She pulled a face. 'It was a truly terrible year. I lived with Mum for a while, it worked better that way. We were both on our own and somehow we got through it together. Then she suggested I move into Lake Cottage. I'd always loved it and it's only half a mile from her house so it's perfect. If I'm called out in the night on a rescue I just drop Jamie with her, or she comes over here. I'm lucky. How about you? How did you get involved with mountain rescue?'

'When I stopped competitive skiing, I started off working as a ski guide to earn money before I went to university. Then I did mountain rescue.' He wanted to

ask whether she'd been on her own right from the start.
Whether Jamie's father had walked out before he was
born. Had she married the guy?

'How did you end up in England?'

He'd been escaping. 'I wanted a change. Do I smell
pizza?'

Meg gasped and grabbed a cloth. 'Jamie will kill me
if I've burnt them.' She pulled them out of the oven and
Dino smiled as he looked at the bubbling cheese and
perfectly cooked crust.

'I thought you told me you were a lousy cook.'

'I am normally. You were the one who reminded
me to get them out of the oven before they were burnt
to a cinder.' She cut the pizzas into slices. 'Jamie! It's
ready!'

They ate pizza together and he watched as she listened attentively to Jamie's questions and answered
them. She was interested in her child, he thought, and
that gave the boy confidence. He tried to remember a
time when his mother had given him that much of her
time, but failed. Families were all different, but this—
this was the way he would have wanted his to be.

After the pizza had been cleared away and Jamie had
gone to get ready for bed, Dino decided that this was
the right time to ask the question he'd been waiting to
ask. 'I have two tickets to the Christmas ball.'

Her shoulders tensed. 'Good for you. I hope you have
a nice time.'

'I'll pick you up at eight o'clock.'

It took a moment for his words to sink in, but when
they did her entire face changed. The tension that had
been simmering below the surface bubbled up. 'Me?
No way. I don't go to that sort of thing.'

'Why not?'

'For a start, I don't dance.'

'Pathetic excuse.'

'That was just one. I have loads more. I can give you a list.'

'And I'm not going to be impressed by any of them.' Dino wondered why it was such a big deal to her. Judging from the expression on her face, he might have just asked her to have his babies.

Was it him? he wondered. *Or men in general?*

'The ball is next Saturday,' he said calmly, 'at the Winter Hill Hotel and Spa.'

'I know when it is and I've already told you I can't make it.' She stacked the dirty plates and took them over to the dishwasher. 'But thanks for inviting me. That was kind.'

'Kind?' Dino put his glass down slowly. 'Is that what you think? That I'm being kind?'

'I'm not thinking at all.' There was a note of panic in her voice as she clattered plates. 'There's no need to think and analyse because I'm not going. Take someone else. I'm sure there's a whole queue of women just desperate to go with you.' One of the plates slipped through her fingers and smashed on the floor. Muttering under her breath, she swept up the bits and disposed of them.

Dino stood up to help her but she glared at him. 'I'm fine—I can sweep up my own mess, Dino.'

'Do you always insist on doing everything by yourself, with no help?'

'Yes. I'm a grown-up. That's what happens when you're a grown-up. It's called independence.'

'Doesn't mean you can't take help.'

'I'm fine, Dino.'

He stood still, wondering what it was about him

that had her so on edge. She wasn't just uncomfortable around him—she was nervous. Jumpy. 'If I'd asked you out to dinner, would you have said yes?'

'Maybe… No…' She shook her head. 'No, I wouldn't. I don't date. It just isn't…'

'Isn't what?'

'Me. My life. Pick another woman, Dino.'

'I just picked you.'

'Well, unpick me!' Her eyes were two huge pools of panic. 'You'd have more fun with someone else. I'm not great at parties. I don't dance, I hate small talk and…' She flicked the wisps of hair out of her eyes with shaking fingers. 'Dino, just forget it. I don't even know why you're asking me.'

'Because you're the one I want to take. We don't have to dance if you don't want to. But that doesn't stop us going out. It's Christmas, Meg. Let your hair down.' He meant it in both a figurative and literal sense. He'd only seen her with her hair down once and that had been when she'd pulled her hat off her head the night they'd rescued Harry. The image of pale gold curls was still embedded in his brain. Using his powers of persuasion, he tried to think what might tempt her to go. 'It's a really smart evening. A good excuse to buy yourself a new dress.'

Another plate almost slipped to the floor but this time she caught it just in time. 'I don't need a new dress because I'm not going.'

Dino cursed himself for being tactless. She was a single mother, wasn't she? She probably had to watch her finances really carefully and here was he suggesting she buy a new dress. He wanted to offer to treat her to something new but sensed that would offend her well-developed sense of independence. Instead, he tried to rescue the situation. 'Just wear anything that's in your wardrobe.'

'Oh, right. I'll wear my best weatherproof jacket, shall I?' Her tone was light but her shoulders were rigid as she clattered around the kitchen, tidying surfaces that were already tidy. 'As I said, it's kind of you Dino, but, really, I don't want to go. You'll have loads more fun with someone else. I won't offer you coffee because I expect you're in a hurry to leave.'

And that was that.

The friendly atmosphere had shattered. The conversation had made her so uncomfortable that she wanted it to be over. She wanted him to leave.

Dino didn't budge. 'Coffee would be great. And I'm not in a hurry. So is it the issue of what to wear that's putting you off going? Because if so, I—'

'You don't give up, do you?' Her interruption was sharp. 'I've told you—that sort of thing just isn't me.'

'So what is you?'

She spooned fresh coffee into a jug. 'I play with my son and my dog. I work. I train Rambo. I walk in the mountains. That's it. That's my life. Maybe other people wouldn't find it exciting, but I love it. I don't need to dress up to enjoy myself. I'm happier in my walking boots than stilettos. Going to parties isn't on the list of things I do.'

Dino stood up and walked across to her, removed the spoon from her hand and put his hands on her shoulders. Rambo lifted his head, tongue lolling. Then his tail brushed over the floor, as if he approved.

'Why does it have to be one thing or another? You make it sound as though they're two different lives, but they could fit alongside each other. We had a deal, remember?' He cupped her face in his hands, stroking his thumb over her cheek, trying to read what was going on in her head. 'You owe me a date. Time of my choosing. Place of my choosing. Time is going to be next Saturday. Place is going to be the Christmas ball. And you're going to have a nice time. I promise you.'

'Don't you listen to "no"?'

'I'm selective.'

Her eyes gleamed with exasperation. 'Why are you asking me, anyway? Is Melissa busy?'

'Melissa?' Dino frowned. 'You mean the blonde who works in the observation unit? I have no idea if she's busy. I haven't asked her.'

'You should. Judging from the way she was flirting with you earlier in the week, I'm sure she'd say yes.'

'That's why you walked off so abruptly?'

'I didn't want to get in the way of a beautiful romance.' She pushed at his chest and he thought it was interesting that this time Rambo didn't growl a warning. Which was just as well because, dog or no dog, this time he wasn't moving.

'I'm not in a relationship with Melissa.'

'I couldn't care less if you are. It isn't any of my business.' The heat rushed into her cheeks and Dino found himself struggling to concentrate. The scent of her hair numbed his reactions and the soft curve of her mouth pulled him in.

'You think I'd be asking you to the ball if I was seeing someone?'

'You're a popular guy. It's like a hornets' nest around your office on some days. The women are three deep.'

'I'm not involved with anyone.'

'So who did you take to dinner last Sunday?'

'Her name is Anna Townsend. She's a lawyer who

has done some work for me in the past. And it was just lunch.'

'You said the date ended exactly the way you wanted it to.'

'It wasn't a "date" in the sense that you mean,' he said calmly, 'and it did end exactly the way I wanted it to. She went home and I went for a walk in the mountains.' Outside the snow might be falling but here, inside her kitchen, the heat was building between them.

Her breathing wasn't quite steady. 'It doesn't make any difference. I still can't go with you. Even if I wanted to, I wouldn't be able to arrange babysitting at this short notice.'

'Your mum is babysitting. I already asked her.'

Meg's mouth dropped open. 'You *asked* her? You've already asked my mum? Is this a conspiracy to get me into a dress or something?'

'Actually my long-term plan was to get you *out* of your dress.' Dino slid one hand into her hair, amused to see her so flustered. Her soft curls wrapped themselves around his fingers. 'Judging from your expression I gather flirting isn't on the list of things you usually do either. How about kissing, Meg?' He lowered his head so that his mouth almost touched hers. 'Is kissing on the list of things you do?' The tension hovered there between them, sharpened by the knowledge of what was to come. For a moment neither of them moved. Sexual chemistry arced through the stillness and he saw her lips part and her breathing grow shallow.

Losing his grip on control, Dino claimed her mouth in what was supposed to be a teasing, exploratory kiss, but the moment their lips touched it was like lighting a fuse. Heat ripped through his body and pulsed across nerve endings. It was scorching and wild and he heard her gasp. Her fingers clutched his shoulders and then she was kissing him back, her body yielding against his as he pressed her back against the cupboard.

'Mum!' Through the haze of passion, Jamie's voice came from upstairs. 'I'm ready for you to tuck me in!'

She jerked in his arms and Dino released her instantly. 'Sorry.' His voice came out rough and raw. 'Bad timing.'

'Yes…' She rubbed her fingers over her scarlet cheeks. 'You— How did you learn to—? Never mind.' Deliciously flustered, she moved away from him. 'I have to go and read to Jamie.'

'Go.' Dino thought about asking whether he could use her bathroom for a cold shower. 'I'll pour the coffee.'

'No. Perhaps we'd better call it a night.' She ran her tongue over her lower lip, her expression dazed. 'By the time I've read to him and tucked him in, you'll be bored. There's no point in you waiting around…' She looked confused, as if she wasn't quite aware of her surroundings, and he understood that feeling. He'd thought about kissing her for a long time, of course; since the first day he'd started working in the emergency department and had seen her talking some drunk out of hitting her. He'd had plenty of fantasies about tasting her smart mouth, but all those fantasies had just been blown apart and replaced by hot, pulsing reality. If Jamie hadn't called out when he had…

'All right, I'll go. This time.' His voice sounded husky. 'But next time, Meg, I won't be leaving before coffee.' Having delivered that warning, Dino grabbed his jacket from the back of the chair. 'Thanks for the pizza. I'll pick you up at eight o'clock on Saturday. And I'm not taking no for an answer.'

* * *

Meg banged into the doorframe and tripped over Jamie's schoolbag.

'Look where you're going, Mummy.' Jamie's voice was sleepy. 'You took a long time. Were you talking to Dino?'

Focus, Meg, focus. One foot in front of the other.

'Yes, we were talking. Just—talking.' Her mind still on Dino, Meg stooped to pick his schoolbag up off the floor, wondering how a single kiss could have a negative effect on balance. The world was hazy and there was a strange buzzing in her head. Maybe it was the champagne.

She ran her tongue over her lower lip again, still tasting the warmth of his kiss. Erotic images exploded in her brain.

'Mummy, why is your face all red?'

Because she was thinking of Dino. 'Because I've been rushing around making supper, pulling pizza out of the oven and generally slaving away all evening.' Turning her back to Jamie, she laid his clothes over the back of the chair, taking her time so that her face calmed down, telling herself that the only reason she felt this way was because she hadn't been kissed by a man for such a long time.

But was that really true?

Since when had she had a burning urge to rip a man's clothes off? When had she ever been so aware of a man, physically?

Cross with herself, she reminded herself about all the women who were interested in Dino. There were so many, she'd lost count. She wouldn't be human if she didn't notice how good looking he was. And as for kissing—well, no doubt Dino Zinetti had a PhD in kissing. Dr Hot indeed.

'Jamie, it's time for you to get some sleep.'

'Can't I have a story? You haven't read to me.'

Meg grabbed the book from the bed and sat down next to him. But instead of seeing the words, she saw the sexy look in Dino's eyes as he'd bent his head to kiss her.

It wasn't the champagne. It was the man.

Jamie sighed, wriggled upright and turned the book the other way up. 'You can't read if it's upside down, silly.'

Meg blinked. 'Oh. Just testing to see if you were concentrating.' She gave a weak smile and tried to focus on the page but her lips were tingling and her pulse was still racing. 'Right—where were we? Dragons…' She read the words aloud without digesting the meaning. *What now?* What was she supposed to say when she saw him at work? Was she going to behave as if nothing had happened? Would he? And what about the Christmas ball? She'd said no at least ten times, but Dino didn't listen to 'no'.

'You're not using the right voices. Normally you do a high voice for the baby dragon and a low voice for the big dragon.' Jamie peered at her. 'Are you sure you're OK? You look sort of weird. Did you bang your head when you walked into my door?'

She felt sort of weird.

She felt…different.

It was just a kiss, for goodness' sake. She rolled her eyes. That was like describing champagne as 'just a drink'. Who was she kidding? As kisses went, this one had blown every circuit in her mind. Judging from the way he hadn't argued about leaving, she guessed it had blown every circuit in his, too.

'I'm fine,' Meg said firmly, concentrating hard on the

dragon story and trying desperately not to think about Dino. He shouldn't have complicated everything by kissing her, but they could move on from this. She wouldn't be going to the ball with him. The mere thought of it filled her with dread. It would show off all the worst parts of herself.

She knew that most of the girls working at the hospital looked forward to it all year. It was the highlight of the Christmas social calendar and there was always a fight for tickets and an argument over who was going to work and who was going to have the night off.

Meg didn't feel that way, which was why she always ended up working.

She gave a slow smile as the answer flew into her head. Of course. Why hadn't she thought of it before? She'd volunteer to work, as she always did every other year. If Dino wouldn't take no for an answer, she'd simply make herself unavailable.

CHAPTER FOUR

MEG was dressing the leg of an old lady who had slipped on the snow and ice when her team pager went off. 'Oh.' She looked down at herself. 'I'm bleeping, Agnes. That's the mountain rescue pager.'

'Someone in trouble on the mountains, dear? The snow was falling all night but I still see walkers trudging past my front door.' The woman flexed her foot. 'That feels very comfortable, thank you. You'd better see what they want, Meg. Don't mind me. I can get my own shoe back on.'

'Don't move until I've talked to you about how you're getting home, Agnes.' Meg dragged the pager out of her pocket and read the message. 'Avalanche? You have to be kidding me.'

'Worst weather conditions for eighteen years. I had to wait three hours for a bus yesterday.' Ignoring Meg's instructions, Agnes stood up. 'It isn't safe to leave the house without crampons. And a young thing like you shouldn't be going out in all weathers. I remember your dad was the same.'

Meg washed her hands quickly. 'Agnes, if you come with me now, I can drop you off on my way to the mountain rescue base. I drive past your house. Then you won't have to stand in the freezing cold waiting for a bus that might never turn up because of the snow. I just need to tell the sister in charge what's happening. Wait there for me.'

She found Ellie, grabbed her coat and her car keys and minutes later she was dropping Agnes off outside her cottage. Having seen her safely inside the house, Meg drove to her mother's house, collected Rambo and made her way through the falling snow to the rescue centre.

'A party of three men were ski touring.' Sean, the leader of the local mountain rescue team, was standing over a map, pointing out the search area. 'They were traversing along the top of this gully when one of them was caught in an avalanche. Their last known position was here, but since then the battery on their cellphone has died, or else they've been caught by another avalanche.'

'Who called you?'

'One of the other three. They were higher than him. The slope broke below them and took him with it.'

Dino strode into the room, zipping up his jacket as he walked. 'Were they carrying transceivers?'

Meg kept her eyes fixed on the map. 'I doubt it.'

'Phone went dead before they could tell me—I'm assuming not.' Sean's face was grim. 'You know how people underestimate the Lake District. Don't any of you do the same. The snowpack is unstable on the south and north-easterly aspects so this is where we need to be careful. Remember that it's loading—adding weight— that causes most avalanches and the fastest way to load a slope is by wind.'

Still not looking at Dino, Meg pushed her hair under her hat. 'And we've had plenty of wind.'

'Precisely. Wind erodes from the upwind side of an

obstacle such as a ridge and it deposits on the downwind side, and wind can deposit snow ten times more rapidly than snow falling from the sky.' Sean sketched a quick picture, showing what he meant. 'Be wary of any slope with recent deposits of wind-drifted snow.'

'So what's the plan?'

'It will take too long to reach them on foot and conditions are clear so, Meg, the air ambulance is going to airlift you, Rambo and Dino straight to the scene. I want you two to work together.'

Great. So much for avoiding him.

Knowing that if she made a fuss she'd just draw attention to herself, Meg gave a nod to acknowledge that she'd heard. Then she kept her head down, preparing herself and Rambo for the challenge ahead. She didn't want to risk looking at Dino in case something showed on her face. If the team sensed that there was something going on between them, she'd never live it down. She was one of the boys. That was the way it was going to stay.

The helicopter dropped them at a safe distance from the base of the gully and Meg immediately put Rambo to work. Lives were at stake. This was no time to be thinking about kissing. Dino apparently felt the same way because he seemed equally focused. Either that or the kiss hadn't affected him the same way it had affected her.

'Can you believe they only have one working mobile phone between the three of them?' Dino scanned the gully. 'You can see where the avalanche started, above that section of wind slab. The others must have been higher up or they all would have been caught.'

'People underestimate these mountains. That's what makes them all the more dangerous.' Meg heard Rambo bark and she pushed herself forward through the deep snow to the bottom of the gully where the dog was already digging.

'He's picked up a scent.' She struggled the final few metres as Rambo carried on digging and barking. 'How long has he been buried? Does he really stand a chance?'

'There's always a chance. Depends how near the surface he is and whether he has space in front of his mouth and nose. Victims often die of suffocation. Off the top of my head I think survival rates drop to about 35 per cent at thirty minutes. On the other hand, friends of mine pulled someone alive from an avalanche in Italy after ten hours, but admittedly that's rare. He was in an air pocket and the weight of the snow hadn't crushed him.'

Dino already had a shovel in his hand and he started to help Rambo. A few minutes later the sleeve of a jacket came into view. Rambo barked and continued to dig. Moments later a man's face appeared, streaked with blood and crusted with snow. He looked at them, dazed, and Meg felt a rush of elation that he was still alive.

'Hang on there. We're going to get you out. Clever boy,' she praised Rambo effusively, and then concentrated on helping Dino dig the last of the snow away.

'I can't feel my feet.' The man was gasping for air and Dino dropped the shovel onto the snow and reached for his backpack.

'That might be the cold, but it's possible that you damaged your back as you fell so we need to be careful as we move you. Can you remember what happened?'

The man screwed his eyes shut, wincing with the pain. 'Visibility was poor, I skied to the far left of the slope. Suddenly my legs went and I was falling. I rolled over and over, couldn't breathe—tried to swim like they tell you to, tried to get my arms up…' He opened his eyes. 'Are my friends safe? They were behind me.'

'They called us before they lost the phone battery. They saw the whole thing but they weren't caught in it. The rest of the mountain rescue team is looking for them now. They were fine when they called.' Meg tried to reassure him while helping Dino carry out the best examination he could in difficult circumstances.

'Does this hurt? Can you feel this?' He was treating the man for head, leg and possible spinal injuries, and Meg used her hands to dig away more of the snow so that Dino had room to see what he was doing.

'Do you want me to contact the search-and-rescue helicopter?'

'Helicopter?' The man groaned. 'I don't think I can get into a helicopter.'

'Trust me, it's the best way. We're going to put you in a vacuum mattress, Dave, to protect your spine,' Dino explained. 'You don't have to do a thing. You'll be winched into the helicopter and they'll get you to hospital.' He nodded to Meg and she quickly made the call while Dino started to prepare the casualty for the transfer.

Dave closed his eyes. 'Can't believe I've been caught in an avalanche in the Lake District. I've walked in the Alps, you know. Can you believe that? This is going to be so embarrassing down at the pub.'

Meg saw Dino's mouth tighten and she knew he was annoyed by that flippant comment.

'You could have died,' she said mildly as she slipped the phone back into her pocket, 'and so could your friends. The outcome could have been a lot worse than embarrassment.'

'If you've done ski touring in the Alps then you must have carried transceivers? Shovels? Probes?' Dino yanked his equipment out of his backpack and the man looked sheepish.

'In the Alps, yes. I guess we were complacent here.'

'Avalanches eat up complacent skiers and climbers. Don't move, Dave. The winchman is going to lower the vacuum mattress and a stretcher and we're going to get you to hospital.' Dino walked across the snow to find a safe place for the helicopter to land while Meg and Rambo stayed next to the injured skier.

Dave put out a hand to the dog. 'I have you to thank for being found. I recognise that guy. It's Dino Zinetti, isn't it? He used to be a member of the Italian ski team.'

'How do you know that?'

'I'm a keen skier. He was a maniac. His downhill times…' Dave laughed. 'Well, let's just say he isn't really in a position to lecture me for being reckless.'

'He wasn't lecturing. It isn't our job to lecture.' As the helicopter drew closer, Meg pulled together the rest of her gear, ready to move out. 'But it is our job to point out where additional equipment might have helped so that people don't put themselves in the same position again.' The downdraft from the helicopter flung powdery snow through the air like a blizzard and Meg shifted her position and tried to protect the man from the sudden buffeting of icy wind.

It was only a matter of minutes before Dino came back with the stretcher and the vacuum mattress and together they moved Dave, careful to protect his spine.

'This will hold you secure,' she explained, as they

pumped up the mattress and strapped it to the stretcher. 'I expect I'll see you at the hospital. Good luck.'

'Thanks.' The man closed his eyes, choosing not to look as he was winched into the hovering helicopter.

As the aircraft became a dot in the distance, Dino turned to her. 'The team have found the rest of his party on the other side of the ridge, so they're going to walk them back down the other track. We'll go back together. Although frankly this isn't a great place to be walking. There's a lot of loose powder snow up there just waiting to bury someone stupid enough to walk beneath it. Watch yourself.'

Meg glanced up at the pile of snow that had almost claimed a life. 'I have to confess I'm not an expert on avalanches.'

'It isn't hard to spot dangerous slopes when you know what you're looking for.' He drew her to one side and pointed, his breath clouding the air. 'Look up there.'

Trying to block out the fact that he was standing within kissing distance, Meg looked at the snow-covered gully. 'I'm looking.' But it was hard to concentrate. She was breathlessly conscious of him. Unable to help herself, she turned her head and glanced at his profile. It was an unmistakeably masculine face—eyelashes thick and dark, his jaw shadowed by stubble. Meg felt something elemental uncurl inside her.

'Can you see where the wind slab fractured above him?' His head turned and his gaze sharpened as he caught her looking at him.

Meg immediately whipped her head back towards the slope, feeling her face turn scarlet. 'Yes,' she croaked, 'I can see.' For a moment she thought she'd got away with it. And then she felt his gloved hand brush against her cheek. He turned her head so that she had no choice but to look at him.

'How long are you going to carry on pretending last night never happened?'

Trapped by his gaze, Meg stared up at him and he slid his hand behind her head and drew her towards him. The blood throbbed in her veins and a delicious, thrilling feeling of inevitability gripped her. As if in slow motion he lowered his head. His eyes held hers until the last moment. And then he claimed her mouth and sent her brain spinning.

Excitement, almost agonising in its intensity, speared her body. Her eyes closed, the world ceased to be grey and white and became a multicoloured kaleidoscope of feelings and emotions. And suddenly there was no doubt left in her head.

Standing in this wild, beautiful place, being kissed by this man, felt completely right. She knew what she wanted. Him. She knew that if he wanted to make love to her here, her answer was going to be yes.

Meg closed her gloved hands on the front of his jacket and leaned into him. His hands were in her hair then on her shoulders and down her back. She tugged at him and he lowered her onto the soft snow, pillowing her head with his arm as he kissed her. And it felt incredible. The skilled brush of his fingers against her face, the warmth of his breath against her mouth as he nudged her lips apart and, finally, the seductive stroke of his tongue as the kiss turned deeper and more explicit.

She'd had no idea, Meg thought dizzily. *No idea that a kiss could feel like this.*

With the snow pressing against her back, she should have felt cold. The air around them was freezing and a few stray flakes had started to fall, but she felt nothing

but scorching heat and burning need. Without discon-
necting the kiss, Dino drew down the zip of her jacket.
Meg gasped as cold air brushed against her flesh and
then moaned as he pressed his mouth to the sensitive
flesh of her throat. She murmured his name and slid
her hands around his neck, her fingers encountering
the collar of his jacket as she tried to get closer to him.
She wanted to touch—*she needed to feel*—but their
outdoor clothing prevented them from anything but the
most minimal contact. With a sob of desperation, she
twisted against him, feeling the fingers of cold penetrate
the neck of her jacket where he'd exposed her flesh. She
started to shiver and instantly Dino hauled himself away
from her and dragged her to her feet.

'*Mi dispiace*, I'm sorry.' His voice hoarse, he yanked
her zip back up to her throat and rubbed her arms to
warm her. 'I can't believe I did that. I don't know what
I was thinking. You are going to get hypothermia. We
shouldn't be doing this here. It isn't the time and it isn't
the place.' As if reorienting himself, he glanced around
and gave an exasperated shake of his head. 'Can you
walk or are you too cold?'

Meg felt numb, but she knew it had nothing to do
with the cold and everything to do with the way he made
her feel. 'I'm fine. Really.' Or she would be once she'd
got herself home and talked some sense into herself.
She had a child. She had a life she liked. Why, after all
these years, was she risking all that?

Misinterpreting her silence, Dino dragged her against
him and held her close, warming her. 'You must be
freezing. I can't believe I lost control like that. It's you—
the way you make me feel…'

Despite the warning bells in her head, his words

caused a buzz inside her and she pressed her lips to his cold cheek. 'You smell good, have I told you that?'

He turned his head to capture her mouth. 'Unless you want to find yourself flat on your back in the snow again, you'd better not say things like that. All these months I've been feeling as though I need to take a cold shower when you walk into the room, and suddenly I discover that even freezing ice isn't going to work.'

Months?

He'd felt like this for months? She'd had no idea. Seriously unsettled by how much that frank confession disturbed her equilibrium, Meg stooped and picked up a handful of snow. 'Want me to help you out with that problem of yours, macho man?'

Laughing, he caught her wrist in an iron grip. 'Put that anywhere near my trousers and we won't be able to take this any further.'

Did she want to take it further?

Confused by the feelings fluttering inside her, she dropped the snow and stepped close to him. 'Dino—'

He smothered her words with a kiss and then stepped back and held up his hands. '*Accidenti,* enough! We need to get going before we are buried in another avalanche or it grows dark.'

It came as a surprise to realise that she really didn't want to go. She didn't want to leave this place. If he hadn't pulled her to her feet, she never would have stopped. She'd been willing to risk frostbite in order to claw her way closer to him. She hadn't wanted the kiss to end. She would have happily gone on kissing him for the rest of her life, rather than confronting just how dangerous falling under Dino Zinetti's spell could be for her.

Looking around, Meg realised just how isolated they

were. The sky was a threatening shade of grey. At some point while they'd been generating heat with each other, it had started snowing again.

Dino hauled his backpack onto his shoulders and secured the waist strap. 'Are you all right to walk?'

Refusing to reveal how shaken she was, Meg gave a mocking smile. 'You may be a good kisser, Zinetti, but even you're not so good I can't put one foot in front of the other.'

'Is that a challenge?' His took her face in his hands and lowered his mouth to hers again. 'Do you know how long I've waited to do this? I was about a day away from just throwing you onto a trolley in the emergency department.' This second frank confession of need made her stomach flip and she laughed against his lips.

'That bad?'

'Worse.' Reluctantly, he lifted his head. 'Much as I'm appreciating the solitude of this place, we have to go. Otherwise our fellow team members will be making another trip up the mountain, this time to rescue us.'

'And that would be almost as embarrassing as being caught in an avalanche in the Lake District.'

Dino helped her slide her arms into her backpack. 'Rambo didn't bark at us. Two bodies in the snow, and he didn't bark. Do you think he knew he was supposed to be discreet?'

'No. He knew we weren't lost.' Meg started to trudge through the snow but it was deep and heavy and the going was exhausting. 'That guy recognised you. Said you used to risk your neck on downhill runs. Why did you stop competitive skiing?' Rambo ran ahead, light on the snow, nosing the ground. She envied his ability to move so easily in the unfriendly terrain.

'I had a couple of injuries. Shoulder...' He flexed

his shoulder under his pack. 'That was a nasty one. Concussion. But in the end I just had to make a choice between skiing and medicine. I couldn't compete at high level and study. So instead I combined my mountain knowledge and my medical knowledge.'

'So you must have seen some real avalanches.'

'That was a real avalanche, Meg. And there could be more.' Glancing back over his shoulder to where they'd come from, Dino frowned. 'We ought to talk to Sean about getting some sort of warning issued. Local radio. Hotels. That sort of thing. The snowpack is too unstable for people to be taking risks. In some ways it's even more dangerous than the Alps because people underestimate what they're dealing with here. That man was lucky. It could easily have ended differently and Rambo would have been barking at a dead body.'

Meg shuddered. 'The weather is closing in. Are we going to make it home before dark?'

'Yes. Why? Don't you fancy a night up here in the wilderness with me?'

Struggling with the deep snow, she smiled. 'You take up too much room in the tent. And anyway, I have to pick Jamie up from my mum's. Tonight is her bridge night or something. I don't want to ruin her social life. Talking of which…' She kept her voice casual. 'I'm afraid I can't make the ball—Ellie needs me to work that shift so I had to swap.'

'Yes, she told me. I swapped it back.' He caught her arm as she stumbled in the deep snow.

'You swapped my shifts?'

'I simply explained to Ellie that you were going to the ball. She was most surprised that you'd offered to switch given that you have a date.'

Trapped, outmanoeuvred, Meg ground her teeth. 'She

won't be able to spare me. It's a nightmare trying to staff that shift.'

'On the contrary, she said that given the number of times you've covered for other people over the years, the least she can do is give you the evening off. You're working a late shift. We agreed that you'd work until eight o'clock. The night staff are going to come on early as a favour. It will mean you'll have to get ready at the hospital, but I don't suppose that matters.'

'Now, wait just a minute—'

'Meg.' He locked his hand in the front of her jacket and pulled her against him, leaving her in no doubt about who was in charge of the decision-making on this particular point. 'Changing your shift isn't going to work. Talking to Ellie isn't going to work. Contracting some mysterious illness isn't going to work. I'm taking you to the ball.'

'What if I tell you I just don't like you enough to go to the ball with you?'

'Then we'll both know you're lying.' Without giving her the opportunity to argue, he leaned in and kissed her. As his lips brushed over hers, her blood heated and for a moment she forgot what they were talking about. Everything important slid out of her mind, leaving a vacant space occupied only by the most intense, sizzling heat she'd ever experienced.

Terrified, Meg shoved at his chest. 'Does that confidence of yours ever get you into trouble?'

'Not so far.'

'You can't run my life.'

'What is it that frightens you? The ball, or me?'

'Both.' Angry with him and suddenly furious with herself too, Meg pulled away from him but he hauled her back against him, his hands firm on her body.

'It's just one evening.' He murmured the words against her lips. 'One evening. If you hate it, I'll take you home after an hour and that's a promise.'

She was about to tell him that an hour was going to seem like a lifetime when she remembered the way she'd felt when he'd tumbled her into the snow. Maybe it wouldn't be so bad. Maybe she should stop being stupid. He was right, wasn't he? It was just a ball and it had been years since she'd been to anything like that. Maybe she'd feel differently about the whole thing now that she was older. It wasn't as if she was going to be standing against the wall, waiting for someone to ask her to dance. She had a partner. And not just any partner—she had Dr Hot.

'All right, I'll go on Saturday,' she said finally. 'If that's really how you want to spend an evening. But don't say I didn't warn you when you come back with bruised feet. You're going to regret this.'

She had a feeling that she would, too.

Rambo sat watching Meg, his tail wagging.

'It's all very well telling me to wear whatever I have in my wardrobe, but I don't have anything in my wardrobe. One dress. That's it.' Meg pulled it out and hung it on the outside. She brushed the dust off it. Her mother had bought it for her years before when the mountain rescue team had thrown a party to celebrate her eighteenth birthday. Frowning at the plain black dress, she shook her head. She had absolutely no idea what to wear to a Christmas ball, but she knew she wasn't looking at it. She didn't own anything suitable, which meant that now she needed to go shopping and she absolutely *loathed* shopping for clothes. Buying a new pair of hiking boots was easy, but endless rails and racks of different dresses turned her brain to useless mush. She didn't know which colours or styles were in fashion. She didn't know what looked good on her. All she knew was that Dino Zinetti was going to take one look at her and wish he'd never invited her.

Daunted by the prospect of trying to find something to wear, Meg picked up the phone and rang Ellie. 'You're taking me shopping. Since you're the reason I'm going to this stupid ball, the least you can do is help me choose a dress that doesn't make me look awful.'

The fact that Ellie agreed immediately confirmed Meg's suspicions that her friend and colleague was matchmaking.

They met in the shopping centre a short drive from the hospital.

'This is going to end in tears, you know that, don't you?' Meg scowled as Ellie virtually danced up to her, a smile lighting her whole face.

'It's not going to end in tears.' Ellie slid her arm through Meg's. 'It's going to end in romance. And great sex.'

'Perhaps you should speak a little louder. I don't think those toddlers at the far end of the shopping mall quite heard you.'

'What do you have against sex?'

'El, you're doing it again. A few octaves lower would be good here, otherwise we're going to be kicked out before we've bought anything.'

'Sorry. I'm just so excited that you're going to the ball!'

'That makes one of us.'

'You're not excited? Seriously?'

'I'd rather sing the "Hallelujah Chorus" while standing naked on London Bridge in the rush-hour.'

'Gosh, you are weird.' Ellie bounced up to an exclusive boutique. 'It's a good job I'm excited enough for both of us.'

Meg took one look at elegant dresses in the window and stepped backwards, narrowly missing a mother with a pushchair. 'If you're even thinking of this shop, forget it. I can't afford it.'

'Look at the sign. Early sale. This is your lucky day.' Ignoring Meg's protests, Ellie tugged her through the revolving glass doors into the daunting hush of the up-market designer boutique. 'You're going to look perfect. This is going to be a real Cinderella moment.'

'Are we talking about the moment where her clothes fall off or the moment where she loses a shoe?' Meg muttered, but Ellie was already sifting through dresses. Envying her confidence, Meg stood awkwardly, waiting for someone to ask her to leave.

'What colour do you look good in?' Ellie squinted at her and Meg shrugged, hideously embarrassed.

'No idea. My thermal top looks OK on me—that's a sort of emerald green.'

Ellie rolled her eyes. 'Stop talking about thermal tops. On Saturday night you are not Meg, wolf-girl, you are Meg, sex-girl.'

'We are definitely going to be arrested.'

'You should be thinking silk and satin.'

'I'm thinking get me out of this nightmare.' Meg caught the eye of one of the shop assistants. 'Ellie—can we go somewhere more anonymous? We're the only people in this shop and those women are looking at me, wondering what on earth someone like me is doing in here.'

'Rubbish. You're their only customer and they're thinking, I hope she buys something.' Ellie was rifling through the rails. Occasionally she paused and narrowed her eyes before moving on. Finally she pulled a dress out and held it up. 'All right. This is the one. It's stunning.'

'It doesn't have any straps. How does it stay up?'

'It's fitted at the waist and your boobs will keep it up.'

'That's not reassuring. Ellie, I really don't think—'

'Try it. It's really sexy. You could wear your hair up. Do you have a necklace of some sort?'

'No.'

'Well, what do you normally wear around your neck?'

'A wool scarf.'

'I meant when you go out.' Ellie was laughing. 'What do you wear around your neck when you're not trudging through mountains?'

'Nothing.' Meg shrugged awkwardly. 'I don't really wear jewellery. Where would I wear jewellery? If I'm not in the mountains, I'm with my son.' She frowned. 'Actually, I do have something, now I think about it. Mum gave me a gold necklace that used to belong to my grandmother but I've never worn it. It's been in my drawer for seven years.'

'Sounds perfect.' Ellie thrust the dress towards her. 'Try it. Changing room is over there.'

'But—'

'Go. I'll find you some shoes to go with it.'

'Make sure they're flat.' Meg threw an embarrassed glance at the sales girls and gestured to the changing rooms. 'All right if I—?'

They waved her in and she slid into one of the cubicles and closed the door, cursing Ellie for getting her into this mess. It was one of the coldest winters on record and she was about to strip off and try on a strapless dress for an evening she absolutely didn't want to attend. Rolling her eyes, Meg removed her coat and pulled her sweater over her head. Pulling on the dress, she stared at herself sulkily. 'I look stupid.'

Ellie opened the door of the cubicle and looked at her. 'That's because you're wearing boots on your feet. Take them off and try these.' She held out a pair of gold stilettos. 'They'll look really sexy. The dress is completely gorgeous. Meg, no kidding, you look stunning. Is your cleavage real?'

'Of course it's real. You think I got a boob job when no one was looking?' Snappy and irritable, Meg toed off her boots and wriggled her feet into the gold shoes. 'Ouch, ouch, ow! They hurt. Do people seriously wear these things?'

'Yes, because they look fantastic.' Ellie stared down at Meg's feet. 'They also look tight. I'll fetch you a bigger size. Wait there. Don't go anywhere.'

'Trust me, I'm not going anywhere wearing this totally embarrassing dress with these things on my feet. There's half a metre of snow on the ground. I'm going to get frostbite.' Wincing, Meg dragged off the shoes and flexed her toes. 'Why do women do this to themselves?'

Fortunately the next pair Ellie brought her was an improvement. 'How do they feel?'

'As if I'm tipping forwards. I'm going to fall on my face.'

'You just feel like that because you're not used to heels, but you're going to be fine. Now, hair…' Ellie pulled a clip out of her bag and twisted Meg's hair into a knot at the back of her head. 'Looking good.'

'Looking weird.'

'It looks weird because you're just not used to seeing yourself like that. Meg—you're really beautiful. Why do you hate the way you look?'

Meg thought for a moment. 'Actually, I don't hate the way I look. Not really. It's men who hate the way I look.'

'You're talking about one man, Meg, not men in general.' Ellie's voice was tight and there was a flash of anger in her eyes. 'One man didn't like the way you look. And if I ever bump into him I'll break his nose and reposition his features.'

'You won't bump into him. You have two kids and he's allergic to anything remotely domestic.' It pleased her that finally she could talk about him without feeling as though she was going to fall apart. 'Last thing I heard, he was living it up in Ibiza. Dancing on the beach every night with women who spend most of the day getting ready for the night.' The sort of women she'd never understood.

Ellie pulled her into a tight hug. 'With any luck he'll catch some vile disease and his vital organs will drop off. He's history, Meg. It's over and done. And you've protected yourself for long enough. Get out there. Have fun.'

Meg stood frozen in her grasp. 'It isn't fun for me. I can't make people understand that. To me, a ball, a dance, a party—whatever—just isn't fun. It's non-stop stress. Am I wearing the right thing? Is everyone staring? Is everyone laughing at me? The answer to the first is almost always no, and the answer to the second two is almost always yes.'

Ellie sighed and tightened her grip. 'You're as rigid as my cat in a temper. Hug me back. It will make you feel better.'

Knowing when she was beaten, Meg hugged and instantly felt better. Friendship, she thought. Friendship was good. 'For a girl who straightens her hair and wears make-up, you're all right, Ellie.'

'I'm more than all right. And you're going to be more than all right, too. Dino isn't taking you because of your hair or your make-up, Meg. He's taking you because you're *you*. It's you he lo—likes. Remember that.'

Meg pulled away. 'Stop turning this into a big romance. It's one night, that's all. El, this dress is too tight. I can't sit down.'

'It's not tight. It's perfect. And you won't be sitting down, you'll be dancing. Or kissing. I want to be there when Dino first sees you. I know you don't wear much make-up, but this dress needs some make-up.'

'That's the dress's problem, not mine.'

'Do you even own make-up?'

'Of course.' Meg thought about the ancient tubes at the back of the bathroom cabinet. 'Somewhere. Everything has probably dried up by now.'

'If you haven't worn it for years, it will be the wrong make-up. We'll start fresh. Not because you need it, because you don't, but because wearing it will make you feel better.'

An hour later they were sitting in a coffee shop surrounded by bags.

'I honestly can't see myself wearing glitter on my eyes. I'll look like something that fell off the Christmas tree.' Meg poked the foam on her cappuccino. 'And the lipstick is too dark. I look like a vampire.'

'You look great. I'm really excited! I've been dying to see you take a chance on a man.'

'I'm not taking a chance. I'm just going to a Christmas

ball, for goodness' sake. We're talking about one date, not a future.'

'Every future starts with one date. You're so wary of everyone, Meg. Matt from Orthopaedics asked you out loads of times, but you said no. Last year it was that really nice doctor from New Zealand whose name escapes me—Pete, that's it. You turned him down too. This is the first time you've said yes. You must really like Dino.'

Meg's palms were damp. Realising that she *did* really like Dino made her want to hyperventilate with panic. How had that happened? *How had she lowered her guard enough to let someone in?* 'Dino?' Her mouth was dry and she struggled to keep her voice casual. 'He's fine.'

'Fine? *Fine?* He's completely, insanely *gorgeous.* Do you know how many of the nurses are trying to get his attention all the time?'

Meg pushed her cup away, feeling slightly sick. 'Yes. Yes, I do know.'

'So you should feel really special. He wants to go with you. He really likes you. You have so much in common. For a start, you both love the mountains.'

'Yes, but being in the mountains is different from being on a date. I'm not worrying about how I look all the time. I'm just me.'

'And it's just you he's invited to the ball,' Ellie said logically. 'So it's no different. It's just that you'll be doing it in a dress. And it's a gorgeous dress. You're going to have a great time. I know you are.'

Meg gave up trying to make Ellie understand. Instead, she shifted the focus of the conversation. 'What are you going to wear?'

'No idea. I have a red dress that I bought before I had

the children so if I can still fit into it, I might wear that. Then I have a black one that is good for "fat" days.'

'Wow. More than one dress.' Meg made a joke of it, but deep down she was in full-on panic mode. Maybe she could develop flu. Or maybe her mum could be persuaded not to babysit. Or maybe… With a sigh, she slumped in her chair. It was no good. She was going to have to go.

The whole thing was her worst nightmare.

CHAPTER FIVE

AT LUNCHTIME on the day of the ball, Dino slammed his way through the doors of the emergency department, his bleep sounding and his phone ringing simultaneously. 'Is someone trying to get hold of me?'

'Dino, thank goodness.' Unusually flustered, Ellie pushed equipment into his hands. 'There's a car stuck in snow on the Wrynose Pass. They can't go forwards and they can't go back. You need to go and help. Meg is going with you. I've packed everything I think you'll need.'

'How about a winch?' Dino lifted an eyebrow. 'Since when did we start operating a vehicle recovery service?'

'It's not the vehicle you're recovering, it's the woman inside. She's very pregnant. She was on her way over the pass to stay with her mum, because it's closer to the hospital and she's afraid of being snowed in, but she's now stuck in the snow. Before you say anything, no, it isn't funny.' Ellie stuffed two more blankets into his arms. 'Do you want the rest of the good news?'

'That was good news?'

'This is her second baby. The first one was a precipitate delivery. Thirty minutes from start to finish.'

Dino rolled his eyes. 'In that case, she needs to be airlifted.'

'The helicopter has just been grounded—they've found a fault. They're trying to get another one but in the meantime the only vehicle that can get you up there is the mountain rescue ambulance. Meg's already outside, waiting for you, revving up the engine.'

Dino strode towards the door and flung the extra equipment into the back of the four-wheel-drive vehicle that was used by the mountain rescue team. 'I'm driving.'

'No way.' Meg fastened her seat belt. 'I'm already sitting at the wheel. Get in, macho man.'

'I'll get in when you move into the passenger seat,' Dino drawled, leaning across and undoing her seat belt. 'Move over. I'm not kidding.'

Meg tightened her grip on the wheel and refused to move. 'Chauvinist.'

'Actually, you're wrong. If it were Ben or Sean sitting in the driver's seat, I'd still move them. I'm Italian. I don't like being driven. Move, Meg, before this woman gives birth in a snowdrift.'

With a sigh, she flounced across into the passenger seat. 'Fine. I'm only doing this because we can't waste any more time. Just don't come squealing to me for help when you've slid off the road because you don't know the bends of the Wrynose Pass. If you're in the wrong gear, you'll never make it.'

'I'll make it.' His hands confident on the wheel, Dino headed along the valley and turned onto the narrow road that led to the beginning of the pass. A snow plough had clearly been along the road before them and the snow was banked high against the stone walls that bordered the fields. 'Why did they pick this route?'

'Because they were desperate and panicking. The forecast for the next few days is really awful. They were afraid that if they waited any longer, they'd be snowed in. One of the disadvantages of living in a remote area.' Meg tucked her hair under her hat and sorted through the equipment. 'Watch yourself on this corner, the road suddenly gets a lot steeper and there's only room for one car. There are passing places, but most of them haven't been cleared since last night's snowfall.'

Dino glanced at her. 'How many times have you driven this road in winter?'

'Plenty. See? You should have let me drive. I know every rabbit hole.' She gave him a cheeky smile. 'The best way to get good at something is to practise. I practised. Driving the mountain passes is one of the best forms of entertainment.'

He was tempted to suggest a few other forms of entertainment that were less life threatening, but he decided this wasn't the time or the place. As they crested the top of the slope, he felt the back wheels of the ambulance slip and heard Meg gasp.

'Relax.' Dino handled the vehicle carefully, feeling the way it responded. 'I'm going to put chains on for the next hill. It's too slick and there's a drop on the right.' He jumped out and fastened the chains to the wheels. The landscape around them had been transformed by the heavy snow and a few abandoned vehicles lay half-buried by the side of the road. It took him less than five minutes to finish the job but that was long enough to freeze his hands.

The snow fell onto the windscreen in big fat lumps and Dino jumped back into the driver's seat, flicked on the wipers and turned the heating up to full. 'That should improve the grip. It's cold out there.' He flexed his fingers. 'I think the mountain rescue team will be called out tonight.'

'If that happens, we'll miss the ball.' Meg checked her phone for messages and he had a feeling that was exactly what she was hoping would happen.

'I'm flattered to know you're looking forward to our date, *tesoro*.'

'I warned you I wasn't good at that sort of thing. Look, I've said I'll go. What more do you want?'

'Enthusiasm?'

She bit her lip. 'I've bought a dress, so I suppose it would be nice to at least have the chance to wear it.'

'A dress? *Bene*. I look forward to seeing your legs for the first time.' Because he was concentrating on the road, Dino didn't see her frown. 'Is that the car? The red one.'

'Yes, looks like it.' Her voice was strange but when he glanced at her she simply glared at him.

'Keep your eyes on the road or you'll drive off it.' She turned back to look out of the windscreen, narrowing her eyes to see through the falling snow. 'The guy is waving. Why is he waving? He ought to just stay in the warm until we get there. There's no reason to—' She broke off and turned her head slowly. 'Oh, no—do you think…?'

'Possibly, knowing our luck,' Dino gritted, 'but if I drive any faster than this we'll end up in the ditch alongside them. Get on the phone and check on the helicopter situation. Failing that, get the police to meet us at the head of the pass.'

'Any excuse to break the speed limit.'

Dino smiled. 'I'm Italian. That's enough of an excuse.'

While Meg made the necessary calls, he negotiated

the switch back turns of the mountain pass and finally pulled up by the red car. Normally it would have been a dangerous place to stop but today, with the world transformed into a white, faceless desert, they were the only people on the road.

'Quickly.' His door was dragged open by the man who had been waving his arms at them. 'Are you the doctor? What the hell took you so long? I'm going to put in a complaint when all this is over. The baby's coming. I'm not kidding. God, you have to do something.' He choked the words out, hyperventilating, and Dino closed his hand over the other man's shoulder, trying to calm him down, choosing to ignore the rudeness.

'Breathe slowly. Deeply. That's better.' He jumped down from the vehicle and found himself in snow up to his knees. The cold immediately clamped his ankles and seeped through his clothing. 'When did her contractions start?'

'About ten minutes ago. I think it's the stress. We never should have left. But I took our little boy to his grandmother's a couple of days ago to give Sue a rest, and Sue was fretting, wanted us all to be together at her mother's for Christmas. If we hadn't left we would have been stranded, and—'

'Hi Mike, it's me.' Meg struggled through the snow and slapped the man on the back. 'Stop panicking. It's all going to be fine, I promise. We just need to get our equipment and then we'll sort her out. Go back and sit with Sue. And stop looking so worried or you'll scare her. Looking at your face is enough to make me go into labour and I'm not even pregnant. Everything is going to be fine.'

The man sucked in two deep breaths and swore. 'It isn't fine, Meg.' His voice was savage and he was clearly on the edge. 'Not every woman is tough. Sue isn't good in cold weather at the best of times. She's delicate and feminine—nothing like you.'

Dino saw Meg's face change.

'Right,' she said tonelessly, 'then we'd better get her out of there, hadn't we? It will be fine, Mike. Trust us.'

'Don't patronise me with all that false reassurance stuff. We're stuck on a mountain pass in the snow and my wife is in labour,' Mike snapped. 'There's nothing fine about it.'

'All right. If I admit we're in trouble, will you stop whining and let us do something about it?' Meg grabbed her bag out of the mountain rescue vehicle and staggered under the weight. 'We're here, and we're good at what we do. Dr Zinetti here has an Olympic gold medal.'

Mike rubbed snow from his face. 'Olympic gold medal? Do they award one of those for delivering babies?'

'Men's downhill, you idiot. Go back to Sue. We'll be with you in a minute.' Meg gave him a push. 'And smile. Tell her everything is going to be OK. We're right behind you.'

As Mike struggled back to the car through the snow, Meg reached into the vehicle for a spare coat. 'What a total idiot. That guy always did have a low burn threshold. Maturity doesn't seem to have improved things.'

'You know him. Is he an ex-boyfriend?' Dino only realised how cold his tone was when she sent him an astonished glance.

'Do you really think I'd hook up with a wimp like him? We went to school together. He was as spineless then as he clearly still is now. The sort who has to have a really, really fragile woman in order to feel big and manly.' She paused, her hand on the strap of her bag. 'What's the matter with you? You look as though you're about to thump someone. What is your problem? I know Mike can be beyond irritating, but you just have to take a breath. To be fair on him, you'd be tense, too, if your wife were about to give birth in a snowdrift.'

Dino fastened his jacket. 'He was rude to you.' *And that had triggered a primitive response far beyond anything he'd experienced before.* 'I didn't like it.'

'I didn't like it much either, but that's life. Some people are rude.' She didn't say anything, but he knew that Mike's nasty comment had hurt her feelings.

Knowing that this wasn't the time or place to deal with it, Dino made a mental note to tackle the subject later.

'So let's check on your friend, Sue. What did the air ambulance say?'

'Still grounded, but paramedics are going to be waiting for us at the head of the pass so we just have to deliver the baby and get them back up this hill.' Surefooted, she picked her way through the deep snow to the car.

'I'm not sure the relevance of telling them about the Olympic gold medal.' Dino used a ski pole to measure the depth of the snow. 'Being able to ski downhill at stupid speeds in tight Lycra isn't much of a qualification for delivering a baby outdoors with a wind chill of minus fifteen.'

'I was trying to impress him. He was one of those sporting jocks at school. Football captain—that sort of thing. Appreciates manly sporting endeavour.' She stopped for a moment to take a breath. 'Winning a gold medal shows grit and determination. A will to succeed and be the best. Not to mention a certain recklessness that might just come in useful given the situation we're in.'

'I'm never reckless with my patients.'

'Today, you might not have a choice. Come on.' Meg pulled open the car door and slid inside quickly. 'Sue? Fancy bumping into you here—I've been dying to catch up with you for ages, although this wasn't quite what I had in mind.'

Hearing Sue giggle, Dino gave a smile of admiration. No matter who the patient was, Meg always seemed to put them at ease. Even with Mike, she'd managed to control the situation.

Putting his head inside the car, he had his first glimpse of the woman. Short red hair framed a face that was as white as her husband's, and Dino saw instantly that 'delicate' was a fair description. Any thinner and she would have risked being blown away by a gust of wind. Against her slender limbs, her swollen belly looked grossly disproportionate. 'Sue, we need to get you to the ambulance. There's more room and we have better equipment.'

'I can't move. Honestly, I can't move. There's too much pain and I'm scared of the snow. I might slip and that would hurt the baby.'

Dino bit back the comment that being born in a snowdrift wasn't going to do wonders for the baby either, and tried to give her the reassurance she so clearly needed. 'I won't let you fall, I promise.'

'I really don't—'

'Sue, I've been timing your contractions.' Meg's voice was firm. 'They're coming every two minutes, fast and furious. We really have to move you to the ambulance. We're going to wait until the end of the next contraction and then we're going to get you out of the car and on your feet.'

'I won't get across there before the next contraction starts.' Sue's voice was reed thin and shaky and Mike swore and punched his fist into the seat.

'Can't you see she can't walk? Just get a helicopter or something!'

'She can walk if she does it between contractions.' Meg wrapped an extra coat around Sue's thin shoulders. 'All right. Get ready to swing your legs out of the car. I'm going to help.'

Sue shrank back. 'These boots are new. They're an early Christmas present from Mike. I'm going to ruin them if I walk in the snow.'

Hanging onto his patience with difficulty, Dino exchanged a fleeting glance with Meg. 'I'll carry you.'

Sue's eyes widened and she looked at his shoulders. 'You'll put your back out.'

'No, I won't.' Ignoring Mike's blustering, Dino moved to the car door. 'Slide forward. Put your arms around my neck—that's it.' He swung her into his arms. Checking his footing carefully, he trudged his way through the snow to the four-by-four in less than the two minutes it took for another contraction to start. Meg was already there, opening the doors at the back, and moments later Sue was safely inside what was a comparatively warm place, her new boots dry and untouched by the snow.

Dino tucked blankets around her. 'Keep the doors closed. I'm just going to help Mike secure your car then we're going.'

'I don't think there'll be time.' Groaning in pain, Sue doubled over and Dino slid out of the way and let Meg take his place. He saw her reach for the Doppler probe, ready to listen to the foetal heart.

He heard her say, 'When exactly is this baby due?' and then the only sound was the angry squeal of the wind as it buffeted his body.

He helped Mike clear their belongings out of the car. Piles of brightly wrapped Christmas presents, two suitcases and a hamper of food all needed to be transported to the mountain rescue vehicle and then finally they were ready to leave.

'Baby's heart is one-forty. We all feel better for having heard that. There's a car park just down there on that bend.' Meg leaned forward to talk to him. 'It means going further down the road, but you can turn safely there. There's no way you can turn here, the road just isn't wide enough. You'll go over the edge.'

Sue gave a whimper of fear and Mike's knuckles were white on the seat.

By contrast, Meg's eyes sparkled with the challenge. She was in her element here and Dino suddenly wished they didn't have company in the back of the vehicle.

'You need to be careful when you turn,' she told him, 'otherwise your tyres will spin out and you don't want to lose traction this high up on the pass.'

'All right—tell me where the turning place is.'

It was the most difficult drive of his life and he was relieved Meg knew the road so well.

'Breathe, Sue.' She was in the back with the labouring woman, encouraging her and keeping her warm.

Dino was just cresting the hill and making the final descent down towards the end of the mountain pass when Sue gave a sharp scream.

'Oh—that's so painful…' She started to sob and Dino pushed his speed as much as he dared.

'I suspect you're in transition, Sue.' He spoke the

words over his shoulder, his eyes fixed on the road ahead. 'Meg, you can give her gas and air.'

'One step ahead of you on that one, Dr Zinetti. You just concentrate on the driving. Can you go any faster?'

Not without killing them all. Dino shifted gear and coaxed the vehicle down the final two bends in the road. An ambulance and a police car were waiting.

'Dino.' Meg leaned forward to speak to him. 'There is no way Sue is going to be able to change ambulances.'

'We'll drive her straight to the hospital. With a police escort we can make it in about five minutes.' Dino rolled down his window, had a succinct conversation with the police officer and moments later they were roaring through town behind the police car, sirens blaring and lights flashing.

'It's coming, Meg.' Sue was panting. 'I can feel the head.'

'You have to get her to hospital,' Mike bellowed, his face scarlet as he flapped around in a total panic. 'You have to get her there right now! Aren't you listening to what she's saying? It's coming!'

'I'm listening, Mike, and we don't have to get her to hospital.' Meg's voice was calm. 'If necessary I can deliver a baby here, in the back of our ambulance. No worries. Don't push, Sue. I want you to pant like this...' She demonstrated and Dino smiled to himself.

No worries? Who was she kidding?

Fortunately her confidence seemed to reassure Sue and she was able to relax slightly and control her breathing.

He could hear Meg tearing open a delivery pack and talking quietly to Sue, encouraging her all the time.

Somehow she'd managed to block out Mike's pointless ranting and focus on the problem in hand.

Dino pulled up outside the emergency department as close to the entrance as possible. Leaving the engine running for the warmth, he vaulted into the back of the ambulance to help Meg.

'Sterile gloves to your left.' She gestured with her head. 'You're doing so well, Sue. Everything is fine.'

By the time he'd snapped on the sterile gloves the head was crowning. Dino used his left hand to control the escape of the head, murmuring encouragement to the labouring mother.

As the head was delivered, Mike made a strangled noise in his throat and crumpled to the floor of the vehicle with a dull thud.

Sue made a distressed sound and Meg grinned.

'We'll never let him forget that one. He'll be fine, Sue. He's better off staying there until we're done. If we sit him up, he'll just faint again, and at the moment you are our priority. What a fantastic Christmas present—a new baby. You're doing brilliantly. Nearly there. Dino, tell me when to give syntometrine.' She had a syringe in her hand and Dino delivered the anterior shoulder and glanced at her briefly, surprised to see tears in her eyes.

'What? What are you staring at? I like babies. What's wrong with that?' Meg blinked furiously and glared at him, clearly angry that he'd witnessed her emotional response to the situation. 'Do I give this stuff now?'

'*Sì*, now.'

She gave the injection and with a shocked cry Sue delivered the baby into Dino's waiting arms. 'You have a daughter, Sue. Congratulations.' The baby gave a thin wail and he quickly lifted her into Sue's arms. 'Hold her against you. We're going to transfer you to a wheelchair and get you inside because it's too cold out here.'

'A daughter?' The tears started to fall. Tears of relief. Tears of gratitude. Tears of joy. 'I'm going to call her Mary because she was born at Christmas.'

Opening the door of the ambulance, he found a crowd of staff from the obstetric unit waiting to help him and moments later Sue and the baby were inside in the warmth.

Having handed over to his colleagues, Dino returned to the ambulance to find Meg sitting with her arm around a white-faced Mike.

'Actually, I've known several,' she was saying, and she looked up and smiled as Dino approached. 'Just telling Mike he isn't the first father to fall over and bang his head when a baby is born. Everything all right with mother and daughter?'

'The paediatricians are examining Mary, but every-thing seems fine. In a moment they'll take her up to the postnatal ward.' Dino cleared up the remains of the delivery pack and Mike rubbed a shaky hand over his forehead.

'I can't believe I missed it. It's a little girl?'

'That's right.' Meg jumped down from the vehicle and glanced at her watch. 'I'll take you up there now. Come on. What do you want us to do with all these Christmas presents?'

Mike looked at them blankly, clearly in shock. 'I—I have no idea. Sue's parents are on their way to the hos-pital now.'

'In which case we can leave the lot just inside the doors with the girls on Reception and you can transfer it all to the car when you're ready.'

Meg closed the door and Mike grabbed her arm. 'Listen—'

'It's OK.' Meg smiled. 'You're welcome.'

Mike looked at her intently. 'You always did have more balls than most men.'

Meg's smile faltered. 'Right. Well—thanks. Have a good Christmas, Mike.'

Looking at her tense shoulders, Dino frowned and was about to ask her what was wrong when Ellie appeared in the entrance.

'Meg? Can you come? I've just spoken to Ambulance Control and they're bringing in a nasty RTA.'

'Why are people still driving their cars in this weather?' Meg slithered across the icy ground and into the warmth of the emergency department. 'Everyone should just stay at home and watch Christmas TV instead of dicing with death on the roads.'

Ellie looked harassed. 'We're incredibly busy. Dino, can you go straight to Resus? At this rate we're going to be lucky if any of us make it to the ball tonight.'

The rest of the shift was so hectic that Meg didn't even have time to grab a drink. By eight o'clock the emergency department had calmed down a little and it was decided that the staff attending the ball could leave.

Dino glanced at his watch. 'Good job we planned to change at the hospital because there's no time to go home. You have twenty minutes to get ready before the cab arrives. It's never going to be enough, is it?'

Twenty minutes? How long did he think it took a girl to pull on a dress? Meg opened her mouth to tell him that there was no way it would take her anywhere near that long, and then she realised that all the other women he dated probably took three times that length of time to get ready for an evening out with him. He was gorgeous, wasn't he? Any woman spending an evening with a man like him would want to look their best. All the time in the world wasn't going to turn her into the sort of woman he normally dated. Why on earth had she agreed to this? Why was she putting herself through this torture? 'Twenty minutes will be fine,' she said tonelessly, 'I'll do a rush job.'

He gave her a searching look. 'Take as long as you need. I'll drive us. That way it doesn't matter if we're late.'

Yes, it did, because the last thing she wanted to do was make a grand entrance. She wanted to arrive along with everyone else. She wanted to blend into the background. With a shaky laugh at her own expense, Meg hurried towards the staffroom. When had she ever blended at that sort of thing? She was going to stand out like a single poppy in a cornfield.

Ellie was waiting for her in the staffroom. 'Hurry up! I've already heated the tongs. I'm going to straighten your hair before I go and get changed myself.'

Meg flattened herself against the door. 'I was planning to just wear it up like I always do. I prefer it that way.'

'I think you should wear it loose. You have beautiful hair. It's time you showed people how amazing it is.'

Meg allowed herself to waste five of her twenty minutes having her hair straightened. After that it took only a couple of minutes to change into the dress and push her feet into the shoes.

'What are your plans, Ellie? Is Ben picking you up here?'

'He's gone to see someone in the imaging department. I'm meeting him there when I've finished with you. We're going home first, because our house is on the way. Close your eyes while I do your make-up.'

'Don't make me look too made-up.'

'Meg, you're going to the ball. Made-up is good. But I haven't overdone it. You look gorgeous. Just lipstick, then I'm done… There… You can look in the mirror.'

Meg looked. Normally she quite liked her face, but the make-up seemed to accentuate all the worst aspects of her features. The lipstick made her mouth look too big. The freckles on her nose, earned from so many hours spent outdoors, stood out. Resisting the urge to grab a tissue and rub it all off, she smiled because she didn't want to offend Ellie, who looked genuinely delighted with what she'd achieved. 'Thanks. Wow.'

Ellie's mobile rang and she gasped. 'That's Ben. I need to get going. We'll see you there, Meg. You look fab. Dino is going to be blown away. I wish I could stay to see his face.' She sprinted out of the room, leaving Meg on her own with all her insecurities echoing in her head.

Staring at her reflection, she sighed. She didn't look like herself. She didn't *feel* like herself. Turning sideways, she kept her eyes on the mirror. All right, maybe she didn't look awful. Just weird. Different.

The dress was nice.

Actually, she looked better than she'd thought she would.

Remembering Ellie's comment that Dino would be blown away, Meg picked up the gold clutch bag that Ellie had persuaded her to buy along with the shoes. He wasn't going to be blown away. She didn't expect that. She didn't have the sort of looks that would turn heads. But she looked OK. Decent. Hopefully he wouldn't be embarrassed to be seen with her.

He'd asked her, she reminded herself firmly. He'd worked with her long enough to know what she was like. He'd kissed her when she'd been dressed in her windproof jacket. She had to look better than she did when she was being blown to bits by a gale.

Meg opened the door of the staffroom and was about to go in search of Dino when she saw him standing in the corridor. He was deep in conversation with a woman wearing a short scarlet dress. It was covered in sequins that sparkled and glinted under the lights.

Short? Meg's stomach plummeted. Was she supposed to have worn something short? Why had no one told her? The invitation had just said 'Black Tie' and she'd interpreted that as meaning that everyone would wear a long dress. Ellie hadn't said anything about the dress being unsuitable. But perhaps Ellie didn't know. As a mother of two young children, she didn't get out much either, did she?

Meg's mouth dried and her heart started to pound.

She looked completely wrong.

Then Meg recognised the woman—Melissa. Staring at her sexy dress, which clung to her body and ended at mid-thigh, Meg wondered why on earth Dino hadn't just invited her to the ball. In all probability he was wishing he had. He certainly seemed to be enjoying the conversation, his laughter echoing down the corridor.

Meg looked down at herself and felt her face burn with embarrassment. It was all too easy to imagine what his reaction would be when he saw her. The comparisons he was going to make. She was going to be a laughing stock. Everyone at the ball was going to be staring at her and feeling sorry for her. *She has no sense of style. No idea how to dress.*

Her palms damp with sweat, Meg closed the door to

the staffroom, yanked off the gold shoes and quickly pushed her feet into her trainers.

No way. No way was she putting herself through this. She'd rather fling herself over the edge of a gully, naked. Dino was blocking the only exit, which meant…

Hesitating for only a fraction of a second, she grabbed her coat and opened the window. The freezing night air poured into the staffroom but Meg didn't care. The cold was the last of her worries. Praying that no one would notice her, she hauled the dress up to her waist, slid nimbly out of the window and moments later she was sprinting through the darkness, the silk dress winding itself around her legs as she fled through the thick snow that covered the grass and on towards the car park. Her feet were soaked in an instant. Twice she tripped and landed on her hands and knees in the snow.

'Stupid, stupid dress.' Her palms stung with pain and she struggled to her feet for the second time and yanked the offending dress up around her waist. Her breath came in great tearing pants and every minute she expected to hear Dino's voice coming from the open window, or footsteps pounding after her. Except that Dino probably wouldn't have bothered following her. He'd probably just think he'd had a lucky escape.

The flash of guilt she felt at having left him standing there with no explanation was eclipsed by the knowledge that she'd done him a favour.

It was only when she realised that she couldn't actually see her car that Meg discovered she was crying. She was so cross with herself. Why, oh, why, had she allowed herself to be talked into going to a ball?

Ellie was wrong. It wasn't fun at all—it was a nightmare. In order for it to be fun, you had to be part of that female club who giggled over the contents of their make-up cases and drooled over dresses, and she did neither of those things. And it was perfectly obvious that Dino was never going to be interested in someone like her. He would have been embarrassed to be seen with her.

She reached her car and pressed her key, some of her panic receding as she heard the reassuring bleep and the clunk as the doors unlocked. Later, she knew, she'd feel guilty. But for now she was just relieved to have made it as far as her car.

Pulling the dress up to her knees so that it didn't get tangled in the pedals, Meg turned on the engine, reversed out of her parking space and accelerated forward.

All right, so Dino seemed to find her attractive, but that was just up on the mountain, when they were working together. Here, doing everyday normal things, she didn't fit and it was no use pretending that she did. She wasn't any of the things he was looking for.

Tears blurred her vision and she brushed them away, struggling to keep her car on the road in the hideous weather conditions.

She contemplated driving to her mother's house, but then decided that would trigger a whole load of questions she didn't want to answer, so instead she took the road that ran along the side of the lake and to her cottage. Her mother wasn't bringing Jamie back until the morning so she had until then to get herself back under control.

Five minutes later she was in the bathroom, scrubbing off the make-up Ellie had so carefully applied, the green dress lying in an abandoned heap on the floor.

She'd just pulled on a cosy bathrobe when she heard the hammering at the door.

Meg froze. Oh, no, no, no. She should have hidden the car. She should have turned off all the lights. She should have—

'Meg! *Maledezione.*' Anger thickened his accent. 'Open this door right now!'

She didn't move. Had he come here just to shout at her? Probably. She deserved it, didn't she? She'd left him standing there. He was a senior consultant and people were expecting him to attend the ball. Because of her, he wasn't going. Because of her, everyone would be talking.

Braced for him to hammer on the door again, she almost died of shock when she heard the sound of a key in the door. Before she could move, he was at the top of the stairs.

Meg took one look at the thunderous expression on his face and flattened herself against the door of the bedroom. 'Where did you get a key to my house?'

Dressed in a black dinner jacket that shrieked of expensive Italian tailoring, he looked sensational. And furious.

Guilt ripped through her. 'Go ahead, yell at me. I know I deserve it. I know I behaved like a coward and I'm prepared to take what's coming to me. Just do it. Get it over with and then you can leave. You're all dressed up and it probably isn't too late for you to find a woman you'd like to take.'

'*You* are the woman I wanted to take! But you climbed out of a window and ran across two flower beds.' He ran his hand over the back of his neck, his handsome face a mask of incredulity and disbelief. 'What is going on? *What is the matter with you?*'

Her heart was hammering against her ribcage. 'Where did you get a key to my house?'

'Your mother. It was the first place I looked for you.'

'Then you wasted your time because I'm not going.'

'I didn't look for you in order to force you to come,' he gritted. 'I looked for you because I was worried.'

Thinking about the lecture she was now facing from her mother, Meg made a sound that was halfway between a sob and a laugh. 'She had no right to give you the key to my house. She had no right to interfere.'

'She's trying to stop you sabotaging every relationship.' Dino loosened his bow tie with impatient fingers. '*Why* are you sabotaging it, Meg? Explain. Is this to do with Jamie's father? Or is it that you don't like my company?' When she didn't answer he took a deep breath and tried again. 'There are banks and safety deposit boxes that are easier to break into than you. Do yourself a favour and drop the self-protection for a few minutes. I'm trying to understand you.' He undid the first few buttons of his shirt and she wondered if he were doing it on purpose to make things harder for her. Was he trying to remind her about their chemistry?

'You know I like your company,' she croaked. 'It isn't that.'

'Then what is going on?'

She'd hurt his feelings. She was a bad person. 'I don't blame you for being angry but I honestly don't know why you would *be* this angry because it can't possibly matter to you that much.'

'I'm *not* angry,' he breathed, 'at least, not with you. If you want to know the truth, I'm furious with myself for not taking notice when you said you didn't want to go to the ball. Instead of pushing you, I should have asked you why.'

Her heart skittered and jumped. 'You're not angry with me?'

'Exasperated, yes. Puzzled, definitely. Angry? No. How could I be angry? You must be extremely traumatised to be prepared to launch yourself out of the window into a snowdrift to escape me. Am I that scary?'

'Not you. I wasn't escaping you. I was escaping the evening.'

He looked at her and shook his head. 'Are you going to explain any of this to me?'

Meg dragged her gaze away from the bronzed skin at the base of his throat. He deserved an explanation, didn't he? That was the least she could do after leaving him standing. She took a deep breath, trying to stay calm as she spoke of the past she'd tried so hard to forget. 'The night Hayden told me he was involved with another woman…' It was an effort to force the words through the barriers she'd erected. '…we were supposed to be going to a ball. I'd just told him I was pregnant and he thought it was important that I know right away we didn't have a future. That he didn't want to keep up our relationship. He said that I was wrong for him. That he didn't want to be with someone like me.' Her voice thickened and she cleared her throat, desperately choking back tears. 'Someone who was more at home in the mountains than a nightclub. He said I just wasn't glamorous enough for him.'

'Hayden is Jamie's father?'

Meg's voice hardened. 'Well, that sort of depends on your definition of father. Given that he's never actually seen Jamie, I wouldn't exactly say he ever really earned himself the title of father.'

'Right. So we've ascertained he's emotionally impaired, intellectually challenged and monumentally self-ish. Did anyone ever diagnose his visual problem?'

'Visual problem?' She stared at him in confusion

'You're beautiful, Meg.' Dino stood strong and firm in front of her, not budging an inch. 'Really beautiful. If he couldn't see that, he obviously had a visual problem. Myopia? Cataracts?'

'He just had a thing for well-groomed women. And who can blame him?' She lifted her head and looked at him, forcing herself to meet his eyes as she revealed the most humiliating part of it all. 'Do you know the thing that hurt most? The night he told me I wasn't glamorous enough, I'd really made an effort. He'd wanted to go to this stupid ball and I'd decided that I ought to support him, so I spent ages on my hair and face and I thought I looked good. Until he said that. And just to make sure I knew how far short of the competition I was, he'd brought my replacement in the car with him.' Meg's knees shook slightly as she remembered the horror of that moment. 'She was sitting outside the whole time he broke up with me. He took her to the ball instead. I haven't been to one since. I decided to stop trying to be something I wasn't.'

'Meg—'

'I'm sorry I messed up tonight. I'm sorry I embarrassed you,' she croaked. 'When it comes to social stuff, I'm a coward. And that is why this is never going to work between us and why you should just turn right around and walk back out of that door. Because if we carry on with this relationship, I'll just do it to you again. And then you'll hate me.'

'*When* we carry on with this relationship, I'll make sure you don't do it to me again and I'm certainly not going to hate you.'

His words terrified her. 'You need a woman who isn't afraid to dress up and stand by your side. The truth is, we're colleagues. You're a fantastic doctor and you've got a killer smile and you just happen to kiss like a sex god, but none of that is going to make this work.'

'Colleagues? A few days ago we almost had sex in the snow. Call me old-fashioned, but I don't normally behave like that with a "colleague".'

'That was a one-off, probably triggered by the intense adrenaline rush of the avalanche threat.'

'If it was a "one off", how do you explain the kiss in your kitchen? We have a relationship, Meg.' He closed his hands over her shoulders, his grip firm and possessive. 'No matter how determined you are to fight it. Answer me one more question—despite the way you felt, you obviously did intend to come to the ball tonight. Why did you change your mind?'

'Because I got it wrong again.'

'What did you get wrong?' Dino frowned. 'You mean the way you dressed?' His eyes narrowed and he turned his head to look through the open door into the bathroom. Muttering under his breath in Italian, he strode into the room she'd just vacated and picked up the dress from the floor. 'You were wearing this tonight? This was the dress you chose for the ball?'

Knowing exactly what he was thinking, Meg felt her face turn scarlet. 'Yes. Sorry. I didn't know.'

'Didn't know what?'

'That we were supposed to wear short dresses,' she blurted out. 'That's why I don't go to these things, Dino. I avoid them for exactly that reason. Hayden was completely right that I don't have a clue! I never know what to wear, or what bag to carry, or w-what height of heel I'm supposed to pick—I don't know anything.' Her voice rose. 'I'm rubbish at that sort of thing. Completely, totally useless. Always have been. When other girls were playing with Barbie dolls, I was learning to fit crampons to my boots. You heard Mike. He told me I had bigger balls than a man! He told me that Sue was delicate, whereas I'm not. No one worries about me ploughing through snow because I'm as strong as a horse.'

'I wouldn't want to be with a woman like Sue,' Dino gritted. 'She would drive me mad and I would very probably want to kill her within two minutes, which isn't a good basis for a long-term partnership.'

'Stop being nice to me. It's making me feel even more guilty.' Meg rubbed the palm of her hand over her face and noticed black on her fingers. 'You see? This is why I don't wear make-up—now I have mascara everywhere and I probably look like a panda.'

He grabbed a towel from the bathroom and gently wiped her face. 'You don't look like a panda.' His gentleness was the final straw and the last of her control crumbled.

'I'm sorry I left you standing there. I never should have said I'd go with you. I'm a truly horrible person and I feel really bad. I wish you'd just shout and rant.' She gave a hiccough. 'And now I'd be really grateful if you'd go away and leave me alone. I need to hide under the duvet.'

But he didn't let her go. Instead, he folded her into his arms and hugged her tightly. 'You saw me talking to Melissa, didn't you? She caught me just as I was about to come and get you. You saw Melissa and that's when you turned and ran.'

Crushed against hard male muscle, Meg felt her limbs melt. 'You should have taken her.' He smelt so good. *He felt so good.*

'I didn't want to take her. And your dress was perfect, *tesoro*.' His voice was husky. 'I just wish I'd seen you wearing it. You should have walked out of that room with your head held high and I would have been proud to have you as my date.'

'Not when you saw how I stacked up against everyone else. Everyone would have been staring at me. And feeling sorry for you.'

'If they stared it would have been because you are beautiful, not because you were dressed inappropriately. And if they felt anything for me, it would have been envy. You shouldn't be insecure about the way you look.'

'I'm not insecure. I like the way I look.' Meg sniffed and pulled away, noticing black smudges on his shirt. 'It's just that the way I look doesn't suit all that social stuff. I like wearing walking boots and tramping through the mountains, I just don't like wearing dresses and putting on make-up. I haven't got the right sort of face or body for that.'

'You have a beautiful face and a woman's body,' Dino drawled, 'and even though I think you look seriously cute in your walking gear, it would be a novelty to see your legs once in a while.'

'Why? Honestly, why are you bothering?' Her throat was clogged with tears. 'All right—yes, I saw Melissa this evening. I thought she looked gorgeous. She looked sexy and feminine—everything I'm not. I'm wolf-girl, Dino, and putting a dress on me doesn't change that. Even if I'd worn Melissa's dress, I still wouldn't have looked as good as she did. I'm just not a girly girl. I'm the person who can manoeuvre a car out of a snowdrift, but I can't apply mascara. You heard what Jamie said— I'm just not that feminine.'

'Really?' His eyes glittering dark, he slid the robe off her shoulders and Meg gasped and made an abortive grab for it.

'What are you doing?'

'You told me you're not that feminine. I prefer to make my own decisions about these things.' He trailed a leisurely hand over the curve of her hip. 'Sorry, but I'm going to have to disagree with you.'

Meg made another grab for her robe. 'Dino, please...' Scarlet with embarrassment, she tried to cover herself but he dropped it on the floor behind him.

'You think I care what dress you're wearing? You think that's why I want you? So how do you explain the fact that I wanted to strip you naked when you were wrapped up in layers of thermal insulation on the mountain?' The heat of his mouth was a breath away from hers and she could feel hard muscle through the thin fabric of his shirt. 'You think I'm interested in the way you wear your hair?'

Transfixed by the look in his eyes, Meg felt the room spin. 'Dino—'

'Just for the record, I don't care about any of that.' He backed her against the door in a purposeful movement. 'I care about the woman underneath. If you want the honest truth, there is nothing sexier than a sleek, athletic body, and yours is the best I've ever seen. Is this your bedroom?'

Her heart hammering, Meg nodded and he swept her up, strode into the bedroom and deposited her in the centre of the bed. Then he threw off his jacket and came down on top of her, pinning her arms above her head so that she couldn't wriggle away. Stretching out his free arm, he flicked on the lamp by the bed and a soft golden light spread across the room.

Mortified, Meg twisted under him. 'Let me go. I'm going to punch you in a minute.'

'Then there's no incentive to let you go, *tesoro*.' His sensual mouth curved into a devastating smile. 'I have you captive. No more running. No more avoidance tactics. For tonight, you're mine.'

'At least turn the light off.'

'No. How can you not know you're beautiful? You have an incredible body and working alongside you for so long has been driving me crazy.' He lowered his mouth to her neck. Licked at the sensitive spot below her ear. 'What are you scared of, Meg? Why are you always pushing me away?'

Her body was quivering. 'Because that's what I do. Because you're going to hurt me and then you're going to hurt Jamie and I'm not going to let you.'

He lifted his head, his eyes deadly serious. 'Let's get one thing straight.' He took her face in his hand, forcing her to look at him. 'I'm not going to hurt your son, Meg. That's just not going to happen.'

'But if—'

'It is *not* going to happen.'

Which meant what, exactly? She tried to work it out but he was kissing her again and suddenly her brain was too fuzzy to make the necessary connections. Meg writhed underneath him but he didn't budge. He just kissed her until she thought her brain was going to explode—until her body was shrieking with a need that only he could satisfy, and all the time his clever fingers touched, caressed, explored. 'Don't do that.' Her voice was a soft plea. 'Damn you, you're not playing fair.'

Ignoring her, he trailed his mouth down her neck and lingered on the swell of one breast. 'Who said anything about fair? We stopped playing fair when you decided to run from me without explanation.' He closed his mouth over the peak of her nipple and Meg felt an explosion of sexual excitement spear her body.

'Don't—please.' She gasped the words. 'When you do that I can't...'

'You can't what? You can't resist me? You can't think straight?' Dino lifted his head and looked at her from under lowered lids, his eyes glittering in the dim light. 'Good. Because that's how I feel about you. By the time I've finished with you, you're going to be in no doubt that you're a woman. It doesn't matter how you're dressed, Meg. In fact, clothes are an irritation if I'm honest. I just want to strip you naked.'

Meg felt as weak as a newborn kitten. She knew she should push him away, but her body and brain appeared to be disconnected. As he tortured her with fingers, lips and tongue, she lost contact with the part of her brain responsible for decision-making. She wriggled and writhed underneath him, driven wild by his skilled touch. Her head swam, her body trembled, and when he brought his mouth back down on hers, she felt as though she'd lost her mind. Hot, hard and demanding, he took her mouth in a searing kiss that left her in no doubt as to how their evening was going to end. It was crazy and desperate, his tongue meeting hers in a skilled, know-ing assault that was shattering in its intensity. When he dragged his mouth from hers, she moaned a protest and locked her hands behind his head.

'Don't stop. You can't stop. You started this...'

'And I'm going to finish it. I love your hair,' he breathed, sliding his fingers through the silky mass, 'I love your hair loose like this—that night after we rescued Harry, that was the first time I'd ever seen you with your hair down. Every day since then I've wanted to see it again. Can you feel what you do to me?'

He moved her hand down his body and Meg felt her heart leap and her mouth dried as she touched him intimately.

Oh, yes, she could feel.

She could feel the throbbing heat of him against her—could feel the power and size of him. And she knew he could feel what he did to her because his fingers were touching her, skilfully exploring the hot, moist core of her body, and it felt so unbelievably good that Meg gave a moan of disbelief. It felt as though she was being burned at the stake, her body devoured by a dangerous cocktail of sexual heat and wicked anticipation, the throb in her pelvis almost agonising in its intensity.

Finally, when she was ready to beg, he pulled away from her, but it was only a brief pause before he came back over her, his eyes glittering dark as he lifted her hips.

'Look at me!' His voice was thickened by raw passion. 'I want you to look at me. I want you to know it's me.'

'I know it's you, Dino.' With difficulty, she galvanised her dazed brain and looked. And looking added another dimension to the whole sensual feast because his eyes blazed almost black with a raw passion that threatened to explode out of control.

Beyond the windows, a thick layer of snow covered the ground but here, in the intimate atmosphere of her bedroom, scorching heat simmered between them. The outside world had ceased to exist.

Meg felt him, hot and hard against her, and then he was inside her, entering her with a series of slow, purposeful thrusts that took him deep. For a moment she didn't dare breathe, and then a wild rush of excitement shot through her and she wrapped her arms around him tightly, feeling him with every nerve ending and fibre of her body. He was still wearing his shirt and she tore at the last of the buttons, frantic to touch him, desperate to run her hands over the satin-smooth muscle of his shoulders.

He murmured something in Italian and then thrust deeper, his body sinking into her tender, sensitised flesh, and Meg went up in flames. Scorching, explosive excitement engulfed her and he started to move, each skilled stroke designed to drag the maximum response from her. His shirt hung loose and she sank her fingers into the sleek muscle of his hard shoulders, completely out of her mind with the pleasure he created.

It was wild and out of control, her teeth on his shoulder, his hand in her hair as he drove into her, sending them both rocketing skywards. Meg felt her body shatter into a million sparkling pieces and she heard him groan her name as he hit the same peak. His mouth came down on hers again and they kissed all the way through it, the erotic stroke of his tongue adding to the intensity of the moment.

It had to end, because nothing so intense could possibly last. Meg felt him shift his weight from her, his breathing unsteady as he rolled onto his back and covered his face with his forearm.

Feeling nothing like herself, Meg stared blankly at the ceiling. She could have told herself that she'd reacted in such a wild way because she hadn't had sex for so long, but she knew that wasn't true. The truth was, she'd reacted in such a wild way because Dino drove her wild. He was the sexiest, hottest man she'd ever met and when she was with him her body had a will of its own. She'd wanted him so badly she hadn't thought about anything else.

Slowly, he turned his head to look at her. '*Mi dispiace, tesoro*—sorry.' His voice was husky, his tone holding a mixture of apology and amusement. 'I had hoped for a little more finesse than that. But I have wanted to get you naked for such a long time, my control was seriously challenged.'

He'd wanted her that badly?

Not for anything would she admit how flattering it was that a man had wanted her so badly he hadn't even bothered undressing. He lay next to her, his shirt undone to the waist, exposing a powerful chest and hard, defined stomach muscles. 'You're not even undressed.'

'I was in a hurry,' he purred, 'but any time you want to do something about that, just go ahead.' He locked his hands behind his head, his eyes challenging her.

Meg swallowed. 'I really am sorry I ruined your evening.'

He gave a slow, satisfied smile. 'My evening turned out extremely well, *tesoro*. How was yours?'

Blushing, she snuggled against him, resting her head on his shoulder. 'Not bad.'

'Not bad? *Not bad?*' Laughing, he rolled her onto her back. 'Then I'd better try again, because I want a lot more from you than "not bad".'

He kissed his way down her body, ignoring Meg's gasp of shock.

'Honestly, Dino, you can't…'

But he did. And when she was pliant and trembling, he rolled onto his back and lifted her so that she straddled him. Her hair flopped forwards, brushing his chest, and this time he entered slowly, his hands hard on her hips as he filled her. His eyes never leaving hers, he made it the most intimate experience of her life. She saw the faint sheen of sweat on his brow and the tension in his powerful shoulders. And then he started to move inside her and she closed her eyes as she felt her body accommodate the whole silken length of him. And nothing had ever felt more right. It was all about the moment. Not the past, or the future, just this one moment.

'*Belissima*. You're beautiful,' he said thickly, his dark eyes hot. 'You feel incredible.'

'So do you.' She gasped the words and then leaned forward and kissed him, her hips matching the perfect rhythm he set.

He groaned her name and tightened his grip on her hips. 'Slow down, *tesoro,* or I'll—'

'You'll what?' Feeling her feminine power, Meg smiled and licked at his mouth. 'You'll what? Struggling to hang onto control, macho man? Have you got a bit of a problem there?'

His jaw hard and set, he muttered a curse and drove into her hard, and her ability to tease him evaporated in the sudden heat of their passion. She couldn't speak or think. As he hit his peak she felt her body do the same, convulsing around the thrusting length of him and exploding into the heavens.

CHAPTER SIX

'Mum? *Mum!*'

'Oh no!' Waking in a panic, Meg shot out of bed, her heart hammering. Light peeped through a gap in the curtains and she grabbed the clock and tried to focus on the numbers. 'It's nine o'clock? Dino, we overslept. I didn't mean you to stay the whole night. Jamie's home! You have to go. Quickly! Oh, why didn't I set the alarm? I'll take them into the kitchen and you sneak out the front door.' Flustered and panicking, she grabbed the first thing she could find, which just happened to be a pair of ancient jeans she'd worn the day before to clean the bathroom. Thrusting her arms into a jumper, she freed her hair and turned to look at him.

It was a mistake.

He was six feet two of sleepy, gorgeous man. The sight of his powerful shoulders and shadowed jaw was enough to make her want to leap straight back in to bed again. He had to be the sexiest man alive.

'Mum?'

'Dino, move!' In desperation, Meg threw his dress shirt at Dino, forcing her mind from sex to mother-hood. It was an uncomfortable and unfamiliar transition. 'Put something on, quickly. I'm so cross with myself...'

Shaking, she pushed herself into her trainers. 'We shouldn't have done this. I don't want to hurt Jamie.'

'*Calma, tesoro*. Calm down. No one is going to hurt Jamie.' His voice still husky from sleep, Dino swung his legs out of the bed and she had a brief glimpse of wide shoulders and rippling pectoral muscles before he shrugged on the shirt she'd thrown him.

It was impossible not to notice that he was aroused and Meg gave a gulp. 'Dino…'

'It will be fine now you're not walking around naked.' A wry smile touched his mouth as he intercepted her glance. 'Go to your son, Meg, before he comes to you.'

For a second their eyes held and, in that single breathless moment, Meg felt something shift inside her. Whatever they'd shared in the darkness of the winter night hadn't gone. It was still there. And it felt good. *And confusing*.

Her head in a spin, she turned and shot out of the room, closing the door firmly behind her just as Jamie came thundering up the stairs. 'Hi, sweetheart! Did you have fun at Grandma's house?' *Did she look as though she'd spent the night having sex?*

No, of course not.

As far as Jamie was concerned, she'd spent the night alone.

'Hi, Mum.' Snowflakes dusted his coat and his cheeks were pink from the cold. 'Where's Dino?'

Or maybe not.

Meg tightened her grip on the door handle. *So much for sneaking him out of the house.* 'Wh-why are you asking? What makes you think that Dino—?'

'His car is parked outside the front door.' Jamie

bounced up to her and hugged her round the waist. 'Did he do a sleepover? I'm really sad I missed it.'

'Yes, he did a sleepover. He had to do a sleepover because he…er…he…well, it really doesn't matter. Tell me what you did with Grandma. Did you wrap presents?' Meg swung Jamie up into her arms before he could charge into the bedroom and carried him back down to the kitchen. 'You're getting too heavy for me.'

'I'm going to get even heavier because Grandma is making us pancakes.'

Which meant her mother wasn't planning on leaving any time soon. Feeling as though she was facing a firing squad, Meg walked into the kitchen. Hoping Dino would take the chance to escape, she closed the door behind her.

Moments later it opened and Dino walked in.

Ignoring Meg's appalled glare, he ran his hands through his ruffled hair and smiled at her mother, who was assembling the ingredients for pancakes. '*Buongiorno*. I must apologise for my appearance but I wasn't planning on staying the night.'

Meg's mouth fell open and she caught a glimpse of her mother's smug smile before Jamie threw himself at Dino. 'You had a sleepover.'

'*Sì*, a sleepover.' Dino swung the boy into his arms and smiled at him while Meg watched, her heart in her mouth. His jaw was dark with stubble and eyes had the same sexy, dark brooding quality that had seduced her out of her knickers the night before. And seeing him with her child made her feel…

Vulnerable.

It wasn't just about her, was it? It was about so much more than her. He'd promised not to hurt her child, but no one could make a promise like that, could they? He wasn't even Jamie's father. Not that you'd know that by looking at the two of them together.

Jamie was clinging, his arms locked around Dino's neck like bindweed. 'I didn't know you were doing a sleepover.'

'I'm afraid the Batmobile let me down. Really she is a warm-weather car. You know that. She has a high-performance engine and that makes her very temperamental. She loves the warm weather, but I insist on driving her in the winter so occasionally she punishes me by refusing to start. All that snow yesterday upset her. I was stranded here. Your mum kindly let me stay.'

Impressed by his impromptu excuse, Meg relaxed and then spotted the sceptical look on her mother's face. The excuse might work on Jamie, but it wasn't going to work on Catherine Miller. She was a much tougher audience to convince.

Jamie bounced in Dino's arms. 'Wow—so now you're here you might as well stay the whole day. Sundays are my favourite day because we have pancakes for breakfast. Say you'll stay—*please*. Do you like pancakes? I have them with maple syrup and chocolate.'

Dino winced. 'Together?'

'Yup, that's how I like them. And then we're going to buy our Christmas tree. You could come.' Jamie held his breath and so did Meg because she couldn't bear to see his disappointment. And she knew that he was going to be disappointed. There was no way Dino would want to spend the day choosing Christmas trees, was there?

Her lower lip clamped between her teeth, Meg waited for Dino to deliver a smooth excuse, but instead he nodded. 'Thanks for inviting me, I'd love to come. As long as we call in at my house on the way so that I can change my clothes. I can't choose a Christmas tree wearing a bow-tie.'

'I could lend you something...' Jamie looked at his shoulders doubtfully '...but I don't think I have anything that would fit you. You look like a real live Superhero.' He squeezed Dino's shoulders with his hand, completely unselfconscious. 'How do you get muscles like that? I want to have muscles. I want a six-pack. I do sit-ups, but so far I haven't even got a two-pack. Will you show me how?'

Dino grinned and lowered him to the floor. 'I think you might have to wait a few years for a two-pack. When the time comes, I'll show you how. Meg, can I use your bathroom for a shower?'

The thought of him in her shower sent the colour flooding into her cheeks. 'Of course.' Her mind was in a spin as she attempted to decipher what was going on. Why had he agreed to spend the day with them?

Displaying none of her reticence, Jamie grabbed his hand. 'I'll show you where the bathroom is. Do you need a towel? You can borrow one of mine. Would you prefer Superman or The Incredible Hulk? Did you bring a sleeping bag for your sleepover?'

Meg watched them, man and boy, her heart twisting as she saw hero-worship and trust in her son's eyes. This is what it should have been like. How it should have been for Jamie. Didn't every child have a right to that?

Part of her wanted to reach out and hug him close—warn him that trusting came with a high price. But another part of her—a small part—wanted to walk further down the path and see where it led.

As the door closed behind them, her mother handed her a cup of coffee. 'Jamie really likes him. Relax.'

'The fact that Jamie really likes him is the reason I can't relax. Jamie is so trusting. He just doesn't see bad in anyone. I'm afraid…' Meg curled her hands around the mug. 'I'm afraid he's going to get hurt. How far do I let this go? How close should I let him get?'

'You can't protect him from everything.'

'No, but I can try.' And by allowing Dino into her life she was risking not just her own happiness, but Jamie's. When Dino decided that he'd had enough of her, it wouldn't just be her that suffered, would it?

Her mother measured out flour and added it to a bowl. 'I know what you're thinking, and you're wrong. Sometimes, Meg, you need to take big strides through life, even if that means falling over. You fell, hard. And now you need to get up again. You need to be brave.'

Meg was affronted. 'I am brave.'

'Yes, when you're walking through a blizzard, or hanging off the end of a rope. But then you've never been scared of the physical stuff. If it doesn't frighten you then it isn't brave. And what frightens you is the emotional stuff.' Catherine added eggs to the flour and whisked. 'I'm glad he stayed the night.'

'I didn't plan that. But you gave him a key so he barged his way in.'

'Good. You can thank me any time you like. I'm not sorry about that. I am sorry we caught you unawares. I should have thought of that and phoned first.'

'Nothing happened, Mum.' Horribly uncomfortable, Meg pushed her hair out of her eyes. 'He slept in Jamie's room.'

'Meg, I may be old but I'm not stupid. And neither are you. If you let that man sleep in Jamie's room then you are even more of a desperate case than I think you are.' Her mother gave a tiny smile. 'Really, you don't have to lie to me. I know I'm your mother, but frankly I'm delighted that you've finally had sex. Looking at Dino, I have every confidence that it was excellent sex. I'm thrilled to see you finally letting your guard down. Can you pass me some milk from the fridge?'

Meg dragged open the fridge door and stood for a moment, hoping that the cool air would reduce the heat of her face. 'I don't want him to come and get the Christmas tree with us.'

'Why not?'

'Because it's a family trip. Our routine.' She closed the fridge door and handed her mother the milk. It was impossible to contain her fears. 'And because he's just being polite. I'm sure the last thing he wants is to spend the day with us.'

'You don't know that. He doesn't strike me as a man who has a problem with decision-making. If he didn't want to come, he would have told you. I think you're spending too long second-guessing him. Sometimes you just have to take people at face value.'

'I did that once before, remember?'

'Yes, I remember.' Catherine poured milk slowly into the batter mixture, whisking all the time. 'But you can't let that one episode of bad judgement affect all your life choices.'

Meg frowned. 'You think Hayden was bad judgement?'

'Appalling judgement. It was completely obvious that he was shallow, selfish and totally focused on himself.'

'It was obvious?'

'Right from the first day.'

Meg scowled. 'But you didn't think to mention it?'

'You were nineteen. Would you have listened if I'd mentioned it?'

'Probably not.' Meg put her coffee down on the table in a huff. 'But given I'm so much older and wiser now, perhaps you'd better tell me now what you think about Dino.'

'I think he's clever, good looking, responsible, strong…' Her mother whisked skilfully. 'Sexy, of course, but I'm sure even you can see that bit without me pointing it out.'

'So he's Mr Perfect.' But her mother was impervious to Meg's sarcasm.

'No. There are shadows there. Scars.' Her mother frowned. 'He's led a real life. A life with ups and downs and traumas. A life like any other. But he's man enough to face those things head on and deal with them. Learn from them. He's not the sort to run from anything awkward or difficult.'

Meg gaped at her. 'How long have you spent with him?'

'I don't need long. It's one of the advantages of getting on in years. You have plenty of past data to draw on. Can you rinse some blueberries? Dino didn't look too excited at the combination of maple syrup and chocolate. The least we can do is feed him something he enjoys.'

'Mum, I don't have any blueberries! I don't have anything in my fridge except the basics, you know that. I know how to cook food a seven-year-old likes. Spaghetti. Meatballs. Chicken in breadcrumbs.' Meg's mood dropped even further. Good sex wasn't enough to sustain a relationship, was it? 'If the way to a man's heart is through his stomach, I'm doomed.'

'Well, let's hope Dino likes chicken in breadcrumbs.

Just remember to throw out mouldy cheese. There are blueberries in the basket by the door. I brought them with me. And a Christmas cake that I iced for you.'

'Thanks.' Her mind in turmoil, Meg smiled absently. 'Jamie will love that.'

There was a pause while her mother put the bowl to one side. 'Why didn't you go to the ball?'

Meg dug through her mother's basket and retrieved the fruit and the cake. 'I don't want to talk about that.'

'I was very surprised to see Dino at my door.'

Guilt squirmed in her stomach. 'I'll pay for the tickets.'

'I don't think he was worrying about the money.' Her mother rinsed the blueberries and tipped them into a bowl. 'He was worried about you. He likes you, Meg.'

Meg thought about the night before—*about the passion they'd shared.* 'Maybe.'

And she liked him. Which made the whole thing all the more terrifying.

'Why not let the relationship take its course?'

'Because when it crashes to the ground, I don't want Jamie caught in the rubble.' Meg broke off as Jamie bounded back into the room, Rambo at his heels.

'Dino didn't actually need any help, so I let him shower on his own.' He climbed onto a chair and helped himself to a handful of blueberries. 'He's going to go with us to buy a tree. Isn't that cool?'

Was it cool? Meg wasn't sure what she thought about it except that the whole situation was an explosion waiting to happen.

She felt as though she was free-climbing, clinging to a vertical rock face without the support of a rope.

How far was she going to fall?

* * *

'This is your house? Wow.' Jamie slid out of the car and stood staring.

Meg stared too. Looks *and* money, she thought. Recipe for disaster.

Her brain was in a total spin. She'd expected him to slink out before dawn and here he was, smiling at her child. Coming with them to pick a Christmas tree. Playing happy families. Playing puppets, with her heart at the end of the strings.

Only if this went wrong it wasn't going to be one heart that was broken, she thought. It would be two.

'It's just a house, Meg.' Apparently reading her mind, Dino urged her forward. 'I have a friend who is an architect. I persuaded him to sell it to me. He throws himself into a project but once it's completed he's immediately bored and he's ready to start on something else. At the moment he's building something incredible on the coast somewhere with sea views. Come inside.'

The house was built on three floors, one of them below ground level.

'Gym and cinema,' Dino said, intercepting her glance.

'Cinema?' Jamie looked as if he were about to explode with excitement. 'You have a cinema in your own home? How?'

'I live on my own. I can use the space any way I choose. Come and see.' He led them downstairs and opened a door.

'Mum, look!' Without waiting to be invited, Jamie shot inside and aimed straight for the wall that was lined from end to end with DVDs. 'This is *so* cool. Where are the cartoons? Do you have *Ice Age*? Can I watch in 3D?'

Dino gave him an apologetic look. *'Mi dispiace*, I'm

sorry, Jamie.' He cleared his throat. 'I haven't built up my collection of cartoons yet, but I'm planning to do that soon. Perhaps you could give me a list of your favourites.'

Jamie's face fell as he scanned the spines of the DVDs. 'So you only have films with real people?'

'Yes.' Dino smiled at the description. 'Real people.'

Meg stood still, taking in leather and luxury. So he had money. That didn't have to make a difference, did it? The fact that she was talking herself round shocked her and made her realise she was in deeper than she'd ever intended.

She wanted this to work.

Scared, she took a step backwards, as if by leaving the room she could also leave behind the thought. The beat of her pulse quickened.

Jamie didn't share her discomfort. 'It's a shame you don't have any good films.'

'Jamie, this is Dino's house,' Meg forced herself back to the present. 'He's an adult. Why would he have animated films?'

'*You* love *Ice Age* and you're an adult.' Jamie lifted his chin and looked at Dino. 'Have you ever seen it?'

'No.'

'Then how do you know you won't like it?'

'I'm sure I will like it and next time you come, I'll have a section of cartoons, I promise.'

'I could just bring my favourites over here and watch them,' Jamie said helpfully, and Meg gasped.

'Jamie! You can't just—'

'That's an excellent idea.' Dino took the little boy's hand and pulled him across the room. 'There's the projector so you sit on one of those sofas and watch it there—try it for size.'

Jamie sprawled full-length on the sofa. 'It's massive. There's room for me and five friends. Will there be popcorn?'

Dino didn't hesitate. 'Definitely popcorn.'

'This is amazing, isn't it, Mum?'

It was certainly amazingly expensive. Which, try as she may to convince herself otherwise, simply gave him another reason why he wouldn't want to be with a scruff like her for long.

Meg turned away, but not before she'd caught his eye.

'Now what?' His voice was soft. 'If you're looking for more excuses why it won't work, you're wasting your time.'

Suddenly she wanted to ask him why he wanted her. She was complicated, wasn't she? Not just because her head was completely messed up after Hayden, but because she had Jamie. She came as a pair.

A tour of the rest of the house did nothing to calm her fears. The place was sleek, sophisticated and not at all child friendly. Constructed in wood and designed to blend into the forest around it, there were balconies outside the bedrooms, and the huge walls of glass created a feeling of light and space. It was a place to chill out with fine wine and good music. And not a plastic superhero in sight.

'It's a perfect bachelor pad,' Meg said tonelessly, and Dino gave a faint smile.

'It would also make a perfect family home.' His face was inscrutable. 'It's a very adaptable living space. Take a look around. I'm just going to change and then we can buy that Christmas tree.' He disappeared through a set of doors, leaving them alone in the beautiful living area.

'It's like living inside the forest,' Jamie breathed, incredibly impressed as he nosed around the house. 'Wow, this place is *enormous*. Mum, I could use my skateboard inside this room—the floor would be brilliant.'

'Jamie, don't touch anything,' Meg said quickly, grabbing his hand before he could touch a delicate bowl. 'Just—just stand still with your hands by your sides.'

Jamie stood rigidly. 'Why? Why can't I move? Mum, Dino has a swimming pool. He can swim every day. Isn't that awesome?'

'It's awesome.'

Meg moved away, staring out over the forest and the peaks beyond. Her mind, exhausted from worrying and analysing, drifted. Suddenly she saw herself curled up on the deep, comfortable sofa, enjoying the warmth of the fire after a long day in the mountains, gazing at that view. She imagined making love with Dino on the rug, or in the enormous bed she'd spied through one of the open doors. She imagined eating lunch on the balcony on a sunny day, and Jamie playing a game of superheroes in the forest...

'It must be a wonderful house for entertaining. Just think of the parties you could have here.' Catherine Miller looked ecstatic and Meg's own vision of the place suddenly twisted and morphed into something different.

Parties. Her mother was right; this would be a perfect place for entertaining.

It was contemporary, sleek and stylish—like the man. And Dino would entertain, wouldn't he? He was a senior consultant with an extended network of friends and colleagues.

She put out a hand to touch one of the tall, exotic plants and saw her own nails which Ellie had painted quickly the night before. Yes, they were shiny, but they were still short, neat and practical.

The wrong sort of nails. Just as she was the wrong sort of woman.

Furious with herself for tearing everything up before it had even started, Meg whirled round and paced to the other side of the room. Thick rugs covered wooden floorboards in a pale maple and the walls were lined with books. Somehow, the house managed to be cosy and spacious at the same time. Why couldn't she live here? Why couldn't it work? She had to stop doing that thing—what did psychologists call it?—catastrophising or something. Believing that the worst was going to happen.

'I'm having a party here next week.' Dino walked in, a sweater in his hand. 'I'd like you to come. And before you start thinking of excuses, it's just a few friends. People from the hospital. Mountain Rescue Team. Very informal.'

'I'll babysit,' Meg's mother said immediately, but Dino shook his head.

'I'd like you to come. And Jamie. Ellie and Ben are bringing their kids, and Sean and Ally. They can all go downstairs to the den and watch a film. Jamie can choose his favourite.'

'Wow, thanks.' Jamie was buzzing with excitement. 'We can come, can't we, Mum? A Christmas party. Will Santa be here?'

Dino didn't miss a beat. 'He'll be here.'

Meg hesitated. A party with the mountain rescue team and children present wouldn't be formal, would it? No more long dresses and wearing things that she just didn't feel comfortable in. 'I'd like that. Thanks.'

'Good.' He looked at her for a long moment and then smiled. 'So, don't we have a Christmas tree to buy?'

'This one?' Dino winced as another fir tree tried to lacerate his skin. They'd been in the forest for an hour and still they hadn't found a tree that satisfied Meg.

He knew, because he was watching her face all the time. He couldn't stop looking at her. Somehow, after the passion of the night, her hair had curled again and it bounced around her face in golden curls. Her mouth was curved in a permanent smile as she laughed with her child. She looked slightly ruffled, natural, as if she'd just climbed out of bed.

Which she had.

Lust thudded through him. If it hadn't been for the child, he would have tumbled her down onto the floor of the forest and had her gasping his name within seconds.

'Not the right shape. Try that one.' She pointed and Dino lowered the tree he was holding to the ground and picked up the other one, unable to see the difference. They all looked the same to him. A tree was a tree, wasn't it?

'I like that one, Mum. Can we have it?' Jamie jumped on the spot and Dino watched him, envying the child's ability to live in the moment. For a child, it was all about now. Yesterday was gone and tomorrow was too far away to merit a single thought.

He thought about Hayden, and wondered how any man could be stupid enough not to want to be a part of his child's life. People could be selfish, he knew that from his own family experience. And then the child suffered. Except that no one could think Jamie was suffering. Not with Meg as a mother.

'Turn it around—I want to see the back.' Blowing on her hands, she peered at the tree from every angle and eventually pronounced it perfect.

'Are you going to buy a tree, Dino? You're going to need a really big one for your house. Or maybe two trees.' Jamie was glued to his side and Dino was about to answer when he saw the expression on Meg's face.

She was watching Jamie and her heart was in her eyes.

She was so afraid he was going to hurt her child.

'I'm not planning on buying a tree, Jamie.' He focused his attention on the boy. 'I'll be on my own on Christmas Day, so it isn't worth it.'

Jamie looked puzzled. 'How can you be on your own? Where's your family?'

Doing their own thing, as they always had.

'My parents spend Christmas in the States. My sister goes to stay with her husband's family.'

'And they don't invite you?'

Dino wondered how best to deal with the questions without shattering the child's illusions about the world. 'I'm a grown-up, and grown-ups don't always get together with family at Christmas.'

'Yes, they do.' Jamie frowned. 'Grandma is grown up. And she always spends Christmas with us. We all have Christmas together. I think it's mean that they didn't invite you. You can't be on your own. It isn't right, is it, Mummy? You can come to us. Grandma always cooks a turkey and it's massive. We eat it for weeks. You could help.'

Unbelievably touched, it took Dino a moment to answer. 'That's kind of you, Jamie—'

'So you'll come? Great. That's great, isn't it, Mum? Dino is going to spend Christmas Day with us.'

Meg's face was pink. 'Jamie, he may not want to—our house is really small, and—'

'I'd love to.' Dino watched her face, trying to read her mind. They hadn't had a chance to talk about what had happened since she'd bolted from the bed that morning. About where this was going. But he knew where he wanted it to go.

All the way.

But he saw the fear in her eyes and knew he had to take it slowly. 'So, Jamie, do you think I need my own tree?'

'Of course. Otherwise where do you put your presents?'

Charmed by the innocence of the conversation, Dino struggled to find the right answer. 'When you reach my age, you don't tend to have too many presents.'

'Why not?' Jamie looked shocked. 'What about your mum and dad and your sister?'

Dino kept his expression neutral. 'My parents give me money and I choose something for myself. That's what we've always done.'

'What? Even when you were little?' Jamie looked appalled. 'That's awful.' He slipped his hand into Dino's. 'This year, you should try writing to Santa. I know you're big, but you never know. I write to him every year and he *always* comes.'

Finding it difficult to speak, Dino cleared his throat. 'You think he'd come if I wrote to him?'

'Sure. I think so.' Jamie frowned. 'Maybe you ought to tell him that you save a lot of people's lives, just in case he doesn't know that you do that kind of thing. I mean, that's good, isn't it? It's got to be worth something.'

Dino nodded. 'Maybe.' He rubbed his hand over his jaw. 'Where do I post the letter?'

Jamie gave him a puzzled look. 'You put it up the chimney. It just goes.'

'Up the chimney. Right.' He didn't point out that his contemporary fireplace was surrounded by glass. 'Maybe you can help me write it. Have you done yours?'

'Last week.' Jamie tugged at his hat. 'I asked for a Batmobile toy, and a Nintendo Wii, but I know I won't get both because it's too expensive. I sort of asked him to choose. He knows what would suit you. He's clever like that. What would you ask for?'

Dino looked at Meg, who had wandered off to help her mother choose a tree. 'I have a feeling Santa probably can't give everyone what they want,' he said huskily, and Jamie looked at him and then turned his head.

'You like my mum, don't you? You look at her all the time. And she looks at you, but mostly when she knows you're not looking.'

Digesting that information, Dino dropped down to his haunches so that he was at the same level as the boy. 'I do like your mum, Jamie. I like her a lot.'

Jamie glanced over his shoulder and then leaned forward and whispered, 'If you like my mum, then you need to have a plan, because pretty soon she'll drive you away. That's what she does. She puts men off. I've heard Grandma talking to her. Grandma says she needs to stop shutting people out. I don't quite know what that means, but I know she doesn't kiss anyone. Is that going to be a problem?'

Dino thought about the night before, about Meg stretched out naked underneath him and above him. 'I think I can handle it.'

'The thing that really worries her is that a man might like her and not me.' Jamie fiddled with one of the branches of the tree. 'Not everyone likes kids. My real dad didn't like kids.'

Dino found that his hands had curled into fists. Forcing himself to breathe slowly, he relaxed them. 'Jamie—'

'I used to think it was that he didn't like me, but Mum told me that was wrong. He didn't even wait around for me to be born, so it couldn't have been because he didn't like me, could it?' There was a flicker of uncertainty in his face and Dino put his arms around the boy and dragged him into a hug.

'No, it most definitely could not have been because he didn't like you. Your mum is right, he must just not have wanted kids. If he'd known you there is no way he could have walked away.' Over Jamie's shoulder he saw Meg looking at them. *Saw the anxiety in her eyes.* He gave her a smile and saw her relax slightly. But she kept glancing towards them as she helped her mother choose a tree.

'Mum says it was her fault. Because she's not a girly girl. She says my dad wanted someone who wore a dress all the time and painted her nails pink.' Jamie pulled away. 'Would you want Mum to paint her nails? Because generally she thinks it's a waste of time.'

'I think,' Dino said slowly, 'that I'd want your mum to do whatever she wanted to do. If she wanted pink nails, that would be fine. If she didn't, that would be fine, too.'

'Right, well, that's good. And I know you don't mind that she likes the mountains, because you like them too. Most of the time at weekends we're up in the mountains, training Rambo. And when I'm older she's promised to get me my own puppy to train.' He looked at Dino. 'So what do you think? Do you think you could get to like me? Because I sort of come with my mum, a bit like getting a free toy in the cereal packet.' There was a tremble in his voice and Dino tried to remember another occasion when he'd felt as though his heart was jammed in his throat.

'I already like you, Jamie. I like you a great deal.'

Jamie stood for a moment. 'So the only problem is how to get Mum to stop being scared of you.'

Dino frowned at that interpretation. 'You think she's scared of me?'

'She's scared you might go away, like my dad. Some men do that.' Looking older than his years, Jamie studied the tree. 'I suppose you just have to show her you like her and that you're not going anywhere. But I don't know how you do that. I expect she'll push you away. It's what she always does.'

'I'm not going to let her push me away, Jamie.'

'It will be hard.'

'I don't mind.'

'That's because you're a superhero.' Jamie slid his hand into Dino's. 'Superheroes don't mind when things get tough. That's when they're at their best.'

'I'm not a superhero, Jamie. But I won't let your mum push me away. That's a promise. How old are you again?'

'Seven years and twelve days. I don't know the hours.'

'Well, Jamie…' Dino cleared his throat. 'for seven years and twelve days and I don't know the hours, you are very wise.'

'No worries. Any time you need any advice about girls, just ask.'

CHAPTER SEVEN

'So you didn't make it to the ball.' Ellie gave her a wink and a suggestive smile and Meg gritted her teeth.

'Actually, it wasn't—'

'Honestly, you don't have to explain. I'm thrilled for you.'

'Ellie, we're not—'

'I knew the moment he saw you in that dress, he'd rip it off.'

Remembering exactly what had happened that night, Meg coloured and Ellie punched her gently on the arm and wandered off in the direction of the radiology department, leaving Meg to stew over her relationship with Dino.

Having not thought about sex for a few years, she suddenly couldn't think about anything else. And it didn't help that she seemed to be working every shift with him. Every time she turned round, he was there. And she'd started noticing things she'd never noticed before—like the way he really looked at the patients when he talked to them. The way he paid attention. Listened. The way he kept a cool head no matter what emergency came through the doors of the department. And he was razor sharp. He had a way of sifting through the evidence in front of him and homing in on the important bit that was going to give him the answers. Just watching him work sent a thrill running through her because he was so incredibly clever. She felt a rush of pride and then realised that was ridiculous. What right did she have to feel proud? He wasn't hers, was he? One scorching night wasn't a guarantee of a future. She knew that better than anyone.

As the days passed, Meg started to wonder whether their colleagues were engineering it so that she and Dino worked together as much as possible and decided that they probably were. People thought it was a bit of fun, didn't they? They didn't realise that they were playing games with something that had the potential to explode and wreck a life. *Two lives.*

On the fourth day after the ball, she finally lost it. 'This is meant to be an emergency department,' she snapped at Ellie, 'not a dating agency. Why am I in Resus with Dino for the fourth time this week?'

'Because you make an unbeatable team.' Leaving that ambiguous statement hanging in the air, Ellie scurried off to meet yet another ambulance while Meg was left standing there, wondering why everyone felt they had to interfere. First her mother then Jamie and now her colleagues.

She felt a flash of exasperation, mingled with fear.

Were they all going to pick up the pieces when everything fell apart?

With a growl of frustration, she removed the packaging from a bag of IV fluid and hung it from the drip stand, ready for the next patient unlucky enough to find himself in the resuscitation room.

'Finally, we're on our own.' Dino's voice came from behind her and her breath caught. Awareness came like a blow to the stomach and Meg tried to calm herself before she turned.

'Alone, apart from about a few hundred staff and patients.'

'I've missed you. This has been the longest four days of my life.' He curved his hand around her face, his gaze slumberous and sexy. 'Can I interest you in hot sex on the trolley? Against the wall?'

Her heart skipped and danced. 'Show a little finesse, Dr Zinetti.'

'Finesse? What's that? In case you hadn't noticed, where you're concerned I don't have any.' His smile was at his own expense. 'Remind me.'

It was impossible not to be flattered by the masculine appreciation burning in his eyes. 'You're obviously feeling rather—'

'Desperate?' There was a husky note to his voice. 'You could say that. I want you, Meg. Every minute of every day. And every minute of every night, but let's not go there.'

His words cut her off at the knees. 'I want you, too.' *It was true, so why was she fighting it?* 'Jamie is sleeping over at my mother's tonight because she's taking him on a secret shopping trip tomorrow.'

'Secret?'

'To buy my Christmas present. I'm not supposed to know. So, Dr Hot…' Her heart jerked. 'Do you want to go out tonight? Dinner? Movie?'

'Neither.' He smiled, the stroke of his thumb against her cheek a sensual prelude to the night ahead. 'If I have you all to myself then I want to stay in. All the entertainment I need is right here.' His eyes told her exactly the form the entertainment was going to take and her insides turned to liquid.

'I assumed you'd want to do fancy restaurants and candles and all that sort of thing.'

'If we're only going to have a few hours alone, I don't want to be in the company of others.'

Her protective antennae twitched. 'You find it hard having Jamie around.'

'No. I love having Jamie around.' He lowered his forehead to hers. 'But I also want to rip your clothes off and I don't want to do that in front of your child.' His mouth hovered close to hers and Meg felt suddenly dizzy.

'Right, well, that's…good, because I don't want to shock him.' She leaned in for his kiss but he released her and took a step backwards.

'Better not.'

'No.' She cleared her throat. 'Because it's unprofessional.'

'Actually, it's more that I'm not sure I'll be able to stop. Which I suppose could amount to the same thing. I'll see you tonight, Meg. Don't bother cooking. I'll do something about replenishing the calories we use.'

In the end they didn't bother replenishing calories. Instead, they feasted on each other, making love until the cold winter light slid across the room and sheer exhaustion had her snuggling against him. She tumbled into clouds of warmth, cocooned by the delicious feeling of being close to another human being, and slept deeply.

This time when they woke, there was no rush to move. No subterfuge.

Meg made fresh coffee and plates of scrambled eggs with toast and they ate in bed, talking about everything and nothing.

'What time will Jamie be home?' Dino leaned back against the tangled bedding. 'Should we get dressed?'

'I'm picking him up from my mother's so that there is no repeat of last time.' Meg put the tray on the floor. It came as a shock to realise she could get used to seeing him in her bed. 'We have another hour, at least.'

'A whole hour?' His eyes gleamed with humour. 'How are we going to fill the time?'

It was fun to tease. 'We could go for a run.'

'If it's exercise you want, I have a better idea…' He rolled her underneath him and his mouth came down on hers just as both their pagers went off.

Cursing in Italian, Dino leaned across and dug his pager out of the pocket of his trousers. 'This had better be something really, really important.' Hair tousled, eyes sexy, he squinted at it. 'A climber has fallen in Devil's Gully. We're closest and they want us to make a start. For the first time in my life I'm thinking of resigning from the team.'

Meg laughed, but she was already out of bed and pulling on her clothes. 'Do we have exact co-ordinates?'

'Yes.' His eyes skimming her body, Dino sighed. 'The guy had better not have taken a stupid risk or I'm going to give him a lecture for ruining my Sunday. I'm not giving this up for anything less than a life-threatening situation.'

'You're not allowed to lecture.' Meg pulled layers over her head and hopped around as she pulled on her socks. 'Don't just lie there staring. Get dressed!'

'If one of us has to abseil into Devil's Gully, it's going to be me. I just want to get that straight right now.' He dressed quickly and she stole a glance, admiring the curves and definition of his muscles.

'Just because you're sleeping with me doesn't mean

you can suddenly get ridiculously protective. I can abseil as well as you can. We'll do what needs to be done.'

He fisted his hand in the front of her fleece and pulled her against him. 'I'm protective,' he said huskily, 'that's just the way it is. Get used to it because it isn't going to change.'

'I don't need protecting.'

'Yes, you do.' He claimed her mouth in a brief but devastating kiss. 'Mostly from yourself. You seem to have a talent for smashing anything that comes too close. Come on. We need to move.'

In under three minutes they were in the mountain rescue vehicle. Rambo was in the back, ears pricked, alert.

'What do you mean, I need protecting from myself?' Meg drove and took the fastest route to the car park that was closest to Devil's Gully. 'I don't smash things.'

'Tell me you're not thinking of a thousand reasons why our relationship is never going to work.'

'Not a thousand.' Annoyed that he was so perceptive, she shifted gear jerkily. 'Even I can't come up with a thousand.'

'That's because I've been keeping you occupied.' He zipped his jacket, wincing as the vehicle hit a bump in the road. 'Keep your eyes on the road. If I have to be driven, the bare minimum I expect is for the driver to look at the road.'

'My eyes are on the road. Don't tell me how to drive.'

'You're so scared of being hurt again you've shut everyone out.' He pushed his hands into gloves, understanding but ignoring her snappiness. 'But you're not shutting me out.'

'Is that a warning?'

'It's just the way it is, so there's no point fighting it. Car park's ahead. If you pull in by the gate, I'll sort out the equipment. And I'm driving home.'

From the car park, it was only a fifteen-minute hike to the top of Devil's Gully, which was just enough time for her to brood on his comments. It wasn't true. She didn't smash anything that came too close. She didn't need protecting from herself. That was a ridiculous thing to say. Her life had been stable over the past seven years, and that was because she'd taken great care to keep it that way. She liked her life.

But she also liked being with him.

And that terrified her.

'I see someone on the path—this must be where they fell.' Dino quickened his pace and they met up with two walkers who were hovering at the top of the gully.

The woman had obviously been crying. 'He was climbing. We were watching him. He was so good. And then he just fell right past his girlfriend. She was screaming but she's stopped now. I think she's paralysed by fear. And he's been dangling from the rope for at least an hour. Any moment now it could snap. But we don't have any equipment. We had no idea what to do so we just called the police.'

Meg stared down into the gully. She saw the girl clinging to the rock face. 'She doesn't look too good.'

Dino was hauling equipment out of his backpack. 'He's hanging from emergency ropes.'

The woman was shaking. 'At first he was just swinging. We kept thinking the rope would snap. And he smashed into the rock face when he fell. He managed to tie something round his thigh but he's still bleeding. He hasn't moved for the last few minutes.'

'I'm on my way.' Meg had her hand inside her

backpack, pulling out her own gear. 'I'll abseil down to him. I'll try and cut a seat in the snow or something for him to sit on while we wait for the helicopter. I know this climb—there are places. There's a ledge just below him.'

'You're not abseiling down.'

'The rock is crumbling here. It's really unstable. That's probably why he fell. I'm lighter than you. It makes sense for me to go.'

'Meg—'

'You're too heavy, Dino. We're wasting time.' She checked the anchors that would hold the rope, looking for signs of corrosion, fractures and movement in the rock. 'If he's been hanging there for a while, the cold is going to be our biggest problem. Once I have him on the ledge, lower me a sleeping bag—something warm, because if he's been hanging there for half an hour, he's going to be cold.'

'You're not going.'

Meg adjusted her harness and jammed a helmet on her head. 'Are you speaking as my lover or as a member of the mountain rescue team?'

A muscle flickered in his cheek. His internal battle was played out across his handsome face. 'Back up your anchors and keep the rope clear of loose rock and sharp edges. Abseil smoothly and directly down the fall line.'

She pulled on gloves and tossed the rope. 'You think I'm doing this for the adrenaline rush?'

He didn't smile. 'Use an autoblock as a back-up to hold the control rope if you let go.'

'I'm not going to let go.' Looking at his face, she felt warmth build inside her. *He cared.* And it felt scarily good. 'I'm tying a French Prusik. Happy? That way, if

I decide to live dangerously and let go, I'm not going to fall.' Calm and confident, Meg made five wraps around the rope and then clipped the two ends into the karabiner.

'Get him onto a ledge.' Dino leaned forward and checked her harness. 'Use your radio.'

Meg went over the edge carefully, checking her anchors and the pull of the rope. The first thing she noticed was the bitter cold and the evidence of new snowfall. She cursed as her feet dislodged loose snow and sent it showering over her. She wondered if the weather had contributed to the man's fall. Overhead she heard the clatter of the search-and-rescue helicopter but she forced herself to focus and concentrate on her own descent.

Finally she was next to the injured climber, her cheeks numb with cold. How much colder must he be after being exposed to the weather in this place?

'Hi, there—can you hear me?' She moved her feet across the rock face so that she was next to him, keeping an eye on the rope. 'I'm Meg. I'm with the mountain rescue team.'

His face was a whitish grey, shocked. Blood had stained one leg of his trousers. 'Nick. I'm bleeding. Not good.'

'Well, this is your lucky day because I'm going to do something about that, Nick.'

His lips barely moved. 'C-cold.'

'I know. I'm going to do something about that too.' She glanced at the rock face. Judged the distance. 'Nick, I'm going to move you onto that ledge and see if I can sort out the bleeding. It will be quicker than getting you to the ground.'

'Fiona—my girlfriend…'

'We'll get her down in a minute. You're the priority.

Can you move?' Descending half a metre, Meg moved across the rock face and climbed up to the ledge that she knew was under the layers of snow. With her gloved hand she formed a snow shelf. Dino's voice came through the radio and she talked to him briefly, updating him, telling him about the bleeding. Then she carefully helped the injured climber onto the shelf. 'OK, let's see what we're dealing with. Can you undo your trousers? They're an expensive brand—I don't really want to cut them off.'

Nick gave a weak laugh. 'That sounds like an indecent suggestion.'

'Nick, it's minus five.' Meg ripped open a sterile pad and then helped him slide his trousers down to expose the wound. 'Sex isn't exactly the foremost thing on my mind right now. I—' Blood spurted into the air and she slammed the pad down hard on the wound, pressing with her hand 'Right, that's quite a cut you've got there. You must have caught an artery.'

'I gashed it on the rock—it spurted.'

'Still spurting.' The pad was soaked within seconds. Meg increased the pressure.

Nick leaned his head against the rock. 'I tried a tourniquet. Kept releasing it and tightening it but it wasn't easy. Just leave me. Get Fiona.'

'I'm not leaving you.' Her fingers were slippery with the blood. Using her free hand, Meg spoke into her radio. Her own pulse was racing because this wasn't the place to be dealing with a major injury. She had no room to manoeuvre. 'Dino, I'm dealing with a bleeding femoral artery.' She was going to have to apply another tourniquet, up here on a ledge in freezing conditions. What equipment did she have? What could she use? She had another rope in her backpack. Maybe she could cut that—

'Meg.' Dino's voice came over the radio. 'I'm sending down a sleeping bag and Celox. Use Celox to stop the bleeding. Pour it into the wound. Apply pressure for three minutes.'

'Celox. Damn.' Meg blinked. 'I'd forgotten about Celox.'

Nick's eyes opened. 'What's Celox?'

'It stops bleeding by bonding with red blood cells. It gels and produces a clot. It's amazing stuff. Originally developed for battlefield injuries, I think, but now we're using it. Had our first training session last month.' Careful with her balance, Meg took the pack that Dino lowered. Trying to remember what she'd been taught in the last training session, she ripped open the packet and tipped the Celox into the wound. Then she tore open a fresh pad and applied pressure. 'Let's just hope it's as good as they say it is. Apparently it takes less than thirty seconds to clot. It even works in freezing temperatures, which is just as well because that's what we're dealing with here. See?' Relief poured through her as the bleeding ceased. 'It's magic. Otherwise known as a powerful haemostatic agent. You're going to be fine, Nick. We're going to get you out of here and— Nick? Oh, no, don't do this to me—not here…'

'It's all right, Meg, he's still breathing.' Dino spoke from right beside her and she turned with relief, realising that she hadn't even heard his descent.

'What are you doing here? The rock is crumbling and you must have come down far too fast.' Her voice was croaky. 'If I admit that I'm pleased to see you, are you ever going to let me forget it?'

'Probably not.' His hands were over hers, reassuring and strong. 'How's the bleeding?'

'It's stopped. That stuff is like a miracle.'

'You're the miracle, *tesoro*.' Dino took over. He checked Nick and then signalled to the winchman, who was slowly lowered with the stretcher. 'I'm going to get some morphine into him and then we're going to get him onto the stretcher and into the helicopter. It's only a five-minute flight from here.'

The transfer to the helicopter went smoothly. Having discharged his responsibility towards Nick, Dino abseiled down to help Fiona, who was still clinging to the rock face, frozen with fear.

It took him another twenty minutes to calm her sufficiently to be able to help her down the rock face. Finally, when she was safely secured to him, Dino carefully helped her down to the valley floor. Back in the mountain rescue vehicle, they wrapped her in layers to warm her.

'Will Nick be all right?' Her teeth chattering, Fiona huddled deeper inside the coat. 'When he fell, I thought—I thought…'

'He's going to be fine.' Meg cleaned herself up as discreetly as possible, sloshing water over her hands. 'We're taking you to the hospital now, so you can check that out for yourself.'

Ellie met them as they walked into the department. Her eyes sparkled knowingly as she saw Meg and Dino together. 'Enjoying your Sunday?' Without saying anything else, she smiled and slid her arm around Fiona, escorting her to where Nick was being assessed.

'Not subtle, are they?' Meg gritted her teeth. 'I should have got you to drop me off.'

Dino sent her a speculative look. 'I don't see a reason to hide our relationship. Do you?'

Meg shrugged awkwardly. 'Well, we're colleagues. I suppose it's just I don't want everyone knowing. I don't want them all taking bets on how long it is before you go off with some long-legged blonde.'

'You're a long-legged blonde, *amore*.' Dino slid his arm round her waist and pulled her against him. 'And I'm with you.'

Conscious of their surroundings, Meg tried to ignore the sizzle of awareness in her body. 'We're at work.'

'No, we're not. It's our day off.' His mouth was close to hers. 'Stop thinking like that, Meg. Stop thinking this relationship is doomed before it starts.'

'Right. Yes. I'm going to stop.' Meg tried not to think about Hayden. Instead, she found herself thinking about her replacement, the gorgeous Georgina, waiting in the car, her hair smooth and sleek and her mouth a glossy red. *Damn the woman.* 'I'm just going to nip to the staffroom and clean up. Then we can go and pick up Jamie and get your car.'

'Come back to my house for the evening.' Dino stroked her face with his fingers. 'I'll cook some pasta. We can open a bottle of wine.'

'I have Jamie.'

'He can eat my pasta. And I've bought a selection of DVDs for him.'

'You're kidding.' Meg started to laugh. 'You bought *Ice Age*?'

'I bought every animated film that has been produced in the last ten years, just to be on the safe side. And a mountain of popcorn.'

'Be careful. If you make it too comfortable, we'll move in.'

Something flickered in Dino's eyes and Meg took a step backwards, seriously shaken up by her own thought process. Why had she said that? What was she thinking? 'I—I need to go and clean up. I'll meet you in the car park.' Without giving him time to answer, she shot into the staffroom and into the shower room.

She turned on the hot water and scrubbed her hands, soaping them to remove all traces of the dramatic rescue. Moving in? Since when had sex turned into moving in? Get a grip, Meg. It was all too fast.

She closed her eyes tightly, trying to wipe out the picture of the three of them curled up on one of Dino's huge, deep sofas, watching a movie.

He liked her, yes. And he liked Jamie. Otherwise why would he have bought an entire collection of movies he was never likely to watch on his own? And he genuinely seemed to find her attractive, even when she was dressed in her walking gear.

So why was she just waiting for it to fall apart?

Reminding herself that Dino wasn't anything like Hayden, Meg dried her hands and opened the door of the shower room. A couple of nurses from the department were making tea and Melissa, the nurse from the observation unit, was in the middle of telling a story about some unfortunate girl whose trousers had split.

'It would help if she ate less chocolate,' she said bitchily, and then broke off as Meg appeared. 'Oh— hi, Meg. Gosh, what have you been doing with your Sunday? You look a total wreck.'

A total wreck.

Angry, Meg pushed her hair away from her face. 'I rescued a man from certain death from a cliff face,' she said coldly. 'What have you been doing with your Sunday, Melissa? Painting your nails?'

Flirting with doctors?

'Apart from working, I've been planning what to wear for Dino Zinetti's Christmas party.' Melissa made herself a herbal tea and declined the offer of a biscuit from one of the other nurses. 'No, thanks. My dress is so-o-o tight there's barely room for me, certainly no room for a biscuit. I want to look like a woman, but not that much of a woman.'

Meg felt sick. Dino had invited Melissa to his party? A few friends, he'd said. Friends from work and members of the mountain rescue team. Since when had Melissa been a friend? He knew it was seeing Melissa that had upset her on the night of the ball.

Nina, one of the other nurses, helped herself to two biscuits. 'So what are you wearing, Meg?'

Meg looked at her blankly. What was she wearing? What sort of a question was that? The party was two days away. Who started thinking about what to wear two days before an event? Dino had told her it was informal. She'd planned to tug open her wardrobe half an hour before she left the house and pick something.

'Meg will wear jeans.' Melissa fished her tea bag out of her mug. 'Meg always wears jeans. And I don't blame you.' She smiled at Meg. 'Jeans are always safe, aren't they? And your legs are quite muscular.'

Muscular?

Meg had an overwhelming temptation to kick one of her muscular legs straight into Melissa's glossy smile.

She wanted to say something witty that would wipe the smirk off the other girl's face, but her mind was completely blank. No words came. Later, she knew, she'd think of something cutting. Later, when it was far too late to say anything, and then she'd spend weeks cursing herself for not thinking of the right thing to say at the right time. But for now there was nothing. So she simply muttered something non-specific and left the room, hating herself for letting them get to her.

Meg will wear jeans. Meg always wears jeans.

What was wrong with that?

What was so clever about pouring yourself into a tight dress that left nothing to the imagination? Any idiot could plaster themselves with make-up and pout, couldn't they?

Angry and hurt, she stomped towards the back entrance of the department. She'd actually been looking forward to Dino's party, but now she didn't want to go. It was going to be another one of those social events that felt like a competition. *I love your shoes. Oh, that dress is so gorgeous.* A room full of gorgeous Georginas all staring at her and judging.

Meg always wears jeans.

Maybe she'd just tell Dino she wasn't well. But then Jamie would be horribly disappointed and she'd earn herself another lecture from her mother.

Pushing open the doors of the emergency department, Meg paused as the cold air rushed forward to meet her. In the distance she saw the jagged outline of the mountains, topped with snow and sparkling under the winter sun. Just looking at them made her feel instantly better.

Really, she had to get over this. It was just a party. One party. Not a big deal. Nothing worth getting herself into a stew over. She was being pathetic.

Meg breathed in the fresh mountain air and suddenly felt stronger.

Two girls dressed as elves hobbled past her into the building, chatting together. A mother with a pushchair loaded with Christmas shopping negotiated the icy pavement on her way home. Life, Meg thought. A mixture of good and bad. Easy and difficult.

The door swung closed behind her and she saw Dino waiting for her, the collar of his jacket turned up against the cold, his phone in his hand as he scrolled through his messages.

She could ask him why he'd invited Melissa. She could tell him she wasn't coming. Or she could play this another way.

Meg gave a slow smile.

And have some fun.

CHAPTER EIGHT

DINO checked on the caterers and adjusted the volume of the music. People had been arriving for the past hour but there was still no sign of Meg and Jamie.

A tinkle of female laughter scraped against his nerve endings and he clenched his jaw and glanced over his shoulder at Melissa. She stood with her back to the fire, the shimmering light turning her skin-tight black dress transparent. He wondered if she knew her underwear was on display and decided that she did. Melissa did nothing by accident. He knew her type well. Her dress was a message. *I'm yours.*

Except that he didn't want her.

He hadn't invited her, but she'd arrived as part of the group of nurses from the emergency department. Given that the purpose of the party was goodwill, he'd decided to overlook it. But now he was remembering that Melissa had been the reason Meg had run out on him the night of the ball. Had she found out that Melissa intended to show up? Was that why she wasn't here?

If she didn't know, she was going to find out soon enough. And she was going to take one look at Melissa's ultra-short dress and shiny red mouth and turn and run. Again.

Dino felt tension ripple across his shoulders. He'd

told her it was casual, hadn't he? He'd set this whole thing up as somewhere comfortable and safe where she could socialise without worrying about what everyone was wearing. He hadn't factored in that it was Christmas and most of the women were looking for an excuse to dress up and flutter their feathers.

Meg was going to arrive in her jeans and feel out of place.

He wondered whether he should call her mobile and warn her. But if he did that, she would definitely freak out and not show.

'Hi, Dino, great party.' One of the consultant radiologists shook his hand firmly and introduced his wife, who was heavily pregnant. 'This is a fantastic place you have here.'

Looking at the throng of people filling his house, Dino gave a humourless smile. Interesting, he thought, how a house could be full of people and yet still feel empty just because of the absence of one person.

Extracting himself from small talk, Dino glanced through the expanse of glass, watching for headlights. People were arriving in a continuous stream, but there was still no sign of Meg.

He was just exchanging a few words with an equipment officer from the mountain rescue team when the room suddenly fell silent. The steady buzz of conversation faded to near silence. Exploring the cause, Dino turned his head and saw Meg standing in the doorway. She was wearing a sparkling blue dress that made Melissa's choice of semi-transparent black look positively dowdy.

Scanning her from the tumble of golden curls to the long, graceful length of her legs, Dino tried to remember how to breathe. What had possessed him to invite all these people when there was only one person who interested him? Why hadn't he just invited her and made it a private party for two? She looked stunning.

And sophisticated.

A pair of killer heels made her legs look impossibly long and the shimmering dress skimmed her athletic physique in a way that suggested rather than shrieked.

'Dino!' Jamie flew across the room, dressed as a superhero, his cape flying behind him. 'Sorry we're late. We were on a mission.'

Dino scooped the boy into his arms, his eyes still on Meg. For a moment she didn't move. She just looked at him. Then she smiled and walked across the room, head held high.

'Dino.'

He'd expected to see insecurity in her eyes but instead he saw fire and fight and felt the tension pulsing from her. Picking up on it, his eyes narrowed in silent question.

Something, or someone, had upset her and she'd come out fighting.

And you didn't have to be a genius to guess who. 'I was beginning to think you weren't coming.'

'Why wouldn't I come?' Her tone was slightly brittle and she helped herself to a glass of orange juice from one of the waiters who were circulating with drinks and canapés. 'This is fantastic. I thought you said it would be just a few friends. Informal.'

'It started out that way but it escalated, and I don't have time to prepare food for this number of people so I thought it was easier to get caterers in. This isn't how I planned it.'

She relaxed slightly and stayed by his side. They chatted about the day and then a couple of members of the mountain rescue team joined them and they all started talking about their latest rescue.

Halfway through the evening 'Santa' appeared with a sack of presents for the children.

As Jamie and the other children leaped around with excitement, Dino watched Meg. Finally she'd relaxed. Drink in hand, she was laughing as Jamie ripped the paper off his present to reveal a large plastic Batman figure.

Dino threw a questioning glance at Meg. 'I know he already has one…'

'It's great. Really thoughtful.' She smiled up at him. 'You can never have too many. I'm trying to work out who is concealed under that Santa suit. It looks like Rob Hamilton from Orthopaedics but he isn't quite that portly. Unless he's hit the mince pies big time.'

'We added some padding to his costume. He has the deepest voice. Not to mention the fact he was one of the few who was prepared to do it. Come on—' He held out his hand. 'Let's dance.'

She hesitated, her cheeks pink. Then she slowly put her glass down on the table and gave a hesitant smile. 'All right, but I ought to warn you I—'

'Dino!' Melissa bounced over to them, her breasts in danger of making a guest appearance. Grabbing his other hand, she pulled. 'This is my favourite track. Dance with me.'

'I don't think so.' Frowning, Dino extracted his hand but Meg was already backing away, her smile frozen to her face.

'You go ahead. I'm useless at dancing anyway. And I need to see Jamie.'

'Meg—'

'Honestly, dance.' She waved her hand towards the centre of the room. 'I'll catch up with you later.'

Dino reached out to grab her but she melted into the crowd, vanishing in the sea of shimmering dresses that closed in front of him, blocking his path.

She was a complete fool.

Meg stood in the bathroom, staring at herself in the mirror. It was always going to be like this. What had she expected? That she could turn herself into some supermodel overnight? That putting on a pair of high heels and a sparkling dress would make her feel any different inside?

'Meg?' Dino's voice came through the door. 'Are you in there?'

She froze. 'Give me a minute.'

'I need to talk to you.'

Tugging open the bathroom door, she pinned a smile on her face. 'Hi. Everything all right? The kids haven't discovered the champagne, have they?'

'Why do you do that? You just walked away.' His eyes were very dark and very angry. 'You always walk away when things get tough. You should have stood your ground and fought her.'

'I didn't want to make things awkward for you.'

'Awkward? You think I care about awkward? *Maledezione*, Meg, what do you think is going on here?'

'I think all the women in the room are interested in you—as usual. I think they all spent most of the last week planning what they were going to wear to catch your attention.'

'There is only one woman in the room who interests me. And, no, you're not leaving until we've had this out.' He rested his arm against the wall, trapping her, his eyes stormy. 'If you'd hung around you would have heard me telling Melissa that I'm not interested. That she's wasting her time.'

'It isn't just Melissa.' Meg found that her hands were shaking. 'There will always be another Melissa. That's the sort of man you are.'

His features hardened. 'What's that supposed to mean?'

'You can't help it, Dino. You're super good looking, sexy, rich—basically gorgeous. You only have to smile and women want to rip their clothes off.' Meg gave a hysterical laugh. 'There will always be some woman who wants you. Always some woman trying to knock me down to get to you. Maybe you don't notice Melissa, but sooner or later one of them is going to attract your attention if they try hard enough. And then it's going to be Georgina all over again.'

There was a long silence. 'That was her name?' His voice was harsh. 'The woman he dumped you for?'

Meg shrugged. 'That doesn't matter. What does matter is that the world is full of Georginas. I can't compete. And, actually, I don't want to. I don't want to live my life on a knife edge, wondering whether this is going to be the day you find someone prettier.'

'Have you any idea how insulting that is?' He pulled away from her, his expression black. 'You're implying that I have no control over my own emotions or behaviour, that I'll tangle the sheets with every pretty girl who crosses my path. Is that what you think of me? Is that who you think I am?'

'You're human. You're a man, for God's sake.'

'Yes, I'm a man. A grown man, not some teenage boy who hasn't learned control. Damn it, Meg, I can forgive you for thinking I'm ruled by my libido because that's how it seems whenever I'm with you, but I find it hard to forgive you for thinking I'm so shallow that I'd chase after any woman who throws herself at me. I need more than mindless sex in a relationship. Until you came into my life, I had no trouble at all with the word no. Believe it or not, I'm adult enough to make my own choices. And if a woman comes on to me, it's still my choice, even if her dress is up round her bottom and her boobs are thrust in my face. For your information, Melissa is the type of woman I avoid. I know her type too well.'

'But—'

'No, there are no "buts" on this one Meg.' His tone was hard. 'Maybe you've spent too much time alone with Jamie. You're treating me like a child, assuming that every shiny new toy I see in the store I'm going to want to buy.'

Her heart pounded. 'I'm not treating you like a child.'

'Then trust me, Meg. Trust me to make my own decisions and exercise control. That's what being an adult is all about. I know what I want out of life. And it isn't quick sex with any woman who will put it out there.' A muscle worked in his jaw. 'I wait until I see something good, something special, and when I do I'm not afraid to go for it. Unlike you.'

'I'm not afraid.'

'Yes, you are. You're terrified of being hurt again the way Hayden hurt you, and I understand that. But we can't have a proper relationship if I'm having to look over my shoulder all the time, checking there are no pretty girls in the vicinity in case you're about to go into meltdown. I can't live like that. There has to be trust, Meg.'

He didn't understand. He had absolutely no idea. Meg felt tears prick her eyes. 'I can't live like that either. I can't live my life wondering whether today is going to be the day you tell me I'm not the woman you want to be with. Wondering whether this is going to be the day you walk out and go off with the more glamorous model waiting in the wings. I sometimes wonder if you even realise how sexy you are. You walk into a room and there isn't a woman who doesn't look at you! And I don't think I can stand by and watch a never-ending string of glamorous woman dress up and try and attract you away from me. And maybe that's defeatist, but it's the way it is. I don't want to live my life with a knot of anxiety in my stomach. It isn't fair on me and it isn't fair on Jamie. And it isn't fair on you because I don't think I can change. And I know this is just me being stupid. I know that. But I can't change the way I think.' Her breathing was shallow.

'You're right that I'm afraid. I admit it, I'm terrified! Terrified that I'll put Jamie through what I went through. Terrified that I'll have to answer another load of questions about why another man left him. I just don't want to risk that. I can't.' She waited for him to give a sympathetic nod or acknowledge in some way that he understood what she was feeling.

Instead, he pulled away from her, his eyes cold. 'If you think I'd hurt your son, you don't know me at all.'

'It isn't about not knowing you. It's about reality.' She struggled to make him understand. 'Relationships break up every single day.'

'Not all of them. Have you thought about that,

Meg? Some relationships actually work out. The good ones.'

'But how do you know?' Her voice was a whisper. 'If I get this wrong, Jamie gets hurt. I can't do that to him.' And she couldn't do it to herself.

'So you'll trust me with your life on the end of a rope, but you won't trust me with your heart.' His tone was raw. 'Is that right?'

Meg stared at him.

She wanted to tell him that she trusted him. But the words couldn't break free from the cold ball of terror inside her.

Dino watched her for a long moment. Waited. And then turned and walked away, leaving her standing alone, drowning in a sea of her own fears.

Meg drove home, Jamie asleep in the back of the car.

Twice she had to stop because she was crying so hard and she couldn't see the road. She'd blown it. She'd totally blown it. Ruined everything.

As she drove through the town on the way to her house, she saw crowds of people pouring out of restaurants and bars after Christmas parties. They wore silly hats and tinsel and clutched presents. They were all laughing and chatting and they seemed so *normal*. Whereas she—she was so messed up she didn't have a clue how to fix herself.

Why couldn't she just have said she trusted him? Even if it all went wrong, could it honestly feel any worse than this?

She could have carried on, couldn't she, hoping that he kept looking at her and no one else?

But she was exhausted with being on her guard and watching for competition. Wiping the smile off Melissa's face should have been fun, but she'd felt nothing except a bone-deep tiredness.

Flicking her indicator, she took the road that led out of the town towards the lake. Was Dino with her now? Had he turned to her for consolation?

As she drove down the lane that led to her house, the moonlight reflected off the snow and the mountains stood out clearly. It was midnight, but she could see the contour of every peak and she could name them. She'd climbed most of them with Dino by her side. He was right when he'd said she trusted him with her life. She did. Out here, in her world. In the place that mattered to her, she trusted him.

Here, she could be herself. Here, it didn't matter who designed your handbag or whether your dress was 'last season'. Here, it was more important to know whether there might be a new snowfall overnight, bringing more risks to walkers in the morning. Here, you had to be able to recognise wind slab and know how to use an ice axe. Here, she was comfortable.

Functioning on automatic, Meg pulled up outside the cottage and gently lifted Jamie out of the back seat of the car. He snuggled against her, his arms tight around her neck. For a moment she held him against her, taking comfort from the feel of his warm, solid body crushed against hers. He was her world. Her whole world.

'It was a lovely party, Mummy.' His voice was sleepy. 'Popcorn. *Ice Age*. And tomorrow is Christmas Eve. I love Christmas Eve because Christmas is still to come and it's so exciting.'

Struggling to find even a glimmer of excitement inside herself, Meg picked her way through the fresh snow. 'What about Christmas Day? Don't you like that?'

'Christmas Day is the best. I can't wait to see Dino again.'

Meg held him tightly with one arm and pushed her key in the door. Looking at the mistletoe, she lifted her hand and pulled it off the door. No more mistletoe. No more dreams and delusions. Flinging it onto the snow, she took a deep breath. 'He's not coming, Jamie.' Her voice was gruff. 'He can't make it for Christmas Day. I'm sorry.' She carried him into the house and Jamie lifted his head groggily. Still sleepy, he focused on her face.

'He *is* coming. He promised.'

'No. No, he's not. It's not his fault.' Her voice cracked. 'It's my fault. It's all my fault.'

'He said he was coming!' Fully awake now, Jamie wriggled out of her arms. 'He promised! He promised he wouldn't let you push him away! He promised he wouldn't let that happen. *He promised!*'

'Jamie…' Shocked, Meg held out her arms to him but he backed away, tears pouring down his cheeks.

'He promised. Just leave me alone! I hate you and I hate Dino! I thought he was a superhero but he isn't. He isn't. He's just a man and I hate him.' Sobs tearing his little chest, Jamie ran upstairs to his bedroom and slammed the door.

Meg closed the front door and leaned her head against the wood, beating herself up for choosing to tell him now and not wait until the morning when he'd slept and was better able to cope with disappointment. She'd told him, she realised numbly, because she'd needed to talk to someone. But that shouldn't have been Jamie, should it? He was a child.

She was crying too, hot tears smudging the mascara she'd applied so carefully only a few hours earlier. She wanted to go after Jamie, but she knew he needed a few minutes to calm down by himself.

In a minute she'd go upstairs and tuck him in. Read to him. Stories where a superhero always stepped in when life got hard.

If only...

She needed to explain to him that none of this was Dino's fault. It was her, wasn't it?

She was a coward.

She'd fallen over once, hurt herself badly, and now she was afraid to run again. Her mother was right—hanging from a rock face from a thin rope wasn't brave because she wasn't afraid of that. Brave was when you did something that terrified you. Tonight, she'd stared her biggest fear in the face. And she'd turned and run.

'Jamie is quiet, considering it's Christmas Eve.' Meg's mother sprinkled icing sugar over the Christmas cake to look like snow. Outside, the sun shone on the snow crystals, adding sparkle and light. 'Is he just tired or has something happened?'

'Do you really need to ask? Don't put any more sugar on that, Mum, or our teeth will fall out.'

'I assume this has something to do with Dino?'

'That's right. I messed it up. As always.' Her tone brittle, Meg emptied cranberries into a saucepan. 'How much water do I add to these?'

'Just a tablespoon. And the zest of an orange. So are you going to fix it?'

'Dino broke up with me, Mum.'

She frowned. 'Really? That surprises me. He doesn't strike me as the sort who walks away.'

'No, that's usually my role.'

'Did he say why?'

'He was angry that I wouldn't trust him. Angry that I was worried he might go off with someone.' She swallowed. 'He said he couldn't live like that.'

'Waiting for you to destroy something good? I don't blame him. You're enough to give the most patient man an ulcer. Don't stir those so hard—they're nicer when they're still whole. I like bite and texture.'

Meg stopped stirring. Her eyes were gritty from lack of sleep and her head ached. But none of that came close to the agony that burned inside her. 'I feel…h-horrible. Miserable. And so, so guilty about Jamie. He wanted it to work out so badly. And the crazy thing is I wanted that too. I wanted us to be a family. I wanted that.' Her voice cracked. 'What have I done, Mum?'

Her mother made a distressed sound and crossed the kitchen. 'Oh, sweetheart…' She folded Meg into her arms and held her tightly, crooning as she had when Meg had been a small child. 'You haven't done anything. You're just sorting out your thoughts and the way you feel and that takes time. You're too hard on yourself.'

Meg sobbed into her mother's shoulder, unravelling in the safe cocoon of warmth and love. 'No, I've wrecked everything and it could have been good because Dino is just gorgeous, not to mention clever, and he's so lovely with Jamie and he's incredible in bed.' She sniffed. 'Sorry—I'm so sorry.'

'Don't apologise.' Her mother stroked her hair away from her face. 'I'm so proud of you and everything you've done. And now you're going to listen to me. You've done a fantastic job with Jamie. You're a wonderful mother, but there are times when you need to put yourself first and this is one of them. Stop worry-

ing about Jamie and think about yourself. Why do you
think you're so scared, Meg?'

'Apart from the fact that I'm a crackpot?' Meg
found a tissue and blew her nose. 'Because of Hayden,
I suppose.'

'You were young and vulnerable when you met
Hayden. A girl, not a woman. You were attracted by surface sparkle and you didn't notice the lack of depth.' Her
mother urged her gently to a chair. 'If Hayden walked
through that door now, what would you do?'

'Kick him out again. I know he wasn't right for me,
Mum. I know it would never have lasted, but knowing
that doesn't help.'

'When Hayden left you were young, you were pregnant, you were alone. But you survived. And you would
survive again. People do.' Her mother's face was sad and
Meg leaned forward and hugged her, feeling horribly
selfish.

'When we lost Dad I was worried you wouldn't survive. I was worried you wouldn't want to live your life
without him.'

'I learned to live a different life.' Her mother's voice
was quiet. 'There isn't a day when I don't miss your
father and I'd be lying if I said it never hurts, but that
doesn't mean I'm not happy. Loving and being loved
is the greatest gift of all. It's what life is all about, and
that's what I want to see in your life. I don't want to see
you turning love away because you're afraid of what
will happen if you lose it. If you do that, you've already
lost.'

'Love? Who said anything about love?' Meg stared,
her heart pumping hard. 'I'm not— I don't…' She
gulped. 'Oh…'

'Why do you think you're so very scared?' Her

mother's voice was gentle. 'Why does it matter so much?'

Meg sucked in a breath. 'Because I love him. I love him so much it's like this huge glowing thing inside me. When I'm with him I feel as though I'm a light that's suddenly switched on. I love him, *I love him*, but I couldn't say it, and now—now—'

'That's why you're scared. Not because of Hayden or that stupid Georgina girl. But because this time you really care and when we really care it makes us vulnerable.'

Meg pressed her hand to her chest and looked at her mother. 'What do I do? Tell me what to do.'

Her mother smiled, love in her eyes. 'I think you already know the answer to that one.'

'I think I need to find out if he loves me. But he's never said—what if he doesn't?'

'He's human too. He's not going to put it all out there unless he thinks there's a chance, and you've been pushing him away from day one. How many months have you worked together?'

'Eight? Nine?' Her brain was a mess. 'I don't know.'

'And he's been biding his time.'

'He flirted with everyone. He only asked me out recently. Why?'

Her mother smiled and stood up. 'Why don't you ask him?'

'Right now?' Meg found it difficult to breathe. 'Wh-what are you going to do?'

'Stay with your son.' Her voice calm, Catherine opened the fridge. 'Go. You have a whole life to live, Meg. And I have a turkey to stuff.'

CHAPTER NINE

THE house looked empty. Quiet after the noise of the night before, the huge windows reflecting the green of the forest and the bright winter sunshine.

There was no sign of life.

Meg left her car and stood for a moment, breathing in the scent of pine. The whole place smelt like Christmas.

They could live here, she thought. They could make a life together. Be a family.

If that was what he wanted. If she wasn't too late.

Walking towards the front door, she wondered if he'd seen her arrive. No, because he wouldn't ignore her, would he? She refused to be that paranoid. If he'd seen her arrive, he would have answered the door. He wasn't the sort to run and hide in the basement.

Her hand shook as she pressed the bell.

If her mother was wrong then she was about to make a total fool of herself. She was about to put her heart out there—everything she felt. She was giving him the chance to squash it.

Except that he wasn't answering.

Which meant he obviously wasn't sitting around brooding or getting blind drunk.

He'd gone out. Unless—unless he was inside and he already had company.

Feeling her courage drain away, Meg bit her lip, realising that the party had probably gone on long after she'd left. As far as he was concerned, their relationship was over. What was to stop him finding someone else?

The cold seeped through her jumper but Meg barely noticed.

She'd ruined everything. She should have been brave.

But she hadn't.

And now she'd lost him.

It was over.

'Mummy, wake up! He's been! Can I open my stocking in your bed?' Without waiting for an invitation, Jamie dragged his lumpy, bumpy stocking into the bed and Meg struggled to wake up.

She glanced at the clock and realised she'd been asleep for less than two hours.

'It's still only seven o'clock, Jamie, so don't make too much noise. Grandma is asleep and she doesn't want to be woken up this early.'

'Do you need coffee or something?' Jamie peered at her. 'You look funny.'

'I just haven't quite woken up yet.' Meg sat up and tried to shake off the sleep. 'But I'm working on it. Right. What's in this stocking?' Even half-asleep and broken-hearted, she enjoyed watching him dig the presents out of the stocking and rip off the paper. They were just small things, but from the look on his face he might have been given the world. Watching his delight at discovering a Batman torch that had cost her less than a cup of coffee, she felt a rush of pride and gratitude. He was such a sweet-natured boy. So undemanding compared to so many of the other children she saw, who were only interested in the label or the 'next big thing'.

'This is so cool.' He lay on his back on her bed, flashing the torch at the ceiling. 'Watch, Mum. The beam is the shape of a bat.'

'I'm watching.'

'Isn't Santa clever, Mum? He knows exactly what I want.'

Meg swallowed. The one thing he really wanted she hadn't been able to give him.

She'd failed at that.

Racked with maternal guilt, she wrapped her child in her arms and hugged him tightly. 'I love you.'

'I love you, too. Can I give you my present to you now?'

'You don't want to wait for Grandma?'

'Grandma helped me choose. Please? I want to see your face when you open it. You're going to be so thrilled.'

His enthusiasm was so infectious that Meg grinned. 'Go on, then.'

'Are you excited?'

'I'm excited.'

Jamie flew off the bed and reappeared moments later with a parcel. The wrapping paper was falling off and the whole thing was loosely bound together with metres of sticky tape. 'I wrapped it myself.'

'I see that. Good job.' Meg handled it carefully, trying to extract her fingers from all the sticky tape. 'Wow. What is it?' She eased the present out of the wrapping and smiled. 'Mrs Incredible pyjamas. How perfect.' She swallowed. No matter what she did, however many mistakes she made, to him she was still Mrs Incredible.

Meg studied the pyjamas through a mist of tears.

'They're red. And when you put them on, you look exactly like Mrs Incredible.' Jamie beamed at her. 'Super-Mum, that's you. I chose them myself. Do you like them?'

'I love them.' Her voice was thickened. 'They're the nicest thing anyone has ever given me.'

'So are you going to put them on?'

'Absolutely. Right away. I'll wear them for breakfast.' Glad of an excuse to leave the room and get herself under control, Meg picked up the pyjamas and walked to the bathroom.

Jamie called after her. 'While you're getting changed, I'll just eat the chocolate from my stocking.'

'Before breakfast?' Meg brushed the tears from her cheeks. 'Yes, why not? Enjoy. Don't get chocolate on my bed.'

They'd be all right, she told herself. They'd get through. But it was an effort to put on the pyjamas and an effort to drag herself down to breakfast.

Her mother had switched on the Christmas tree lights and Meg's living room looked cosy and festive.

After Jamie had opened his other present from her, a Nintendo Wii that she'd saved up to buy him, she left him playing and found her mother in the kitchen.

'He seems happy.'

'Of course he's happy. He's a child. Children are resilient. More resilient than we give them credit for. I've made a pot of coffee. Strong coffee.' Her mother handed her a mug. 'You look as though you need it, Mrs Incredible.'

'Thanks.' Meg looked down at herself. 'I don't deserve these. He should have bought me Mrs Make a

Mess of Everything. They didn't have a pair of those in the store, did they?'

'Mum! Grandma!' Jamie tore through the house, his eyes shining. 'Look outside! I thought the Wii was the best present ever—oh, Mummy, thank you, thank you.' Still in his Batman pyjamas, he dragged open the door and ran into the snow, Rambo barking at his heels.

'Wh-what? Jamie, put a coat on!' Appalled, Meg followed him, shivering in her own thin pyjamas. 'It's *freezing* out here! What do you think you're…?' She stopped, her jaw dropping as she saw the sleek Batmobile crouched on her front lawn. It was child-size, perfect for a boy of Jamie's age. 'What? What is going on?'

'Oh, Mummy, thank you, thank you.' Jamie was almost incoherent with excitement as he slid into the driver's seat. 'How does it work?'

'Jamie I have no idea. I didn't— It isn't from me.'

'It's from me. I hope you don't mind.' Dino walked across the snow towards her, his black hair gleaming under the sun.

Meg stood still, shocked into silence by his unexpected appearance. 'Dino…'

'Merry Christmas, Mrs Incredible.'

Suddenly remembering that she was still wearing Jamie's Christmas present, Meg tugged at her pyjamas self-consciously. Great. If she'd had to meet Dino straight from bed, she would have chosen to be wearing some shimmering slip of silk. Not novelty pyjamas. 'I didn't expect to see you. What are you doing here?'

'You invited me to spend Christmas Day with you.' He slid his hand under her face and held her gaze for a moment before turning back to Jamie. 'It works on the snow. It will pretty much drive anywhere, but we can work out the best places together. Come inside and put on a coat and then we can try it out properly.'

Jamie was completely still, his eyes huge and wary as he stared at Dino. 'You left.' His tone was accusing. 'You said you wouldn't let her push you away, but you did.'

'No, I didn't. Sometimes girls need a bit of space to think things through and I was giving her space.' Dino dropped into a crouch so that he was at eye level with the little boy. 'I didn't let her push me away, although she tried pretty hard. That's why I'm here now. I came back.'

Jamie's fists clenched on the steering-wheel. 'Are you going to go away again?'

'Never.'

'What if she tries to make you?'

'She won't. Not when I've had a chance to talk to her properly.' Dino stood up and held out his arms to the child. 'I'm glad you like the present, but you need to be wearing a few more layers before you play in it or you'll give your mum a reason to be angry with me. Let's go inside and come out again when you're dressed.'

As Jamie sprang into Dino's arms, Meg discovered she was shivering, but whether it was the cold or the fact that Dino was there, she didn't know.

What did he mean when he said he wouldn't go away again?

Her mind spiralled round and round and it was only when she was back in the warmth of the living room that she realised that Jamie and her mother had left her alone with Dino.

'There are things I need to say to you.' Uncharacteristically hesitant, he shrugged off his coat and threw it onto the sofa. 'Things I probably should have said to you a long time ago.'

'There are things I need to say to you, too. I went over to your house. I wanted to see you. To talk to you.'

'You did? I wish I'd been there and then perhaps both of us wouldn't have suffered another sleepless night. I went for a walk. I needed to think.' Lifting his hand, he brushed the dark shadows under her eyes with his fingers. 'I owe you an apology for what I said the other night. I was way out of line.'

'You weren't out of line. Everything you said was true. I do sabotage every relationship. It is a ridiculous way to live. I am a terrible coward. All those things are true.'

'I was too hard on you, but I was offended that you didn't trust me. Offended that you'd think I was the sort of person who would go after Melissa just because she likes to walk around with most of her body on show. As if I didn't have a brain or a mind of my own.'

'Dino—'

'And then I realised that the reason you didn't feel secure in our relationship is because I've never given you any reason to feel secure. I've been holding back telling you how I feel because I didn't want to scare you off. And that's stopped you understanding why our relationship is going to work. I love you, Meg.' He cupped her face in his hands and stared into her eyes. 'I love everything about you. And I'm not talking about a sparkling blue dress or a pair of high heels. I'm talking about what's inside you. I love your energy and your spirit. I love the way you won't hesitate to risk your life to save an injured child, the way you'll make split-second decisions when it's life and death but haven't got any confidence to choose a lipstick.'

Meg's knees were shaking. 'I suppose I'm just basically weird.'

'Gorgeous.'

'I'm messed up.'

'Human. And very beautiful.'

Her heart skipped and danced. 'You can't possibly think that.'

'Meg, I grew up in a family that was completely obsessed with appearance and material things. I came to England to escape from the oppressive expectations of my family. Our home was like a museum and my mother was like one of those mannequins that you see at the waxworks. Beautifully dressed but with no heart or soul. In my entire childhood I don't ever remember her hugging me. Not once. Yes, her nails were perfect and I never once saw her without lipstick, but she wasn't a real person to me. You're a flesh-and-blood woman with feelings and emotions, and you let it all hang out there. You're so open and honest, so warm and emotional. You don't do anything by halves and I love that. I love you, *tesoro*. Every single thing about you. I've waited for you all my life.'

Her heart clenched and she hardly dare breathe in case she disturbed the moment. 'Truly? That's how you feel?'

'I thought it was obvious.'

'No.' She forced the word out. 'No, it wasn't obvious to me.'

'Then perhaps you weren't looking.'

'I just didn't think— I'm not…' She gave a helpless shrug. 'You're so good-looking.'

'I'm glad you think so.' His smile was slow and sexy. 'Say that to me again later when I'm in a position to do something about it, Mrs Incredible.'

'I don't deserve to be wearing these.' Meg bit her lip. 'I'm not Mrs Incredible.'

'To your son, you are. And to me.' He lowered his

mouth to hers and kissed her gently. 'I just didn't realise Mrs Incredible was this sexy.'

She laughed against his lips. 'Oh please—sexy? It's hardly sophisticated lingerie, is it?'

'No—' his eyes were amused '—which just goes to prove my point. It isn't what you're wearing that interests me. Although just for the record I think the pyjamas are cute. I'm assuming they were Jamie's choice.' He pulled her against him, leaving her in no doubt about the way he felt. 'If you can do this to me wearing Mrs Incredible pyjamas, I don't even want to think what you can do to me in sophisticated lingerie.'

She threw herself against his chest, her sob of happiness muffled against his chest. 'I was so scared of getting involved with you. Right from the first day you strolled into the department with your lopsided Italian smile and your fancy car and your incredible body, I avoided you like measles.'

'I know. It took me a long time to win you round. You're a hard nut to crack, Meg Miller.'

'Do you know why I was so afraid?' Meg sniffed and lifted her head to look at him. 'Because I love you so much. If I lost you it would really matter.'

'I know you love me. I worked that out during my long walk yesterday. And you're not going to lose me, *tesoro*. Not now, not ever.'

'Other women look at you all the time. Wherever we go, they look at you.'

'If other women look at me, that's their problem.' He stroked her hair away from her face. 'I make my own choices. And I choose you.'

Meg couldn't breathe. 'Dino—'

'Let me finish. You told me you don't want to spend each day wondering whether this will be the day when

I tell you I don't want to be with you any more. Well, you're not going to be wondering that, Meg, because each day I'm going to be telling you how much I love you and how much you mean to me. You're not going to be wondering, *amore*, because you're going to *know*. You're going to know I love you.'

Meg made a sound somewhere between a laugh and a sob and he brought his mouth down on hers in a possessive kiss.

'Grandma, they're kissing! You were right about the mistletoe. It's magic.' Jamie's voice came from the doorway and both of them jerked backwards. 'I want to play in my car. Dino, are you ready?'

'*Sì*, yes.' His voice was rough and his eyes were still on Meg, 'I'm ready, but first I have a present for your mother.'

'A present?' Jamie leaped onto the sofa, his Batman cape flying. 'Can I watch while she opens it? Grandma!' he yelled at the top of his voice. 'Dino is giving Mum her present. What is it? Do you need any help opening it, Mum?'

'I don't know, I...' Bemused, Meg stood in the middle of the room and gasped as Dino pulled a small box out of his pocket. 'Oh.'

Jamie's face fell and he looked at her sympathetically. 'It's really small, but it's the thought that counts, Mum.'

Fingers shaking, Meg undid the silver wrapping paper. A shower of tiny silver stars fell to the floor and she stared down at the black box with her heart bursting out of her chest.

Dino removed it from her hand and opened it. A huge diamond solitaire sparkled against midnight-blue velvet.

'Dino…' Meg whispered his name, her feelings over-flowing.

'Gosh!' Jamie stood on tiptoe and peered at the box. 'It's a ring. Mum doesn't really wear jewellery. She doesn't wear rings, Dino.'

'She'll wear this one. This one says she's mine.' He took her hand in his and slid the ring onto the third finger of her left hand. 'Marry me, Meg. I want to be with you and Jamie for ever.'

Tears scalded the back of her throat. 'I don't know what to say.'

'You say yes.'

She smiled through her tears. 'Yes—oh, yes—of course, yes.'

Jamie stared up at them, his eyes bright with tears. 'For ever? You mean Dino is never going away again?'

'I promised you I wouldn't.' Dino scooped him into his arms. 'I promised you I wouldn't let her push me away. I never will.'

Jamie buried his face in Dino's neck, his small hands clinging. 'Mine. You're going to be all mine. My very own superhero.'

'No, Jamie.' Dino's voice was husky as he held the child. 'I'm not your very own superhero. I'm going to be your dad. We're going to be a family.'

Meg closed her eyes, breathing in happiness and thinking of the future.

A family. Her family. A million moments, lived together.

Mistletoe and magic.

'Talking of families…' Her mother's voice came from the doorway. 'If you'd all like to come to the table, we have a turkey to eat.'

THE
CHRISTMAS BABY
BUMP

BY
LYNNE MARSHALL

All the characters in this book have no existence outside the imagination of the author, and have no relation whatsoever to anyone bearing the same name or names. They are not even distantly inspired by any individual known or unknown to the author, and all the incidents are pure invention.

First published in Great Britain 2010
Harlequin Mills & Boon Limited,
Eton House, 18-24 Paradise Road, Richmond, Surrey TW9 1SR

© Janet Maarschalk 2010

ISBN: 978 0 263 87926 1

Harlequin Mills & Boon policy is to use papers that are natural, renewable and recyclable products and made from wood grown in sustainable forests. The logging and manufacturing process conform to the legal environmental regulations of the country of origin.

Printed and bound in Spain
by Litografia Rosés, S.A., Barcelona

Dear Reader

The Christmas season is a special time of year. Ideally, it is a time of happiness and goodwill towards others. With that in mind, I was hesitant to give my lovely Stephanie Bennett such a difficult and haunting past to overcome. As for carefree Phil Hansen—well, it just seemed cruel to put him through such an emotional rollercoaster by simultaneously dropping two not-so-perfect people into his life. However…I'm a writer, and it is my job to make life miserable for my characters, so with my editor's blessing I laid it on thick in THE CHRISTMAS BABY BUMP.

Stephanie needs a change of scenery for the holidays, and Phil is coerced into filling in as a caregiver for his preschool-aged half-brother. Unbeknownst to both Stephanie and Phil, these two story elements are the perfect ingredients for a Christmas miracle in the making.

Stephanie has an issue she must face and deal with before she can ever hope to find peace of mind and her fair share of happiness. Fortunately Phil, though at first seeming the least likely, is just the man to help her conquer her past.

I hope you enjoy this Santa Barbara Christmas story, the wrap-up book for my MidCoast medical trilogy: THE BOSS AND NURSE ALBRIGHT, THE HEART DOCTOR AND THE BABY and THE CHRISTMAS BABY BUMP. I've grown to love my imaginary friends at the clinic, and I'm so happy I could help them all find their happy-ever-afters.

With warm holiday wishes coming your way

Lynne
www.lynnemarshall.com

Lynne Marshall has been a Registered Nurse in a large California hospital for twenty-five years. She has now taken the leap to writing full time, but still volunteers at her local community hospital. After writing the book of her heart in 2000, she discovered the wonderful world of Mills & Boon® Medical™ Romance, where she feels the freedom to write the stories she loves. She is happily married, has two fantastic grown children, and a socially challenged rescued dog. Besides her passion for writing Medical Romance, she loves to travel and read. Thanks to the family dog, she takes long walks every day! To find out more about Lynne, please visit her website www.lynnemarshallweb.com

Special thanks to Sally Williamson
for her constant support and for
keeping me on the right path with this story.

CHAPTER ONE

MONDAY morning, Stephanie opened the door of the cream-colored Victorian mansion and headed toward the reception desk. Though the house had been turned into a medical clinic, they'd kept the turn-of-the-century charm. Hardwood floors, tray ceilings, crown molding, wall sconces, even a chandelier made everything feel special. She could get used to showing up for work here.

A man with longish dark blond hair in a suit chatted with not one but two nurses at the receptionist's desk. Nothing short of adoration gleamed from the women's eyes. He looked typical trendy Santa Barbaran—businessman by day in a tailored suit and carefully chosen shirt/tie combo, outdoorsman on the weekends by the tone of his tan. Not bad, if you liked the type.

"Of course I'll help you out, Dr. Hansen," one of the young and attractive nurses gushed.

"Great." He held a clipboard. "I'll pencil you in right here. Anyone else?"

Was he taking advantage of the staff? Unscrupulous.

"Sign me up for Saturday," the middle-aged, magenta-haired receptionist chimed in.

Hmm.

"Got it." As he scribbled in her name his gaze drifted upward. The warm and inviting smile that followed stopped Stephanie in her tracks.

"May I help you?" he said.

Flustered, and not understanding why—okay, she knew exactly why, the guy was gorgeous—she cleared her throat. "I'm Stephanie Bennett. I have an appointment with Dr. Rogers."

"Yes," the older receptionist said, back to all-business. "He's expecting you, Dr. Bennett. I'll let him know you're here."

Before she could take a seat in the waiting room, the man with the bronze-toned suntan (even though it was November!) offered his hand. "I'm Phil Hansen, the pulmonologist of the group. If you'd like, I'll take you up to Jason's office."

"It's nice to meet you," she said, out of habit.

A long-forgotten feeling twined through her center as she shook his hand. She stiffened. Tingles spiraled up her arm, taking her by surprise. No wonder the ladies were signing up on his clipboard. She stifled the need to fiddle with her hair.

"Oh, that's fine," she muttered. Then, finding her voice, said, "I'll wait for him to…" Before she could finish her sentence and drop Phil's hand, another man, a few years older but equally attractive with dark hair, appeared at the top of the stairs. Working with such handsome men, after being celibate for over three years, might prove challenging on the composure front. She'd imagined typical stodgy, bespectacled, aging doctors when she'd signed on as a locum. Not a couple of *Gentleman's Quarterly* models.

"That would be Jason," Dr. Hansen said, his smile narrowing his bright blue eyes into crescents. Instead of letting go of her hand, he switched its position and walked her toward the stairs, as if they were old friends. "Here's Stephanie Bennett reporting for duty."

"Great. Come on up, Stephanie. After we talk, I'll show you around."

Phil brought her to the stairway complete with turned spindle rail, dropped her hand on the baluster, and patted it. "Thanks for stepping in," he said in all sincerity. "You'll like it here."

Considering the odd feeling fizzing through her veins, she was inclined to agree.

Stephanie saw the temporary stint in Santa Barbara as the perfect excuse for missing the holidays with her family in Palm Desert. Thanksgiving and Christmas always brought back memories too painful to bear. Not that those thoughts weren't constantly in her mind anyway, but the holidays emphasized *everything*.

The promise of going through the season surrounded by well-meaning loved ones who only managed to make her feel worse was what had driven her to take the new and temporary job. She'd only been dabbling in medicine since the incident that had ripped the life from her heart, shredded her confidence, and caused her marriage to disintegrate. A huge part of her had died that day three years ago.

The Midcoast Medical Clinic of Santa Barbara needed an OB/Gyn doctor for two months. It was the perfect opportunity and timing to get away and maybe, if she was lucky, start to take back her life.

As she walked up the stairs, she overheard Phil. "Okay, I've got one more slot for Friday night."

"I'll take it," the other nurse said, sounding excited.

Was he full of himself? That fizzy feeling evaporated.

* * *

Phil sat at his desk, skimming the latest *Pulmonary Physician's Journal* unable to concentrate, wondering what in the hell he was supposed to do with a kid for ten days. But he couldn't turn Roma or his father down.

His father had recently survived his second bout with Hodgkin's lymphoma. His stepmother, Roma, who was closer to Phil's age than his father's, had called last night. She'd wanted to talk about her plans to take Carl to Maui for some rest and relaxation.

Reasonable enough, right?

No!

Just the two of them, she'd said. Had she lost her powers of reasoning by asking him to care for Robbie? The kid was a dynamo...with special needs.

Robbie, the surprise child for his sixty-five-year-old dad and his fortysomething stepmom, had Down syndrome. The four-year-old, who looked more like a pudgy toddler, always got excited when his "big brother"— make that half brother—came for a visit. Phil didn't mind horsing around with the kid on visits, because he knew he'd go home later on, but taking on his complete care was a whole different thing. Robbie's round face and classic Down syndrome features popped into his mind. The corner of Phil's mouth hitched into a smile. The kid called him Pill. Come on. No fair.

"And it's only for ten days. Your dad needs this trip and if we don't jump on booking it right now we won't get these amazing resort rates and airfares. Please, please, please!"

Roma knew how to surgically implant the guilt. His father's craggy sun-drenched face, with eyes the color of the ocean, the same eyes Phil had inherited, came to mind. The guy deserved a break.

How could he say no?

Those eyes had lost their sparkle when Phil's mother had left fifteen years ago, the week after he'd first been diagnosed with cancer. How could someone who was supposed to love you do such a thing? Phil had cut his Australian surfing tour short to come home and see his father through the ordeal. It had been a life-changing event for both of them, and he'd never spoken to his mother again. Last he'd heard, she was living in Arizona.

After that, Phil couldn't fathom his dad pulling out of his slump. How could either of them ever trust a woman to stick around?

Carl Hansen had been granted a second chance with Roma, followed by a huge surprise pregnancy. *"Hell, if I wait around for you to settle down and have a grandchild I'll be too old to enjoy it. May as well have my own!"* his father had joked with Phil when he'd first told him the news.

Carl and Roma had had a tough go when Robbie had been diagnosed with Down syndrome after amniocentesis, but they'd wanted him no matter what and hadn't regretted one moment since. Then, after fifteen years of remission, Carl had been hit with cancer again and, on top of being a new parent of a handicapped baby, he'd had to go through chemo. Carl and Roma were nothing less than an inspiration as far as Phil was concerned.

Ten days wasn't a lifetime. Anyone could survive ten days with a kid, right?

"We'll be home in time for Thanksgiving," Roma had said, "and I promise the best meal of your life." Hell, she'd had him at please, please, please.

He'd already started the sign-up sheet for babysitters and backup. Good thing he'd always managed to stay friends with his coworkers and ex-girlfriends—maybe he'd call in a few extra favors.

"You've already met René's replacement, Stephanie Bennett," Jason said, breaking into Phil's thoughts. His partner stood in his office doorway, and beside him the redhead. "She comes with a great endorsement from Eisenhower Medical Center."

All Phil's worries vanished for the time being as he took her in.

Her gaze darted to Jason and back to him, her cheeks flushing pink.

Though noticeably uptight, she had possibilities… Hold it—toddler on board!

"Hi, again. Jason's giving you the official tour, I see." He stood behind his desk. "Let me know if there is ever anything you need, Dr. Bennett."

Her delicate mouth, which sat appealingly beneath an upturned nose, tugged into a tentative smile. "Call me Stephanie," she said, as she tucked the more-red-than-brown, shoulder-length hair behind an ear. "Please."

Though she was saying all the right words, he sensed her standoffishness. He'd never had trouble making friends and acquaintances, especially with women, and sometimes had to remind himself that it didn't come as easy for other people.

"Okay, Stephanie, welcome aboard." He remembered how cool her hand was when he'd shook it, and an old saying came to mind, *Cold hands, warm heart*. It got him thinking about what kind of person she might be behind that cool exterior.

He engaged her sharp gaze, enjoying the little libido kick it gave him. A spark flashed in her butterscotch-colored eyes. Had she felt it too? "Oh, and call me Phil. My extension is 35, same as my age. If you ever need me, I'm right across the hall and I'll be glad to help out."

She nodded her thanks.

"Now let me show you your office," Jason said to Stephanie, ushering her across the waiting room.

As quickly as she'd appeared, she left without looking back. That didn't keep Phil from staring and giving a mental two-note whistle as she followed Jason.

Phil sat and leaned back in his chair, thinking about Stephanie in her copper-and-black patterned jacket, black slacks and the matching stylish lace-lined scoop-neck top. He liked the way her hair was parted on the side and fell in large, loose waves over her cheek and across her shoulders. He liked the set of her jaw, more square than oval yet with a delicate chin. He liked the ivory color of her skin without a hint of the usual freckles of a redhead, and wondered if he might find a few on her nose if he got up close, really close. Just a sprinkling maybe—enough to wipe away that sleek image, enough to make her seem vulnerable beneath her obvious social armor.

And just as he was about to dream a little deeper, his intercom buzzed. It was his nurse. "Your dad's on the phone," she said.

The trip.

Robbie.

How in the hell was he supposed to impress Dr. Bombshell while babysitting his half brother?

Stephanie spent most of the day getting used to the Midcoast Medical OB/Gyn doctor René Munroe's office, as well as the new setup. She'd held a mini-meeting with her nurse, discussing how she liked to run her clinic and telling her exactly what she expected. She wanted to make this transition as smooth as possible, and stuck around later than she'd planned, logged in to the computer, reading patient charts for the next day's appointments. For this stint, she'd concentrate on the gynecological portion of her license.

There had been one stipulation for her taking this job, and Jason Rogers had agreed to it. Though she'd take care of the pregnant patients, she wouldn't be delivering their babies. Fortunately, after perusing the patient files, none of Dr. Munroe's pregnant patients would be at term during her stay. And Jason had eased her concerns by mentioning that it would have been very hard to get her privileges at their local hospital anyway. She'd been in the process of picking up the pieces of her career, knew she could handle the clinical appointment portion, but no way was she ready to deliver a baby again. The thought of holding a tiny bundle of life in her arms sent her nearly over the edge.

Her stomach rumbled and in need of changing her thoughts, she packed up for the day. As she crossed the reception area, the front clinic door swung open and in rushed Phil Hansen with a little dark-haired boy tagging along beside him. The slant of the boy's eyes with epicanthic folds, and the flattened bridge of his nose, hinted at Down syndrome.

"Hold on, Robbie, I've got to make a call," Phil said, shutting off his beeper and reaching over the receptionist's desk to grab the phone.

Robbie smiled at her as only a child with no fear of strangers could. "Hi," he said.

"Hi, there." Her insides tightened and her lungs seemed to forget how to take in air, knowing her son, Justin, would have been close to Robbie's age…if he were still alive. She looked away. Before her eyes could well up, she diverted her thoughts by eavesdropping on Phil's conversation.

"I'll be right there," he said, then hung up and blew out a breath. "Great. What the hell am I supposed to do now?" he mumbled.

She cringed that he cussed so easily around a child.

Phil's gaze found her. A look of desperation made his smooth, handsome features look strained. He glanced at Robbie and back to her. "I need a huge favor. I just got a call from the E.R. One of my patients inhaled his crown while the dentist was replacing it, and I need to do an emergency bronchoscopy to get it out." He dug his fingers into his hair. "Can you watch Robbie for me? I'll only be gone an hour or so."

What? Her, watch a child? "I can't…"

"I don't know what else to do." His blue eyes darkened, wildly darting around the room.

He was obviously in a bind, but didn't he have a child-care provider?

She glanced at the boy, who was oblivious to Phil's predicament, happily grinning at a picture of a goldfish on the wall.

"Pish!" he said pointing, as if discovering gold.

"I'm really in a bind here," Phil pleaded. "The E.R. is overflowing and they need to get my patient taken care of and discharged. I can't very well plop Robbie down in the E.R. waiting room."

Oh, God, there it was, that lump of maternal instinct she'd pushed out of her mind for the past three years. It planted itself smack in the middle of her chest like an ice pick. She studied Phil, his blue eyes tinted with worry and desperation. She'd give the wrong impression if she refused to help out, and she'd come to Midcoast

Medical to help. He'd seemed so sincere earlier when he'd offered his assistance anytime she needed it. A swirl of anxiety twisted her in its clutch as she said, "Okay."

"You'll do it?" He looked stunned, as if he'd just witnessed a miracle.

Well, he had. Never in a million years would she have volunteered to do this, but as he was in such a bind…

She nodded, and her throat closed up.

"Thank you!" He grabbed her arms and kissed her cheek, releasing her before she had a chance to react. "You're the best."

"What am I supposed to do?"

"Just watch him. I'll be back as soon as I can. Be a good boy for Stephanie, Robbie," he said before he disappeared out the door.

Why couldn't she have left earlier, like everyone else in the clinic? Dread trickled from the crown of her head all the way down to her toes. Her heart knocked against her ribs. She'd made a knee-jerk decision without thinking it through. She couldn't handle this. There went that swirl of panic again, making her knees weak and her hands tremble.

The boy looked at her with innocent eyes, licking his lips. "I'm hungwee."

She couldn't very well ignore the poor kid. "So am I, but I don't have a car seat for you, so we can't go anywhere."

She'd spoken too fast. Obviously, the boy didn't get her point.

He held his tummy and rocked back and forth. "Hungweeeeee."

Oh, God, what should she do now? She scratched her

head, aware that a fine line of perspiration had formed above her lip. He was hungry and she was petrified.

Think, Stephanie, think.

She snapped her fingers. The tour. Jason had taken her on a tour of the clinic that morning, and it had included the employee lounge. "Come on, let's check out the refrigerator."

Robbie reached up for her hand. Avoiding his gesture, she quickened her step and started for the hallway. "It's down here," she said, as he toddled behind, bouncing off his toes, trying to catch up.

She switched on lights as they made their way to the kitchen in the mansion-turned-clinic. "Let's see what we can dig up," she said, heading for the refrigerator, avoiding his eyes at all cost and focusing on the task. She had every intention of writing IOU notes for each and everything she found to share with Robbie.

Some impression she'd make on her first day, stealing food.

Heck, the fridge was nearly bare. Someone had trained the employees well about leaving food around to spoil and stink up the place. Fortunately there was a jar of peanut butter. She pulled out drawer after drawer, hoping to find some leftover restaurant-packaged crackers. If the kid got impatient and cried, she'd freak out. Drawer three produced two packs of crackers and a third that was broken into fine pieces. Hopefully, Robbie wouldn't mind crumbs.

"You like peanut butter?"

"Yup," he said, already climbing up on the bench by the table. "I wike milk, too."

Stephanie lifted her brows. "Sorry, can't help you there." But, as all clinics must, they did keep small cartons of juice on hand for their diabetic patients. "Hey, how about some cranberry or orange juice?"

"'Kay."

"Which kind?"

"Boaff."

"Okay. Whatever." Anything to keep the boy busy and happy. Anything to keep him from crying. She glanced at her watch. How long had Phil been gone? Ten minutes? She blew air through her lips. How would she survive an hour?

After their snack, she led him back to the waiting room, careful not to make physical contact, where a small flat-screen TV was wedged in the corner near the ceiling. She didn't have a clue what channels were available in this part of the state, but she needed to keep the boy distracted.

"What do you like to watch?"

"Cartoons!" he said, spinning in a circle of excitement.

She scrolled through the channels and found a cartoon that was nowhere near appropriate for a child.

"That! That!" Robbie called out.

"Uh, that one isn't funny. Let's look for another one." She prayed she could find something that wouldn't shock the boy or teach him bad words. Her hand shook as she continued to flip through the channels. Ah, there it was, just what she'd hoped for, a show with brightly colored puppets with smiling faces and silly voices. Maybe the fist-size knot in her gut would let up now.

She sat on one of the waiting-room chairs, and Robbie invited himself onto her lap. Every muscle in her body stiffened. She couldn't do this. Where was Phil?

His warm little back snuggled against her and when he laughed she could feel it rumble through his chest.

She inhaled and smelled the familiar fragrance of children's shampoo, almost bringing her to tears. Someone took good care of this little one. Was it Phil?

She couldn't handle this. Before she jumped out of her skin, she lifted him with outstretched arms and carried him to another chair, closer to the TV.

"Here. This seat is better. You sit here."

Fortunately, engrossed in the show, he didn't pick up on her tension and sat contentedly staring at the TV.

It had been a long day. She was exhausted, and didn't dare let her guard down. Robbie rubbed his eyes, yawning and soon falling asleep. She paced the waiting room, checked her watch every few seconds, and glanced at the boy as if he were a ticking time bomb. Her throat was so tight, she could barely swallow.

Several minutes passed in this manner. Robbie rested his head on the arm of the chair, sound asleep. Stephanie hoped he'd stay that way until Phil returned.

A few minutes later, one of the puppets on the TV howled, and another joined in. It jolted her. Robbie stirred. His face screwed up. The noise had scared him.

Oh, God, what should she do now?

After a protracted silence, he let out a wail, the kind that used up his breath and left him quiet only long enough to inhale again. Then he let out an even louder wail.

"It's okay, Robbie. It was just the TV," she said from across the room, trying to console him without getting too close. She patted the air. "It was the show. That's all." She couldn't dare hold him. The thought of holding a child sent lightning bolts of fear through her. She never wanted to do it again.

Flashes of her baby crying, screaming, while she

paced the floor, rooted her to the spot. Robbie cried until mucus ran from his nose, and he coughed and sputtered for air, but still she couldn't move.

It took every ounce of strength she had not to bolt out of the clinic.

Phil's patient had been set up and ready for him when he'd arrived in the nearby E.R. The dental crown had been easy to locate in the trachea at the opening of the right bronchus. He'd dislodged it using a rigid scope and forceps, and done a quick check to make sure it hadn't damaged any lung tissue. He'd finished the procedure within ten minutes, leaving the patient to recover with the E.R. nurse.

He barreled through the clinic door, then came to an abrupt stop at the sight of Robbie screaming and Stephanie wild-eyed and pale across the room.

"What's going on?" he said.

She blinked and inhaled, as if coming to life from her statue state. "Thank God, you're back," she whispered.

"What happened?" He rushed to Robbie, picked him up and wiped his nose.

"I was 'cared," Robbie said, starting to cry again.

"Hey, it's okay, buddy, I'm here." Phil hugged his brother as anger overtook him. "What'd you do to him?" he asked, turning as Stephanie ran out the door. What the hell had happened? Confused, he glanced at Robbie. "Did she hurt you?"

"The cartoon monster 'cared me," he whimpered, before crying again.

Phil hugged him, relieved. "Are you hungry, buddy? You want to eat?"

The little guy nodded through his tears. "'Kay," he said with a quiver.

What kind of woman would stand by and let a little kid cry like that? Had she been born without a heart? Phil didn't know what was up with the new doc, but he sure as hell planned to find out first thing tomorrow.

CHAPTER TWO

STEPHANIE snuck in early the next day and lost herself in her patients all morning. She gave a routine physical gynecological examination and ordered labs on the first patient. With her first pregnant client, she measured fundal height and listened to fetal heart tones, discussed nutrition and recommended birthing classes. According to the chart measurements, the third patient's fibroid tumors had actually shrunk in size since her last visit. Stephanie received a high five when she gave the news.

Maybe, if she kept extra-busy, she wouldn't have to confront Phil.

Later, as she performed an initial obstetric examination, she noticed something unusual on the patient's cervix. A plush red and granular-looking area bled easily at her touch. "Have you been having any spotting?"

"No. Is something wrong?" the patient asked.

To be safe, and with concern for the pregnancy, she prepared to take a sample of cells for cytology. "There's a little area on your cervix I want to follow up on. It may be what we call an ectropion, which is an erosion of sorts and is perfectly benign." She left out the part about not wanting to take any chances. "The lab should get results for us within a week."

"What then?"

"If it's negative, which it will most likely be, nothing, unless you have bleeding after sex or if you get frequent infections. Then we'd do something similar to cauterizing it. On the other hand, if the specimen shows abnormal cells, I'll do a biopsy and follow up from there."

"Will it hurt my baby?"

"An ectropion is nothing more than extra vascular tissue. You may have had it a long time, and the pregnancy has changed the shape of your cervix, making it visible."

"But what if you have to do a biopsy?"

How must it feel to have a total stranger deliver such worrisome news? Stephanie inhaled and willed the expertise, professionalism and composure she'd need to help get her through the rest of the appointment. Maybe she shouldn't have said a thing, but what if the test result came back abnormal and she had to drop a bomb? That wouldn't be fair to the patient without a warning. She second-guessed herself and didn't like the repercussions. All the excitement of being pregnant might become overshadowed with fear if she didn't end the appointment on a positive note.

"This small area will most likely just be an irritation. It's quite common. I'm being extra-careful because you're pregnant, and a simple cervical sampling is safe during pregnancy. I'll call with the results as soon as I get them. I promise." She maintained steady eye contact and smiled, then chose a few pamphlets from the wall rack on what to expect when pregnant. "These are filled with great information about your pregnancy. Read them carefully, and afterward, if you have any questions, please feel free to ask me."

The woman's furrowed brow eased just enough for Stephanie to notice. She wanted to hug her and promise everything would be all right, but that was out of her realm as a professional.

"Oh, I almost forgot to tell you your expected due date." She gave the woman the date and saw a huge shift on her face from concern to sheer joy. Her smile felt like a hug, and Stephanie beamed back at her.

"This is a very exciting time, Mrs. Conroy. Enjoy each day," she said, patting the patient's hand.

The young woman accepted the pamphlets, nodded, and prepared to get down from the exam table, her face once again a mixture of expressions. "You'll call as soon as you know anything, right?"

"I promise. You're in great shape, and this pregnancy should go smoothly. A positive attitude is also important."

Stephanie felt like a hypocrite reciting the words. Her spirits had plunged so low over the past three years she could barely remember what a positive attitude was. If she was going to expect this first-time mother to be upbeat, she should at least try it, too.

After the patient left, she gave herself a little pep talk as she washed her hands. *Just try to have a good time. Do something out of the ordinary. Start living again.*

A figure blocked the exam-room doorway, casting a shadow over the mirror. "You mind telling me what happened last night?" Phil's words were brusque without a hint of yesterday's charm.

Adrenaline surged through her, and she went on the defensive. "I don't do kids." She turned slowly to hide her nerves, and grabbed a paper towel. "You didn't give me a chance to tell you."

"How hard is it to console a crying kid?"

Stephanie held up her hand and looked at Phil's chin rather than into his eyes. "Harder than you could ever understand." She tossed the paper towel into the trash bin and walked around him toward her office. "I'm sorry," she whispered before she closed the door.

Phil scraped his jaw as he walked to his office. What in the hell was her problem? Last night, he'd found her practically huddled in the corner as if in a cage with a lion. It had taken half an hour to console Robbie. A bowl of vanilla ice cream with rainbow sprinkles had finally done the trick. Colorful sprinkles, as Robbie called them. For some dumb reason, Phil got a kick out of that.

What was up with Stephanie Bennett?

He didn't have time to figure out the new doctor when he had more pressing things to do. Like make a schedule! He'd put so much energy into distracting Robbie last night, horsing around with him and watching TV, that he'd lost track of time, forgotten to bathe him and missed his usual bedtime medicine. A kid could survive a day without a bath, right?

His beeper went off. He checked the number. It was the preschool. Hell, what had he forgotten now?

Stephanie arrived at work extra-early again the next morning, surprised to see someone had already made coffee in the clinic kitchen. She was about to pour herself a cup and sneak back to her office when Phil swept into the room. Her shoulders tensed as she hoped he didn't hold a grudge. Wishing she could disappear, she stayed on task.

"Good morning," he said, looking as if he'd just rolled out of bed, hair left however it had dried after his shower.

"Hi," she said. She didn't want to spend the next two months avoiding one of the clinic partners. Phil had been very nice at first, it seemed to come naturally to him, and, well, she needed him to forgive her. "Look, I'm sorry about the other night."

"Forget about it. Like you said, I didn't leave you much choice." He scrubbed his face as if trying to wake up. "Didn't realize you had a problem with kids." He glanced at her, curiosity in his eyes, but he left all his questions unspoken.

She had no intention of opening up to him, and hoped he'd let things lie. Maybe if she changed the topic?

She lifted the pot. "Can I pour you a cup, too?"

"Definitely. Robbie kept me up half the night with his coughing."

"Anything wrong?" She leaned against the counter.

"No virus. Just an annoying cough. He's had it since he was a baby." He accepted the proffered mug and took a quick swig. "Ahh."

"So what do you think it is, then?" Discussing medicine was always easy…and safe.

"I've been wondering if he might have tracheobronchomalacia, but Roma, his mom, doesn't want him put through a bunch of tests to find out."

"Is that your wife?"

He laughed. "No, my stepmother. Robbie's my half brother."

"Ahh." She'd heard the scuttlebutt about him being quite the playboy, and she couldn't tolerate a married guy flirting with the help.

A smile crossed his face. "Did you think he was my kid?"

She shrugged. What else was she supposed to think?

"I'm just watching Robbie while my dad and Roma are in Maui." He stared at his coffee mug and ran his hand over his hair, deep in thought. "Yeah, so I want to do a bronchoscopy, but Roma is taking some persuading."

"You think like a typical pulmonologist," she said, spooning some sugar into her coffee. "Always the worst-case scenario."

"And you don't assume the worst for your patients?"

She shook her head. "I'm an obstetrician, remember? Good stuff." *Except in her personal life.*

"You've got a point. But I'm not imagining this. He gets recurrent chest infections, he's got a single-note wheeze, and at night he has this constant stridorous cough. I've just never had to sleep with him before."

"You're sleeping with him?" The thought of the gorgeous guy with the sexy reputation sleeping with his little brother almost brought a smile to her lips.

"Yeah, well..." Did Phil look sheepish? "He was in a new house and a strange bed. You know the drill."

She couldn't hide her smile any longer. "That's very sweet."

He cleared his throat and stood a little straighter, a more macho pose. "More like survival. The kid cried until I promised to sleep with him."

Heat worked up her neck. "That was probably my fault."

He looked at her, and their eyes met for the briefest of moments. There was a real human being behind that ruggedly handsome face. Perhaps someone worth knowing.

"Let's drop it. As far as I'm concerned, it never happened," he said.

Maybe she shouldn't try so hard to avoid him. Maybe he was a great guy she could enjoy. But insecurity, like well-worn shoes you just couldn't part with, kept her from giving him a second thought.

"It's not asthma," he said, breaking her concentration. "If I knew for sure what it was, I could treat it. He may grow out of it, but he's suffering right now. You think I look tired, you should see him. The thing is, he might only need something as simple as extra oxygen or, if necessary, CPAP." He rubbed his chin.

All the talk about Robbie's respiratory condition made her worry about him. Especially after she'd made the poor little guy cry until he was hoarse the other night. She sipped her coffee. "Is there any less invasive procedure that can give the same diagnosis?" Keeping things technical made it easier to talk about the boy.

"Bronchography, but he's allergic to iodine, and I wouldn't want to expose him to the radiation at this age. And all I'd have to do is sedate him and slip a scope in his lungs to check things out. Five minutes, tops. I'll see how things go."

"So where is he?"

"He's in day care with his new best friend, Claire's daughter. Thankfully she took pity on me and chauffeured him today."

No sooner had he said it than Claire breezed through the door. The tall, slender, honey blonde had a mischievous glint in her eyes. "It's called carpooling."

"Ah, right." Phil said, then glanced at Stephanie. "Learning curve."

"Morning," Claire said.

Stephanie nodded. She'd met the clinic nurse practitioner the other day in a bright, welcoming office that came complete with aromatherapy and candles. She was

Jason's wife, and seemed nice enough, but Stephanie hadn't let herself warm to anyone yet.

"So, Robbie didn't want to go with his group after driving to the preschool with Gina talking his ear off," Claire said. "Gina's my daughter," she said for Stephanie's benefit. "He looks so cute in his glasses. When did he get them?"

Phil grinned. "Beats me, but I found them in his things, so I talked him into wearing them."

"See, you're a natural."

He refilled half of his mug. "That'll be the day. Two nights, and I'm already planning to scope him for that cough of his. How does Roma manage?"

"Like all mothers. We follow our instincts. Give it a try." Claire winked at Stephanie, as if they belonged to the same secret sorority. If Claire only knew how wrong she was.

Stephanie took another swallow of coffee, wishing she could fade into the woodwork.

"Do you have any kids?" Claire asked.

"No." Stephanie couldn't say it fast enough. She stared deeply into her coffee, trying her best to compose herself. Phil watched her. "Well, I'd better prepare for my first patient. I have a lot to live up to, filling René's shoes." She reheated her coffee and started for the door, needing to get far away from all the talk of children. Maybe it had been a mistake coming here, but she'd committed herself for the next two months, and she'd live up to her promise.

"You'll do fine," Phil said with a reassuring smile. "I've got to take off, too. Need to make a run to the hospital this morning."

She peeked over her shoulder. He stopped and poured the rest of his coffee into the sink, then glanced at

Stephanie. Eye contact with Phil was the last thing she wanted, so she flicked her gaze toward her shoes. What must he think of her and her crazy behavior? But, more importantly, why did she care?

On her way out the door she passed the cardiologist, Jon Becker, and nodded. He gave a stately nod then headed for the counter and the nearly empty coffee pot.

"Hey," he said. "I made the coffee and now all I get is half a cup?"

Hunching her shoulders, Stephanie took a surreptitious sip from her mug and slunk down the hall. How many more bad first impressions was she going to make?

"Make a full pot next time," she heard Claire say. "Quit being so task oriented," she chided, more as if to a family member than a business colleague. "If you're going to be a stay-at-home dad, you need to think like a nurturer."

"Claire, all I wanted was a cup of coffee, not a feminist lecture on thinking for the group."

Stephanie couldn't resist it. A smile stretched across her lips, the first one in two days. Jon looked at least forty, and he was going to be a stay-at-home dad?

She'd been so isolated over the past three years, and had no idea how to have a simple conversation with coworkers. Maybe it was time to make an effort to be friendly, like every other normal human being.

A familiar negative tidal wave moved swiftly and blanketed her with doubt.

You don't deserve to be alive. She could practically hear her ex-husband's voice repeating the cutting words.

* * *

On her way back to the extended-stay hotel that night, Stephanie realized how famished she was. On a whim, she stopped at a decent-looking Japanese restaurant for some takeout.

After placing her order, she sat primly on the edge of one of the sushi bar stools. She sipped green tea, and glanced around. Down the aisle, there was Robbie, grains of rice stuck to his beaming face like 3-D freckles. Across from the boy, with his back to her, sat Phil. A jolt of nerves cut through her as she hoped Robbie wouldn't recognize her. He might start crying again. How soon could she get her order and sneak out? Just as she thought it, as if sending a mental tap to his shoulder, Phil turned and saw her, flashed a look of surprise, then waved her over.

She couldn't very well pretend she hadn't seen him. She waved tentatively back then shook her head as Phil's ever-broadening gesture to join them was accompanied by a desperate look.

Be strong. He's the one babysitting. It's not your responsibility.

He stood, made an even more pronounced gesture with pleading eyes.

The guy begged, but she couldn't budge. She shook her head and mouthed, "Sorry." He might think she was the most unfriendly woman he'd ever met, but no way was she ready to sit down with them, as if they were some little happy family. No. She couldn't. It would be unbearable.

She avoided Phil's disappointed gaze by finishing her tea.

Fortunately, the sushi chef handed her the order. After she paid for the food, she grabbed the package, tossed Phil one last regretful look, and left.

Strike two.

* * *

Stephanie walked her last patient of the morning to the door. The lady hugged her as if they were old friends. One of the things she loved about her job was telling people they were pregnant.

"Have you got all the information you need?"

The young woman's head bobbed.

"Any more questions?"

"I'm sure I've got a million of them, but I can't think of anything right now except...I'm pregnant!" She clapped her hands.

Stephanie laughed. "Well, be sure to write all those questions down and we'll go through them next time."

"I will, Doctor. Thanks again." The woman gave her a second hug.

Stephanie waved goodbye, and with a smile on her face watched as her patient floated on air when she left the clinic.

"I was about to accuse you of being heartless, but I've changed my mind now," Phil chided.

Stephanie blushed. She knew exactly what he referred to.

"How are things going with Robbie?" her nurse asked Phil in passing.

"Just dandy," he said, with a wry smile. "I finally figured out it's a lot less messy to take him into the shower with me instead of bathing him in the tub by himself."

The nurse giggled. "I can only imagine."

Stephanie fought the image his description implanted in her mind, obviously the same one Amy had. He seemed to be a nice guy. Everyone liked him. Adored him. The fact that he was billboard gorgeous, even with ever-darkening circles under his eyes, should be a plus, but it intimidated her. And after the way she'd treated him and Robbie, she didn't have a clue why he kept coming around.

"You doing anything for lunch today?" he asked.

Could she handle an entire lunch with this guy? "Why would you want to take me to lunch?"

"Why not? You're new in town, probably don't know your way around..."

His cell phone went off, saving her from answering him.

"Cripes!" he said. "Hold on a sec." He held up one finger and answered his phone.

After a brief conversation, he hung up with a dejected look. "Evidently Robbie got pushed by another kid and skinned his knees." He scratched his head, a look of bewilderment in his eyes. "He's crying and asking for me, so..."

"It's a big job being a stand-in dad, isn't it?"

"You're telling me. Hey, I have an idea, why don't we have lunch tomorrow?"

Swept up by the whole package that was Phil, including the part of fumbling stand-in dad, she answered without thinking. "Sure."

The next day, at noon, Stephanie found Phil standing at her door wearing another expression of chagrin. "I completely forgot we have a staff meeting today."

"Yeah, I just got the memo," she said.

"You should come. We've got some big decisions to make."

"I don't have any authority here."

"Oh, trust me, on this topic your input is equally as important as any of ours."

"What are you talking about?"

"We have to decide how we're going to decorate the yacht for the annual Christmas parade."

"It's not even Thanksgiving yet!"

"Big ideas take big planning. Besides, have you been by the Paseo? They've already put up a Christmas tree. Huge thing, too. I took Robbie to see it last night."

His deadpan expression and quirky news made her blurt a laugh. When was the last time she'd done that? "Well, seeing I've never been on a yacht, not to mention the fact that I suck at decorating, I can't see how I'll bring a lot to the table."

"Come anyway. You might enjoy it."

I might enjoy it. Wasn't that the pep talk she'd given herself the other day? Be open to new things? Start acting alive again?

"It's a free lunch," he enticed with lowered sun-bleached brows.

"I'll think about it."

"If you change your mind, we'll be in the lounge in ten minutes."

"Okay."

His smile started at those shocking blue eyes, traveled down to his enticing mouth and wound up looking suspiciously like victory. The guy was one smooth operator.

After he left, Stephanie surprised herself further when she brushed her hair, plumped and puffed it into submission, then put on a new coat of lip gloss before heading to the back of the building for the meeting. She stopped at the double doors, fighting back the nervous wave waiting to pounce. The place was abuzz with activity. Claire called out various types of sandwiches she had stored in a huge shopping bag, and when someone claimed one, she tossed the securely wrapped package at

them. One of the nurses passed out canned sodas or bot-
tled water. Another gave a choice of fruit or cookie.

"I'll take both," she heard Phil say just before he
noticed her at the door. "Hey, I saved you a seat." He
patted the chair next to him. "What kind of sandwich
do you want?"

"Turkey?"

"We need a turkey over here," he called to Claire.

Stephanie ducked as the lunch missile almost hit her
head before she could sit. A smile worked its way from
one side of her mouth to the other. These people might
be crazy, but they were fun.

"Sorry!" Claire called out.

"No problem." She had to admit that she kind of
liked this friendly chaos. It was distracting, and that was
always a good thing. When her gaze settled on Phil, he
was already watching her, a smile very similar to the
one she'd seen in her office lingering on his lips.

"I'm glad you decided to come."

If he was a player, she got the distinct impression
he was circling her. How in the world should she feel
about that? Lunch was one thing, but what if he asked
her out? Hearing how he struggled with Robbie had
shown her another side of him. This guy had a heart
beneath all that puffed-up male plumage, she'd bet her
first paycheck on it. She wasn't sure she could make the
same claim for herself.

"Okay, everybody, let's get going on this." Jason stood
at the head of the long table, his mere presence com-
manding attention. Dark hair, pewter eyes, suntanned
face, she could see why Claire watched him so ador-
ingly. "Last year we came in third in the Santa Barbara
Chamber of Commerce Christmas Ocean Parade, and
this year I think we have a fighting chance of taking

first if we put our heads together and come up with a theme."

"You mean like Christmas at Christmastime?" Jon looked perplexed by the obvious.

"He means like Santa and his helpers, or Christmas shopping mania, or the North Pole," Claire shot back.

"How about trains?" Jon said. "Boys love trains at Christmas."

"What about trains and dolls?" Jon's nurse added, with a wayward glance.

"How about Christmas around the world?" Stephanie's nurse, Amy, spoke up. "We could cover the yacht with small Christmas trees decorated the way other countries do, and the mast could be a huge Christmas tree all made from lights."

The conversation buzzed and hummed in response to the first ideas. It seemed everyone had a suggestion. Everyone but Stephanie. She particularly liked what Amy had suggested.

What did she remember most from Christmas besides the beautifully decorated trees? Santa, that's what. "Could we have a Santa by the big tree?" She said her thought out loud by mistake.

"Yeah, we need a Santa up there," Phil backed her up.

"And I nominate you to be Santa," Claire said, pointing to Phil with an impish smile. "You'd be adorable."

"Me! You've got to be kidding! I scare kids."

"Oh, right, and Robbie doesn't adore you. Yeah, I think you should be Santa and Gina and Robbie can sit on your lap." Claire wouldn't back down.

"No way," he said, with an *are-you-crazy* glare in his eyes. Out of the corner of his mouth he said, "Thanks a lot," to Stephanie.

"Great idea," one of the nurses blurted across the table, before a few others chimed in. "Yeah."

"But I am the *un*-Santa." He glanced at Stephanie again, this time with a back-me-up-here plea in his eyes.

Not about to get involved in the debate, she lifted her brows, shrugged and took a bite of her sandwich.

"Look," Jason said. "We need to get more people involved on the yacht, and you haven't been much help the last couple of years." There was a sparkle in Jason's eyes, as if he enjoyed putting Phil on the spot. "Should everyone be elves?" he asked, his mouth half-full of sandwich.

"What if one person stood by each decorated country's tree dressed in the traditional outfit?" Amy seemed to be on a roll. "You know, lederhosen, kilt, cowboy hat…oh, and what's that Russian fur thing called? Ushanka? And what about a dashiki or caftan, oh, wait, and a kimono, or a sari or…"

"That's a fantastic idea," Claire said.

Revved up, Amy grinned, and Stephanie nodded with approval at her. Phil squeezed her forearm. Okay, everything was a great idea except for Santa.

General agreement hummed through the room, and several people soon chimed in. *Wow. I like that. Good idea.*

The receptionist, Gaby, wearing glasses that covered half of her face, took notes like a court reporter.

"Did you get that?" Jason asked her.

Gaby nodded, never looking up, not breaking her bound-for-writer's-cramp speed.

"Ah, then we shouldn't need a Santa anymore," Phil said, sounding relieved.

"Of course we will," Claire said. "One Santa unites them all, and Phil will be it."

Stephanie's eyes widened and from the side, she noticed his narrow betrayed-looking gaze directed at Claire.

"I say we take a vote on who should be Santa, the captain of the boat or me," he said, just before his beeper went off. "Damn. It's day care. I've got to take this." He strode out of the room, the doors swinging in his wake.

Jason snagged the opportunity. "Okay, everyone agree Phil's Santa?"

Everyone laughed and nodded. Poor guy didn't stand a chance. Stephanie had to admit she sort of felt sorry for him.

Phil stepped back into the room, half of his mouth hitched but not in a smile. "I've got to make a quick run over to day care. Robbie's refusing to cooperate with nap time."

Jason nodded. "Let us know if you need to reschedule some appointments."

"It shouldn't take long. I've just got to make the kid understand he has to follow the rules—" Phil snapped his fingers as if the greatest idea in the universe had just occurred to him "—or he won't get afternoon snack!"

Stephanie laughed. The guy was barely coping with this new responsibility, but he wasn't griping. He seemed to catch on quickly, and, she had to admit, it made her like him even more. She glanced around the table at all the adoring female gazes on him. Okay, so she'd finally joined the club.

"So who's Santa this year?" Phil asked, one hand on the door.

Jason grinned. "You!"

He flashed a glance at Stephanie, pointed, and mouthed, "You owe me."

CHAPTER THREE

PHIL finished entering the list of orders in the computer for his last patient of the afternoon. His mind had been wandering between the appointments, and Stephanie Bennett was the reason. She was as guarded as a locked box. Then out of nowhere today this fun-loving Santa-of-the-world fan had emerged, and it had backfired and landed him on a date with a red suit.

Something held her back from enjoying life, and he'd probably never find out in two months what it was, but romantic that he was, he still wanted to get to know her better. The time restraint was a perfect excuse to keep things casual and uninvolved. Just his style.

But there was Robbie—a full-time job. No way could he squeeze in a romantic fling until his father and Roma came home.

He pushed Enter on the computer program and shut it down.

Good thing he'd lined up Gaby for child care on Saturday morning.

Jason had asked him to stop by his office on his way out today, so he trotted up the back stairs to the second floor. Aw, damn, he'd caught Jason and Claire kissing. He stepped back from the doorway. They seemed to do that a lot and hadn't even heard him. Yeah, they were newlyweds but, still, they were married, with children! He marveled at the phenomenon. Come to think of it, his dad and Roma did a lot of smooching, too.

Maybe players like him didn't corner the market on romance.

He decided to talk to Jason later, then padded down the stairs and veered toward Stephanie's office, a place he'd been drawn to like a magnet lately. Just as he passed Jon's door he heard his name.

"Hey, Phil, come take a look at the latest pictures."

Oh, man, he knew exactly what those pictures would be. Evan, his newborn son, seemed to be the center of Jon's universe these days. Being just outside Jon's office, Phil couldn't very well avoid the invitation.

What was with his partners? They'd all settled down, leaving him the lone bachelor. The thing that really perplexed him was that they all seemed so damn blissful. Well, he wasn't into matrimonial bliss. No way. No how. He liked his freedom. Liked being alone. He glanced at Stephanie's office. At least now he knew someone else who liked being single.

Except for Robbie staying with him, he hadn't lived with anyone since his med-school roommates. And he really didn't miss their stinky socks and dirty underwear tossed around the cramped apartment. Come to think of it, Robbie's socks ran a close second, and the kid knew nothing about putting things away. He smiled at the image of his little half brother strutting around in his underwear with pictures of superheroes pasted all over. Even his nighttime diapers had cartoon characters decorating them. What in the world had his life turned into?

An odd sensation tugged somewhere so buried inside he couldn't locate it, but the feeling still managed to get his attention. *Heads up, dude. Take note. Maybe there's something to be said for a good relationship and a family.*

No. Way. Maybe it worked for other people, but he wasn't capable of sustaining a long-term love affair. Wasn't interested. He knew just as many people whose marriages didn't work out. Hell, his own mother had walked out on them.

Nope. He liked the here and now, and when things got too deep or involved, he was out of there. Maybe he was more like his mom than he wanted to admit. His list of ex-girlfriends kept growing; many of them had since married and he was glad for them. It just wasn't his thing.

Phil greeted Jon and fulfilled his obligation as a good coworker to ooh and aah over Jon and René's new son. Then he patted him on the back, told him he was a lucky dog, and excused himself with a perfectly valid reason. "I've got to pick up Robbie."

On his way out of the clinic, he glanced at Stephanie's closed office door. What were the odds of him running into her at dinner again tonight?

Nope. If he wanted to spend some more time with her, he couldn't depend on something as flimsy as fate. He'd need a plan.

Gaby had signed up to watch Robbie on Saturday morning. Maybe he'd make plans with Stephanie then. As for dinner tonight, he had a date with his kid brother for a grilled cheese sandwich and tomato soup.

Just seven more days.

Stephanie was aware that René mentored nurse practitioner students from the local university once a week, but hadn't realized she'd be taking on this aspect of René's job along with everything else. Thursday morning she was shadowed by a bright and pregnant-as-she-was-tall young woman filled with questions. Maria Avila had thick black hair and wore it piled on top of her head, and if she was trying to look taller, the extra hair didn't help. Her shining dark eyes oozed intelligence and curiosity and her pleasant personality suited Stephanie just fine. After a full morning together, they prepared for the last appointment.

"If my next patient consents, I'll guide you through bimanual pelvic examination."

Stephanie fought back a laugh at the student's excitement when she pumped the air with her fist.

"Have you done one before?"

"I've done them in class with a human-looking model," Maria said.

Stephanie raised her brows. "That's not nearly the same thing. I'll do my best to get this opportunity for you. Now, here's the woman's story." Stephanie recited the medical history from the computer for Maria. "What would you do for her today?"

Maria sat pensively for a few minutes then ran down a list of questions she'd ask and labs she'd recommend. Her instincts were right-on, and Stephanie thought she'd make a good care provider one day.

The examination went well, Stephanie stepped in to collect the Pap smear, and Maria was ecstatic she got hands-on experience. Fortunately the patient was fine with the extra medical care as long as Stephanie followed up with her own examination.

One of the ovaries was larger than normal, and tender to the touch. It could be something as simple as a cyst, but she wanted to make sure. She also wanted Maria to feel the small, subtle mass that she'd overlooked when she'd first performed the exam.

From the woman's history she knew there wasn't any ovarian cancer in her immediate family. She met some of the other risk factors, though. She had never been pregnant, was over fifty-five, and postmenopausal.

"Have you had any pain or pressure in your abdomen lately?"

The woman shook her head.

"Bloating or indigestion?"

"Doesn't every woman get that?" the patient said, with a wry smile.

"You've got a point there." Stephanie grinned back.

When she finished the exam, as she removed the gloves and washed her hands, she mentioned her plan of action. "I'm ordering a pelvic ultrasound to rule out a small cyst." She didn't want to alarm the woman about the potential for cancer due to her age, but finding any pathology early was the name of the game when it came to that disease. "I'll request the study ASAP."

The grateful woman thanked both of them and on her way out she hugged the student RNP, Maria. "Good luck with your pregnancy, and keep up your training. We need more people in the field."

Her comment drove Stephanie to ask, "Are you in medicine?"

"I'm a nurse."

Stephanie figured, being a nurse, the patient was already in a panic about what her slightly enlarged ovary might be.

"Don't drive yourself crazy worrying about the worst-case scenario, Ms. Winkler, okay? The nodule didn't feel hard or immovable. It's most likely a cyst."

The extra reassurance helped smooth the woman's

wrinkled brow, but nervous tension was still evident in her eyes when she left.

Stephanie briefed Maria on possible reasons why she'd missed the subtle change in the ovary and offered suggestions on hand placement while performing future examinations for best results.

They walked back to her office as Stephanie explained further for Maria.

"The worst thing we can do is leave a patient waiting for results, but sometimes our job is like a guessing game. We have to go through each step to rule out the problem. Fortunately, modern medicine usually gives us great results in a timely manner."

"Waxing philosophical, Doc?" Phil's distinct voice sent a quick chill down her spine.

How long had it been since that had happened with a man? Not since the first morning when she'd seen him, to be exact. "Can I do something for you, Phil?"

With a slow smile, he glanced first at Stephanie then at Maria, whose cheeks blushed almost immediately. What was with his power over women?

"Yeah. You can meet me at Stearn's Wharf Saturday morning around nine."

Was this his idea of asking her out? In front of the student nurse practitioner?

"Uh. You sort of caught me off guard."

"Hmm. Like how you bamboozled me into being Santa?"

Okay, now she got it. It was payback time. She grimaced. "If it matters at all, I abstained from voting."

"Warms my heart, Doc." He patted his chest over his white doctor's coat.

But meeting at the beach for what was predicted to

be yet another gorgeous Santa Barbara day sounded more like reward than payback.

Maria cleared her throat. "I should be going and let you two work this out."

"Oh, right." Stephanie felt a blush begin. What kind of impression would she make with her student, making plans for a date right in front of her?

"Thanks so much, Dr. Bennett. You've been fantastic and I've learned a lot today," Maria said.

"You're welcome, and I guess I'll see you next week?"

"Actually, that's Thanksgiving. But I'll be here the week after, that is if I don't go into premature labor first!" The otherwise elfin woman beamed a smile, looked at Dr. Hansen again, subtly turned so only Stephanie could see her face, and mouthed, "Wow!" with crossed eyes to emphasize his affect on her, then left.

Stephanie didn't even try to hide her grin. *Yeah, he's hunky.*

Stephanie couldn't have asked for a more beautiful day on Saturday morning. There wasn't a cloud in the cornflower-blue sky, and the sun spread its warmth on the top of her head and shoulders, making the brisk temperature refreshing. The ocean, like glittering blue glass along the horizon, tossed and rolled against the pier pilings, as raucous seagulls circled overhead. At home, the clean desert air was dry and gritty, but here on the wharf the ocean breeze with its briny scent energized her.

She hadn't exactly said yes or no to Phil's proposition on Thursday. She'd said she'd think about it, and he'd said he was planning to surf that morning anyway, so come if she felt like it. Well, she'd felt like it, and by virtue of the glorious view, she was already glad about her decision.

A group of surfers was a few hundred yards to the left of the pier, and though the odds were stacked against her, she tried to pick out Phil. With everyone wearing wet suits, it proved to be an impossible task.

"Here's some coffee."

Jumping, Stephanie pivoted to find Phil decked out in a wet suit, holding his surfboard under one arm and a take-out cup of coffee in another. He handed it to her as she worked at closing her mouth.

He was a vision in black neoprene. The suit left nothing of his sculpted body to her imagination—from neck to shoulders to thighs to calves, every part of him was pure perfection.

"Thanks," she said, taking the coffee, unable to think of a single thing to say.

"I'm glad you showed up."

"Me, too."

"If you're still around later, I'll meet you on the beach in…" he glanced at a waterproof watch "…say an hour or so," he said, throwing his board over the forty-foot-high rail.

She watched in horror as he hopped onto the wood post and dived into the ocean. Was he crazy?

"Hey, no jumping from the pier!" a gruff voice yelled from behind. The white-haired security guard didn't stand a chance of catching him.

Stephanie gulped and looked over the rail just as Phil surfaced. He swam to his board, straddled it like a horse, looked up and waved. *Yee haw!*

She shook her head, waiting for the surge of adrenaline to wane. "You almost gave me a heart attack," she yelled.

He laughed. "This is the lazy man's way of getting past the breakers," he shouted with a huge grin. "Enjoy your coffee. I'll see you on the beach later."

He paddled off, and like an expert he caught the first wave, dipping through the curl, zigzagging, riding it until it lost its momentum.

As she sipped her coffee, she watched Phil surf wave after wave, never faltering. He looked like Adonis in a wet suit playing among the mere humans. Today the ocean was only moderately roiled up, offering him little challenge and nothing he couldn't handle standing on one leg. But it was still exciting to see him in action. She remembered several pictures on his office wall with his surfboard planted in the sand like a fat and oddly shaped palm tree, and him receiving a trophy from someone, or a kiss from an equally gorgeous girl. What a charmed life he must lead. Doctor by day, surfer by weekend.

She checked her watch after an hour or so and began walking back to the mouth of the pier. After removing her shoes, she strolled along the wet, gritty sand as she watched Phil ride the curl of a strong, high wave almost all the way to the shore.

He stepped off his board as if off a magic carpet, bent to tuck it under his arm, and waded the remaining distance to where she stood.

"You make it look so easy," she said, waving and smiling.

"I've been surfing since I was twelve."

All man—hair slicked back from his face curling just below his ears, sea water dripping down his temples, broad shoulders and narrow hips—the last thing she could envision was Phil as a prepubescent boy.

"Second nature, huh?"

"Something like that. Hey, I know a great little stand that sells the best hot dogs in Santa Barbara. If you like chili dogs, I'll get out of this suit and we can walk over there."

She nodded as he pointed to the street and the amazingly lucky parking place he'd managed to snag. They walked in friendly conversation toward his car, a classic 1950s Woodie, the signature surfer wagon, complete with side wood paneling.

"Oh, my gosh, this is fantastic!" she said.

"My dad gave me this for my sixteenth birthday, when he realized surfing was my passion."

"It's gorgeous." *So are you.*

For the first time that day, Phil made an obvious head-to-toe assessment of Stephanie. She'd worn shorts, a tank top and zipped hoodie sweatshirt. "You're looking pretty damn great yourself."

A self-conscious thought about her pale legs, compared to his golden-bronze skin, made her wish she'd worn her tried-and-trusted jeans, but seeing the pleased look on his face as he stared at her changed her mind.

He unzipped his wet suit and peeled it off his arms and down to his waist, revealing a flat stomach, cut torso, and defined chest. Just as Stephanie began to worry about what a guy wore under a wet suit, he tugged down the garment to reveal black trunks.

Oh, my. Seeing so much of Phil Hansen was making her mouth water.

He threw a pair of cargo shorts over the trunks, ducked his head into a T-shirt, and in record time slid into some well-worn leather flip-flops.

"You ready?" he said, shaking out his hair.

"Sure," she said, completely under his wet-and-wild spell.

"Oh, hey, wait," he said, closing and locking the hatch. "I forgot something." He took a step toward her, pulled her close, and kissed her.

His mouth was warm and soft as it covered her lips ever so gently. They were nearly strangers, and this wasn't how she did things, but she couldn't manage to tear herself away. Shock made her edgy…at first. The kiss, like a calming tide, swept over her head to toe, smoothing and relaxing her resistance. She wanted more and pressed into his welcoming lips.

When his hands went to her waist, she tensed again. Their heat started a mini-implosion over her hips, sending pleasant waves throughout her body. She wasn't ready to touch him back, except for right there on those inviting lips. She inhaled the scent of ocean on his skin, and breathed deeper, tasting sea salt as she flicked the smooth lining of his mouth with her tongue.

Their connection seemed to stop time. Her hands dangled at her sides, more out of concern about where it might lead if she touched his broad shoulders. Though she wanted to. She wanted to explore every part of Phil Hansen, but they were in public on a busy street. This was no time or place for a first kiss of this magnitude.

Still, she didn't move, kept kissing him, savored the sweet, tender, first kiss. A basic, female reaction flowed through her core, warming everything in its path from the tips of her breasts down to the ends of her toes. She hadn't felt this kind of heady response since she'd first fallen in love with her husband.

Her ex-husband.

Okay, that put the hex on this kiss. Aside from the fact that Phil was a good kisser—restrained, not mauling;

gentle, not immediately going for the touchdown—and aside from the fact that she liked how he felt—really liked how he kissed—the thought of her condemning and unforgiving ex ruined the moment.

She broke contact and pulled back. He studied her up close as if reading her mind. He wasn't rude or persistent. He knew they'd had their moment and now it was over, yet his probing stare let her know he understood something was up, and that he'd respect whatever the barrier was…for now.

What she saw in the depths of his eyes unsettled her. Besides everything his kiss had done, from heating her up inside to sending chills over her skin, she could read in his look that it was only a matter of time before they'd be doing this kissing business again.

The unspoken promise both thrilled and scared her.

CHAPTER FOUR

PHIL had promised a world-class hot dog and he hadn't let Stephanie down. They sat at a little metal table on the cement walk in front of a red-and-white striped awning on Cabrillo Boulevard. Still trying her best to recover from Phil's kiss, she concentrated on eating the dog slathered in heart-clogging chili topped with cheese, and not the imposingly appealing man across the table... staring at her.

"You said you started surfing at twelve?" she said.

She could handle lunch with Phil. If she repeated it enough times maybe she'd believe it. Tell that to her pulse, which quickened every time she noticed new things about him, like how his sideburns were perfectly matched and at least three shades darker than his hair, with a tinge of red. Just before she took her first bite of hot dog, she wondered what his beard stubble might feel like first thing in the morning, and almost missed her mouth.

"Yeah. I had a knack." He smiled at her and her heart stepped out of rhythm. He had a "knack" for world-class kisses, too. "I was spoiled and my parents let me do just about everything. By the time I was fourteen, I got recruited for the Corona Pro surf circuit, and the rest…" he delivered another one of his knockout smiles "…as they say, is history."

"Growing up in the desert, surfing wasn't exactly on my list of things to do. I'm more of a volleyball girl myself."

He raised one brow with interest. "Ever played beach volleyball?"

She shook her head and reached for her soda. "Looks too grueling with all that sand."

"They play beach volleyball every weekend right down the street." He pointed behind him with his thumb.

"Oh, yeah, I remember I saw the nets the day I drove into town."

"So what do you say? Want to check out the game tomorrow?"

"What about Robbie?"

He sat straighter. "I'll bring him along."

She gave him a hesitant glance; her throat tightened, making it hard to swallow the tastiest chili she'd ever eaten.

"You see right through me, don't you?" he said. "Truth is, I need some help keeping the kid entertained, and I've already run out of ideas."

"Well, don't look at me," she said, swallowing and taking another bite.

His playful gaze grew serious. "What's the deal? I mean, I've never seen…"

Should she tell him? By all accounts, he was still a stranger…who'd kissed her senseless. Did he deserve to know her deepest secret just because he was curious?

"The thing is …" Two years ago she'd had her tubes tied to cement the point. "I don't do kids." No. Better to keep it vague. Keep the distance.

"But you deliver babies for a living," Phil said, arms crossed over his black T-shirt, brows furrowed, obviously confused.

"I deliver *other people's* babies." She took another bite of her hot dog and did her best to pretend there wasn't anything contradictory about the statement.

Phil finished his first hot dog, washed it down with cola and wiped his mouth. Stephanie intrigued him with this inconsistency—an OB doc who didn't do babies. And she was quickly becoming his dream date. When a woman didn't want kids, marriage didn't seem to be a priority. And since marriage was the last thing on his to-do list, maybe they could have a good time together, for however long this attraction lasted.

Beneath her defiant remark "I don't do babies" he noticed one telling sign—hurt. He could see it in her gaze. Those inviting butterscotch-with-flecks-of-gold eyes went dull at the mention of kids. Something had caused her great pain and the result made her avoid children. He flashed to the moment he'd walked into the clinic the first night, how he'd seen terror in her expression, how she hadn't been able to get away fast enough. He needed to play this cool, or she'd bolt again.

"No wonder you looked so uncomfortable when I left Robbie with you." He wiped mustard from the corner of his mouth.

She gave a wry laugh as a quick blush pinkened her cheeks. "Uncomfortable is a generous description."

"Yeah, okay, more like you freaked out."

She nodded. "Sorry."

"It's all right."

She made a half-hearted attempt at a smile, and his heart went out to her. He needed to lighten the mood. Maybe he could tease her into submission.

"So there's no chance I can change your mind?" He put his hand on top of hers, immediately aware of how fragile she felt.

"Maybe some other time."

"Translation being—get lost, Phil?"

"Not at all." She met his gaze, sending a subtle message, then quickly looked away.

So maybe she was interested in him, just not the whole Phil-and-Robbie package. Once he sent Robbie back to his stepmom and dad, he'd have time to enjoy her company up close and, hopefully, very personal. Especially after that kiss confirmed what he'd suspected since the first day he'd seen her—they had chemistry. And knowing she didn't want to get involved with anyone any more than he did sounded like the perfect setup.

"Okay. I get it. But when my parents get back from Hawaii, and Robbie goes home, I'd like to make an official date with you."

He hadn't removed his hand, and hers turned beneath his. Now palm to palm, a stimulating image formed in his mind. He wished he could take her home and ravish her right on the spot, but she was skittish and he needed to take things slowly.

"Fine." She flicked her lashes and glanced quickly into his eyes, then slid her hand away.

Still high from their kiss, new desire stirred in him. From the jolt he felt, she could have been throwing lightning bolts instead of batting her lashes. They definitely had chemistry.

"Fine?" he said. "Well, then, let's make that date right now, so I'll have something to look forward to."

On Saturday night, Phil watched Robbie sleep. The little guy flipped and flopped and in between he coughed.

His eyes popped open for the briefest of moments, fluttered, then clamped shut as if trying desperately to stay asleep, but the constant irritation of that cough gave him a good battle. The restless spectacle put a hard lump smack in the middle of Phil's throat.

Robbie's world would become difficult enough as he got older and realized that other kids looked at him differently, and maybe they wouldn't play with him because of him having Down syndrome.

"Sweet kid," he mumbled against an alien yet firm tugging in his chest. What was happening to him?

He adjusted the covers for the umpteenth time beneath his little brother's chin before taking a stroll to the kitchen for a glass of water. It had taken a few days, but they were starting to get into a routine at night. Robbie had filled him in on the rule about reading a picture book before bed. Phil had complied. Heck, he even enjoyed some of them. After a couple of nights, Phil was even able to sneak back to his own bed.

Robbie drifted in a sweet oblivious tide of ignorance and bliss hanging out with other toddlers. How much longer would it last? And as long as it did last, Phil wanted nothing more than for him to be well rested and on his best play-pal game at preschool.

When Robbie didn't sleep, Phil didn't either. How in hell had Roma and his dad managed the last four years?

And when Phil couldn't sleep, his mind drifted to Stephanie—the last person he needed to think about if he had any hope of getting rest. Maybe he'd taken advantage of the situation by kissing her at the beach, even though she'd done her share of participation with that kiss. It had been a whim. She'd looked so damn sweet and vulnerable, completely different from work.

Well, he'd wanted to kiss her, and he had. And he was glad.

He hadn't given a no-strings-attached kiss like that since high school. Stephanie's wounded and fragile air made him extra-cautious. It also drew him to her. Ironically, he only had two months, but he vowed to take things slowly, to give her plenty of leeway. Even if it killed him.

He scratched his chest and paced back and forth across the kitchen. Stephanie was sleek, not flashy; intelligent, but not street-smart. Her hair changed colors in the sun from brown with a hint of red to full-out copper. Her eyes often looked like honey. And she was sweet, in a withdrawn sort of way.

He scraped his jaw. Did any of the description make sense? All he knew for sure was a deep gut reaction happened each and every time he saw her. That was not normal. For him.

What he'd give for a little affectionate nuzzling with her right about now, especially if it quickly evolved into hot and panting sex. But he was going to take it slow. *Remember?* He sloshed back a quick gulp of cold water.

Robbie coughed again.

Phil had already ruled out enlarged adenoids on the kid. He'd played the old airplane spoon of ice cream flying straight for Robbie's mouth, but only if his brother promised to open wide. He'd flashed his penlight across the back of his throat, in the guise of making sure the runway was clear, and all had looked normal in the tonsil and adenoid department, even though Phil must have looked a fool in order to find out. To be honest, it was kind of fun. He was getting a taste of parenting, and realized some of it wasn't so bad.

More muffled coughing drew him back to the guest room. Robbie's butt was up in the air and his thumb had found its way back to his mouth. Some picture. The nasal cannula delivering a small amount of oxygen he'd tried as an experiment had been removed, giving the boy's forehead the concentrated air instead of Robbie's lungs. Phil smiled and shook his head. The stinker really was something. He thought about taking a picture, but he didn't want to risk waking Robbie up so instead he closed the door all but four inches. Besides, taking a picture would be acting like Jon, and he definitely didn't want to go down that path.

Robbie coughed again. Phil ran his hand through his hair, frustrated. He needed to do a bronchoscopy on him, document his condition, and get him started on either CPAP or negative pressure ventilation. Right now the bigger question was, when in his busy clinic schedule would he have time to do one?

An idea popped into his mind and wouldn't let go. Weren't people supposed to face their demons in order to move on? Maybe one small step at a time. Yeah, that might work. If things went as planned, he'd have a coerced but hopefully willing helper on Tuesday evening. How bad could a sedated kid be to be around?

Maybe he'd finally have proof his brother had tracheobronchomalacia. And if he played his cards right, he'd finagle some extra time with the lovely doctor from the desert.

On Tuesday afternoon, Stephanie sat in her office with a mug of coffee. Staring out the window through the gorgeous lace curtains to the bright blue sky, she contemplated her schedule for the next week—except her mind kept drifting to a certain moment at the beach on Saturday. Okay, so she was out of practice, but was she such a bad kisser that she'd completely turned Phil off?

She'd only caught glimpses of him at the clinic since then, and even though she shouldn't care what he thought about her or her kissing, it made her feel as insecure as if she were still in high school. As if she'd made a mistake by letting him kiss her. But she'd wanted him to.

She took another sip of coffee, loathing the teenaged insecurity, just as Phil appeared at her door, bringing with him a sudden tingle-fest.

"Got any plans for tonight?" he asked.

Why did her mood brighten instantaneously? She had no intention of telling him she'd planned on a little shopping at the Paseo before she took in a movie, alone.

"A few. Nothing major," she said, playing it coy.

One look at his great smile and she wanted to get angry for his turning her world sideways. She wanted to hate him for being so damn charming! But all she could muster was a mental, *Wow, I'd forgotten how gorgeous you are.*

"Would you consider doing me a huge favor?" he asked.

She had nothing better planned, so why not? "Depends." Heck, he'd been the one avoiding her. Why make it easy?

He scratched his chin. "As in what's in it for me, depends?"

"It depends on what you want me to do."

"How about I start by telling you how I'll repay you?" A single dimple appeared.

Oh, he thought he was a smooth operator, but she

wasn't that easy. No way. "I don't do bribes, Hansen. No babies, no bribes. Sorry."

He nodded, the second dimple making itself annoyingly visible. "Okay, I'll come clean."

He moved closer and sat on the edge of her desk. She immediately picked up the scent of his crisp and expensive cologne. An impeccable dresser, his pinstriped shirt and flashy patterned tie was the perfect complement to the dark gray slacks. And, *sheesh*, without even trying, his hair looked great, waving in all the right places, with an unintentional clump falling across his brow.

"It does involve a kid," he said. "My kid brother, to be exact." He raised a finger before she could protest. "But here's the deal. I need to scope his lungs and I need to do it tonight, and I need some extra hands and credentials to make it legal. You in?"

She stared at him.

"It's not like you'd be babysitting. Think of it as a technical procedure, and I need your help. That's all."

"That tracheobronchomalacia business?"

He nodded. "I want to get it documented and refer him for CPAP immediately."

"What about your dad and stepmom?"

"I finally got their verbal consent over the phone, and while Robbie's with me, I have medical consent."

"I know nothing about pediatric conscious sedation," she said.

"I'll take care of everything. I just need you to monitor Robbie and inject the drugs while I scope him. I'll recover him and you can leave as soon as I'm through."

She considered his request, but made the stupid mistake of glancing into his eyes, which watched and waited and reminded her of the ocean last Saturday at high noon. He ramped up the pressure by tilting his head and giving a puppy-dog can-we-take-a-walk expression. If Phil handled everything, and all she had to do was administer drugs and do the technical monitoring, maybe she could help him out.

"What time?"

"I've got to pick him up from day care in ten minutes. Mmm, how about in half an hour?"

That didn't give her much time to think it over, or change her mind. She pulled out her drawer and, having learned from her snack expedition the other night with Robbie, found a pack of peanut butter with cheese crackers, tore it open with her teeth, and tossed the first one into her mouth.

"You're on," she said, sounding muffled.

As naturally as old friends, he kissed her cheek. "You're the best," he said, and took off, leaving her chomping on her snack, blowing cracker flakes from her mouth when she sighed. And there was that damn feeling he brought along with him every time they talked—flustered.

The new and state-of-the-art procedure suite at Midcoast Medical provided the perfect setting for Robbie's examination. Jason had had the equipment installed after a successful second-quarter report. Every penny they made beyond salaries went right back into their clinic with upgrades and added services. Phil no longer had to rent space at the local hospital to perform his broncho-scopies, taking him away from the clinic, and making his nurse able to increase her hours to full-time as a result.

But this examination was after hours, and he'd lined up a great replacement for his regular nurse—Stephanie.

She hadn't bargained on Robbie being awake when

she arrived, and Phil had to do some quick talking to make her stick around.

"I can't do this on my own, Stephanie. Please. Five minutes. It will only take five minutes. I promise."

She looked pale and hesitated at the procedure-room door, but something, maybe it was Robbie looking so vulnerable and unsuspecting, made her change her mind.

Robbie fought like the devil when Phil tried to insert an intravenous line, and he thought she'd bolt right then and there. Surprisingly, she held the boy's arm steady, and with her help they got the IV in and the keep-open solution running. She'd been an unexpected decoy with her medley of wacky kids' songs. Robbie even giggled a few times. If she didn't do kids, how did she know all those children's songs?

Gowned, gloved and masked, Phil watched Stephanie draw up the quick-acting, deeply sedating medication. He knew there was a fine line between true anesthesia and conscious sedation, and though he wanted to make Robbie comfortable, he didn't want him too sedated, just out of it long enough to get a minitour inside his lungs. After she had set up Robbie with pulse oximetry, heart and blood-pressure monitor, and supplemental oxygen, he directed her to give the standard pediatric dose for fentanyl and benzodiapine instead of a newer, short-acting drug.

"No offense, but I only use Propofol when I have an anesthesiologist working with me." He smiled at her through his mask.

She tossed him a sassy look. "Believe me, no offense taken, I already feel out of my element here." With skilled and efficient hands she titrated the drugs into the IV as he applied the topical numbing spray to

Robbie's throat, and within seconds Robbie drifted into twilight sleep.

"I called ahead to the preschool to hold his lunch, but Robbie loves to eat so much he almost snuck a snack around three today. Fortunately, they caught him, so we shouldn't have a problem with emesis." He flipped on the suction machine, using his elbow to protect his sterile gloves. This would be his backup contingency plan in case Robbie did vomit.

"I'm going to use a pediatric laryngeal mask airway instead of an endotracheal tube." He showed her the small spoon-shaped device. "As Robbie has the typical shortened Down syndrome neck, an endotracheal tube would have been tricky anyway," he said as he lubricated the tablespoon-size silicone mask and slipped the tube inside Robbie's slack mouth. The boy didn't flinch. "See? I don't even need a laryngoscope with this gizmo."

Once the LMA was in place, Phil immediately reached for his bronchoscope and slipped the flexible tube down Robbie's trachea for a quick look-see.

"See that?" he said to Stephanie, who took turns intently watching the procedure on the digital TV screen, keeping track of the heart and BP monitor readings, and watching Robbie in the flesh. Sure enough, due to softened cartilage, his trachea showed signs of floppiness and collapsed while he breathed under the sedation. The same thing happened while he slept each night. "This is classic TBM." Keeping things short and sweet, and already having digitally recorded his findings, Phil removed the scope and quickly followed suit with the laryngeal mask airway. Even though sedated, Robbie coughed and sputtered. "All the kid needs is continuous positive airway pressure while he sleeps, so he won't have to cough every time his trachea collapses."

"That's great news," Stephanie said, watching Robbie like an anxious mother hen.

True to the short-life drug effect, Robbie started to come out of his stupor. "There you go, buddy, we're all done," Phil said. He bent over and looked into his blinking eyes. "Are you in there somewhere?"

The bleary-eyed Robbie tried to look in the vicinity of his voice. Phil set the scope on the counter and prepared to wipe it clean before putting it in the sterilization solution overnight.

"Can you watch him a few minutes while I clean up?" he asked.

She nodded, undoing her mask and letting it hang around her neck, though keeping a safe distance from Robbie.

As with many recently sedated children, Robbie woke up confused, fussing and crying. Phil worked as quickly as he could. "You're okay, Rob. I'm right here, buddy," he said. The boy seemed to calm down immediately. Phil smiled, assuming the sound of his voice had done the trick, but when he glanced over his shoulder, he saw a sight that made him smile even wider.

The I-don't-do-kids doctor was holding Robbie's hand and patting it.

"You at all interested in getting takeout and keeping me company tonight while I help my kid brother recover from major surgery?" He'd lay it on thick, and hope for the best.

She remained quiet for a few seconds, then let go of Robbie's hand.

"I can't, Phil. I'm sorry."

* * *

On Wednesday morning, Stephanie hung up the phone after a long conversation with her mother. She'd used the excuse of being on call—which wasn't completely untrue—for not showing for Thanksgiving. If things followed the usual routine, her sister would be on the phone within the next ten minutes, and Mary was ruthless when it came to arm-twisting. All the more reason to get started with her appointments.

Phil had surprised her last night with both his technical skill and tender banter with his brother. The more she got to know him, the more she suspected his playboy reputation was just a cover. Helping out with Robbie's exam hadn't been nearly as bad as she'd thought it would be, another surprise. Maybe she was getting used to him. She'd watched the boy sleep, and yearning had clutched her heart. If only her son could be alive.

She closed her eyes and bit her lip. Someone tapped on the door.

"Your next patient is ready."

Thank heavens for work.

By midmorning, Amy delivered the latest batch of lab reports and special tests.

Stephanie shuffled through the stack with an eye out for two in particular. The first was great news—it was just an ovarian cyst for Ms. Winkler. The next report wasn't nearly as welcome. Celeste Conroy's Pap smear showed abnormal cells. She picked up the phone.

After she'd calmed the woman down, she suggested her plan. "I'd like to perform a colposcopy, which is a fancy way of looking at your cervix up close with a bright light and magnifying glass."

The proactive next step went over better than the bombshell dysplasia news.

"And while I'm examining your cervix, I'll take a

tiny biopsy of that questionable area. This will give us a better idea of exactly what we're dealing with."

After a brief silence, several questions flew from the young pregnant woman's mouth. Stephanie answered each as she was able.

"The exam is not threatening to your pregnancy, though after I do the biopsy, there may be some mild cramping and light bleeding. We'd have to monitor you carefully to make sure the bleeding was from the biopsy and not from the pregnancy, but the risk is extremely low that your baby will be in jeopardy."

After a few more minutes of convincing the patient to arrange an appointment on Friday, the day after Thanksgiving, she hung up.

And now she had a good reason to stay in Santa Barbara for Thanksgiving. She needed to be well rested and in top form on Friday. Mary could twist her arm all she wanted, but she wouldn't give in to Thanksgiving dinner in the desert.

Her next call was pure pleasure. "Ms. Winkler? This is Dr. Bennett from Midcoast Medical. I've got your ultrasound results back, and you can rest assured that your enlarged ovary is nothing more than a pesky cyst."

She smiled when her patient sang out a loud "Hallelujah!"

By lunchtime it occurred to Stephanie that she hadn't seen Phil in the clinic all morning. She nibbled at her microwaved plate of food, and half-heartedly chatted with a couple of coworkers. It also occurred to her that Thanksgiving was going to be one lonely day. She'd hole up in her hotel room and watch a stack of old DVDs and pretend it was just another day. Maybe she'd eat an open-faced turkey sandwich with dressing and gravy, with a side of cranberries from the deli around the corner, too. Oh, and she'd watch the famous New York Thanksgiving Day parade on TV, she mused with a jumble of faraway thoughts.

"I bet you're wondering where I've been," Phil said, standing beside her.

"What makes you think I've even noticed?" she said, glancing over her shoulder, going along with his playful tone.

"*We* noticed you weren't around," one of the two nurses sharing the community lounge table chimed in. As far as Stephanie could tell, Phil had all the ladies in the clinic wrapped around his finger.

His quirked brow and goofy expression of "see what I'm saying?" made her laugh. It felt good.

"Thank you, Tamara and Stacy," he said. "I'm glad someone noticed."

He sat next to Stephanie, edging out Jon's nurse, though there was plenty of room on the other side of the table, then unpacked a couple of shrimp tacos from his brown bag. "You know, that's what I like about you. You're not under my spell."

She almost spat out her soda. "You have a spell?" She was walking on thin ice because she knew without a doubt he did have a special something that very well could be called a spell, and that she was most likely already under it…especially since their kiss.

"So I've been told."

"He's got a spell," the nurses said together.

She laughed and shook her head. "Well, I don't know about a spell, but I do know you've got a jelly stain on your shirt."

He pulled in his chin and glanced downward. "Oh, that. It's probably from when I made Robbie's sandwich this morning."

With each day, and all the little details she noticed about him, Phil became more irresistible.

Not that she was interested or anything. "So where were you?"

"Where else? The preschool. Seems like it's my second home. How does Roma do it?"

"Don't let this go to your head, Phil, but I think you're doing a pretty good job of pinch-hitting for your parents."

"They're due back tonight, and I'm counting the hours."

The nurses finished their lunch, and announced they were just about to take a walk before the afternoon clinic opened when René Munroe appeared, complete with swaddled baby in her arms and Jon at her side.

"Hi, Dr. Munroe!" one of the nurses said, rushing over to look at the newborn. "Oh, he's adorable. May I hold him?"

"Sure," the dark-haired René said, glowing with new-mom pride.

Phil popped up and took a peek under the blanket. "Hey, he looks just like those pictures."

René rolled her eyes. "Oh, gosh, has Jon been boring everyone with pictures?"

Phil nodded, but the nurses quickly protested, "No! We love baby pictures."

"Oh, hey, René, this is Stephanie Bennett, the doc we hired to cover your patients," Jon said, looking a bit abashed and obviously wanting to change the subject.

They greeted each other and Stephanie already felt as though she knew René from working in her office. While Jon passed the baby around, Stephanie discussed Celeste Conroy's abnormal Pap smear with René and her plans for following up. When René agreed with the next step, Stephanie felt much more confident.

"Would you like me to call and reassure her that I'm in total agreement?" René said.

"That would be wonderful."

"Okay, last chance to hold Evan before I take René out to lunch," Jon said, having taken back his son but seeming ready to share him with anyone who wanted. "Stephanie?"

He offered the teddy-bear-patterned bundle of blanket to her and she froze. Oh, no, what should she do? Would it be completely awkward to refuse? Her pulse sputtered in her chest, and her ears rang. She liked these people and didn't want to insult them.

"Okay," she said, feigning a smile. She held Evan with stiff arms, away from her chest. "Aren't you something?" Memories of her son gurgling and cooing hit so fast and hard she found it impossible to breathe. She blinked back the images as her heart stumbled, and she handed the baby back to René, trying her best to disguise her quivery voice. "You must be so proud."

The huge, beaming smile on René's face gave the answer. She cuddled the baby to her heart and kissed his cheek. "I wuv this wittle guy."

Jon laughed and scratched his nose. "Anyone know a cure for a highly educated woman who suddenly starts talking baby talk?"

The nurses giggled. "It's a requirement of motherhood, Doc," one of them said.

Flushed and edgy, Stephanie willed her hands to stop shaking. She'd looked into those beautiful baby gray eyes and had seen Justin. She'd glanced up to find Phil intently watching her as her lungs clutched at each breath.

Somehow she made it through the goodbyes, but as soon as the couple left she headed for the back door and the tranquil promise of the yard. She needed to breathe, to get hold of herself.

She was staring at the small bubbling fountain and listening to chattering birds in the tree when a hand grasped her arm. It was Phil. He'd picked up on what had just happened. Hell, she'd been so obvious, anyone would have noticed her fumbling attempt at acting normal…if they hadn't been so distracted with the baby.

"I was wondering what you're doing tomorrow," he said.

She welcomed the change in subject, even if it was another sticky topic. How should she best phrase the fact she had no plans for Thanksgiving and not come off as pitiful? Sure, she could go to Palm Desert, but it wasn't going to happen.

She swallowed and said, "I'm having a quiet day."

He glanced thoughtfully at her. "My stepmother is a fantastic cook, and she promised me a Thanksgiving dinner to die for as I've been taking care of Robbie and all, and I thought you might like to be my plus one."

"Plus one?"

"My guest. What do you say? Great food. Even better company. You'll like my dad." He tilted his head, and his crescent-shaped eyes looked very inviting. "Robbie will be so happy to see them that he'll leave you alone. I promise." Phil was the distraction she needed—a guy completely unaware of her past, who didn't ask questions, and with one not-so-subtle thing on his mind.

Did she really need to think about it? Hotel room. DVDs. Deli sandwich. Or plus one.

"You know what? I'd really like that."

The full-out smile he delivered assured her she'd not only made the right decision but she'd also made his afternoon. When in the past three years had she been able to make that claim about a man? And it felt pretty darn good.

He looked as if he wanted to kiss her again, and maybe that's exactly what she needed right now, a kiss to make her forget, but his beeper went off and after a quick glance, a forlorn look replaced the charm. He sighed. "It's the preschool, again."

Late that afternoon, Phil appeared at Stephanie's office door, looking agitated.

"What's up?" she asked.

"The damn weather."

She glanced out her window at another perfectly clear blue autumn sky then back at Phil. "Looks pretty good to me."

"I'm talking about Maui. They're having a terrible storm and the return flight has been canceled until Friday. Looks like Thanksgiving dinner is off."

She couldn't deny the disappointment. Ever since he'd invited her, she'd felt a buzz of expectation, a curiosity about his family, and mouthwatering anticipation of great food. Now a storm on a tropical island had changed everything. "How disappointing…for them. I'm sure they're eager to get home to Robbie and all."

He snapped his fingers. "I've got an idea. Come to my house and I'll order a turkey dinner." His eyes lit up. "It'll be fun, and you can help me warm things up. What do you say?

She'd swung from one end of the emotional pendulum to the opposite over this Thanksgiving, and here was yet a new twist. Hotel. DVDs. Deli sandwich. Or spend an afternoon with a gorgeous guy…and Robbie?

It all came down to one desire. Did she want to have a life again? Or go on living in a vacuum. Hotel. DVDs. Deli sandwich…or…

There really wasn't a decision to make. "What time?"

CHAPTER FIVE

ON THANKSGIVING morning, Stephanie put extra effort into getting dressed. She wanted to look good, but not overdo it. She opted for casual with jeans and boots, a pumpkin-colored top with a flashy hip belt, and a multi-fall-colored knit scarf to ward off the cooler weather.

She'd stopped last night at the bakery she'd recently discovered and got one of the last two pumpkin pies baked that afternoon, the kind of whipped cream you sprayed from a can, and a bottle of deep red wine to go with the turkey. She had no intention of impressing Phil with her culinary skills. Heck, she was living in a hotel, how could she? And wasn't he the one who'd invited her to dinner?

She arrived at his house just before noon, impressed with the rolling brown hills and secluded homes scattered across them. The sprawling country farmhouse was the last type of home she'd expect to see Phil living in. In the distance, and far behind her, the ocean sparkled as if the bold sun had scattered glitter over it. She took a deep breath of fresh air, savoring the special view, suddenly aware that her insides were letting go of that usual tight knot.

Santa Barbara had a completely different kind of beauty from the tall purple mountains that encased her desert home, and the flat breadth between them. Both were special, but the ocean added that extra touch with which, in her opinion, no amount of saguaro cactus or Joshua trees could compete.

With an odd sense of contentment folding in around her, she tapped lightly on his door before ringing the bell. After a short time the door swung open, with Phil grinning and with Robbie riding piggyback.

"Hey," he said, a little breathless. "Come in."

The spacious living room, with a stone fireplace and wall-long French doors and windows, was bright and open. The light-colored hardwood floors were offset by high, dark beamed and arched ceilings. The family room opened into a modern kitchen complete with cooking island and expensive-looking Italian tile floors.

Toys were everywhere. Pillows and books were scattered around the family room, and furniture was obviously askew.

Phil looked happy, and for a confirmed bachelor he was doing a fine job at playing stand-in father. "We were just horsing around, weren't we, shorty?"

Robbie giggled and nodded, and once Phil released him, he ran off toward a beach ball, blissfully unaware of Stephanie invading his territory.

Maybe she was getting used to being around Robbie, because he hadn't set off any internal alarms today. Or maybe she was distracted by the attractive guy right in front of her. He wore jeans and a white tailored Western-styled shirt with the collar open, revealing a hint of light brown chest hair. And he kept smiling at her, his white straight teeth like something out of a magazine ad.

"You look great," he said. "As always."

The compliment stopped her. At the end of her marriage her husband had thought she was despicable.

Couldn't stand to look at her and hadn't minded telling her so. Knowing that, on top of every horrible thought she'd already had about herself, had almost made her lose the will to live. She shook her head, refusing to go there again. She wanted to move forward and she couldn't very well do that by constantly looking over her shoulder, remembering the bad times.

Phil had just told her she looked great. Did he tell all his dates that? "Thank you." She felt her cheeks heat up.

"I mean it." He pinned her with a no-nonsense gaze.

"I believe you." Did she? Did she have the nerve to tell him how fantastic he looked, too?

"Good."

The antsy feeling made her need to change the subject. "This house is amazing," she said.

"Thanks. I've only been here a couple of years, but I like to call it home."

"Oh, here's the pie and some other stuff," she said.

He took her few items into the kitchen, reading the wine label on the way. Instead of sitting, she followed him, sliding her hand over the cool granite countertops and marveling at the state-of-the-art stainless-steel appliances. This was the kind of home a person dreamed about but never intended to actually live in. And what was a bachelor like Phil doing here?

"This seems so unlike you," she said.

"Tell that to my Realtor. I spent a year looking for it. This is the place I intend to stay in."

"A guy like you?"

"Hey, give me a break. I may not be interested in settling down, but a house, well, I have no qualms about where I want to live for the rest of my life."

"We really don't know a thing about each other, do we?" she said, smiling.

His eyes brightened to daylight blue. "Here's something else to surprise you." He washed his hands and opened a cupboard. "I'm cooking today."

The undeniable aroma of turkey hit her nostrils. "I thought you were ordering in?"

"I got to thinking, how hard could cooking a turkey be? My butcher gave me instructions, and they didn't sound difficult."

How many more surprises did he have up his sleeve? "Well, it smells great."

"Hey, you're gonna love the dressing. I made Roma fax the recipe to me last night."

She laughed. For the first time in ages, she felt excited about Thanksgiving.

He washed a few vegetables in the sink. "What would you like to drink?"

"Water is fine." Heaven forbid she should have a glass of wine, relax, and let her guard down.

He delivered her a glass as she sat on one of the stools by the island. "You've got to admit this beats eating in your hotel room, right?"

She gazed across the comfortable and stylish home and nodded. "You win. Hands down, this beats my hotel. I feel like I'm in a *House Beautiful* commercial."

He smiled, obviously liking her description of his home.

"These are from my garden." He held up a handful of new carrots, and medium-size tomatoes.

"You're kidding me," she said. "You garden, too?"

"What can I say? I like being in the sun. I like digging in the dirt and pulling weeds. Don't tell anyone at work, they'd never let me live it down."

"Your secret's safe with me," she said, taking a sip of water and fighting off an ever-growing crush on her surprising host.

"How are you at mashing potatoes?" he asked, just as something hit the back of her butt with a plunk. She jerked around, it was the beach ball, and Robbie had a guilty expression on his face.

"Hey, remember what I said about throwing that thing around in here," Phil chided Robbie.

"Outside, Pill," the boy said. "Go. Peez?"

"I'm busy right now."

"Now!" Robbie said, throwing the ball at Stephanie and hitting her stomach this time.

"Okay, mister, you're in big trouble." Phil headed for Robbie, who didn't take him seriously in the least. The boy must have thought they were playing catch-me-if-you-can, as he ran off on short, squat legs, no chance of escaping Phil's reach.

Phil grabbed him by the collar then held him over his hip. Robbie kicked and griped. Phil glanced at Stephanie, his embarrassment obvious. "Sometimes I just can't control this kid."

"Tell you what," she said, trying not to smile as Robbie continued to squeal with delight. She had half an urge to toss the ball back to him, even though it was against the rules, but Phil was setting limits and she didn't want to confuse the boy. "I'll peel the potatoes while you two work off some extra energy."

"Sounds like a plan." He nodded with a grateful glance. "Okay, buster, you're gonna get what for," he said with mock seriousness.

"No!" Robbie said. "*You're* gonna get what for!"

Stephanie couldn't help but smile. She watched momentarily as they headed outside, an odd sensation taking hold. Ignoring the nudge toward a change of heart, she headed for the kitchen.

Phil's house was laid out so that the kitchen flowed directly into the family room, and the family room opened to a patio, and beyond that the huge expanse of verdant yard was accented by flowering hibiscus in white and red and assorted leafy bushes. From the large ranch-style kitchen windows she could see their wild game of catch or dodge-the-beach-ball or whatever their version of "what for" was called. Seemed as if all Phil's griping about being stuck with his kid brother for ten days was nothing more than a cover. And Robbie was having the time of his life, laughing, throwing, and running all over the place. Looked like kid's heaven to her. And Phil played the role of a benevolent uncle wanting nothing more than to make the kid happy.

Happy.

That was a word that had slipped from her vocabulary these past three years. As she peeled the potatoes, sliced and dropped them into a bowl of cold water, she pondered how inviting the old and nearly forgotten feeling was. Her lips stretched into a broad smile that reached like a warm glove into her chest and squeezed her heart. Welcome back to the living. Happy felt great.

It hit her before the next breath. She'd admitted being happy and she was in the company of a little boy. Wow. Maybe things were finally breaking through that guilt logjam.

Robbie was a sweet kid. Justin was a memory she'd always hold deep in her heart and never forget, but Robbie wasn't Justin. She wasn't Robbie's mother. She wasn't responsible for him. Why be afraid of him? Did she want to spend the rest of her life cowering around *all* children, or was it finally time to face her fear?

She wiped her hands on the dish towel and walked toward the French doors. As she opened them and walked onto the patio, she swallowed and took a steadying breath. "Um…" Her gaze darted around the yard as she picked at her nails.

Phil quit jogging and gave her an odd look. "Is everything okay?"

Her hand flew to her hair. "Yeah. Um…I was just wondering…"

He took a few steps toward her, a concerned expression clouding his good looks. At the moment, passing the medical boards seemed easier than what she wanted to say. Another deep breath.

"Do you have room for one more in that game?"

By the time the potatoes had boiled, Phil had followed Stephanie back to the kitchen. Robbie looked sufficiently pooped out and sat in front of a children's DVD in his little corner of the family room. On a separate large-screen TV the annual Thanksgiving Texas football game was going on.

"I'd better put the yams in the oven," Phil said. "I got this dish from my caterer."

She glanced over her shoulder at the gorgeous-looking casserole complete with pecans on top. Phil opened a top oven, slid the dish inside then checked on the turkey in the lower oven, basting it as if he'd done this before.

"You're making my mouth water," she said, savoring the smell. She'd worked up quite an appetite running around with Robbie and Phil. And it hadn't wiped her out emotionally either. If anything, it had invigorated her.

"It'll be done in another half hour. In the meantime, I'm having a beer. Can I get you anything?"

Could she even remember the last time she'd had a glass of wine? "I'll try that wine I brought."

"You're on."

By the time they'd set the table, made the gravy, and laid out all the food, the few sips of wine she'd managed to find time to take had already gone to her head. The pleasant buzz filtered throughout her body, heating her insides and causing her to smile. A lot. How could a few sips of wine make her feel that giddy? Maybe this great feeling had a lot more to do with Phil, Robbie, and Thanksgiving than the liquid spirits. She took another sip, loving the way the simply laid-out table looked, and before he signaled for her to sit, she grabbed her purse.

"Wait," she said. "I want to take a picture of this. It's so beautiful." She dug out her cell phone and snapped first a picture of the turkey in the center of the table, then had Robbie and Phil pose for one, heads close to the bird. Then she snapped one of herself at arm's length with the two of them beside her and the turkey in the background. In her opinion, all three were keepers, even if the third one, taken at such close range, looked as if they all had oversize noses and heads.

Things had been so busy all afternoon she hadn't allowed herself to examine Phil's proximity to her until now as they studied her photographs. She felt his warmth and it called to her. Reacting before thinking, she turned and reached for him, gave him a hug, and kissed his cheek.

"Thank you so much for inviting me," she said, a little bit of her heart going out of her. Though frightening at first, his welcoming reception gave her courage not to pull back inside. Maybe Phil was someone she could let her hair down around.

"I'm really glad you're here," he said with a sincere glint in his eyes, as if on the verge of kissing her.

"Pill! Eat!"

He rolled his eyes. "Can you imagine how hard it would have been to keep him entertained all afternoon by myself?"

She laughed. He'd given her a compliment then quickly yanked it back.

"Eat now!" Robbie chanted.

"Right," he said. "First order of business."

Once everyone was seated at the table, and their plates were filled, Phil surprised her even more. "Robbie? Will you say grace for us?" He looked at her and winked. "I got a note from preschool saying they've been practicing."

The boy's big brown eyes grew serious. He licked his lips a couple of times, obviously considering what to say, then he clamped his lids together. "Thank you for da peshell food. For my fambly. For Pill. And for Theff-oh-nee."

With her head bowed, big fat tears brimmed as Stephanie blinked and whispered, "Amen."

Thanksgiving dinner had gone better than Phil could possibly have dreamed. After they'd worn him out playing ball, Robbie was on his best behavior. And Phil had almost fallen over when Stephanie had asked if she could join in. She'd chased Robbie around the yard as if she were a kid again, as if it didn't bother her anymore to be around him. After the panic he'd caused her that first night, this was an amazing improvement.

Dinner was exceptional, if he did say so himself. Not one thing got burned, except for the crescent rolls, and that was only a little on the bottoms. They were still edible, especially if you loaded them up with sweetened cranberry sauce straight from the caterer.

Stephanie was more animated than he'd ever seen her. It brightened those gorgeous eyes and made her prettier than he'd previously thought, dazzling him with her easy charm. Too bad his eyelids were at half-mast and his stomach so full that he didn't have the energy to get up and walk across the room to plant a kiss on her. If he didn't move in the next few seconds he'd fall asleep. Some impression that would make.

"You sit, and I'll clean up," she said. "It's the least I can do."

He thought about protesting, but the couch felt great and it was the third quarter in the game and Dallas was only ahead by a field goal. Robbie crawled up and snuggled beside him. That did it. "Thanks!"

By the time Stephanie had finished the dishes, Phil and Robbie had fallen asleep. The sight of the two of them on the couch sent a chill through her heart. A memory flashed of her holding her baby, exhausted, eyelids heavy, the couch inviting her to settle down and rest, just for a moment...

Didn't Phil know how dangerous that was? A pop of adrenaline drove her to rush to the sofa. She delicately lifted Robbie so as not to wake him or disturb Phil. She couldn't very well hold him as if he had a dirty diaper and expect him to stay asleep, so she brought him to her chest. On automatic pilot, Robbie wrapped his legs around her waist, and hung his arms over her shoulders. She anchored him beneath his bottom and across his back, and he nuzzled his head against her neck. A rush of motherly feelings made her feel dizzy. He was so much heavier and bigger than Justin, her four-month-old baby.

She hugged Robbie tight and, determined not to succumb to her woozy feeling, walked carefully down the hall to his room. She could do this. It was time to prove she could.

As she prepared him for his nap, his sublime expression sent her thoughts to Justin. He'd always looked like an angel when he'd slept. *Sweetheart, Mommy will always love you. Please forgive me.*

She bit her lip and fought the pinpricks behind her lids as she wondered how different her life would have been if she'd put her baby to bed that night. Today, through Robbie, she'd pretend she had…

At some point Phil had drifted off to sleep, and the next thing he remembered was a cool hand on his cheek. Her hand. The faint feel of her fingers reminded him of butterfly wings, delicate and beautiful, and easily harmed. Strangely, it made him want to look out for her in the same odd way he wanted to protect Robbie.

He must have stretched out on the couch because she sat on the edge, facing him.

"Are you ready for dessert?" she asked, sending a thought through his brain completely different from what she'd probably intended. "I've made some coffee."

Ah, that dessert.

Through his bleary eyes, her familiar butterscotch-and-cream features came into focus. Without thinking, he took her hand and kissed her slender fingers. "I'd love some," he said, thinking more about what he'd really like right then.

Heat radiated from his gaze, and half of her mouth hitched into a knowing smile as she edged away. "Don't move. I'll bring it to you."

As he woke up a little more, he got suddenly curious.

"Where's Robbie?" He sat bolt upright, a sudden knot of concern lodged in his chest.

"He fell asleep, too. I hope you don't mind, but I put him to bed."

"You put him to bed? How long have I been out?"

"An hour, give or take a few minutes."

He scrubbed his face. "Man, some host I am."

"You've been a perfect host," she said, on her way to the kitchen, practically skipping. This was a side of Stephanie he'd never seen, and definitely liked. She'd come outside and played with him and Robbie, though it had felt like pulling teeth to get her to ask. She'd shared Thanksgiving with them, as if they were a small and happy family—this from the woman who hadn't been able to go near them in the Japanese restaurant. And now she'd put Robbie to bed.

While she was busy preparing coffee and dessert in the kitchen, he wandered down the hall to Robbie's room. The door had been left a few inches open, like Roma had instructed Phil the first night she'd left him. Robbie slept peacefully…in his blanket sleeper.

What kind of a woman would think to put him in his pajamas and leave the door ajar? He thought about some of the women he'd dated over the past year. He'd bet his house that none of them would have thought of it. Hell, they'd probably have left him right on the couch where they'd found him, but not Stephanie.

Phil scratched his head as he exited the bedroom, leaving the door as he'd found it. Who would be that considerate?

A mother, that was who.

Was Stephanie a mother? Then why would she freak out around kids? And if she was a mother, where was her child? Maybe she'd been through a bad divorce, and her husband had gotten custody. Nah, that seemed too outrageous. The woman was a doctor and a great person. Sometimes disgruntled husbands kidnapped their kids. He shook his head, unable to go there, but something tormented her and he intended to find out what it was.

He glanced into the kitchen, at Stephanie pottering around, whistling under her breath. She'd come out of her shell today. He'd just begun to glimpse a different side of Stephanie Bennett, and he liked what he'd discovered. Even with all of his questions, Thanksgiving wasn't a day to dig up her past. He didn't want to spoil her upbeat mood; the lady deserved a break.

A subtle smoothness to her brow made him think she'd made peace with herself today, that maybe she'd conquered a demon or two, and he was glad to witness it.

She looked great, too. Those straight-leg jeans hugged her hips in all the right places, and the silky top revealed the hint of a soft, sweet cleavage. And her hair. What could he say about that gorgeous head of hair, other than he'd love to get his fingers tangled up in it?

By the time he sat down, she showed up with two cups of coffee, handing him one and sitting on the edge of the sofa again. "As I said, you're a fantastic host. I haven't felt this relaxed in ages. Besides, that's the beauty of a huge turkey dinner in the afternoon. You get to nap and wake up in time for a sandwich later." There was that bright smile again. "Oh, and Dallas won."

"Go, Cowboys!" What was it about her smile that drove him over the edge? From this closer range the fine sprinkling of freckles he'd discovered across her nose looked the exact color of her hair. She was a vision he thought he'd never get tired of, and he wanted to hold her, to feel her hair on his face, to kiss those freckles, but he was holding a hot cup of coffee instead.

They'd had a great afternoon together, really gotten to know each other better, and he liked every single thing he'd discovered.

She sat next to him with her leg curled under her. She'd slipped off her shoes, and he noticed polished toenails that matched her top. A fleeting image of her in a bath towel, painting her nails, sent a quick thrill through his veins. He wanted her, pure and simple. He wanted to make love to her, to make her come alive.

No risk, no gain.

He set the cup down, and reached for her. "Come here," he said.

Surprise flickered in her eyes. She put her cup on the table and with no sign of resistance snuggled into his arms. He kissed her cheek then brushed her mouth with his thumb. "You have no idea how much I want to kiss you," he said.

She tasted his thumb. He saw a flash of fire in those butterscotch depths. There wasn't any question what her answer was. She tilted her chin to make better contact as their mouths came together.

He picked up where he'd left off at the beach, slipping his tongue between her soft lips, and found her velvet-slick mouth.

She cupped his face and kissed him hard. He delved deeper, ravenous for her taste, then mated his tongue with hers. They made love with their mouths as time ceased to exist. He had no idea how long they'd necked, all he knew was that she matched his heated response, pressing her body against his, smothering him with her lips. He knew where needy kisses like that led, and there was no going back.

The fine skin of her neck tasted like vanilla. She moaned as if he'd uncovered the most sensual spot on her body. He wanted to explore more, discover every area that drove her mad with desire, but she was fully clothed. He'd have to fix that. Immediately. He cupped her breast, and felt the tightened nipple under the thin fabric of her top. His ears were so hot he thought they might spontaneously combust, and his now-full erection pulsed and strained to be set free.

As difficult as it was, he broke away from her fired-up kisses, stood, and took her hand. "Follow me."

With flushed cheeks and hooded eyes, eyes that confirmed she wanted him as much as he wanted her, she followed him down the long hall.

Stephanie watched Phil throw back the covers of his bed and step toward her. He took her by the neck and kissed her so hard she thought her knees would go wobbly.

This was no time to change her mind. Her mind? Hell, she'd misplaced that right around the time he'd kissed her. If she was going to change her mind it had to be now, but desire shivered through her and the only thing in the world she wanted at this moment was to make love with him. She was on fire. A feeling she hadn't experienced in three years pulsed between her legs, and one thing was very clear. Phil wanted her as much as she wanted him.

Hadn't she been telling herself to start living again? Every sensation coursing over her skin and through her veins shouted, *Do it! Give yourself permission.* Phil's mouth clamped down on hers again, and the no-brainer decision was made.

Completely giving in to the moment, she found a way under his shirt and skimmed the taut muscles on his chest, her hands skating across his substantial shoulders. It had been so long since she'd touched a man this way. She savored the feel of naked flesh. His skin was smooth with a fine sprinkling of hair on his chest, and she wanted to see him. See all of him.

"Let me help you," he said, pulling his shirt over his head, buttons untouched.

She only had time to glimpse his flat stomach and defined arms before he did the disappearing act with her top. A hot rhythm between her thighs drove her to undo his jeans. He yanked them down and stepped out, his erection outlined through his black briefs. With a rush of desire she cupped the full length of him, restless to see him, to feel him inside her.

To feel. Him. She'd been living on anxiety and tension for so long, this surge of lust intoxicated her. Every cell in her body came to life, heightening his touch and sweetening his taste. It empowered her, made her think she could do anything. With Phil. She pulled his briefs down and watched as he stepped out of them. She'd seen his physique in the wet suit the other day, but it couldn't compare to him in the flesh. His powerful legs and full erection was a picture she'd hold in her memory for the rest of her life.

With a dark, hooded stare, Phil studied her. "Your turn," he said. He brushed his warm hands over her breasts, cupping and lifting them as he dropped feathery kisses on her shoulder, and expertly unlatched her bra. "You're beautiful. So beautiful," he said in a hushed, reverent tone, kissing each breast.

Their mouths came together again, his lips full and smooth, as they dropped onto the bed. He unzipped and removed her jeans and lacy thong that matched her bra.

"Cute," he said, eyebrows lifted in approval as he tossed it across the room. It landed on a lampshade.

Phil's natural banter and easygoing manner helped her relax when she briefly felt out of her depth. What the hell was she doing, having sex with a coworker, with a man known for being a playboy? But she looked into Phil's eyes, saw unadulterated desire, and lost her train of thought. Again.

Today she needed to be desired. It was a truth she could face, a gift he offered, and she had every intention of accepting and savoring it.

They rolled together into the center of his huge bed, finally feeling every part of each other. The exquisite feel of his muscles and skin fanned the flames licking in her belly. They kissed and tasted, touched and kneaded each other until she was frantic. "Please," she said, taking him in her hand and placing him between her thighs. She touched her tongue to his, and nibbled his kiss-swollen lower lip. "I need you," she said.

From the flashing depths of his eyes there was no doubt he needed her, too.

"Let me get some protection," he said with a bedroom-husky voice.

"Not necessary. My tubes are tied," she said, pulling him closer.

He cocked his head as if momentarily surprised, but it didn't stop Phil from seizing the moment and making her needful wishes his complete command.

CHAPTER SIX

STEPHANIE crawled out of her postsex haze and glanced at the surfing god beside her. She couldn't believe what she'd just done—she'd slept with a man after only knowing him for a couple of weeks. Was she out of her mind?

She'd let him tug her down the hall to his bedroom and have his way with her. Now nestled in the crook of his arm, she blinked. Come to think of it, she'd pretty much had her way with him, too. Maybe that was the freedom that having her tubes tied had finally given her. She'd never forget this night, no matter what happened next, and that realization felt great.

He definitely knew how to satisfy a woman, yet he was anything but mechanical or practiced. What they'd shared had been nothing short of fan-bleeping-tastic. When he'd filled her, she'd let herself go with basic instincts and savored each and every sensation coiling tighter and tighter until release had torpedoed through her. Now feeling like a huge mound of jelly, she admitted how much she'd needed this. How glad she was he'd taken her there.

They snuggled warmly in the center of his king-sized bed, lights dimmed, breathing roughly, completely satisfied. Now that he'd had her, he still hadn't lost interest.

No. He folded her into his chest—his muscular chest brushed with light brown swirls and curls—and stroked her hair. She loved the soap-and-sex smell of his skin and marveled at how smooth it was and how substantial he felt. She smiled against his chest, her hand on his upper thigh. Phil was definitely substantial.

His fingers lightly played with her matted hair, sending chills over her shoulders. She'd thought she was tingled out, but his touch settled that debate. When she looked up at him, a grin was on his flushed face. He'd had a workout, too.

It had been so long since she'd been with anyone, wasn't this the point where the first-time lovers were supposed to feel awkward and clumsy? She felt anything but as she shared a completely contented smile with him. There wasn't a hint of regret in his clear-as-the-sky eyes.

"I've been fascinated with your hair since the moment I met you," he said, honey-voiced, giving her shivers all over again.

Truth was she'd been fascinated with his hair, too. She'd loved digging her fingers into it and kissing him hard and rough as they'd rolled around his bed. She liked the thickness, and how there was so much to tug and hold on to. She'd even tasted it when he'd covered her with his compact, muscular body and brought her to orgasm.

"Same here," she said.

He laughed. "You like my hair?"

She nodded, digging her fingers into his scalp, further mussing the dark blond cloud of hair. He grinned before sudden concern changed his expression. His crescent-shaped eyes grew wide.

"Damn. Robbie! I'd better go check on him."

He jumped out of bed and pulled on his jeans but not before she enjoyed the view of his sinewy back and handsome behind. He had an obvious tan line left over from summer from surfer-styled trunks.

While he was gone, she stared at the high, beamed ceiling and thought how romantic his French country-style bedroom was. The man had had impeccable taste when it had come to choosing this house. There had to be more to him than met the thoroughly satisfied eye.

He'd also made her feel like a complete woman again. Wow. She stretched and arched in the comfy bed, senses still heightened, enjoying the finely woven sheets against her back. She could get used to this kind of escape. And wasn't that what this two-month job was? An escape from all things?

Phil returned, his smile wide, sexy. "He's still asleep." He stripped and jumped back under the covers with her. "Now, where did we leave off?" He nuzzled her neck and ran a cool hand across her breast. Even if she tried, she couldn't stop her response.

The deliciously warm current he'd started with his fingertips rolled right to her center and, as quickly as that, she was ready for him again.

Robbie's nap ended much too soon, if you asked Phil. He'd have liked to spend the rest of the night making sexy memories with Stephanie on the best Thanksgiving of his life. But Robbie was awake and protesting by banging on his bedroom door.

"Pill! Whar you?"

"Hang on, Robbie, I'll be right there."

"Don't let him see me in here," Stephanie whispered.

"Okay." He took one last glance at her creamy skin

and, yep, her nipples were the same color as her freckles, except, thanks to his attentions, everything about her was much rosier now. He'd have to make a mental snapshot because he had a kid banging on the door.

He hopped into his jeans and strode toward the door, then opened it just enough to squeeze through. "What's up, little dude?"

"I'm hungwee."

"Again?" Phil ruffled Robbie's already messy hair and led him to the kitchen. He smiled at how the boy had put his glasses on lopsided, and how his round belly pushed against the sleeper. The kid was a total wreck, but still managed to look cute.

Did I just use cute *in a sentence?*

He cut up a piece of pumpkin pie, poured him a glass of milk, and sat him at the kid-size plastic table Roma had left. When he was sure Robbie was preoccupied enough with eating, he slipped back down the hall to check on Stephanie's progress.

She'd put her underwear back on, and the sight of her long torso and shapely legs gave him another pang of pure desire. He couldn't wait to unload Robbie back on Roma and his father. If all went well, they'd arrive home tomorrow, and his bachelor life would finally be back to normal.

"Here you go," he said, handing her the clothes he'd found across the room.

"Thanks."

There was still fire in those dilated pupils, and it took a lot of restraint to keep from grabbing her and throwing her on the bed again. If he was lucky, he'd have six more weeks of great sex with Stephanie—a gift he hadn't expected when they'd hired the locum.

He liked her pumpkin-colored top just fine, but it

looked so much better discarded on the floor. And would he ever take those great legs for granted? Not in six weeks, he wouldn't.

Usually, once he'd been with a woman, he was fine with sending her home, preferring his alone time. But he wasn't anywhere near ready to say goodnight to Stephanie. And he still had Robbie to deal with.

"Can you stick around for another glass of wine or some coffee?"

"You know, I've scheduled that colposcopy for early tomorrow morning," she said, clasping the belt over her hips.

He was fascinated watching her, as if he'd never seen a woman dress before. "Then on Saturday night I want to take you to dinner."

She finished zipping her ankle boots, rushed him, and brushed his lips with a moist kiss. "I'd like that."

The simple gesture set off another distracting wave of desire. O-*kay*. They had a great thing going, with no strings attached, and as far as he could tell, they were on the same page.

Stephanie willed all the crazy thoughts about the huge mistake she'd made out of her head. By the time her sex-with-Phil high had subsided this morning, she'd realized her blunder. She'd given herself a pep talk on the drive in to the clinic on Friday. Last night had been a one-time thing. She'd gotten carried away, that's all. Phil probably felt obligated to take her out to dinner. For her part, she'd blame it on that evil sweet-tasting red wine she'd imbibed and the sexy wonders of Phil. Heck, she'd already accepted his invitation for dinner on the weekend and, considering his allure, it would be extra-hard to tell him there wouldn't be a repeat bedroom performance.

Old habits were hard to break, and there was comfort in safety. Why couldn't she figure out what to do?

Celeste Conroy lay on the examination table, prepared for the special procedure. As she'd done countless times before, Stephanie used the colposcope to examine the area of cervix in question and to take a small biopsy.

It only took five minutes.

"You may feel some cramping today. Take it easy. No lifting or straining for a couple of days, and no sex for a week."

The mention of sex sent her mind back to last night with Phil, making her ears burn. She shook her head, hoping to stop the X-rated visions on the verge of materializing in her mind as she made her last few notations on the patient chart.

Celeste, as always, had a slew of questions, and Stephanie was grateful for the distraction.

"I'll need a week to get the results," Stephanie answered, "and I'll call the minute I get them."

The busy morning postponed her curiosity, but by lunchtime, when she still hadn't seen Phil, she asked Gaby.

"He's at the airport, picking up his parents."

He'd made it clear he wanted to take their acquaintance to a whole new level once his parents took Robbie off his hands. The thought made her insides scramble up with anxiety yet excited her at the same time. Soon an unsettled feeling had her finding the nearest mirror and taking a good long look.

Make up your mind, Bennett. Either go for a fling

or keep your distance. Don't leave it up to Phil to decide.

Hadn't she given herself permission to let go last night? And hadn't the results been beyond any fantasy she could have dreamed up? After a long inhalation, a tiny smile curved her lips. She had six more weeks in Santa Barbara before she'd be back in her world—why not totally escape from all things Stephanie? And, besides, she'd had her tubes tied—there was nothing to worry about.

The thought of pursuing a carefree romance with Phil launched a wave of flittering wings in her stomach. Did she have the guts to carry it out?

Well, if this didn't take the prize. If Phil hadn't been so worried about his dad he'd be frustrated by having to hold on to Robbie for a couple more days. The layover at the airport had made Carl sick and Roma had taken him directly to the hospital once they'd landed. He'd picked up a nasty bug and was already showing signs of dehydration. The big iron man Phil had grown up admiring looked far too human in the hospital bed, and it sent a weary wave of dread down his spine.

"I'll keep Robbie for the weekend or until you feel ready to take over," Phil said to Roma.

She sat at her husband's bedside, her dark hair heavily streaked with silver, holding his hand. "If you could bring Robbie by later today, I'd really appreciate it. I miss him so much."

"Go, Roma. You don't have to sit here watching me sleep," Carl said. "Go and see Robbie."

She gave Phil a questioning gaze. How different Roma was from his mother, who'd left when things got tough. His mother's action had jaded Phil and had planted a lifelong mistrust of women. They couldn't be counted on to stick around, so why get serious? Roma broke the mold, but she was the exception.

"Come with me," he said. "Robbie can't wait to see you. I'll drop you back here on my way home."

It dawned on Phil that his fabulous weekend plans, with the hottest lady he'd met in forever, would get put on hold. Again.

Once he sorted things out with Roma and Robbie, he'd give Stephanie a call to give her a heads-up. Either she'd be willing to let Robbie tag along for dinner or they'd take a rain check, but there was no way he'd leave Robbie with a babysitter. The kid would be disappointed enough knowing his mom was back in town yet he still couldn't go home.

How did you explain such a thing to a kid? He'd step back and let Roma do the chore, see how a pro handled it, and maybe learn something.

Later, after he'd heard the latest doctor's report on his father and Robbie was preoccupied with building blocks and making his version of the world's tallest building, or so he'd announced with extra esses and saliva, Phil thought about Stephanie. He thought about how much he'd enjoyed spending Thanksgiving with her, and especially how great it had been to make love to her. And he thought how he'd like to do it again. Soon. But he had to look after the squirt.

So why was there a smile on his face? Because the kid really was a great source of entertainment.

After several attempts, Robbie had made it to ten blocks high, but he'd jumped up and down, knocking the top block off again. Phil stifled a laugh when he glimpsed the expression of frustration cross the boy's face. Phil had to hand it to him, the kid didn't quit. He picked up the same block and balanced it on top of the others, then went hunting for several more.

Phil took the opportunity to call Stephanie. Hearing her soft voice on the phone, it occurred to him how much he'd missed seeing her today, and just how disappointed he was about canceling their plans.

"Looks like I'll be keeping the kid brother for the weekend," he said on a resigned sigh. Though she'd made real progress being around Robbie on Thanksgiving, he wanted her all to himself the first time he took her out to dinner.

Phil felt compelled to give her the whole story about his father's illness, flight home, and current status. Once he'd filled her in they'd settled into an easy conversation, and as Robbie was still erecting the west-coast version of the Empire State building, he kept talking.

Hell, he'd had sex with the woman. They knew each other intimately now. And though completely out of character, he wanted to take the opportunity to get to know her even better.

"Do you have a minute to talk?" he asked. How busy could a person be in a hotel room?

"Sure," she said.

The problem was that, if he wanted to learn more about her, he'd have to talk about himself. Should he take the risk?

He glanced at Robbie, who'd now moved on to scribbling with crayons in his newest coloring book from Hawaii, and decided what the heck.

"It's been bugging me. I mean, how does a doctor with an aversion to kids wind up being an obstetrician?"

To her credit, she blurted out a laugh instead of taking offense. Though maybe she sounded a little nervous? "I guess it does seem odd, and please don't get me wrong,

I love delivering babies. It's just…well, pregnancy and delivery is one thing, and child rearing is another."

"See, now, that's where I get tripped up," Phil said, trying hard to understand her elusive explanation. "It's been my experience that people usually go into a specialty profession because it's their passion. For instance, I chose medicine because of my mother."

Maybe it was the fact that his dad was sick and in a hospital, looking all too frail. Maybe it was because, even after professing to hate his mother all these years, he still missed her, but she'd been on his mind today.

"Your mother wanted you to become a pulmonologist?"

"Actually, she never knew, because I stopped talking to her."

Phil wasn't ready to tell Stephanie the whole story, that he'd been in Australia at a surfing championship when his father had been diagnosed with lymphoma the first time—and that his mother's leaving turned his life upside down. It had made him quit the surfing circuit at twenty to care for his dad and, eventually, head back to school.

"I'm so sorry to hear that, Phil."

He'd confused her. He sensed honest compassion in Stephanie's voice and it felt like a forgiving breath; made him want to be honest with her. Maybe he did owe her an explanation.

"My dad had lymphoma, and when he first got diagnosed, my mother walked out on us. She couldn't deal with his disease. Evidently she didn't give a damn about me either because I never got to say goodbye."

"Oh, God, how awful."

Phil hadn't meant to turn their conversation in this maudlin direction, he'd just wanted to keep her on the phone a little longer, but here he was stripping down barriers and letting the new girl on the block know about the secret of his mother. He could count back ten girlfriends and know for sure they'd never had a clue about his family or whether either of his parents was alive or dead. So why had he opened up to Stephanie?

"Yeah, I haven't talked to her since. I don't have a clue if she knows I'm a doctor or not."

"I see." She sounded suddenly distant.

As he'd gone completely out of character, he decided to get something else off his chest.

"Stephanie, this is a really weird question, but something I noticed yesterday made me wonder if you have a child." The way she'd put Robbie into his pajamas and had left the bedroom door ajar. A novice like himself wouldn't know to do that without being told. But not Stephanie.

She inhaled sharply.

He kicked himself for bringing up the subject. "Are you okay?"

"Yes. Sorry. You caught me off guard, that's all."

He sighed. "Didn't mean to," he said, regretting having mentioned it.

She swallowed. "You and I have something in common."

"How so?"

"You never got to say goodbye to your mother, and I never got to say goodbye to my son."

"Stephanie…" In that moment, he wanted to put down the phone, to crawl inside, and come out the other end. He wanted nothing more than to console her. She had lost a child. "I'm sorry if I—"

"That's okay, Phil. I need to get off the phone now

anyway. I'll see you at work," she said, not giving him a chance to say another word.

Confused, he scrubbed his face. All he wanted was an uncomplicated romance, but having lived thirty-five years and dated for twenty of them, he knew there was no such thing.

When Stephanie arrived at work on Monday morning, all the nurses were abuzz with news about the yacht decorations. Gaby had used the office petty cash to purchase six small fake Christmas trees. "They all came complete with lights!" she said animatedly. "Now all we have to do is anchor them on the yacht."

"Great!" Amy said. "And I found my grandmother's decorations from the old country, and my lederhosen still fit!"

Another nurse chimed in. "I've got a bunch of Philippine Christmas lanterns we can use for one of the trees, too."

Stephanie did her usual fading into the woodwork rather than join in.

Claire appeared, honey-blonde hair pulled back into a long swishy ponytail and green eyes bright with excitement. "Sounds great, guys. Bring everything this Saturday for the decorating party." She saw Stephanie and waved her over. "You're coming, right?"

Stephanie had been keeping a safe distance from the clinic employees. Why get too involved when she was only going to be around for a couple of months? What was the point? Up until this moment she'd planned to blow off the Christmas yacht party, but how could she say no and not appear to be antisocial?

"Um, sure." And, besides, it would give her a chance to see Phil in a perfectly safe environment, one where she couldn't get swept off her resolve to keep a distance.

"Great! I'll send the directions to your email." Claire glanced at her watch and strode for the stairs to her second-floor office. "Talk later."

Well, hell, she'd already had sex with Phil, why not get to know everyone else a little better, too?

The nurses continued to rabbit on about decorating the yacht and what fun it always was as Stephanie smiled and made her way toward her office. After spending an ultra-quiet weekend, she had to admit that she enjoyed the hustle and bustle of the clinic, and with the official invitation now she looked forward to the plans for the coming weekend.

When later that morning Phil loomed in her doorway, her gut clenched. It was the first time she'd seen him since they'd made love. Her heart stumbled over the next couple of beats. He looked amazing with his hair freshly washed and combed straight back. She'd come to notice that however it fell, it stayed, and it always looked great. He'd probably expect further explanation about her weird reaction on the phone on Friday night. She wasn't ready to give it.

"Hey," he said, obviously waiting to be invited in.

"Hi. What's up?" Did her face give her hopeful thoughts away? Was he here to invite her out to lunch or, better yet, a quiet dinner with just the two of them—like the one she'd so looked forward to last weekend? If he did, she hoped he'd keep all conversation superficial.

He carried a large specialty coffee drink in each hand and placed one on her desk. "It's a pumpkin latte. Thought you might like it."

"Thanks." Why did the thoughtful gesture touch her so? Why did it feel so intimate? Before she'd gotten strange on the phone the other night, they'd embarked on a new line of communication. The man had opened up about his mother and because she'd been thinking about Justin after being around Robbie, she'd gone overboard with her response. It must have seemed so strange and out of the blue that she wouldn't have been surprised if he'd avoided her, yet here he was bringing her a drink.

He sat on the edge of her desk and studied her. If the morning sun was brighter than she'd ever seen it, and there wasn't a cloud on the horizon, that's what she imagined the color would be, and it was right there in his eyes.

"So Robbie's going to stay with me the rest of this week, until my dad gets discharged from the hospital." He sounded worn out, like he'd had a super-hard weekend.

As she gazed at him, grateful he hadn't probed more about her son, she caught the telltale signs of sleep deprivation. It looked as if ashes had been faintly smudged beneath his eyes, and his voice sounded huskier than usual. Watching his brother had taken its toll, but Phil wasn't complaining. For a guy who professed to keep things easy and uncomplicated, he'd proved to be deeper than that. And though she wasn't in the market for anything permanent with Phil, this side of his character helped her trust him.

Before he left, he bent over and dropped a sweet kiss on her lips. The simple gesture invited chills. He tasted like pumpkin latte, and after he'd left, she enjoyed sipping her drink and thinking of Phil's kisses for the rest of the afternoon.

Phil had finally gotten Robbie down for the night. All he wanted to do was talk to Stephanie. She'd lost a child and was trying to put her life together. She could use a friend at a time like this, yet she'd chosen to leave the desert during the holidays and spend Christmas with strangers in Santa Barbara.

The last thing he could call himself was a stranger to her, not after their intense lovemaking session the other night. The crazy thing was, it wasn't just about sex with Stephanie. He genuinely liked her. So why not call her, just to talk? The thought made him smile. It reminded him of how in high school he used to have to work up an excuse to call a girl when he liked her. But that had been back in a time of innocence, back when his heart had been eager to fall in love, back when he'd still trusted the opposite sex…back before his mother had walked out.

Yikes, he'd put himself into a lousy mood, and now he needed to call Stephanie to cheer himself up. So that made two reasons, more than enough to make the call.

Robbie came running down the hall in his pajamas. Before Phil had put him to bed, Robbie had talked to his mother and had cried a little. It almost broke Phil's heart. The kid had to settle for second best with him when all he wanted was to sleep in his own bed and get a good-night kiss from his parents. Carl was still in recovery mode, and Roma had her hands full. If Robbie went home too soon, he might feel neglected, and get his feelings hurt.

"I thought I already put you to bed," he said.

"Furgot sumtin'." Robbie used his short, pudgy arms to pull Phil close and tell him, "Wuv you."

Without thinking, Phil kissed him on the forehead. "Back at ya, little dude. Now, skedaddle back to bed."

Robbie giggled and ran off.

A scary feeling crept over Phil. It had felt nice to kiss his kid brother and, yep, he'd miss him when he was gone.

He stroked his jaw. Maybe he should get a dog.

All the cozy feelings and thoughts about having another warm, living, breathing body share his house boggled his mind. It gave him a third excuse for calling Stephanie—distraction!

"Hey, what's up?" he said, when she answered after the second ring.

"Hi!" Her welcoming tone pushed all his worries aside. All he wanted to do was talk about her day.

After chatting superficially for a while, he realized the real point of his call. He wanted more one-on-one time with Stephanie. Just before hanging up, he said, "And tomorrow lunch is on me."

She answered without hesitation. "Okay. If the weather's nice, maybe we can eat outside."

If he could conjure up warm weather and sunshine for tomorrow he would, but he already felt the equivalent of a sunny day right there—he rubbed the spot—in his chest. "Sounds like a plan."

The next day, though the sky was blue, temperatures were low. Phil and Stephanie wore jackets and set off for the shore anyway. He'd ordered a hearty fish chowder and sourdough rolls from the best deli in town, and carried it in a warming bag with one hand. He longed to place his other arm around her waist but, not wanting to put any pressure on her, he withstood the urge.

He hadn't figured out yet where they stood. The other night he'd been positive she was interested in a no-strings fling for the duration of her stay in Santa Barbara. Since that night—the hottest night he could remember—Stephanie had partially rebuilt that invisible barrier. He knew it had something to do with that weird comment she'd made about not getting to say goodbye to her baby.

He shook his head. The day was too beautiful to try to figure things out. And since when did he get all caught up in really "knowing" a woman? All he knew was that right now the sun danced off the golden highlights in Stephanie's hair, making it look like a shiny copper penny. She smiled whenever she looked at him, and if he didn't get pushy about it, he might just get another kiss before they headed back to the clinic.

They found a bench along the bike path with a shoreline view and sat. She squinted from the bright sun and had to slip on her sunglasses, covering those gorgeous caramel-candy eyes. He was glad to see the smile never left her face.

The simple fact they had time alone together had sparks flying and itchy messages flowing through the circuit board of his body. He'd much rather strip her naked than hand her a cup of soup, but he kept his true desire at bay, and when she took the first taste he received a smile of orgasmic proportions, and that smile was definitely worth his efforts.

Stephanie wasn't very talkative today, but that was okay. He was happy to be with her. Just before he finished dunking the edge of his roll into the last of his soup, his cell phone rang. It was Roma.

"They're going to discharge your dad this afternoon, so I won't be able to pick up Robbie."

"I'll make arrangements," Phil said, realizing he'd gotten pretty blasé about carpools and favors and paybacks with the other mothers from the preschool. They all seemed to really get a kick out of the "cool" surrogate dad on campus. Normally, he would have played the distinction to the hilt. He'd flirt, use them for all the favors they could offer, and maybe even find out if any of the moms were single. But out of respect for his kid brother, he'd done the right thing by taking care of him and hadn't abused the special circumstances.

And, besides, he'd been completely preoccupied with Stephanie.

"Do you want me to keep him tonight, so you and Dad can get settled?"

"That would be wonderful," she said, after an obvious sigh of relief.

Stephanie looked at him as if he were a superhero or something. In that moment he admitted it: he might just miss the kid once he went home. Maybe…just a little.

He flipped through his contacts on the phone and made a quick call. "Hey, Claire, can you do me a huge favor and pick up Robbie today when you get Gina?" After almost two weeks, he finally understood the bartering side of child care. "Thanks, and I'll drop her off at your house from day care after I get off work."

Stephanie's arms flew around his neck and she planted a cold kiss on his cheek. It wasn't the sexy kind of kiss he'd been hoping for, but he wouldn't complain. He turned the angle of his face so their lips could meet, and dropped a peck on her mouth. This was all way too affectionate for his taste. He preferred sexy and hot, but the weirdest thing was, he kind of liked it.

"I guess we better be getting back to the clinic," he said. "Looks like Robbie and I are roommates for one more night."

CHAPTER SEVEN

THURSDAY morning lab results planted a rock-size knot firmly into Stephanie's stomach. Celeste Conroy's biopsy showed squamous cell carcinoma. After last Thursday and Thanksgiving, Maria was back today, sitting on the other side of Stephanie's desk, waiting expectantly for the day's assignment.

"Well," Stephanie said, handing the printed pathology report to the RNP student. "This is a perfect example of what makes this job a challenge."

"Wow," Maria said. "She's pregnant, right? How do you handle something like this?"

"I tell her the truth. We need to find out how extensive the cancer is and I'll need to do a conization of her cervix."

She'd remove a thick cone-shaped wedge of tissue from the area in question of the cervix, extending high into the cervical canal. Her goal would be to leave a wide margin of normal cells around the area of cancer.

"Risks?" Maria queried.

"Yes, but we must always balance them against the benefits. I'll do everything in my power to keep both the mother and the baby healthy." Stephanie glanced over her calendar for the earliest possible appointment. "I want to do the biopsy on Monday so I can get this mother-to-be some good news before Christmas." She shuddered, thinking of all the potential possibilities, and willed a positive attitude.

"Would it be okay if I came in to observe?" Maria patted her protruding pregnancy as worry lines etched her brow.

"Of course."

Stephanie's pulse had worked its way into her mouth. She punched in the phone number, willing her quivery hand to settle down, then cleared her throat. She needed to sound confident when she gave the diagnosis, for the patient's sake.

Stephanie couldn't believe the choreographed chaos on Saturday morning at the harbor. Even halfway down the harbor she could hear lively Christmas music over the loudspeaker. The pungent sea air seemed to heighten her senses, making her feel alive and excited. She stopped in midstep, having never seen a more gorgeous boat. As promised, everyone from the clinic had showed up with their contribution. She'd even made an extra effort to buy several strings of Christmas lights for the yacht.

Jason greeted her with a captain's smile and waved her aboard. Before she boarded, she noticed the name on the bow—*For Claire*. Something about that special touch pinched at her heart. She'd heard bits and pieces about Claire and Jason's love affair. It hadn't been easy for either of them to admit they'd fallen in love, yet now they made a perfect couple. She shook her head. Why were people so slow to figure things like that out?

"This is my latest indulgence," Jason said, grinning and patting the rail. "I wanted to upgrade, anyway."

Claire, wearing a teal-colored windbreaker and

matching ball cap, with her long ponytail sticking out the hole in the back, stood at his side, smiling up at him. "He made sure there were plenty of shady spots when he designed this boat, because of my lupus. Come on, I'll show you around."

Amy and Gaby worked diligently on placing the small Christmas trees at key positions on the bow, stern, port, and starboard. Other nurses and aides helped stabilize and decorate them. They waved hello, and the simple greeting made Stephanie feel like part of the clinic family. Maybe it would have happened sooner if she'd reached out to them. Well, better late than never.

Just when Claire was about to take Stephanie below deck, she saw Phil rushing down the dock with a huge pink box in his arms. He waved at her and smiled, and her insides got jumbled up. Jason met him dockside and shook his hand.

"I brought doughnuts," Phil said.

"Yay," Amy said, as Gaby applauded.

"I'm making cocoa," Claire called over her shoulder, leading Stephanie by the arm down to the galley. Stephanie was grateful for the distraction to buy time to straighten out her suddenly fuzzy thoughts.

Wow. Stephanie had never seen a more modern galley on a boat. Granted, her experience with boats was woefully limited, but still. Stainless-steel appliances, perfectly stained woodwork and cupboards; the compact galley oozed class.

As Claire stirred a huge pot of milk, adding cocoa liberally, she seemed her usual self from work, but more relaxed and completely carefree. "I'd never been on a sailboat until I met Jason. Now I'm ready to give up my practice, homeschool Gina, and sail around the world with him." A soft laugh gently bubbled out. "Don't worry, we won't quit our day jobs. Too many people need us at that clinic, and I love it there. But maybe someday…"

"You must take some great weekend getaways," Stephanie said, gathering the red paper cups decorated with wreaths and garland trim and placing them on a large tray.

"Not as often as we'd like, but we have plans for a longer trip this summer. Thought we'd sail up to San Francisco and back."

"Wow," Stephanie said. "That's impressive." She held the tray close so Claire could ladle out the cocoa into the cups then she shook the whipped cream can and sprayed a dollop on top of each.

"If all goes well, maybe the year after we'll set sail for Hawaii."

"Sounds like a dream come true."

Before she could say more, a familiar bedroom-sexy voice vibrated from the doorway into the main saloon. "You ladies need a hand?" Phil hung in the doorway, opening up his broad chest, cutting a V down to a trim waist. Her throat went dry, so strong was her reaction, and she suddenly needed a sip of cocoa. "I think we've got this covered."

She did her best to act casual, as if the mere presence of the man didn't scatter her nerves.

He jabbed a thumb over his shoulder. "The folks have already eaten most of the doughnuts, but I saved you ladies a couple."

"Thanks. We'll be right up," Claire said, oblivious to the caveman-sexy gaze streaming from Phil's sea-blue eyes and directed at Stephanie.

How in the world would she make it through the day without mauling the man?

She'd been losing sleep, having hot and restless dreams of tussling in bedsheets with a strange man. The dreams had been so realistic; she could practically feel the man's weight on her body, driving himself into her. Hell, she knew exactly who the guy was. Phil. One time she'd woken up with the covers on the floor, throbbing thighs, sheets wadded in her fists, panting, and *very* frustrated. How in the world should she handle her desire where Phil was concerned?

They were both adults—why not enjoy each other?

Later, as she and Phil put the finishing touches on the mainsail Christmas lights, she jumped at his touch.

"Sorry," she said, as electricity powered through her veins.

"You seem a bit flinchy," he said, drilling her with a stare.

"I'm just a little uptight with all the new patients and work and all."

Phil lowered his voice and lifted her hair, hooking it behind one ear. "It's Christmastime, pretty baby, loosen up." The raucous version of *Rockin' Around the Christmas Tree* nearly drowned out his words. "You know, a little TLC might be just the thing you need."

A vision of tender loving care, compliments of Phil, whirled through her mind. She couldn't breathe for a second. He'd spoken the words she'd been afraid to acknowledge. He seemed to know exactly what she'd been thinking, and now her cheeks were probably betraying her by blushing hot pink. She glanced around the busy deck. Fortunately, everyone seemed oblivious to them.

Why not? Why the hell not have a fling? Was she such a wretched person that she didn't deserve a little pleasure in life? Phil had already proved what a fantastic lover he was. He hadn't pushed her into doing anything she hadn't wanted to. Hell, she'd come up with all kinds of ideas in her dreams lately. It could be fun to try them out...with Phil.

Did she really want to balance on the precipice of sexual frustration for another month, or slide back into that incredible place he'd taken her before?

How many times did she need to give herself permission to live?

Her cheeks flamed and her palms tingled, thinking about it. Slowly, she glanced into his darkening and decidedly sexy stare.

"Robbie went home last night," he said, eyes never wavering from hers. "And I owe you that dinner out. What about tonight?"

What about tonight? She knew what he meant, what he wanted.

He'd sounded the same when he'd made love to her. Phil's voice, full of intimate intention, massaged her rising senses, snapping to life key areas and a powerful drive to scratch the itch with him.

So strong was her physical reaction that if everything else could just disappear, she'd be on him, knocking him down and ripping off his clothes right this instant.

Nearly trembling with desire, she found her voice, if only a whisper. "Yes. Tonight."

That evening, Stephanie had talked herself down from the frantic sexual cliff, but excitement still washed over every cell in her body. She couldn't wait to see Phil again, to be alone with him. The permission she'd given herself to be with him had been so incredibly freeing.

He picked her up at her hotel looking impeccable. He wore a perfectly tailored sport coat, dark slacks, and a pale blue shirt open at the collar. Did he realize how the color brought out his eyes? His hair, brushed back from his forehead, curled beneath his earlobes. And that smile—did she stand a chance resisting it? She didn't want to!

She'd rushed to the Paseo after they'd finished decorating the boat that afternoon and bought a little black dress. Now, standing before his scrutinizing eyes, she tugged at the skirt with shaky hands. Maybe tonight's seduction wouldn't be as easy as she'd fantasized. She didn't want her nerves to ruin things.

"Wow," he said. "You look spectacular."

His reaction nearly knocked her off her spiky heels. It was exactly what she'd wanted to hear. He liked what he saw, and that made her ecstatic. In her fantasy, she was a vamp, but here, in front of Phil, all she could say was, "Thanks."

His gaze lingered several moments then he scanned from her hair to her brightly polished toes. As if his head was a glass globe, she could practically see his thoughts. He liked what he saw and wanted to indulge. Just as quickly, he snapped out of the spell.

"I hope you've got a warm coat," he said, brushing a light kiss across her cheek. Man, he smelled as good as he looked. "We'll be eating outside."

What did she care? It would give her an excuse to cuddle up close to him.

They entered the restaurant, called Bouchon, through a shrubbery-hidden portal, and the first thing Stephanie noticed was shiny light wood floors. The decor was understated yet classy, utilizing matching light wood tables and chairs, and cream-colored tablecloths. Huge modern art canvases supplied needed color on the walls. Her first impression was that the total dining effect was as warm and welcoming as Phil's hand pressing against hers.

Phil seemed to know the proprietor of the restaurant and had gotten them a perfectly placed table on the patio. He guided her with his palm at her waist, the barely there pressure at her back already setting off chill rockets. Even though every seat was taken, their cozy corner felt as intimate as Phil's eyes. The brisk evening air mingled with radiant restaurant heat lamps to create the best of both outdoor and indoor worlds.

Stephanie inhaled and rolled her shoulders, inviting the long-overdue relaxation to settle in.

Phil's taste was flawless. The wine crisp from nearby vineyards, appetizers made from local farmers' market ingredients, and the main course free range from Santa Barbara microranches.

Stephanie savored the exquisite taste of plump sea scallops, sharing the appetizer with Phil and with a perfect glass of Chardonnay. He'd insisted she try the seared duck as her main course, the signature dish of the great chef. Who was she to argue?

He took her hand in his and gazed appreciatively into her eyes. "I'm really glad we finally got our date."

So this was what it had all come down to. She hadn't planned on sleeping with him on Thanksgiving, but hadn't regretted it for a second. She'd backtracked a bit from her permission, but seeing Phil as a whole person, committed to his job and connected to his family, drove her to know him more. The decision to take the moment by the horns and ride it for all it was worth, or walk away a frustrated and closed-off woman, remained in her hands.

She glanced at Phil, latticed moonlight shadows

making him all the more intriguing. The decision seemed obvious.

She couldn't help but smile as warm tingles worked their way through her insides. She could blame it on the wine and great food, but she knew better. Only Phil could set that kind of reaction twisting through her. Her decision final, she'd skip dessert at the restaurant, instead saving up for the special delights that Phil Hansen had to offer.

Three hours later, flat on her back, Stephanie lay panting, staring at the ceiling, flushed and tingling...everywhere! Phil should have a doctorate in making love.

Never in her life had she given in to her desires, completely exempt of expectations, and gone with her mood. Until now. With Phil. He had a way of drawing that out of her. She didn't feel tawdry about it, either. With him, making love came as naturally as breathing, and, boy, was she out of breath.

He nuzzled her neck, sending yet another wave of chills across her skin. "That was perfect," he said, husky and still revved up.

She slipped her arm across his torso and curled into his shoulder. Secure in his embrace, and content beyond words, she sighed. "We'll have to do this again sometime."

His devilish laugh vibrated through his chest. "Why not right now?" He got up on his elbows and looked deep into her eyes. "You're incredible, you know that?"

Did she know that? Had her husband ever told her she was incredible? They'd been in love once upon a time—she'd known that much for sure. When she'd become pregnant, she'd been happier than she'd ever been, but months later things had changed.

Her hand brushed over her abdomen, imagining the fallopian tubes she'd had tied off. She was safe. She'd never get pregnant again.

Phil's mouth pressed gently against her jaw. He glanced into her eyes again, as if he'd seen her secret fleeting thoughts. The next kiss he delivered was warm and caring. The tender gesture nearly split her heart.

She kissed him back, ragged and hard, her fingers digging into that glorious hair. If she was having a fling with Phil, she couldn't allow emotions or any feelings beyond passion and excitement to get in the way.

Sunday, after making her breakfast in bed—Phil had *been* breakfast—he talked her into hitting the beach for a game of volleyball.

She couldn't help but grin at the invitation. Surfing may be his turf, but volleyball was definitely hers. After a few warm-up shots, they *thwopped* the ball back and forth across the net. Her toes dug into the sand, the fresh sea breeze making her skin feel as vibrant and warm as Phil's touch had the night before, as warm as the sun heating her scalp and shoulders. Phil popped a ball off his fingertips, and out of reflex she spiked it over the net, hitting him smack between the eyes. Shock quaked through her body as she rushed to him.

He rubbed his nose, looking dazed. "Great shot, Bennett!"

After she made sure he was okay, the surprised look on his face set her off laughing. She crumpled to her knees, overcome with the giggles.

He swooped her up into his arms and ran toward the water. Weak with laughter, she didn't protest, until he ran knee-deep into a wave and tossed her into the chilly ocean. Her scream was cut short by salt water. Once she regained her bearings, she chased Phil toward the beach and made a poor excuse for a tackle, only managing to grab his ankles and falling flat.

This carefree feeling felt as foreign as having that ocean, crashing and constant, in Palm Desert. She welcomed the new sensation, breathing deeper and feeling more vital than she had in years.

He broke away from her grasp and sat back on his ankles, grinning. His high-pitched laugh and corny smile egged her on. She crawled toward him and threw her arms around his neck then planted a wet and salty kiss on his mouth. Though clumsy at first, the kiss soon turned passionate, his hands wandering, holding her as if he never wanted to let go. With their lips smashing and tongues mingling, she thought how close to heaven it felt being here on the beach with Phil. How he managed to wipe away her worries with a single heart-stopping kiss.

As they rolled around, their kisses became invaded by sand, and soon her sexy moment turned to awareness that every crease and crevice of her body was sticky with beach grit. And after he'd made the same discovery, they lay side by side, flat on their backs, laughing together.

It seemed the playboy of Santa Barbara had resuscitated her life. Yeah, to use his own words, their fling *was* just what the doctor had ordered.

After he'd taken her to the hotel to shower and clean up, they went to lunch at the yacht club. During a long walk along the seashore, Phil invited her to his house again. The memory of being lost in his body, oblivious to her thoughts, lured her back to his bed.

Though anything but rehearsed, their lovemaking became more familiar. They'd explored each other's bodies with abandon, and she'd delighted in discovering his sensitive spots. She loved the texture of his skin, so many shades darker than her own. The ease with which he responded to her touch made her smile. She felt as though she could weave magic with him, especially when he was deep inside her, expertly guiding her to her final release.

Sex with Phil was nothing short of enchanting, and she hoped to stay under the spell for as long as she stayed in Santa Barbara.

Once completely sated, she flopped limply on top of him, and lifted her hair from her hot and sticky shoulders.

He blew lightly on her neck. "Stay with me tonight."

Reality checked back in. "I can't. I've got to be well rested for the conization tomorrow morning."

"Come back tomorrow night, then," he murmured, his hand playing with tendrils of her hair.

"I thought you were a love-'em-and leave-'em kind of guy?" Her true thought about his reputation had tumbled out before she could censure it.

In one quick move, he grabbed her and flopped her onto her back. Settling himself between her thighs, he gazed confidently into her face. "I'm just getting started with you."

It wasn't the most romantic thing she'd ever heard, yet, as he nibbled her earlobe, it thrilled her just the same. He hadn't grown tired of her yet, and, heaven knew, she wasn't even close to getting bored with him. Couldn't imagine it. Yet she wasn't as easily lured into his spell this time. Her mind wandered.

As life and her job wedged into her thoughts, she switched to the practical side of her life, and pragmatic words followed. "How does it work with you? How do you know when it's time to move on?"

The leftover fairy dust from their heated sex vanished.

He rolled onto his back and stared at the ceiling. "Where'd that come from?"

"I'm curious. That's all."

He rose up onto one elbow. "I'm not nearly as callous as my reputation."

"I didn't call you callous. All I did was ask how you know when a 'fling' is over."

He took her hand and kissed her fingers, cleverly diverting her attention. "Let's just say I'm nowhere near that with you."

The perfect answer from a master. He was a playboy after all, and she couldn't forget it.

Stephanie saw so much potential with Phil, yet he seemed a man of contradictions. Regardless of his stereotypical-playboy dating pattern, he lived in a house perfect for a family. He liked to dawdle in the kitchen, and garden! And when push came to shove about looking after his kid brother, he'd proved himself worthy. Phil was full of potential. Not that she was looking for anyone. No. Not that he'd ever consider her for more than a few nights of great sex.

She glanced at him, as if seeing for the first time the truth of their bond. They had nowhere to go but here, his bed. She was thankful for him forcing her out of her shell, but reality had a mean spirit and it had just smacked her in the face.

Phil took her hand and kissed her fingertips.

How long would she be able to overlook his playboy ways? Would it tear her heart out when he lost interest and moved on? Would he have the courtesy to wait until she'd moved back to Palm Desert? He'd been evasive when she'd questioned him.

She glanced into his unwavering eyes. He smiled at her, but she couldn't return it, wondering instead if anyone would ever be able to tame him. These were not the thoughts of a woman having a fling. She shouldn't be concerned with them. Yet she was.

She fought off a wave of regret, refusing to let it blemish their fantastic weekend. Then with a sudden need to retreat back to her protective shell, to hide behind the medical profession, she kissed his forehead.

"I've got a big day tomorrow." With nothing further to say, she slipped out from under the sheets, gathered her clothes strewn across the floor and bedroom love seat, and padded toward the bathroom.

"I'll let myself out," she said.

CHAPTER EIGHT

PHIL rubbed his temples and squinted. What in the hell had just happened? He and Stephanie had had great sex over the weekend, he'd enjoyed every minute he'd spent with her, then whammo! She'd slipped back into stranger mode.

He sat at the bedside and gulped down a glass of water. His head pounded behind his temples. Sex was supposed to release endorphins, and they were supposed to make a guy feel great. And they had…until she'd withdrawn.

He thought of Stephanie wrapped in his arms one minute and gone the next. He wasn't sure what he wanted with her beyond what they already had—great fun, great sex, good times—but then what? She'd leave for the desert.

Buck naked, he paced the length of his bedroom. Give her a day to herself. Bring her lunch. Invite her for Chinese food after work another night. No pressure. He'd do what he did best—charm the hell out of a woman.

And though it would be hard, he'd keep his hands to himself, because he didn't want to lose what little ground he'd gained with her.

The Christmas lights parade was on Saturday, and he

hoped she'd be there. If the magic of Christmas couldn't break down the last of her barriers, nothing would.

He stopped in midpace and stared at his feet. Stephanie had given him the perfect opportunity to let another relationship slip away. Letting a woman loose had never bothered him. Over the years he'd learned new and creative ways to let his lady friends down gently. He'd buy them an expensive bracelet or necklace, tell them they deserved so much better than him. Yeah, he'd even stooped so low as to use his "busy career" as an excuse. And if he saw that special twinkle in the lady's eyes, he'd announce that he never wanted to be a father, even though in reality his own father meant the world to him.

There were always other women out there. But this time around he wanted Stephanie. Hell, he liked her. A lot. He thought about her lilting laugh when they playfully wrestled on his bed. Up close and personal, those tiny freckles bridging her nose turned him on more than he cared to admit. And her skin. Damn, she felt like velvet under his gardener's calluses. And she was a fantastic doctor. Everyone at the clinic had commented, now that she'd started mixing with them, on how well she fit in. Truth was, he liked the whole Stephanie Bennett package.

Complete silence echoed off the walls and drowned out his thoughts. He had to admit that at times like this he missed the thudding of Robbie's pudgy feet, and he definitely missed Stephanie Bennett in his bed.

Was this foreign feeling loneliness?

Maybe it was time to get a dog. In the meantime, he'd see if a football game was on TV.

On Monday morning, Christmas music streamed through the office speakers, grabbing Stephanie's attention. Gaby had obviously been busy decorating over the weekend. Maybe the boat-decorating party had put her in the mood. She'd set up a miniature Christmas village behind the reception window, complete with mock snow and twinkling lights. Wreaths hung at each doctor's door, and a banner wishing everyone a happy holiday was draped across the entryway to the waiting room.

The cheery atmosphere seemed contrary to what Stephanie had scheduled first thing that morning in the clinic. She got settled in her office and did a quick mental rundown of how the procedure would be carried out then noticed Maria standing expectantly in her doorway. She welcomed her in—having Maria as moral support was nice.

"I'm planning on doing a cold-knife conization. It may produce more bleeding than other procedures, but it doesn't obscure the surgical margins as much as the two other techniques, which is very important."

Stephanie drew a diagram for Maria. "While were there, I'm going to go ahead and perform a cerclage to minimize the bleeding and to protect from premature labor down the road." She sketched as Maria looked on, outlining how she planned to remove the wedge of tissue then stitch the cervix together to keep it tight until delivery.

"Amy is having Celeste sign the consent in the procedure room. Are you ready?"

Maria nodded, her espresso-brown eyes wide and intelligent. She tottered beside her as Stephanie made her way to the special-procedure room. Even though it seemed impossible for Maria's pregnant belly to look any bigger, it did, and Stephanie wondered how she could possibly hold out until her due date.

Stephanie greeted Celeste Conroy with a firm hand-shake as the patient reclined on the table with a paper shield across her lap and her feet in place in the stir-rups. Amy had already set her up for the cervical cone biopsy.

"You remember Maria Avila, the nurse practitioner student?"

Celeste gave permission for Maria to observe, and Stephanie was glad of the extra pair of hands.

Amy had given Celeste a mild sedative on her ar-rival and Stephanie administered a local cervical block. As they waited for it to take effect, Celeste had more questions.

"The consent said a lot of scary things," Celeste said. "Can they all happen?"

"The consents have to list every single possibility. Will they all happen? No. Will any of them happen? Not likely. Please don't let it scare you. The main thing I want to make sure about is the bleeding. Pregnancy increases blood flow to the uterus and cervix, so it might get tricky, but I'll be extra-careful."

"What if we don't get all of the cancer out with this procedure?"

"There is a very low risk that your lesion will prog-ress during the course of your pregnancy. My job is to remove it all today, and I'm confident I can. Let's take this one step at a time."

Reluctantly, Celeste agreed, and as the sedative wove its spell, she plopped her head back on the exam table and stared off into the distance. Stephanie could only imagine the thoughts she must be having.

Once the wedge of tissue was excised and placed in a specimen container, Stephanie used electrocautery to control the rapid local bleeding, then, as planned, performed the cervical cerclage.

"Maria, I'm going to assign you to Recovery. I want to watch Mrs. Conroy for the next four hours. Amy, will her husband be on hand to drive her home later?"

Amy nodded.

Stephanie ran down a long list of things Celeste needed to avoid for the next week, and wrote everything down. Knowing her patient had been sedated, she planned to go over everything again later when her husband was present and ready to take her home.

"Let me know if there's any unusual bleeding," Stephanie said to Maria on her way out.

"Will do."

Stephanie went about the rest of her morning clinic, only occasionally allowing Phil to slip into her thoughts. She wasn't looking for a husband or a future father. She'd gone that route and failed miserably, and had ensured she'd never be a mother again. All she wanted to do was put the pieces of her life back together, and maybe, while she was here, have a little fun. So if he was only a guy to have fun with, why was she thinking about him so much? Maybe it was because he'd turned out to be so great with Robbie. She'd seen him go from clueless to expert in less than two weeks. The guy had father potential written all over him. In a twisted sort of way, after she left, she hoped he'd find a woman who could give him a family one day.

"Dr. Bennett?" Amy interrupted her confusing thoughts. "Maria sent me to tell you that Mrs. Conroy has soaked through several pads already."

Alarm had Stephanie picking up her phone and dialing Jason Rogers's office. He met her at the patient's gurney, as she finished her examination.

"I need to cauterize more extensively, and then I'd like to admit the patient for overnight observation," she said.

"I'll call the hospital and tell them we're sending her," Jason said.

"I don't have privileges there, so I'll need you to admit her."

"No problem," he said. "Whatever you need."

Having such support and backup from her boss meant the world to her. And after the second round of cauterizing the wedge margins, the cervical bleeding already showed signs of slowing. Still, she couldn't be too careful with her patient, and, more importantly, with the pregnancy.

The transporters arrived, and Maria volunteered to ride over with Celeste so Stephanie could finish her clinic appointments. She'd head over to the hospital as soon as she was finished.

By the end of the day, Stephanie hadn't seen even a glimpse of Phil, and she figured if he was avoiding her she deserved it for pulling back and leaving without a proper goodbye. What did he expect? They really were nothing more than bed partners so she had no obligation to him. Then why did him avoiding her bother her so much? She bit her lip and sighed.

Because she cared about him.

"Is Dr. Bennett in?" Phil asked Gaby on his way into the clinic on Tuesday morning.

"She's at the hospital, discharging one of her patients."

He'd decided to ask her to lunch today, and was eager to see her again. When he got to his office and booted up his computer, a calendar alert popped up at the moment Jon strode through his door.

"You ready?" Jon asked.

Damn, he'd forgotten the symposium in Ventura he and Jon had signed up for months ago to attend together today.

So much for lunch with Stephanie.

On Wednesday, Phil got called into the E.R. for an emergency thoracentesis in the morning, and by the time he'd caught up with his patient load that evening, Stephanie had already left for the day.

He could give her a call and ask her out for dinner, but he knew how easy it was to blow someone off over the phone, so he decided to wait until Thursday morning when he could see her face-to-face.

On Thursday, when there was no sign of Stephanie at the clinic, Phil discovered through Jason that she'd been invited to the local university to speak to Maria's fellow nurse-practitioner students.

Things weren't looking good, and, though contrary to his natural desire to see her as soon as possible, he decided to wait until Saturday evening at the postholiday-parade party at Jason's house. He'd missed her all week, and wanted to iron out that wrinkle in their relationship, the unspoken knowledge about his dating history. He understood how it must look to a woman like Stephanie. He couldn't make any guarantees, of course, but she seemed worth delving deeper into—dared he use the word?—a relationship. He scraped his jaw. It wasn't just any girl he'd ask to help with the task he had planned.

This is nuts, Stephanie thought as she drove back to her hotel from the university. Maybe the move to Santa Barbara and starting to practice medicine again had been more stressful than she'd expected. Each night this week she'd been dead tired, and the springboard of emotions that getting to know Phil had created couldn't be denied. Maybe she was premenstrual? She rubbed her forehead and mentally did some math. It was December 9 and she was supposed to have started her period on December 2. She'd been like clockwork ever since she'd had her tubes tied. Today she felt a little foggy headed and maybe a little tender in her breasts. She'd probably get her period any day now.

But she was a week late, and hadn't so much as spotted.

She shook her head as she pulled into her parking space at the hotel. It had to be stress.

California had a reputation for perfect weather, and on this Saturday in mid-December, while the rest of the country dealt with snowstorms and arctic cold snaps, the sky was clear and the temperature was in the high sixties. Rain was predicted for early tomorrow morning, but you couldn't prove it by the sky overhead.

Stephanie shaded her eyes with her palm and enjoyed the sight of the setting sun over the glistening blue ocean, then took a deep breath of salty air as she walked down the docks to Jason's berth.

An hour earlier she'd come off the phone from a conversation with Celeste Conroy, who continued to improve since the bleeding scare earlier in the week. The best part of all was being able to tell her they'd successfully removed the small cancerous area on her cervix, and the tissue margins were all clear. If all continued to go well, the cerclage would keep her from going into premature labor later on.

Stephanie decided to compartmentalize her professional and personal life. With her duties as a physician completed today, she removed the mental stethoscope and…oh, hell…prepared to be Santa's helper. Nerves tangled in her stomach at the thought of confronting Phil after walking out on him the other night.

A memo had gone out at work, "Wear your most outrageous Christmas sweater," and she'd made a quick run to the Paseo to find something to fit the theme, but was too embarrassed to put it on until she got there.

Jason's yacht was decked out with the Midcoast Medical employees' handy Christmas decorations, and from this vantage point the boat promised, when lit up later, to thrill the spectators.

She smiled, even as her stomach fought off another wave of nervous flitters. She hadn't seen Phil all week except for fleeting moments coming and going at the clinic. She'd avoided his gaze once, and another time he made an abrupt turn and entered Jon's office. She'd failed miserably as fling material.

Claire waved and greeted her from the deck. An adorable curly-headed child with huge blue eyes stood by her side, and another baby, getting pushed back and forth in a stroller, sat plump and contentedly swaddled in extra blankets.

"This is my daughter, Gina," Claire said, then nodded toward the stroller. "And this is Jason Junior."

Looking more petulant than shy, Gina hugged her mother's thigh and buried her face rather than say hello. Claire smoothed the girl's hair with her free hand.

Stephanie gave herself a quick pep talk about not letting the children make her nervous. They were Claire's children, not hers, and from the look of it, Claire handled the job with aplomb. It was Christmas, a child's favorite time of year, and there was no way Stephanie could avoid missing her son, but just for today she vowed to not let it get her down. Just for today she'd let Christmas joy rub off on her and she'd smile along with everyone else on this festive occasion. Then, on Christmas Day, she would withdraw into her shell with her constant companion of grief.

She boarded the boat, her sweater in the original shopping bag, and almost immediately lost her balance when someone grabbed her knees. She reached for the boat rail and glanced down in time to hear a familiar squeal of hello. "Robbie, what are you doing here?"

"I get to thit on Thanta's knee," he said, pride beaming from his eyes.

"Me, too!" Gina had found her voice and chose to use it to stake her rightful claim.

Robbie made his version of a mean face at Gina—the silly scrunched-up look almost made Stephanie laugh—and crossed his arms. "He my brother."

"This was my bright idea," Claire said, looking apologetic. "Maybe I should have thought this through a little more."

Phil seemed to materialize from thin air. A sudden pop of adrenaline quickened her pulse. She'd pretend, for Claire's sake, that everything was normal.

Phil hadn't noticed her yet, but Jason and Gaby had obviously noticed him, and laughed. He'd gone for Surfer Dude Santa with belly pad beneath a reindeer-patterned Hawaiian shirt and red velvet pants with suspenders. And good sport that he was, he'd stuck an all-in-one Santa hair and beard combo on his head like a helmet. A huge grin made his eyes crinkle at the edges as he modeled his ridiculous outfit. His California version of Santa might raise brows, but it would fit right in with Santa Barbara and was the perfect touch for their Christmas-themed yacht.

He made a slow turn, hands out to allow Jason and Gaby to see the entire costume, including the surfboard-toting reindeer on the shirt. They blurted out a laugh. He'd been hoodwinked into the job and, instead of griping, he'd good-naturedly put his signature on it. The thought tugged at Stephanie's heart, and a bizarre notion catapulted through her brain. She could fall in love with a guy like Phil…if she didn't watch out.

Phil finally noticed her, and she saw a subtle change in his self-mocking. When their eyes met for a brief second, he nodded and her legs turned to water. She nodded back, unsure if she'd be able to talk coherently to him. Gina and Robbie, rushing to greet Santa, put a quick stop to her fears.

"Santa, Santa," the children chanted.

Suddenly distracted, Phil hugged both of them. An irrational sense of hurt made her fear she'd blown everything by leaving on Sunday night.

"Claire, I tell you, Roma and Dad will do anything for a cheap babysitter and a night out." He gave a good-hearted shrug, as if he was putting on a carefree performance for her sake. "It's a good thing I've got two knees," he said. "Ho, ho, ho."

Though sounding more resigned and not even close to a real Santa impersonator's laugh, he still delighted the kids. And Stephanie thought he might feel as much at a loss as she did about how to handle things between them.

"He's coming to my house first," Gina chided Robbie.

"Nah-uh," Robbie was quick to reply, arms tightly folded over his chest. "Mine."

"Go get dressed," Gaby said from over Stephanie's shoulder. She wore a gaudy red Christmas sweater that clashed with her magenta hair, and nudged Stephanie toward the stairs. "I want to take group pictures before it gets too crowded."

Whisked away to change, Stephanie barely had a moment to think about anything but putting on the Christmas sweater complete with a string of flashing Christmas lights on the appliquéd quilted tree. Aside from her mixed-up feelings about Phil, it actually felt good walking among the living again.

When she went up on deck, Jason had already turned on the lights. Everything twinkled and shone and the sight took her breath away. They really had created a winter wonderland. A dozen colorful strings of lights had been extended from the tip of the mainsail, from where they fanned out and were attached to the deck in a Christmas tree shape. At the top was a huge white lighted star. The half-size internationally decorated trees blinked and blinged, and with the added touch of a Scotsman, a Russian, a cowboy, a Dane and a Filipino standing next to them, they painted an impressive picture. Several lighted wreaths were hung strategically along the boat railing, and pine garland loaded heavily with glittery balls and blinking lights outlined the rails.

To top things off, two huge flashing neon Merry Christmas signs adorned both the bow and the stern. The remaining clinic employees sat on deck, wearing knitted caps and mufflers, assorted loud holiday sweaters and singing Christmas carols. If they didn't win first place in the Santa Barbara Chamber of Commerce Christmas lights parade, they should at least win the gaudiest-boat award!

Swept up with the holiday spirit, Stephanie couldn't help but laugh to herself. She hadn't felt this excited about celebrating Christmas in years, and it felt pretty darn great…until she came face-to-face with Santa.

He looked as uncomfortable as she felt. If only she could think of something witty to say. Something that would break this awkward trance they seemed stuck in.

"Nice sweater," he said, with the hint of teasing in his eyes.

It was the perfect excuse to lighten things up between them, to call a truce, and she grabbed it. "I like your suspenders, too."

They smiled cautiously at each other. His solid bedroom stare cut through her facade and flustered her. She focused on his white cloud of hair and beard for distraction, realizing she'd never think of Santa the same way again.

"Hey, let me get a picture," Jon said, camera in place, ready for his shot.

"Me, too," Gaby chimed in, at his side.

René stood smiling behind Jon, holding a bundle of baby wrapped in half a dozen blankets. "You may as well let them," she said. "They'll just keep pestering you until you pose."

Phil took Stephanie by the arm, pulled her closer, and whispered, "Smile pretty for the camera."

His unflappable charm disarmed her, all the apprehension she'd clung to vanishing. Maybe she was in over her head, but she couldn't deny her attraction to him.

"Great," Jon said. "Now let's go for a group shot."

Jason appeared, decked out in a captain's cap with minilights that blinked on and off. Everyone else lined up around him.

Almost as if being transported back in time, the magic and mystery of Christmas overcame Stephanie. Her skin became covered with goose bumps and her eyes prickled. It felt too good. She didn't deserve to feel this happy…during the holidays.

"Okay, that's enough," Phil said, clutching her arm and nudging her toward his appointed chair as if sensing her mood change. "We have work to do. How did I get talked into this again?" He stared into her eyes, where tears were threatening. "Oh, right—you!"

"I abstained, remember?" she said, grateful that everything seemed back to normal between them. It helped snap her out of the weepiness.

Deeply grateful for this night and all the distractions, she took her place and waved toward Jon on the docks as he snapped several more group shots. Then Jason backed the vessel out of the berth, laying on the air horn for a long and attention-getting blast.

Claire lifted first Gina and then Robbie onto Phil's lap. He pulled his chin in, as if aliens from planet Xenon had just been dropped from a spacecraft.

"Listen up, you two." Claire held each of their chins in a hand. "Do not get down from Santa's lap. Do you understand?"

Mesmerized by her firm clutch, they gave her their undivided attention and both nodded.

Though more relaxed with Robbie, Phil looked completely out of his element, with Gina bouncing excitedly on his knee. Stephanie hid her smirk. At least he wasn't complaining.

It seemed as if it took forever to line up the participating boats and set sail in Santa Barbara bay. They'd head toward Stearns Wharf, sail around the end and along the other side, then down the coast for a few miles before starting back toward the harbor.

The magnificent sight of a fleet of decorated boats reflecting off the blackening sea made Stephanie's eyes prickle again. When she looked back toward shore and saw the rolling hillsides and houses heavily covered with holiday lights, and the palm tree silhouettes dotting the beach, she couldn't hold back her feelings. For the first time since Justin's death she'd explore the goodness of the season. She couldn't bring him back, but she could celebrate his short existence by refusing to let the sadness dictate her life. Even if it was only for tonight.

Overwhelmed, she let her tears brim and dribble down her cheeks. They weren't the usual tears that burned with guilt. Not today. They were tears of joy and goodwill…and letting go. Today she'd extend that goodwill to herself. A huge weight the size of Santa's gift sack seemed to lift from her shoulders. Suddenly feeling as buoyant as the ocean, she anchored herself to the rail and waved to the passing judges' motorboat, her smile genuine and filled with the spirit of the season.

Jason released the cork from the champagne bottle in his living room, sending it flying through the air as everyone ducked. While he splashed the bubbling liquid into several outreaching glasses, he beamed with satisfaction.

"Here's to a well-deserved win," he said. "We finally did it!"

Everyone cheered.

Phil saw Stephanie standing beside Claire and René, applauding along with everyone else.

The sight of her earlier on the boat had knocked him

off balance. He'd felt compelled to make things right, but wasn't sure if she wanted anything to do with him, and he wanted to respect her feelings. He hadn't felt that lacking in confidence and confused over a woman since high school. All he knew for sure was that she'd left abruptly a week ago, and he hadn't been the same since. And that damn ticking clock counting down the days until she left for home didn't help either.

Under the bright lights of the Rogerses' family room, Stephanie's hair was decidedly red. The royal-purple satin blouse she wore accented the color even more. She'd taken off her ridiculous sweater, and he definitely liked what he saw.

He'd miss her when she was gone. Hell, he'd missed her all week. She'd stay here until the first of the year, and if he played his hand right, he'd get things back on track and hopefully have her back in his bed before the night was over.

He snagged an extra glass of bubbly and delivered it to her. "Here's to our win."

Her bright eyes widened and her generous smile let him know she was happy to see him. "And kudos to you for juggling two squirming kids all evening."

He shook his head. "Man, since Robbie has been sleeping with CPAP he has even more energy. I was ready to throw him overboard a couple of times, but I kept thinking Roma would be really mad at me."

She laughed. "You'd never do that."

"Figure of speech." He enjoyed the little patches of red on her cheeks and neck. He'd spent enough time around her to know that meant she was nervous. He still made her nervous. Was that a good thing? Hell, she made him nervous, too, and he liked it.

"Admit it, you love that kid," she said.

"He is my brother." Talking about kids wasn't exactly what he had in mind. He'd had a whole week to devise his plan. "Can I talk to you for a minute?" With his hand on her lower back, he guided her to a quiet corner of the room.

"What's up?" She gazed at him with suspicion.

"We're friends, right? And we're supposed to be honest with each other," he said, noticing her eyes soften at the edges and her lusciously alluring lips pout ever so slightly. He wanted to kiss her, but they were in a room full of fellow employees. Even though whispers and suspicions traveled the watercooler circuit at the clinic, he wasn't about to flaunt their private relationship. "That's why I want you to know that I'm ready to take the next step."

Wide-eyed disbelief had returned. She took a quick sip of champagne and nearly choked on it. He tapped her back as her eyes watered.

"Sorry, didn't mean to shock you."

She coughed and sputtered. "What are you talking about—take the next step?"

"Listen," Phil said. "I know it's kind of hard to take a man dressed in a surfin' Santa suit seriously, but I want you to know I've really been doing a lot of thinking over the last week."

The suspicious glint returned to her eyes.

"Yeah, and the thing is I've decided to try commitment out."

"What?" She blurted a laugh. "Just like that? You're putting me on."

"Well, maybe one step at a time. Seriously, don't you think that's progress for a guy like me?"

"Hey, that's great. Really, I think it's great," she said, but the subtle slope of her shoulders and that naggingly suspicious gaze wasn't very encouraging. She obviously didn't believe he'd changed a bit.

"So you have any plans tomorrow?" he said.

The champagne flute was halfway to her mouth when she tossed him a surprised glance.

"I thought I'd hit the local shelter. Maybe you can help me pick out a dog?"

Bad timing. She'd taken another sip, and along with her wry laugh she blew champagne out of her mouth.

"What? You don't think I can handle a committed relationship with a dog?"

All she could do was shake her head and point her finger at him with a one-day-I'll-get-you-back-for-this glower.

He knew he was pushing the limit, but he couldn't help playing with her, especially when her reaction was so satisfying. "What do you say, are you in?"

Having wiped her mouth, and found her voice again, she said, "I wouldn't miss that for the world."

What had gotten into Phil? He'd brought her a glass of champagne and strung her along with his newfound wisdom about relationships, then got her good. She shook her head and laughed to herself. The guy was completely spontaneous, and she thoroughly enjoyed him. She pushed aside the quick thought about love she'd had earlier.

He was ready to commit…to a dog.

She couldn't very well leave him to his own resources over such a big decision. The guy—the charming and sexiest Santa she'd ever laid her eyes on—needed help choosing a dog. How could she refuse?

Phil had hoped to bring Stephanie home with him to-night, but he didn't want to blow any progress he'd made by imposing his desires. He'd have to wait another day, get her all worked up over some canine's big brown eyes, have her help him make the dog at home then ask her to stay for dinner. If things worked out the way they usually did when the two of them were alone together, he'd put Fido in the yard and bring Stephanie back to his bed.

Not that he was using a dog simply to impress Stephanie. Once he'd thought about it and made the decision, he really wanted one. Loyal. Dependable. Warm. Loving. A dog would never leave him, and was exactly what he needed for companionship.

Phil turned the final corner to his street, rubbed his jaw, and smiled. Being Santa had been a blast. Who could have guessed? If Stephanie hadn't pushed him into the job, he never would have known. And the constant smile on her face on the boat made all the humiliation worthwhile.

Something seemed different about her, he thought as he parked in his garage. He'd never been known for being intuitive, but he could have sworn she'd left half of her usual baggage behind tonight.

He'd picked up on her playful spirit and tested out the limits. He shook his head and grinned as he unlocked his house door. He'd imagined Stephanie Bennett doing all kinds of sexy things, but he'd never expected to see her spit champagne across the room. A hearty laugh tumbled from his throat as he stepped inside. It echoed off the empty house walls, and once again he was reminded how big and lonely his bachelor pad was.

The rows of metal cages, with every size, breed, and shape of dog filling every single one, almost broke Stephanie's heart. She could hardly bear to look into any of the dogs' eyes. The cages lined the walls of the cement-floored warehouse/shelter, where the smell of urine and dog breath permeated the air.

"I wish I could buy all of them," Phil said, echoing her sentiments.

His sincerity had her reaching for his hand.

He squeezed her fingers and gave her a tender glance. "This is going to be harder than I thought."

On the drive over, on a gorgeous sunny day, they'd discussed the kind of dog he was looking for—big, sleek and muscular. To Stephanie's ears his "kind of dog" sounded a bit like him. If she had her choice, she'd go for something petite and furry. Hmm, was that like her?

Loud barking and yipping made it almost impossible to carry on a conversation as they walked the length of the shelter. Some jumped and yipped incessantly, others hovered in the corners of their cages, and still others paced restlessly back and forth with anxious eyes taking everything in.

"Lots of these dogs got left behind when home owners walked away from their mortgages. With the lousy economy, other people couldn't afford to have a dog anymore," the shelter worker said. "We're hoping the Christmas season will help find some of these dogs homes."

Stephanie spotted a little bundle of cream-colored wavy fur with round brown eyes getting overrun by two other small dogs. It looked like a puppy.

The shelter worker must have picked up on her interest. "That one is a terrier mix. She's a bit older than most of the others."

"Hey, look at this one!" Phil called her attention

away, but she glanced over her shoulder one last time at the so-called older dog, before moving on.

Amidst several cages of Labrador retrievers and German shepherds was a medium-size dark-furred dog.

"That one's a collie-Lab mix. One year old. Owner had to move out of state."

Phil petted the dog on his head, and the dog licked his hand.

"Both breeds are smart and they generally have good dispositions. Mixed breeds are often healthier than purebreds, too. They love their owners. Very loyal."

As if it was the easiest decision in the world, Phil nodded and smiled. "What's his name?"

"Daisy."

"It's a her, huh?"

"And she's been spayed."

"Good to know. Hey, Daisy, you like big yards and sunset walks along the beach?" The dog whimpered and licked his hand again.

Stephanie laughed at Phil's ability to charm females of all species.

"What do you think, Steph? Would Daisy and I make a good pair?"

His willingness to open his home to a forgotten pound dog warmed her insides. The change in his attitude since taking care of Robbie was astounding. She had the urge to give him a big kiss and hug, but touched his face instead. He hadn't shaved that morning, and the stubble made a scraping sound as she ran her fingers down his jaw.

"I think you and Daisy will make a great couple, and I promise I won't get jealous about your new female friend."

He smiled and nodded. "Then I'll take her."

As he filled out the paperwork and paid the fees, Stephanie kept going back to the little terrier mix up front. "Hey, sweetie," she whispered. The dog timidly explored the front of the cage, trying to sniff her fingers but not letting her touch his head. There seemed to be a world of sadness in his eyes. "You need a home, huh?"

"We'll take this one, too," Phil said from over her shoulder.

"What are you doing?" she said, rounding on him.

"I know love at first sight when I see it." He gave a magnanimous grin. "Consider him a Christmas present."

"I can't have a dog—I'm living in a hotel."

"The dog can stay with me until you go home. You have a town house in the desert, right?"

"Yes, but I…"

"Hey, don't analyze everything. Let's save two dogs today." Before she could respond, he looked for the shelter worker again. "What's this one's name?"

"Sherwood."

He laughed. "Sherwood. There you go. Stephanie and Sherwood. Sounds like a match made in heaven."

"How old is he?" she asked.

"He's older. Seven. His owner passed away."

That cinched it. The dog was grieving, something she understood completely. Though she felt inept, the shelter worker opened the cage and handed the dog to her. The trembling, compact dog fit perfectly in her arms. Fur partially covered soulful eyes, and a little pink tongue licked her knuckles. He was so trusting, and obviously missed his owner. The thought tied a string around her heart and squeezed. Phil was on to something. Maybe caring for a dog was the perfect stepping-stone for her lagging confidence. She could do this. She could take care of one small dog.

"You'll keep her until I move home?"

"I've got enough room for six dogs in my yard. Let's do it. Come on."

With more warm feelings washing over her, she hugged him and the dog yipped.

"Okay, Sherwood. Looks like you've got yourself a new mommy," she said, holding the dog to her face and enjoying the tickly fur.

The warm feeling that had started at the animal shelter continued to grow as Stephanie spent the afternoon with Phil. They'd shopped for leashes and beds and the proper food for each breed and, most importantly, travel cages.

Now that they'd unloaded everything at Phil's house, Sherwood had timidly gone into his cage, almost as if it was a security blanket, and Stephanie tried to coax him out.

"Come on, sweetie. I won't bite," she said, down on her knees, head halfway into the cage. She reached for him and he let her hold him then licked her face again.

"Maybe you should carry him like that for a while, until he gets used to the new house," Phil said, his dog dancing around his feet.

She nodded, stirring that warm bowl of feelings brewing stronger and stronger for Phil. He'd been a prince today. For a guy who didn't know the first thing about committing to a woman, he sure had no problem bringing a dog home.

"I can't figure out why I never did this before," he said, petting Daisy's silky black-and-white fur.

"I guess you just needed a nudge."

As if they'd known each other all their lives, he kissed her while each of them held their new dogs. His warm and familiar mouth covering hers felt so right she hoped the day would never end.

And later, when he asked her to spend the night with him, and she followed him down the hall to his bedroom, she realized the best part of the day was only getting started.

CHAPTER NINE

THE next week went by in a whirlwind. Stephanie and Phil were inseparable. She'd go to his house every day after work: they'd walk the dogs; catch up on any left-over paperwork from the clinic; cook dinner; make passionate love; have breakfast together; and head back to work. By Thursday, Phil suggested they carpool.

A red flag waved in Stephanie's mind. Wasn't carpooling a thinly disguised assumption that she'd return to his house again that night? Why couldn't he come right out and ask her to move in with him? Was this how all of his "flings" progressed, him keeping a subtle barrier until he tired of the woman and quit finding ways to spend time with her?

She only had two more weeks in Santa Barbara—did she really need to complicate her stay by thinking in such a manner? If she'd mentally agreed to "a fling," why were her emotions lagging so far behind?

Giving herself a silent pep talk, she agreed to drive to work with him then mentally ran down the pros and cons of her decision. This was a fling—an unbelievably wonderful fling with a guy who made her happy in all respects, a guy who never asked questions or made demands.

"You think this carpool business is a good idea?" she asked.

"It's good for the environment." He grinned.

She shook her head and rolled her eyes.

"You're already staying here every night. Sherwood wants you around." He glanced across the front seat at her then quickly back to the road. "I kind of like having you around."

This from a guy who supposedly didn't like to get involved or commit to relationships. She really needed to get her mind straight over this fling business.

"What are you really asking me, Phil?"

He pulled into his assigned parking place at the clinic and parked then turned toward her with an earnest expression. "Since our time together is limited, I'm asking you to spend as much of it as possible with me." He reached for her hand and rubbed his thumb across her knuckles, igniting warm tingling up her wrist to the inside of her elbow. "We should explore this thing we've got going on."

So that was it. They had a "thing." Well, heck, she'd known they had a *thing* since the first time they'd kissed.

That red flag waved again. *He wants to have you in his bed every night, not have you move in or get involved or anything. He knows your time is limited. It gives him freedom to do whatever he wants with you... knowing you'll leave after Christmas.*

"Talk to me," he said. "I can see a million thoughts flying around your mind. Share one of them with me." His voice was husky and sincere. "Please."

She took a deep breath. "This is all so new to me. I guess I just need to know the rules."

"I'm the king of no strings, Steph. I think you know that."

She hesitated with a long inhalation. "No strings. Right."

Their eyes met and fused. For long silent moments they searched each other's souls for the truth. She wasn't positive what she read in his stare other than it made her feel dizzy and fuzzy-headed. She wasn't ready to tell him that it was too late, she'd probably fallen a little in love with him. How silly of her to think that. Love wasn't something you could do a little of. Love was like being pregnant—you either were or you weren't. Was she in love?

Hell, she'd really messed up with this fling thing. Next time, if there ever was a next time, she'd sit on the sidelines and leave it to the experts. Like Phil. He knew how to keep a sexy and satisfying relationship in its place. Just do it. Have a good time. Don't make any promises. Maybe it was a surfer's creed: ride the wave for all it's worth then move on to the next.

Apparently, Stephanie didn't have the no-strings gene.

Phil put his hand on the back of her head and pulled her toward him. His kiss was tender and meltingly warm. He kissed her as if he loved her, but that was her interpretation, her head was mixing everything up again. She'd blame it on being hormonal and still waiting for her period.

What he offered and what she felt were two different things. She needed to remember that. He only wanted her for two more weeks.

His lips kept nudging her, asking her to give back, to kiss him as if she meant it. She couldn't resist another second. Whatever words he'd just avoided saying, he

communicated beautifully with his lips. I. Want. You.
With. Me.

Did she need to know anything more than that?

As predicted on the previous night's news, the storm
front moving down from Alaska had worked its way
along the coast, first bringing gray skies, clouds, and
cold temperatures on Thursday night, and by Friday
morning, a week before Christmas Eve, full-out rain.

As the morning wore on, Stephanie became aware
of something worse than stormy weather—nausea.
Realizing exactly where she stood with Phil—
nowhere!—had affected her more than she'd thought.

She sat with a new patient in her office. As she cal-
culated the pregnant woman's expected due date, it hit
her. Her hand trembled to the point of being unable to
write.

She cleared her throat and verbally gave the due date,
then used her best acting skills to hide the anguish brewing in her heart. "Congratulations. You'll have a late-
summer baby. August, to be precise."

The young woman clapped her hands and beamed
with joy. The complete opposite of how Stephanie felt.
A late-summer baby?

The instant she'd ushered the ecstatic woman from
her office, she got out the lab kit and drew a vial of
blood from her arm, labeled it with a bogus name, and
hand carried it to the laboratory for a STAT test.

After lunch, spent sitting in the darkness of her
office, Stephanie frantically flipped through her reports, looking for the single most important lab of her
life. She knew it was preposterous. She'd had her tubes
tied! What were the odds? They certainly weren't in her
favor—she'd looked it up—three different times. But

defying the odds, she'd missed her period and showed early signs of pregnancy with fatigue, tender breasts, and mild nausea. It simply couldn't be!

With dread and a trembling hand, she continued to skim through the reports, and after a few more, there it was—her pregnancy blood test—and it was positive.

Her stomach protested as if she'd taken a five-hundred-foot free fall. Her pulse surged. She couldn't breathe. Her body switched to fight-or-flight mode.

She surged from the chair and strode toward the door on unsteady legs, her footsteps soon turning to a jog. She reached the clinic entry in a full sprint and just as she saw Phil on the periphery of her vision, she sprang outside and down the street, through the icy, pouring rain.

With all systems on automatic panic, she ran without a destination, unaware of the weather. She ran from her breaking point, she ran in a futile attempt to keep her sanity, her only goal to prolong the inevitable, to avoid the truth—she was pregnant.

"Stephanie, come back here!"

What in hell was she doing running down the street? Didn't she know it was practically hailing?

Phil raced down the sidewalk, slipped in a puddle, and nearly crashed into a bush. He recovered his balance, knocked a rolling trashcan out of his way then hurdled another, all while keeping Stephanie in his sight.

Not waiting for the streetlight, she crossed Cabrillo Boulevard, recklessly dodging a car, and headed for Stearns Wharf.

He didn't have a clue what had made her snap and take off for the pier in a storm like this, but he sure as hell planned to catch up and find out, if she didn't get herself killed first!

She'd reached the beach, and headed for the pier. It may not have been such a great move, clearly not well thought out, but he had no choice. If he wanted to catch her, he'd have to tackle her, and finally he got close enough. He lunged and brought her down with a mild thud onto the wet sand.

She rolled onto her back, squealing. "What are you doing? Are you crazy?"

"I'm not the one sprinting between cars in the rain, darlin'," he panted. "Now, are you going to tell me what's going on?"

"Let go of me." She squirmed to break free.

"Not gonna happen. Calm down and talk to me." He pinned her arms above her head.

She sighed like an outsmarted teenager, wagging her head back and forth. Her tears blended with the rain. "I'm pregnant."

A rocket left his chest, headed straight toward his head, and exploded. The shock waves zapped every ounce of strength left in his hands. "What? You're what?"

"I'm pregnant!"

"But your tubes are tied!"

She glanced up at him. "See? There's a reason I was running."

He sat back on his knees, raking his hands through his soaked hair. His vision blurred from the combination of rain and disbelief.

"I'm kicking myself for tackling you." He hopped up, pulling her up with him, before he spit out some sand. He couldn't leave her floundering on the beach. "Come here." He drew her into his rain-drenched arms, into a gritty, sand-wrapped hug. "What do we do now?" He felt her trembling and wondered, coupled with his jarring reaction, how much he was contributing to it.

"I can't have this baby." She wouldn't look him in the eyes. She kept shaking her head.

"I know you don't do kids, but maybe this is a good thing. Maybe you can get beyond that hang-up now."

"No!"

"Okay. Maybe just give yourself time to think this over."

"You don't understand." She sounded tormented.

Maybe he'd been too wrapped up in his own reaction. Sure, he was shocked, but the craziest thing followed— he wasn't upset about it. She obviously had an issue about the pregnancy, hence the jogging on the beach in the pouring rain. This was all new territory for him, too. He needed to handle her delicately, find out what she was thinking—because he cared. He gave a big fat damn about her and her feelings, and, most importantly, about the baby they'd made. "Try me. Tell me why you can't have this kid."

She tried to pull away, but his strength had returned and he didn't let her.

"Let me go!"

"No!" He clenched his teeth and fought to keep her near. "Tell me why you don't want the baby."

"I killed my baby." She spit out the words as if they were poison.

"What?" His pulse paused; a distant rumble of thunder helped jump-start it. "I don't believe that."

"I killed him. I let him fall." Her head drooped so low, he could barely hear her.

Lightning snapped and forked into branches over the ocean. Her confession deserved wisdom that he didn't have, but he wanted more that anything to do right by her. He'd never experienced anything close to this new-found desire in his life.

"Let's sit down. Get out of this rain." He led her to the covered bus stop a few feet away by the porpoise fountain. "Tell me what happened. I want to know everything." He took her by the shoulders and forced her to look at him. "You've got to tell me."

"You'll hate me when you find out."

"No. I won't." And he meant it. By God, he meant it.

She paced within the small confines of the bus stop as if she was a panicked animal, gulping her tears, gasping her words.

"Justin was a super-colicky baby. He never grew out of it. He was four months old and this time he'd cried three nights in a row. You have no idea how terrible it feels not to be able to console your child." She shuddered, and he fought the urge to wrap her in his arms for fear she'd quit talking.

"No matter what I did, he wouldn't calm down. I paced and sang. I rubbed his back. I gently bounced him. I walked and walked…all night long."

She hiccuped for air, hugged herself, hysteria emanating from her eyes. He wanted to console her, but couldn't fathom how. No wonder she'd freaked out with Robbie that first night.

"My arms ached. My back throbbed. I was exhausted. No matter how long I walked, no matter how I held him, sang to him, kissed him, he kept crying. Then finally the crying stopped. Justin had calmed down and gone to sleep in my arms. I didn't know what to do. If I moved he might start up again."

She spoke as if reliving the moment—locked in

another time and place. Phil knew she couldn't have killed her baby. He knew there was a logical explanation, one she couldn't accept.

"If I put him in his crib I knew for certain he'd wake up. I eased onto the couch and he kept sleeping on my chest. So peaceful. So beautiful. For the first time in hours I found comfort. Comfort in the feel of my precious baby in my arms, and comfort for my aching back, my burning, sleepy eyes. I laid my head against the cushions and my son's gentle breathing lulled me to sleep."

A feral flash in her eyes alerted him that the hysteria was back. "I fell asleep!" she said, pain contorting her face. She continued her story as if he wasn't there. "I fell asleep," she sobbed. "And the next thing I knew… Oh, God, my baby!"

She dissolved into tears, crumpled to the bench. Phil rushed to lift her, to hold her up, to embrace her. After she settled down a bit he cupped her shoulders and stared into her eyes. "Tell me, sweetheart. Tell me everything."

She hiccuped another sob. "Justin fell off my chest, he fell off the couch, and…" She cried so hard she heaved, fluids pouring from every orifice on her face. She wiped her eyes with her palms, even as she cried more. "He hit his head on the table…"

Phil had never heard a woman cry like this in his life. He'd never seen such primal torture. He'd never imagined the depth of pain ripping at her.

"It damaged his brain." Then, as if finally giving in to the nightmare, her shoulders slumped in total defeat. "He died the next day."

Phil held her so tight he worried she might not be able to breathe, but she held him back, all trembles and shivers. "I never got to say goodbye, Phil," she whimpered, collapsing against his chest.

"Baby. Oh, honey. No. No, it wasn't your fault. Who let you believe it was your fault?" He pulled back to look at her. She avoided his eyes. "You weren't a single mother. Your man should have helped. You shouldn't have had to do it all yourself. Don't you see, he should have been there for you." Feeling anger at the bastard who'd let her down, Phil kissed her cheek.

They held each other tight for several minutes. What the hell should he do now? A maelstrom of emotions, fears, and doubts knocked him off balance. He could only imagine how Stephanie felt. She thought she'd killed her baby, didn't deserve to ever be a mother again, had had her tubes tied to make sure she never would be, and still wound up pregnant.

And he was the father.

He didn't know what else to do, so he put his sopping wet jacket over their heads, and escorted Stephanie back to the clinic. When they got close, he flipped open his cell phone and called Jason as he steered Stephanie away from the clinic and toward his car.

"Jase, I'm taking Stephanie home. She's not feeling well."

Phil undressed Stephanie. She'd slipped into a stupor, trembling from the cold. He was in near shock, too, but one of them needed to function. He turned on the shower and waited for it to heat up then thrust her inside. She gasped, but didn't fight him.

He ripped off his wet and gritty clothes and climbed in with her, easing her head under the water, making sure her body warmed up.

"Come on, honey, turn around. Let the water hit your

back." The steamy shower felt good. He dipped his head under the stream and shook it.

What in the hell were they supposed to do now?

Sherwood and Daisy came sniffing around the bathroom, obviously aware that something wasn't right.

With Stephanie still out of it, Phil tried to gather his thoughts. He'd never been in this position before. He watched her through the water. She stared blankly at the tile. His heart ached for her. He could only imagine the torture she'd lived through, the guilt, the self-hatred, and now her hibernating nightmare had been reawakened.

He washed her hair and lathered his own. The excess sand and mud gathered around the drain.

"Are you warmer now?"

She didn't respond.

"Let's get you dried off then I'll put you to bed."

Her worst fear may have materialized, except there was one thing different this time around.

He was the father.

CHAPTER TEN

PHIL bundled a second blanket over Stephanie, but she still trembled. He made a snap decision to share his body warmth, and climbed under the covers then spooned up against her. She snuggled into his hold. Heavy rain sounded like Ping-Pong balls on the roof, and crackles of thunder in the distance made the cuddling even more intimate.

After the shower, he'd blow-dried and brushed her hair, and now it splayed across the pillow, tickling his face. It seemed odd to smell his standard guy shampoo in her hair instead of the usual flowers-and-dew-scent shampoo she used. Up on one elbow, he pushed the waves away from her shoulder and dropped a kiss on her neck.

"We'll get through this, Steph," he whispered.

They'd leaped a thousand steps ahead in their relationship with today's news. What should they do? He'd just finished a crash course on parenting with Robbie and had barely made the grade, but this was different. They'd made a baby. Together. Was he ready for this?

And what about Stephanie? The last thing in the world she wanted was a child. He'd never been in this position before. One thing was certain; he didn't want to run away from the challenge. A part of him was excited about being a father.

A swell of tender feelings made Phil pull her closer. He pressed another kiss to that special spot on her shoulder.

Stephanie needed oblivion. She needed to find one tiny corner of her mind and hide there. She didn't want to think. Couldn't bear the truth.

A vague memory of Phil bathing and drying her then brushing her hair filled her heart with gratitude. Even in her haze, she could sense the delicate way he'd treated her. Now his warm hands surrounded her and pulled her close. His breath caressed her neck. He kissed her... there. Chills fanned across her breasts and she suddenly knew how to keep from thinking about anything but Phil.

She turned into his arms and eager mouth. His kiss was different. The passion was still there, but this one felt warmer than all the others had. Phil handled her gently, lovingly, taking their kisses slowly, yet building each on the next until she longed for more of him. She needed his hands touching her everywhere, and guided one to her breast. He didn't require schooling on the rest. She cupped his head at her chest as he kissed and taunted her. Desire burrowed through her, down to her belly.

As his arms explored and caressed every part of her, her legs entwined with his locking him tight. With his passion obvious, she moved against him, placing him at her entrance. His hand moved between them, touching and teasing her, making her squirm for more. She needed to forget everything, and Phil's deep kisses and sex would soothe all the aching in her soul.

His tongue delved into her mouth as he simultaneously entered her with a slow, determined thrust. She gasped as she stretched and gloved him. He kissed her harder and quickened his rhythm, the building heat pulsing through her center. Her inner muscles throbbed as he edged farther inside. His breathing went rough and ragged and he cupped and tilted her hips for deeper access. She gulped for air and ground against his powerful penetration, her muscles and nerves winding tighter and tighter with every lunge.

He held her at the peak of pleasure with the steady pace, and she thrived on every sensation swirling through her body. She never wanted the exquisite feeling to end and, languishing there with her, it seemed his only desire was to please her. Feeding on the suspended moments of bliss, her hunger grew. He'd made her frantic and dependent on him to take her all the way. As if reading her thoughts, he doubled his rhythm, pushing and nudging her to the brink, holding her there until she begged for release and he erupted.

Tears streamed down her cheeks as she quivered and gave in to the pulsations pounding through her body, floating her outside of time and mind and, like a heavy sedative, numbing her to harsh reality.

Phil had taken her there—to oblivion.

Stephanie cracked open an eye. The room was still dark. She'd been sleeping, one glance at the bedside clock told her, for hours. Phil breathed peacefully beside her, his warmth like a snug cocoon. Sherwood had curled into a ball at the foot of the bed, and Daisy sprawled out on a nearby rug.

The snapshot of domestic tranquility shocked her back into the moment.

An odd fragment of thought repeated itself in her mind. *Who let you believe it was your fault? You weren't a single mother. Your man should have helped. You shouldn't have had to do it all yourself. Don't you see, he should have been there for you.*

She blinked and sat up as the course of the afternoon came roaring back through her mind. Phil rustled and turned. She studied him. Had he said those words merely to console her or did he really believe them?

Was a guy like Phil capable of committing to one woman? Would it matter if he could? She shook her head—she couldn't handle this pregnancy. She never deserved to be a mother again.

She lay back on the pillow and stared through the shadows at the ceiling, desperately in need of sorting through her problems.

She studied Phil's mop of dark blond hair, his straight and strong profile. She ran her finger along the length of his red-tinged sideburn. In other circumstances, she could see herself waking up next to a guy like Phil for the rest of her life. If things were different.

It was a fool's dream.

You don't deserve to be happy. You're a murderer.

Out of reflex, she curled into a ball and covered her eyes. The negative thoughts her husband had charged her with day after day until they'd divorced became so strong she couldn't ward them off. A queasy feeling took hold in her stomach, and self-hatred pulled her deeper inward. She definitely couldn't keep the baby.

"Are you all right?" Phil took her by the shoulders and shook her. "Hey, what's going on? Are you having a nightmare?" He pulled her to him and kissed the top of her head.

"Yes," was all she could whisper. "A nightmare."

"Come here," he said, rubbing her back and kissing her again.

He wanted to protect her. Had her ex-husband ever offered to protect her at the worst moment of her life? No. He'd blamed her. He'd called her out as the monster she was.

What kind of person would do that? he'd accused.

Along with the vivid memory, Stephanie whimpered, and Phil drew her closer to him. His warm chest and strong arms gave little solace. She didn't deserve solace.

"Let me take care of you," he said. 'I don't want anything bad to happen to you."

What happened to two weeks of good times? No strings attached? Now, only because she was pregnant, he wanted to take care of her? If she weren't pregnant, would he still want her? Could she trust a man like Phil to be there if she needed him?

He was practically a stranger, and she needed to think things through.

Confused and unable to respond to his caring words, she bolted from the bed.

He looked like a man about out of patience.

"Phil…" She paced the length of the rug. "This wasn't supposed to happen with us."

"You're right. But it did, and now we have to figure out what to do."

Why did he sound so reasonable?

The jumble of feelings and fears caused that queasy sensation to double into a fist of nausea. Before she could think another thought, she sprinted for the bathroom.

Phil sat outside the washroom door, listening to Stephanie heave as if exorcising a demon. He scrubbed his face. What in hell was he supposed to do now? Was he anywhere near ready to be a father? At the moment it seemed the bigger problem was that Stephanie felt determined *not* to be a mother again.

What kind of mind game had her ex-husband played on her to make her feel so unworthy of a second chance?

Behind the door, the toilet flushed and the faucet was turned on. For Stephanie's fragile sake, no matter how much he wanted to, he wouldn't dare broach the subject that *they* were having a baby until she brought it up.

Maybe he could distract her. Why not pretend things were the same as they were two days ago? What normal activity would they have done this weekend before everything had changed?

"I was thinking that maybe today we could shop for a Christmas tree," he called through the door, feeling completely at a loss for what to say or do. All he knew was that he wanted to make things easier for her. Maybe he could distract her with something fun and frivolous like buying a Christmas tree. It was the season.

She didn't answer.

Lame idea. Okay, he'd think of something else. He'd help her get through the shock of it by keeping her busy, and maybe in the process he'd manage to work out his own feelings. "Or we could take the dogs to the beach."

Still no answer.

A few minutes later, she emerged from the bathroom fully dressed.

He went on alert.

"I'm going away," she said. "I need to be alone."

He jumped to his feet. "What? Don't I figure into this?"

With eyes as flat as stone, she looked at him. "Ultimately, it all comes down to me and what I decide to do."

He words were like a slap to the face. Just like that, she'd shut him out. He needed to buy time, to keep her there. "At least let me fix you something to eat."

"I don't want anything."

"You can't just think about yourself anymore." Ah, damn, that had been the wrong thing to say. Why was he such an idiot?

She gave him a measured look. He wished he could see inside her mind, to figure out what was going on. He was at a loss and she wasn't having a thing to do with his fumbling attempts to keep her there.

Stunned silent, he watched her gather up her purse and leave.

Phil couldn't stand staying in his house alone, so he herded the dogs into his Woodie and drove to the beach. Sherwood stayed close to his side as Daisy romped through the waves, chasing the Frisbee he threw again and again.

Never in his life had he been more confused about a woman. He'd covered for his true feelings when he'd insisted they carpool to work together. He hadn't wanted to scare her off by asking her to move in with him for the rest of her time in Santa Barbara, though that was exactly what he'd wanted. Hell, these new feelings scared him enough for both of them. The problem was, for the first time in his adult life he was open to exploring where this "thing" between him and Stephanie might lead. And she'd have nothing to do with him.

He'd never cherished a woman in his life, yet last night, after she'd told him her darkest secret and they'd made love, he'd felt the subtle shift of his heart. She'd transformed from hot girlfriend to the woman he loved…and she was carrying their child. Had he just admitted he loved her?

He swallowed, wanting nothing more than to prove he could be the kind of man she deserved. A man who believed in her, who'd never let her down. Was he capable of such a thing?

He'd learned an important fact about himself when Robbie had been thrust on him. When he set his mind to something, he could do it. No matter how foreign or hard, he could make it work. He and his little brother were closer than ever before, and Phil was quite sure he could do even better by his own kid. The thought excited him, and he wanted to make things work out with Stephanie. He'd never wanted anything so much in his life.

Yet, just like his mother, when life had gotten tough, she'd split.

Daisy scampered toward him, soaking wet, and dropped the slobbery Frisbee at his feet. Deep in thought, he hardly noticed he'd thrown the toy back to sea. Sherwood snuggled on his lap. Without thinking, he rubbed the dog's ears.

"Don't worry, boy, she'll be back for you. I'm the one she left."

Phil couldn't sleep all weekend. He felt like hell on Monday, and with a million lectures planned for Stephanie, he was surprised to find out she'd called in sick. As hard as it was, he'd given her the weekend to sort things through, but she still wasn't ready to face him. Or their baby.

Frustrated, he scraped the stubble on his jaw. Damn, he'd forgotten to shave, but it didn't matter. He was far more concerned whether Stephanie had made a rash decision or not. Damn it, he deserved to be in on *any* decisions she made about their baby, but she wouldn't answer her phone. He'd called by the extended-stay hotel, only to be told she'd checked out.

He dialed her cell number again and it went directly to messages, then he shoved it back into his pocket. Gaby give him a strange look.

"What?" he said.

"Nothing." She went back to her task as if it was the most important thing on the planet.

Jason buzzed him on the intercom. "Hey, just wanted to tell you that Claire is going to pick up as many of Stephanie's patients as she can. I'll see a few myself."

"I'm a pulmonologist." Phil censured the expletive he wanted to utter. "I don't know squat about gynecology. Can't help." He clicked off without giving Jason a chance to respond.

Stephanie cried about everything. What to eat. What to wear. Whether to get out of bed. Whether to run away to the desert. Every single thing about life set her off.

She'd changed hotels, and gave strict instructions that no one was to know which room she was in. Yet deep inside she wished Phil would find her. And that made her cry, too.

With each passing day, she grew more aware of the life forming inside her, and with that knowledge she forged a private bond with the baby. The thought of giving it up…made her cry.

She couldn't fight her desire to be in Phil's arms any more than she could resist his easy charm, so she'd opted to stay away. When she'd bared her soul to him, he'd acted more like a prince than a playboy. He'd gathered her close to his chest and stroked her cheek with his thumb, and she'd almost believed that things could work out for them. Almost.

She'd seen all the evidence over the past month. He'd professed to be a confirmed and happy bachelor, yet he owned a house fit for a family. He loved to putter around in the yard and garden just as much as he liked to surf. And he was a great cook, better than she was.

When she saw how he was with Robbie, she knew he'd make a great father for some lucky child some day. And when he'd suggested they each buy a dog, it had almost been as if he'd wanted to test the waters on commitment.

But that was her side of the story. What he really thought or felt would remain a mystery, because she couldn't face him. Not with what she had planned.

She sighed and pulled the comforter closer. Besides, he deserved a lady who wanted kids, and she'd finally made up her mind what she was going to do. And the decision…made her cry.

CHAPTER ELEVEN

STEPHANIE'S sense of duty drove her back to work on Wednesday. That and the fact she couldn't bear to be alone with her tortured thoughts another day.

She entered the MidCoast Medical clinic cautiously, peeked around the door and edged her way inside.

The first voice she heard was Phil's and she almost ran the other way. A fist-size knot clenched her stomach, forcing her to stand still.

"Gaby," he said, "I asked you to bring Mr. Leventhal in this morning. Why is he still on the schedule for this afternoon?" He sounded irritated.

"It didn't work with his schedule, Dr. Hansen." Smooth professional that she was, Gaby didn't let his snit bother her. "Welcome back, Dr. Bennett."

Stephanie had never seen Phil look so horrible. He had dark circles under his eyes similar to football players' black antiglare paint, and when was the last time the man had shaved? His hair was in need of a good combing, too, and…did he actually have on two different-colored socks?

He stopped in his tracks when he noticed her. She didn't look any better than he did. His consuming stare made her forget how to breathe. All she could do was nod and make a straight line for her office. She felt his glare on her back the entire way, and prayed he wouldn't follow her.

With a trembling hand, she reached for the doorknob. How would she make it through the day?

Feeling emotionally and physically drained, she wondered how much longer she could keep going like this. After the New Year, she'd move back to Palm Desert, but first she had to get through Christmas, and she owed the medical clinic the time she'd signed on for. After she put on her doctor's coat, she wrapped her hands around her waist and realized she'd been doing that a lot lately. The baby was quickly becoming a part of her every thought.

Maria Avila came waddling into the clinic. "My back is killing me," she said.

"Why don't you go home, take a load off your feet? You don't have to do this today," Stephanie said.

"Are you kidding? This is what I live for. If I go home, I'll have two kids under the age of five to chase around. Heck, I know where I'm better off." She gave a wry laugh, and her face lit up with her usual infectious grin. "Besides, I need to make up for that clinical day I missed on Thanksgiving."

Stephanie couldn't help but smile back as she shook her head. "Here's our first patient. Why don't you do the honors?" At least one of them wanted to be there.

Maria snatched the chart. "Great!"

All morning Maria shadowed Stephanie. Occasionally, she rubbed her back and sighed, but never complained about the highly charged pace Stephanie insisted on keeping. It was the only way to keep her mind off Phil and their baby.

At lunchtime, Stephanie holed up in her office with

a sack lunch, and Maria waddled off to the nurses' lounge.

"I'm gonna go put my feet up," Maria said, on her way out of the office.

No less than five minutes later, just as Stephanie finished a small sandwich, a rapid knock alerted her to someone at the door. Her heart stammered, and she prayed it wasn't Phil.

The door swung inward as it became evident her prayer hadn't been answered. He closed it and strode toward her desk, his intense gaze knocking the wind out of her.

"Have you made up your mind yet about what you plan to do?"

She stared at her desk. There wasn't the slightest tone of compassion in his voice. He hadn't wasted one second on preliminaries. If he wanted to be direct, she'd join him. "I'm going to give the baby up for adoption."

Her decision hit Phil as if a boulder had dropped on his chest—it crushed him and made it hard to breathe. Give their baby up? He'd been on the verge of telling her he loved her the other morning, the day she'd left. She'd put him through hell this week while he impatiently waited for her to make her decision. Now she'd made the second-worst decision he could have imagined. Give up their baby?

Could he honestly love a woman who would walk away from her child? She wasn't an unwed teenager— she was a well-established adult who could easily care for a child. Yet she wanted to give the baby away. It didn't make any sense, but he'd never been in her shoes. He couldn't imagine how it must feel to bear the brunt of a child's accidental death.

He wanted more than anything to be angry at her for resisting this special gift, but he couldn't. The fact was he loved her. He wasn't sure if she felt anything for him, though. Her careless disregard for his feelings proved otherwise.

"The baby is mine, too. Remember?" he said. "We made it together."

She glanced at him, as if it had never occurred to her that he might want to be involved in the decisions.

He stood before her, hands at his sides, opening and closing his fists. "How selfish of you. You haven't even asked me what I'd do."

Surprise colored her eyes. She sat straighter. Had it really never occurred to her that he'd want to be involved with any decision she made about their baby? Things were more screwed up than he'd imagined.

"I'm sorry if that's what you think. Doesn't it always fall on the woman?" She stood and met him eye to eye. He fought the urge to grab her arms and shake her. "You've got your carefree life. You've never given me a hint that you were interested in anything more than sex and a good time, and suddenly I'm supposed to consult you because I got pregnant? Is that it?"

She'd challenged him, and he needed to tell her the truth. If nothing else, she deserved the truth.

"The day I met you," he said, "I was really turned on by your looks, but the more I got to know you, the more I knew you'd been hurt in life. I just wanted to be your friend and, if I was lucky, maybe be your lover. I never would have dreamed what followed."

"That I'd screw things up and get pregnant?"

He ignored her defiant tone. "That I would fall in love with you."

Stephanie needed to sit down.

Tingles burst free in her chest and rained over her body. She squeezed her eyes closed, and soon large tears dripped over her cheeks. She clenched her jaw to keep from blubbering. If only she weren't pregnant, she'd be free to love him, too. "Phil…"

"I want you to know where I stand." He knelt in front of her and looked into her face. She bowed her head to hide her tears.

At a loss for one single word, Stephanie withdrew into her thoughts. She loved him; *he* loved her, so why couldn't they have a happy ending? Because she couldn't bear to lose another child—she still didn't trust herself.

"If you're giving up the baby," he said, "give it to me."

"Give it to you?" Oh, God, how could she do that? She loved Phil, and he wanted to keep their baby. Remembering the special love she'd felt from him last Friday night, and how he'd taken care of her like a mother hen, she believed he loved her, but would he want her if she wasn't pregnant? Now she'd lose both the baby and Phil. Could she remove herself so easily from the equation? If she changed her mind and wanted to keep the baby, would he want her, too? Or would he hate her?

"I'll do the best I can as a father."

She couldn't believe what he was telling her.

By putting him in this situation, not by choice, she'd never know if he stayed with her out of love or obligation, and not knowing for sure would kill her and eventually ruin their relationship. Oh, God, her mind was so mixed up, she couldn't think straight.

"Please don't hate me, Phil. You can't understand…"

He shook his head and paced the floor. "Yes, losing

your baby was a tragedy. I can't imagine how it must feel, but, Stephanie, you're alive, not dead, and you've got to let it go. That was three years ago. It's time to move on."

He was right, she knew he was right, but she was so damn stuck in her self-loathing rut...

Amy came rushing through the door. "Maria's water broke, and she's having contractions!"

Stephanie jumped to her feet, her legs having turned to rubber bands. Maria had gone into labor, as she'd been threatening for six weeks since Stephanie had first met her.

Words, as dry as the desert, crawled out of her mouth. "Have you called the paramedics?"

"She wants you, Doctor," Amy said, eyes huge from adrenaline.

She hadn't signed on for this. It said so in her contract—no delivering babies.

"Where is she?" Stephanie asked in a wobbling voice, following Amy to the procedure room.

Phil remained at her side, supporting her elbow and walking briskly with her. "You know what to do, and I'll be here, right here. We'll get through this together."

His words of encouragement meant more than she could say.

Stephanie rushed into the procedure room, where Amy had left Maria between contractions. Phil was right on her heels.

"Maria, do you think you can make it to the hospital?" Stephanie said.

"Feels like the kid's head is between my knees!"

Claire appeared. "I'm here if you need me." Word had traveled fast through the clinic.

Surrounded by her clinic family and Phil, Stephanie

felt confidence spring back to life. She'd delivered more babies than she could count. She could do this. She went to the sink and splashed water on her face and washed her hands, then gowned up and gloved. "Let's have a look," she said.

This was Maria's third baby, the woman knew the drill.

She'd check for effacement, dilatation and station. "One hundred percent, ten centimeters, plus three. I guess your baby doesn't plan to wait for an ambulance," Stephanie said, her heart kicking up a couple notches on the beat scale.

Amy rushed around the room gathering everything they might possibly need.

Stephanie glanced over her shoulder at Phil, who was looking a little pale, but was still there.

He touched her arm and nodded. "You'll do fine. Now I'm going to step out of your way, but holler if you need me."

As if on cue, Maria let out a guttural sound.

Stephanie saw Maria's abdomen tighten into a hard ball. Now was the time to click into the moment and do what she'd been trained for. All other thoughts left her mind. Half an hour later, she positioned herself at the birth canal before giving a terse command. "Push!"

A tiny head with dark hair matted with vernix crowned.

"Keep pushing!" She slowly guided the baby's face-down head through the birth canal. "Okay, now stop pushing." She made a quick check to make sure the umbilical cord wasn't wrapped around the baby's neck. It wasn't. "Push. Push."

Soon the entire body flopped into her waiting hands, and the baby let out a wail.

Stephanie held the newborn as if he was made of porcelain. The squirming bundle of perfection mewed and tried to open his eyes. A booster shot of adrenaline made her hands shake. *What if I drop him?* Her arms felt as if they carried the weight of the world.

Phil appeared at her side, and put his gloved hands around the child for added support. His eyes met hers and she saw all the confidence she lacked right there. He believed in her. That look told her he knew she could do it. He'd never doubted her. He knew she could handle her own baby, too.

She bit her bottom lip to stop herself crying. Hadn't she done enough of that lately? "It's a boy!" Emotionally wrung out, she held the baby close enough for Maria to see. "He's gorgeous."

Maria grinned and nodded in agreement as Stephanie laid the newborn on her stomach.

"May I?" Phil asked, snipping the umbilical scissors in the air.

"Be my guest," Maria said, cuddling her baby to her breast.

Phil glanced at Stephanie. "I wanted to get a little practice in before our baby arrives," he whispered into her ear, before severing the cord.

His words meant more than anything in the world just then.

After the placenta was delivered, and the ambulance arrived to transport Maria, Stephanie cleaned up and went back to her office. Phil was right at her side. His eyes were bright with the buzz from Maria's delivery as he closed the door.

"You were fantastic. You can handle anything you set your mind to," he said.

The high from the delivery had boosted her confidence, and Phil's support meant everything to her. He stepped closer and touched her shoulder.

"We're going to have a baby. Steph. Look at me. In case you're wondering, I want you and I want our kid."

She gave him a questioning glance, her heart thumping so hard she thought it might crack a rib.

"I'm ready to make the leap," he said. "And it's all because of you, sweetheart."

If she'd ever doubted that he loved her, that doubt vanished. Even though he knew her tragic secret, he still loved her. He was the best man she'd ever met.

"Nothing will sway me. Now that I've discovered you, I can't let you go," he said. "I've fallen crazy in love with you." He took her into his arms. "I'm here to tell you I'm ready. I want you. You're the woman I love. But there's one thing that will hold us back, that is if you don't love me, too."

Why hadn't she told him? He'd opened his soul and she'd been wallowing in self-pity. He hadn't cursed her and run off when he'd found out she'd dropped her baby. He'd forced her to open her heart with small steps and a dog named Sherwood. He'd made love to her as if she were a goddess. He'd forced his way inside her fortress and conquered her heart. The guy deserved to know how she felt.

"I do. I love you, Phil. More than I can ever express."

A relieved grin stretched across his face and he covered her mouth with his, whispering over her lips, "It's about time you admitted it."

After he'd kissed her thoroughly, leaving her breathless and weak-kneed, he held her at arm's length.

"You need to forgive yourself. *Really* forgive yourself.

Your ex-husband let you down. He was a jerk. These horrible things happen in life, and somehow we have to dig deeper and keep going.

"I love you and I promise to never let you down. And if I do, you have my permission to call me on it. I won't run. I won't hate you. I'll love and respect you. I'll always love you, Stephanie."

She crumpled into his embrace on another wave of tears, and he welcomed her with open arms. With the deepest feeling of connection to another human being she'd ever felt, she hugged him back.

They belonged together, both broken and jagged along the edges but a perfect fit. Filled with hope, she knew without a doubt that his unconditional love would finally help her heal.

"So what do we do now?" he said, against her ear.

She pulled back and gazed into his sea-blue eyes. As he'd said everything she needed to hear, and she had admitted exactly how she felt, there really wasn't much left to say or do. Except one silly thought popped into her mind. "Let's go and buy that Christmas tree."

His full-out laugh was the second-best sound she'd heard all day, the first having been the newborn baby's cry.

On Christmas Eve, Stephanie had come down with a mild cold. Phil insisted she stay in bed, but she didn't want to miss such a special holiday, her first Christmas with the man she loved.

Their decorated tree blinked and twinkled in the corner of the family room. A few gifts, mostly for the dogs, were wrapped and tucked beneath. Christmas carols played quietly in the background. The incredible aroma of roast beef filled the air as it cooked in the oven, along with Yorkshire pudding, making her mouth water.

Carl and Roma arrived with hyperactive Robbie. What was it about Christmas that got kids so wound up?

She grinned at the boy, and stooped to his level before he had a chance to tackle her. Her legs were still sore from Phil's tricky maneuver at the beach the week before, and Robbie's version of hugging was to throw his body against hers.

"Pill," Robbie said, quickly losing interest in Stephanie when he noticed his big brother.

"Dude!" Phil hugged him, and Stephanie had to blink when he kissed his brother on the cheek. "Merry Christmas."

Robbie's gaze darted everywhere. "Wow, did Santa come to your house already?" He saw the gifts and ran for the tree.

Daisy and Sherwood intercepted him, hopping in circles and demanding their fair share of attention. Easily distracted, Robbie giggled and jumped around with them.

Stephanie grinned, thinking the dogs were protecting their doggy cookies and leather chews but knowing they loved any and all attention they could get. She watched Robbie roll around on the floor with them, and soon felt a hand on her shoulder.

It was Carl.

"Thank you," he said.

She looked into the same blue eyes she'd woken up to that morning, and imagined how Phil would look thirty years down the road. She liked what she saw.

"For what?" she said.

"For making my son happy. For helping him finally grow up."

She shook her head and hugged Carl. "He's done the same for me."

Christmas evening, one year later...

Stephanie sat bundled in a blanket and snuggling with Phil on the couch. She stared at the Christmas tree in the dimmed living room. It really was the most beautiful tree she'd ever seen. The decorations reflected the colorful blinking lights across the family-room ceiling, and the effect was nothing short of magical.

Their family and friends had come and gone and they were finally alone. She looked up at her husband, who bore a mischievous grin.

"I've got an idea how to make an already perfect day even better," he said. He dipped his head and kissed her neck, sending feathery tickles over her chest. She reached for him and kissed his jaw, enjoying the evening stubble and waning spice of his aftershave.

"That sounds wonderful," she whispered.

He stood, held her hands, and pulled her to her feet.

Baby gurgles and coos came through the nursery intercom. From their brand-new Santa-delivered dog beds, Daisy's and Sherwood's ears perked up.

Stephanie smiled at Phil. "Shall we wait to see how long before she realizes she's hungry?"

They looked at each other briefly and said in unison, "Nah."

Phil led her down the hall and together they peeked in on the center of their universe—their four-month-old daughter, Emma.

The contented baby lay on her back in her crib, reaching for the tiny stuffed animals dangling from the mobile over her bed. Her foot made contact with a teddy bear and she squealed with delight.

Stephanie and Phil laughed quietly. They loved watching her, and wanted to steal a few more moments enjoying the show before she noticed them. But it was too late. The baby glanced at the doorway and squealed even louder when she saw them. She flapped her arms and legs as if she might fly to them.

Stephanie rushed to her and lifted her into her arms, smothering her with kisses. Emma cooed and gurgled, and laughed. She'd reached a euphoric stage in her life, and everything seemed to make her happy.

Phil wrapped his arms around both Stephanie and Emma and hugged them tight. "How're my girls doing this Christmas night?"

Stephanie pressed her cheek to Emma's and glanced up at Phil as if she was posing for a picture. "Just fine, Daddy. We couldn't be happier."

MILLS & BOON®
HAVE JOINED FORCES WITH THE LEANDER TRUST AND LEANDER CLUB TO HELP TO DEVELOP TOMORROW'S CHAMPIONS

We have produced a stunning calendar for 2011 featuring a host of Olympic and World Champions (as they've never been seen before!). Leander Club is recognised the world over for its extraordinary rowing achievements and is committed to developing its squad of athletes to help underpin future British success at World and Olympic level.

'**All my rowing development has come through the support and back-up from Leander. The Club has taken me from a club rower to an Olympic Silver Medallist. Leander has been the driving force behind my progress**'

RIC EGINGTON – Captain, Leander Club Olympic Silver, Beijing, 2009 World Champion.

Please send me ☐ **calendar(s) @ £8.99 each plus £3.00 P&P** (FREE postage and packing on orders of 3 or more calendars despatching to the same address).

I enclose a cheque for £ _____ made payable to Harlequin Mills & Boon Limited.

Name _____

Address _____

_____ Post code _____

Email _____

Send this whole page and cheque to:
Leander Calendar Offer
Harlequin Mills & Boon Limited
Eton House, 18-24 Paradise Road, Richmond TW9 1SR

All proceeds from the sale of the 2011 Leander Fundraising Calendar will go towards the Leander Trust (Registered Charity No: 284631) – and help in supporting aspiring athletes to train to their full potential.

All the magic you'll need this Christmas...

When **Daniel** is left with his brother's kids, only one person can help. But it'll take more than mistletoe before **Stella** helps him...

Patrick hadn't advertised for a housekeeper. But when **Hayley** appears, she's the gift he didn't even realise he needed.

Alfie and his little sister know a lot about the magic of Christmas – and they're about to teach the grown-ups a much-needed lesson!

Available 1st October 2010

2 FREE BOOKS
AND A SURPRISE GIFT

We would like to take this opportunity to thank you for reading this Mills & Boon® book by offering you the chance to take TWO more specially selected books from the Medical™ series absolutely FREE! We're also making this offer to introduce you to the benefits of the Mills & Boon® Book Club™—

- **FREE home delivery**
- **FREE gifts and competitions**
- **FREE monthly Newsletter**
- **Exclusive Mills & Boon Book Club offers**
- **Books available before they're in the shops**

Accepting these FREE books and gift places you under no obligation to buy, you may cancel at any time, even after receiving your free books. Simply complete your details below and return the entire page to the address below. You don't even need a stamp!

YES Please send me 2 free Medical books and a surprise gift. I understand that unless you hear from me, I will receive 5 superb new stories every month including two 2-in-1 books priced at £5.30 each and a single book priced at £3.30, postage and packing free. I am under no obligation to purchase any books and may cancel my subscription at any time. The free books and gift will be mine to keep in any case.

Ms/Mrs/Miss/Mr _____ Initials _____

Surname _____

Address _____

_____

_____ Postcode _____

E-mail _____

Send this whole page to: Mills & Boon Book Club, Free Book Offer, FREEPOST NAT 10298, Richmond, TW9 1BR